Maggie-Now

Maggie-Now

BETTY SMITH

G.K.HALL &CO.
Boston, Massachusetts

1982

Library of Congress Cataloging in Publication Data

Smith, Betty, 1904-
   Maggie-now.

   1. Large type books. I. Title.
[PS3537.M2895M3   1982]   813'.52   81-20329
ISBN 0-8161-3303-4   AACR2

Published in Large Print by arrangement
with Harper & Row
Set in 16 pt English Times

Maggie-Now

Chapter One

YOUNG Patrick Dennis Moore wore the tightest pants in all of County Kilkenny. He was the only boy-o in the village who cleaned his fingernails; and his thick, black, shiny hair had the widest, cleanest part in all of Ireland—or so it was said.

He lived with his mother. He was the last of a brood of thirteen. Three had died, four had married. Three had been put in an orphan home when the father had died, and had been adopted or bound out to farmers and never been heard from again. One had gone to Australia; another to Dublin. The Dublin one had married a Protestant girl and changed his name to Morton. Patrick Dennis was the only one left with his mother.

And how she clung to her last baby—Patsy Denny, she called him. In her young days, she had had her babies like kittens. She nursed them at her huge breasts, wiped their noses on her petticoat, cuffed them, hugged them and fretted when they toddled away from her skirts. But when they grew older and stopped being utterly dependent on her for life itself, she lost interest in them.

Patsy Denny was a change-of-life baby. She was in her middle forties when he came along. (His father died four months before Patsy was born.) She had been awed and surprised when she found herself "that way" with him, having thought surely she was too old to have another child. She held his birth to be a holy miracle. Believing he was a special dispensation from heaven, and realizing he was the last child she'd ever bear, she flowed over with maternal love and gave him all she had denied her other children.

She called him her "eye apple." She did not ask that he work and support her. She worked for *him*. All she asked was that he *be*. All she wanted was to have him with her for always—to look her fill at him and to cater to his creature comforts.

She was the one who convinced him (and he wasn't hard to convince) that he was above common labor. Was he not the talented one? Sure! Why, he could dance a jig, keeping his body rigid as he jumped into the air, no matter what intricate figures his feet beat out.

He had a friend known as Rory-Boy. The friend had a fiddle. Patsy and Rory-Boy entertained at the public houses. Rory-Boy banged his bow on the fiddle strings and wild, incoherent music came out to which Patsy

2

pranced, jogged and leaped. Sometimes someone threw a copper. Patsy's share didn't come to much—just enough to keep him supplied with the lurid-colored handkerchiefs which he liked to wear around his neck and knotted under his left ear.

What was there said about Patrick Dennis in the village? Much that was bad and little that was good—except that he was sweet to his mother. And so he was. He loved her and treated her as though she were a girl he was forever courting.

Sure, he had a sweetheart. She was seventeen. She was a pretty thing with black hair and azure eyes with charcoal-black lashes. She was walking proof of the legend that sometimes God's fingers were smudgy when He put in the eyes of an Irish girl baby. She lived with her widowed mother and her name was Maggie Rose Shawn. She was beautiful, she was poor. And mothers of marriageable sons warned them against Maggie Rose.

"And what would she be bringing to a marriage except her beautiful self? And it's soon enough the bloom would leave that rose when the man would have to take the mother with the daughter for the Widow Shawn is not one to live apart from her only daughter.

"No. The Widow's only son won't take the old lady. Sure now, he's a constable in Brooklyn, America, and it's grand wages he makes. And it's the constable's wife, herself, with her American ways, who looks down on her man's mother and his sister. Or so 'tis said.

"No, my son, there is others to marry. Our Lord put more women than men in this world, especially in this village where the young men leave almost as soon as they're weaned, to get work and to lead the wild life in Dublin or some other strange part of the world and leave the village girls behind."

The boys listened but looked on Maggie Rose with desire, and many there were who thought the care and support of her clinging mother was a cheap price to pay for such a darling of a girl.

But Maggie Rose would have none of their intentions. Patrick Dennis was dear one. He was the one; the only one.

Lizzie Moore was not too concerned when her eye apple of a son started walking out with Maggie Rose Shawn. She knew she had a strong mother-hold on her son.

"Why would he marry," she said, "and play second fiddle to the girl and third to the Widow and him a king alone in me cottage?"

She was sure, too, that Patsy was too lazy and selfish and too scared of hard work to marry a poor girl.

"And what can the girl bring to marriage with a honest boy-o? No bit of land, no sow, no cow, no bag of cloth with a few pieces of gold in it. Nothing! Nothing but a keening mother and a handful of picture postal cards from her brother, the constable in Brooklyn."

She gave out ugly rumors about the girl. "Marry, you say? And why should me last son marry the likes of her? A man marries for the one thing when he can't have it no other way. But ah, me boy-o don't have to go to the trouble of *marrying* for that—the way he is good looking and all."

Patrick Dennis and Maggie Rose were together day and night except when he ate with his mother or performed in the taverns with Rory-Boy. Soon, all of Maggie Rose's other suitors gave way. There was talk.

"The shame of it . . ."

" 'Tis against nature . . ."

"A healthy boy-o and a beautiful girl together all the time, it follows that . . ."

So spoke the drink nursers in the taverns. The village biddies, arms folded and lips stern, nodded knowingly as they agreed that if the couple were not married, sure and they should be.

None of these things were true. Maggie Rose was a good, decent, churchgoing girl. But the talk came to her mother in time and Mrs. Shawn invited Patrick over for supper and had it out with him.

"Sonny lad," she said, "I will talk to you about marrying."

"I'm a-willing," said Patrick.

"To marry?"

"To talk."

"And aren't you the one for talking. And

5

making talk, too—the way they talk about me only daughter and all the fault of you and your ways with her.''

"I'll thrash any man what speaks against Maggie Rose—no matter how big he be's.''

"You'll have to be thrashing most of the women of the parish too, then.'' She gave him the question point-blank. "Now when will you be marrying me daughter?''

Patrick felt trapped and frightened. He wanted to run away and never see either of them again. Not that he didn't care for Maggie Rose. He did. But he didn't want to be gunned into marriage. His gift of gab came to his aid.

"Would I not be the proudest man in the world could I marry Maggie Rose and she willing? But I made a great promise to me old mother: never to marry the while she lived. For who else does she have in all the world? Only meself—poor thing that I am.'' He appealed directly to Maggie Rose. "You would not be wanting a man what was cruel to his mother, would you now?''

Dumbly, and with eyes cast down, she shook her head "No.''

"Is it not so that a son what is bad to his mother,'' he said, "is bad to his wife? Ah, nothing but bad cess would come of it. Think on the poor children what would be born to us—and them blind and crippled—our Lord's punishment was I to destroy me promise to me poor old lady.'' He wiped an eye with a corner of the magenta handkerchief knotted under his left ear.

"And the while you're waiting for your poor old mother to die on you," said the Widow Shawn, "and she the one to make old bones and live to a hundred, me Maggie Rose is losing her chances with the other boy-sis."

" 'Tis true, 'tis true," moaned Patsy. "I don't be having the right to stand in her way." He turned to the now weeping girl. "Me poor heart breaks in two giving you up, me Maggie Rose. But is not your good mother right? So I'll not be standing between you and some other fine man. I'll be bidding you good-by."

To his astonishment, he burst into tears. *Is it a good player that I am,* he thought, *or is it that I love the girl?*

He rushed out of the cottage. Maggie Rose ran down the path after him, weeping and calling out his name. He turned and waited for her. She put kisses on his face and buried her tear-wet cheek in his neck.

"Don't be leaving me, darling," she sobbed. "I'll wait ever for you for I want no one else. I'll wait till your mother dies. And may that be years to come," said the good girl, "for I know how you love her and I would not have you grieve. Only don't leave me. Do not leave me because I love you so."

Things went on as before. Patsy kept on courting Maggie Rose and enjoying it more because he knew now that he didn't have to give

7

up his freedom. Sure, he intended to marry her someday maybe. But for now . . .

His mother was jubilant. She told her cronies: "Her and her mother together: They tried to thrick me boy into marrying the girl and for all I know saying there was the reason for it. And maybe so. Maybe so," she said insinuatingly. "But if so, 'twas not me Patsy Denny was the feller. A girl like that, and sure, it could be anybody a-tall."

Rory-Boy told Patsy Denny he was lucky. "Is it not so that the old cow's got no husband and the sweet girl no living father to beat the hell out of you for not going to the priest with her? I tell you nowhere in the world is there such free love. Not even in America where all is free."

There was a tug at Patsy's heart. *Should I not be sheltering her against the dirty talk,* he thought, *by standing up in church with her? Ah, yes. But would I not be a poor stick of a man if I married me Maggie Rose because the old lady said: do you do so, now.*

Mrs. Shawn took to waylaying the boy and inquiring after his "dear" mother's health. "And how's your mother this day?" she would ask.

"Ah, she's as well as might be," he'd answer, "and me thanks to you for asking. But," with a sigh, "she's getting older . . . older."

"And so's me daughter," she'd answer bitterly.

The harassed woman decided to put a stop to

the affair. She told the girl she'd have to stop seeing Patsy or go into a convent.

"I will not do so," said the girl.

"That you will. 'Tis meself has the say of you and you not eighteen yet."

"Do you try to force me, Mother, I'll . . ." she searched for a word she didn't know. ". . . I'll stay with him in the way bad girls stay with men and they not married to each other."

"To talk to your mother so," wailed Mrs. Shawn. "To dig me grave by breaking me heart. And you—such a good girl before you were spoiled by that black'ard! You who went to church every morning to receive . . ."

Mrs. Shawn went into a time of weeping and keening. When that was out of the way, she sent for Bertie, the Broommaker, who was also the village letter writer. Bertie brought his book along: *Epistles for All Occasions*. There was no form letter that suited the Widow's exact occasion. The nearest one was: *Epistle to Be Written to a Relative Across the Water Announcing the Demise of a Dear One*. Bertie said he'd copy it off and make it "fit" by changing *demise* to *my daughter's fix* whenever *demise* came up, and to substitute *my esteemed son, Timothy* for *my esteemed great-uncle Thaddeus*.

After the letter was carefully addressed to: *Constable Timothy Shawn, Police Department, Brooklyn, U.S.A.*, Bertie inked in his trademark on the back of the envelope.

9

Chapter Two

OFFICER Timothy (Big Red) Shawn sat in the parlor of his East New York flat. His beat was the Bowery in Manhattan, but he lived in Brooklyn because he liked to live in the country, he said, and because his wife wanted to live near her mother. It took him more than two hours to get home each night. He had to journey by ferry, horsecar and foot.

Now, his day's work done, he sat in his parlor in his undershirt soaking his poor feet in a dishpan of warm water in which Epsom salts were dissolved. The stiff red hairs on his chest pushed through the cloth of his undershirt like rusty grass seeking the sun.

"Why don't you soak your feet in the kitchen and save the parlor rug?" asked Lottie, his American-born wife of Irish descent. She asked the same question each night.

"Because me home is me castle." He made the same answer each night.

He surveyed the parlor of his castle. The

narrow windows that looked down on the street were hung with lace curtains. They were sooty but starched. A taboret, fake Chinese, stood between the windows. Its function was to hold a rubber plant in a glazed green jardiniere. The unfolded top leaf of the plant always had a drop of rubber milk on its tip. A gaudy and fringed lambrequin draped the fake marble mantelpiece over the fake onyx fireplace. On the mantelpiece was a china pug dog lying on its side and with four pug puppies lying in a row, frozen eternally in the act of taking nourishment from their mother.

"We got bedbugs again," said his wife conversationally.

"Where'd the buggers come from?"

"From the people upstairs. They *always* come from the people upstairs. Where the cockroaches come from."

"Ah, well, they got bedbugs at Buckingham Palace, too," he said. He sniffed the air. "What are we got for supper tonight?"

"We got boiled dinner for supper tonight, being's today was washday."

"If there's anything what I like," he said, "it's a boiled dinner like you make it."

"Want to eat now, then?"

"Let's see." He lifted a foot out of the dishpan and watched it drip. "Not yet. My feet ain't done yet."

He was content. He looked fondly at his wife. She was teasing a lock of hair; making it frizzy

11

by holding one hair and pushing the others up on it in a tangled ball.

He was proud of her. No matter how hard she worked in the house or taking care of their son, she always dressed up for his homecoming. She got into her corsets and tied on a bustle pad (not that she needed one) and pinned the lace ruffles to her corset cover (not that she needed them either). The bustle and ruffles filled her out more and Big Red liked a well-filled-out woman.

Her dusty blond hair was in dips and waves and the rat made her pompadour stand up high. That was the way she had worn it when he first met her and she hadn't changed her hair style a bit in ten years.

Big Red sat in his parlor, then, contented, soaking his feet and trying not to think too deep. Lottie was folding towels and singing her iceman song under her breath.

> . . . of one thing I am sure.
> There's something about his business
> That affects his temperature.

"Where's our boy Widdy?" he asked.

"Over to Mama's."

"Why?"

"He's eating supper over there."

"What for?"

"Well, Mama took him to the butcher's with her and they had these rabbits hanging outside a barrel with hair on? *You* know. So Widdy wanted a rabbit foot for luck and the butcher wouldn't sell just a foot so Mama had to buy the whole rabbit and she couldn't eat it all by herself so he's eating over there.''

She got up, went to him and ran her fingers through the few red curls left on his head.

"Why'n't you tell me before?'' he said.

He gave her a slap on the backside. He felt that, with their child out of the house, he could take a liberty. He lifted one foot out of the dishpan. It looked like a mummy's foot.

"Listen, Timmy,'' she said. "Dry your feet and go down to Mike's for a pint of beer and we'll eat.''

"Sure.'' But he looked ill at ease. "But first—I got a letter today. It came to the station house.'' He stiffened, reached back, and pulled a letter out of his hind pocket.

"Who from?''

"Me mother.''

"What does she want now?''

"*Now?* And 'tis five years since I heard from her last?''

"What does she say?''

"I don't know. I saved it to read in front of you.''

"Aw, Timmy, that's all right. You could've read your letter in the station house.''

"We share.''

"I know. That's what keeps us sweethearts.''

"From Ireland.'' He turned the letter over and back. "County Kilkenny.'' He dreamed:

"Ah, I can see it plain, Lottie, the medders and all. And me mother's sod shanty with the rushes always blowing off the roof and the clay hearth and the black pot ever on the hob and the skinny cow and the few bony chickens and the praties we scratched out of the ground . . ."

And, thought Lottie, not bitterly, *his mother standing in the doorway and holding out her hand once a month for the letter with the ten-dollar bill in it that he sends and his mother and sister never writing to say, yes, no, or kiss my foot.*

"And," dreamed Timmy, "the village walk and the girls with no corsets on and the skirts turned back to show the red petticoat and their hair flying in the wind . . ." He sighed. "Ah so. And I wouldn't go back there for a million dollars."

"Will you read the letter now," she said, a little piqued about the girls not wearing corsets, "or will you frame it?"

He opened the letter and read:

Esteemed Son: I take my pen in hand to compose this sorrowful epistle . . .

"Me mother can't read or write," he explained.

"Go on!" she said in disbelief.

"Bertie, the Broommaker, wrote it for her. I bet you he's still living! Why, he must be seventy . . . no, eighty years . . ."

14

"Will you read or will you frame?" she asked. He read:

. . . to convey to you, esteemed son, the sorrowful tidings that one who once was with us and who had a loving place in our hearts and who was esteemed by all, has heeded the call of a Higher Being, and is now In A Fix.

"Who died, rest his soul?" asked Lottie.
"Nobody yet. Let me read."

Oh, better, esteemed son, "that we two lay sleeping in our nest in the churchyard sod," than to endure the grief of The Fix she is in.

Big Red paused to wipe a tear from his eye and to give his wife a pleading look.
"You read it to yourself, Timmy, dear," she said, "and tell me after."
He mumbled through some more of the letter and suddenly let out a snarling cry and stood upright in the dishpan of water.
"What?" she cried out. "Oh, sweetheart, what?"
"The black'ard!" he snarled. "The durrrtee black'ard!" He stepped out of the dishpan and strode up and down the parlor with Lottie following him with a towel. "Oh, me baby sister. Me baby sister," he moaned.
She tried to comfort him. "We all got to go someday, Timmy darling."

"She's not dead. But 'twas better if she was."

"Oh, why, my sweetheart?"

"Because a black'ard by the name of . . ." he consulted the letter, ". . . P. D. Moore, Esquire, scandalized her name and now he won't marry her." He sobbed in big gulps.

"Sit here," said Lottie gently, "and I'll dry your poor tired feet."

She knelt before him and patted his puckered feet dry. He wept until his feet were well dried. Then he made a fist and shook it at the ceiling.

"I'm going to Ireland and beat the be-Jesus out of him, God willing," he said.

Chapter Three

THE tavern was smoky, crowded and smelled of warm, spilled beer. Rory-Boy's fiddle was squealing wildly and Patsy Denny was jigging his heart out. It was a noisy Saturday night. The door opened and a big, red-headed stranger came in. He wasn't exactly red-headed, being almost bald, but there was a rusty glow where his hair had been. A clot of ale-drinking men at the bar opened up to let the stranger in and then closed about him; absorbing him, as it were.

Rory-Boy saw the stranger come in and his Irish intuition told him that the stranger was Maggie Rose's big brother come all the way from Brooklyn to beat the hell out of Patrick Dennis. He was too scared to warn Patsy. He forgot the notes of "The Irish Washerwoman" as his fingers froze on his fiddle strings. His desperately sawing bow brought out a continuous one-note, high wail. Patsy thought the tune was ending and he went into the frenzied leap into the air where he usually clicked his

17

heels together in a finale.

"Never have I le'pped so high!" he called to his friend as he went up.

Indeed his leap was prodigious. He went up . . . up without the volition of his legs and he *stayed* suspended in the air. For a second, he felt like an angel with wings, then he wondered what made his pants so tight. He found out.

Timothy (Big Red) Shawn had slipped out of the knot of men, and at the moment of Patsy's leap he had, like a trained acrobat, gotten a purchase on the seat of Patsy's pants and on the scruff of his neck and had given Patsy's leap a grand fillip. As Bertie, the Broommaker, who happened to be there, later wrote in a letter for a gossiping client: *All conviviality ceased and silence reigned.*

Big Red held Patsy in the air and shook him as though he were a rag puppet. Big Red had rehearsed a speech coming over in the steerage. He had planned to give it as a prelude to a thrashing, but he forgot it entirely and had to ad-lib.

"You durtee, wee, little black'ard you!" he said loud for all to hear. "I'll learn youse to break the only heart of me only mother and . . ." (Shake! Shake!) " . . . scandalize the name of me baby sister. You jiggin' monkey! You durtee bog trotter, you!"

"What do you mean, bog trotter?" gasped Patsy, scared but insulted. "I never cut peat in all of me life."

Finally Big Red set him down and gave him one of those old-time lickings. When he had finished, he threw Patsy in the general direction of the exit and dusted off his hands.

"And don't forget, fancy man," he said, "there's more where that come from."

Patrick Dennis backed out of the tavern. He wasn't taking any chances of being kicked in the behind.

The next day, Sunday, a scared, chastened Patsy went to Mass with his mother. He saw his girl wedged in between her simpering mother and her burly brother. Patsy started to feel sick as he stared at Big Red's broad back.

Father Crowley came down from the altar and stepped to one side of it before the railing to make the routine announcements of the week. Patsy hardly listened to the rise and fall of the voice until, as in a nightmare from which there is no awakening, he heard the sound of his name.

" . . . weekly meeting of the girls' Sodality." The priest cleared his throat. "The banns of marriage are read for the first time between Margaret Rose Shawn and Patrick Dennis Moore. Your prayers are requested for the repose of the soul of . . ."

Lizzie Moore gave a hoarse honk like a wild goose calling the flock in for a landing. There was a stir like a great sigh as the congregation turned to stare at Patsy and his mother. Big Red turned around and gave Patsy a grin of victory.

His lips silently formed the words: *There's more where that came from.*

Patsy was caught and he knew it. *Trapped,* he moaned to himself. *And by what thrickery did he get me name up for marrying and me the one should have the say of it? Caught! Before two weeks is out I'll be married forever.*

His mother wept foggily into the hem of her top petticoat. *He kept it from me,* she mourned. *Me lyin' son. He went to the priest with the girl and gave himself up. And Big Timmy was sent for to give the girl away and she having no father to do so. Oh, for me son to treat me so, and he me last baby and the hardest to bring into God's world with his head the size of a hard, green cabbage at the time.*

She wept and Patsy was ashamed. He left during the final prayer. Maggie Rose, kneeling, turned as he got up and made an instinctive movement to follow him but Big Red pulled her back down.

Patsy felt friendless and disgraced. He was sure that by now all the village knew he had been licked by his girl's brother. Before night the whole village would know whatever trick Big Red had used to get the banns read and he, Patsy Denny, would be the laughingstock of the county.

It came too late to Patsy—too late—the knowledge that he loved Maggie Rose and would never love any other woman. Why, oh, why hadn't he married her when their love was fresh and new—before it had been dirtied by scandals and beatings and public disgace?

'Tis not to be endured, decided Patsy. *Oh, better to be dead—to go to America . . .*

America!

He'd heard that the steamship company paid your way and got you a job in America. And there was a little office in a village not ten miles away where the steamship man from Liverpool arranged everything. He almost whistled as he sneaked home in a round-about way.

His mother wouldn't speak to him when he got home. She had her good, black dress and a pair of black stockings she'd been hoarding for twenty years laid out on the bed. She was polishing her black shoes from a tin of caked blacking. He chattered, trying to get her to speak to him. But she had nothing to say until he asked politely

"Are you going a-visiting, Mother?"

"And who would I go see, the way I'm 'shamed to show me face in the village? No, I'm getting me good black clothes ready—the clothes I'm wishing to be laid out in."

"Not for many a year yet, God willing."

"Soon. Soon. The day you marry is the day you'll see me in me casket."

"Don't die on me," he begged.

"You marry on me and I'll die on you." She buffed the shoe which gloved her hand.

"I'll never marry the while you live."

"Ah, so. Never marry, he says, after having

21

the banns read and all!"

It took him an hour to convince her that the banns were said without his consent or knowledge. She refused to believe him until he told her of the beating he'd had from Big Red.

"And so he licked you, me poor boy, and you saying you fell off your wheel."

" 'Twas shame made me say it."

"And he'll lick you many a time till you say, 'I do.' "

"I'll die first!"

"You won't die first or last. You'll be made to marry the girl."

"I can't be made if I go to America."

"And you'd be leaving me like me other chilthren did?"

"Only for a while. I'll send for you before the year is gone."

"You'll not be sending for anyone. You'll bide here with me. Die if you have the wish. But you'll not marry and you'll not leave me."

" 'Tis hard to die," he said, "and our Lord forgive me for saying I would and me not meaning it a-tall. I will stay, Mother dear, and marry Maggie Rose, and I will be shamed in the county all the days of me living and I'll not be caring, because I love Maggie Rose."

"You *say* so."

"I would do so."

She put the lid on the tin of blacking. "In a year you say? You'll send for me?"

"I swear it."

" 'Tis for the best." She put the blacking away. "Go, then, to America and make a place for me and I will come to you."

The next morning, he cycled ten miles to the next village. The Liverpool sport who represented a steamship company made things easy for Patrick Dennis Moore. Passage was arranged and everything was free—free for the time being.

Yes, Patsy would have to pay for the ticket in time, but that was easy, too. There was a job waiting for him in America. One Michael Moriarity—and, oh, he was Lord Mayor of Brooklyn or something near as grand, was the sport's opinion—would pay Patsy all of five dollars a week and give him room and board. And all for what? For nothing. For taking care of two darling carriage horses.

Staunchly, Patsy promised to pay the passage money back. That he would, the sport assured him. A man from the steamship branch in Brooklyn would come once a week and take two dollars from his wages until the ticket was paid up. Patsy agreed with the sport that the remaining three dollars was a "forchune"—in America or anywhere else.

Patsy put his name on a paper.

"You'll be wanting some loose change for the trip," suggested the sport.

"Glory be," said Patsy. "Does the company give out spending money, too?"

"Well, hardly. But your wheel. You'll have no use for it when you're gone. I'll take it off your hands for two pounds. You ride over on it Tuesday when the coach leave for Cóbh Harbor and I'll take ownership then and give you the pound notes."

Big Red wasn't happy. His mother and sister forever found fault with him. Maggie Rose was not a bit grateful. She told her brother she hated him because he had thrashed her love and shamed him and herself in the village.

"Now he'll go from me forever," she wept.

"Over me dead body," vowed Big Red.

"Why did you come a-tween us?" she sobbed. "I was willing to wait till his mother died. Why did you make him the clown of the county?"

"Anyone," he said bitterly, "who would marry a sharp-tongue girl like you—his mother living or dead—is a clown born and not made." He was instantly sorry. "Forgive me wild talk, Maggie Rose, do," he said.

There was that pain coming in his left temple; a sure sign that he was thinking deep. *God forgive me,* he thought, *if I did a wrong to this boy what never knew me, by giving him a licking and putting his name up to be read in church with me sister's.*

His mother's reception of the wedding gift his Lottie had sent by him wasn't appreciated by Big Red. It was a pair of pillow shams with hand-crocheted edges. Mrs. Shawn claimed the linen was coarse and that Lottie had changed crochet

24

patterns in the middle of an edging.

" 'Tis not so," shouted Big Red. "Everything my Lottie does is beautiful."

"Ah, the sloppy house she must be keeping for me only son," sighed the Widow.

"So help me, God, Mother . . ." he shouted.

"Raise your voice to me again," she interrupted, "and I'll give it to you. Big as you are!"

Holy Mother, he prayed, *let me not be losing me temper and me here for only a bit of a while with the mother what bore me and me only baby sister.*

By agreement, Patsy and his mother pretended to be all for the marriage the following Sunday. When the priest read the banns for a second time and the congregation turned around to gloat, Mrs. Moore smiled and bowed graciously and Patsy smiled tenderly at the Shawn family. This threw the villagers into confusion. After Mass, they gathered in groups outside the church and held worried, whispered consultations. Had something gone wrong, they asked each other. Would he marry the girl after all? It was a big letdown. Big Red relaxed and was happy. He felt he had done the right thing after all.

Two days later, Patrick Dennis strapped a homemade knapsack, made of coarse linen, on his back. It held all he owned: six colored handkerchiefs, his other shirt and a pair of woolen socks knitted by his loving mother.

"And you will send for me before the year is out?" she asked for the tenth time.

"That I will, Mother dear."

"Swear!"

He swore on the little black leather prayer book she had given him when he made his First Communion.

"May I drop dead," he swore, "if I don't send for you within the year. As God is my witness."

"Amen," she said, as she tucked the book in his knapsack.

He looked around once more before he mounted his bicycle. The soft, green, rolling hills . . . the blue sky and tender white clouds and the pink, wild roses tangled on the tumble-down, gray, rock wall around the cottage.

And he didn't want to go—he didn't want to go. But he was caught up in the momentum of all the events and the arrangements were made and it was easier to go than to stay.

Patsy jigged with impatience while his mother sprinkled the bicycle and himself with holy water and ceremoniously pinned a St. Christopher's medal to his undershirt. When that was done, he got onto his bike in one frenzied leap. His mother's parting words were:

"God grant, me son, that her bastid of a brother don't ketch you sneaking out of Ireland."

He turned to wave and wheeled out of his mother's life, and out of Ireland forever.

Chapter Four

PATRICK DENNIS MOORE stood on American soil once removed by the slate pavement. His first impression of America was that half the people in the new world were riding bicycles.

Sure, he thought, *here they must give them away with a pound of tea for where would all these people be getting money to buy them?*

He stood on the curb, knapsack on back and card with Moriarity's address clutched in his hand. "Ask a cop," a man in the steerage had instructed him. "Be sure to call him 'officer' and he'll tell you how to get the ferry to Brooklyn." Patsy saw a cop across the street but the traffic confused him so he didn't know how to cross.

Great beer trucks, some drawn by six Percherons, pounded by; horse-drawn cars clanged along on iron tracks. A funeral procession, composed of a hearse, an open carriage full of floral pieces and ten coaches of mourners, crawled along. The dead man, likely as not ineffectual in life, was important enough in death to hold up traffic for ten minutes.

Two-wheeled carts, some loaded with fruit, others with junk, were pushed along by men with long, patriarchal beards. The junk carts had cowbells on a leather strap across the top. The bells made an unholy, discordant jangle in the jungle of noises. A lot of cursing, most of it directed at the bearded men, seemed necessary to keep all the vehicles moving.

Bicycles skimmed in and out, confounding all traffic. The riders irritated everyone by their nervous tinkling of the bicycle bells. The men rode looking constantly over a shoulder, which made the bicycles swerve from here to there.

A bell-clanging fire engine thundered by and the horses' hoofs drew sparks from the cobblestones. Patsy stared in amazement at a spotted dog that ran along under the fire truck, avoiding, by some miracle, being ground to death by the fast-turning wheels.

There were hansom cabs and lacquered traps and varnished carriages drawn by nervous, shining horses and with elegantly dressed dandies and ladies lolling back on the cushions.

The cop across the street was moving away. Patsy was afraid he'd lose him so he made an attempt at crossing the street. Bedlam! Whistles blew, bells tinkled, gongs clanged, drivers cursed, horses reared and a man fell off a high-wheeled bicycle. People yelled at Patsy:

"Get out-a the gutter, yer Goddamned greenhorn!" This was Patsy's first greeting in the new world.

"Wipe-a behin' ears, doity mick," yelled an Italian fish peddler. This was the first instruction Patsy received.

And, "Go back where you come from, why doncha," from one of Horatio Alger's newsboys, was the first piece of disinterested advice Patsy received in America.

Patsy scuttled back to the sidewalk, thinking: *I'll get to know the language in time, for 'tis almost like English.*

A hansom cab worked its way over to the curb where Patsy was standing. The driver sat high up on the back of the cab. Of course he had a red nose and a battered top hat.

"Cab, sir?"

Eagerly, gratefully, Patsy held up the card which had Moriarity's Brooklyn address. "Would you now, old Da', take me to this place?" he said.

"Not all the way, me boy, sir. Horse can't swim. But I'll take you to the dock and you take the ferry from there."

"How do I get in your wagon, then?" asked Patsy. "Or do you be having room up there with you where I can see the sights of the town?"

"Let's see the color of your money first," said the driver. Patsy showed him a pound note. "Counterfeit!" gasped the cabbie. Then he said: "Oh, no, you don't, sport. Lucky I don't turn you over to the cops." He flicked the horse with his whip and worked his way back into the stream of traffic.

A businesslike young man, with a sheaf of papers in his hand, who had been watching Patsy for some time, now approached him.

"Name, please!" he said briskly, giving Patsy a keen look.

"Patrick Dennis Moore," said Patsy obediently. The young man riffled through his papers.

"And you are going . . . ?" Patsy gave him the card. The young man read the name and address. "Ah, yes," he said. He pulled a paper out of the sheaf. "Here it is. Phew!" He wiped his face with his hand. "I thought I lost you. I've been looking all over for you since the ship docked."

"You know me, then?" asked Patsy, astonished.

"I know who you are. I work for Mr. Moriarity, too." He extended the hand of friendship. Deliriously happy, Patsy wrung it. "Gee, Mr. Moore," said the young man appealingly, "please don't tell Mr. Moriarity that I was late meeting you. He'll sack me."

"Things have been said of me," said Patsy grandly, "but never that I was an informer."

"When I first spotted you," said the young man, "I could tell you was true blue. Now," he said briskly, "where's your luggage?"

"All I own in the world is strapped to me back."

"I'll relieve you of it."

"I'll keep it. 'Tis no burthen a-tall."

The young man consulted the paper. "Mr. Moore," he read aloud, "is to be given every consideration. You are to carry his luggage. . . ." The young man shrugged. "Boss's orders," he said cheerfully.

Patsy gave him the knapsack. The young man rolled it up and tucked it under his arm. "Let us be on our way," he said, "to your new home in America."

Skillfully, he piloted Patsy across the street. "I'll put you on a horsecar," he said, "and that will take you to the ferry dock. You get on the boat and when it stops you get off and Mr. Moriarity will be waiting for you there with his carriage, to drive you to his home."

"I'm that obliged to you . . ." began Patsy.

"Don't thank me, Mr. Moore. This is all part of my job. Now!" He gave a furtive look up and down the street. "Do you have any money on you?" Patsy's eyes narrowed suddenly. "I mean for carfare and the ferry?" added the young man quickly.

"Well . . ." began Patsy cagily.

"Here, then," said the young man. He gave Patsy four nickels. "That will get you over to Brooklyn and buy you a beer in the bargain."

Patsy was ashamed of his suspicions. "I got two notes," he said, "but the cabby said they was counterfeet."

"Let's see 'em." Patsy gave him the notes. The young man examined them carefully. "Why, these bills are just as good as gold," he said indignantly. "Only you have to get them changed into American money." He took another furtive look up and down the street. "Wait! I'll run in here and 'change them. Only take a minute. Be right back."

He darted through the swinging doors of a saloon. He did not come back in a minute. As Patsy waited, he became heavy with premonition. He waited a few minutes longer. Then he went into the saloon.

The place was empty save for the man behind the bar. He was a big man with big mustaches and roached hair. A smell of wet sawdust, stale beer and dank graveyard air seemed to rise from the barkeep like a vapor.

"Yah?" he asked.

"Where's the man what just came in here?" asked Patsy. "The man who came in to change me pound notes?"

"No Mann ist hier," said the barkeep.

"I *saw* him come in. He told me to wait."

"Oudt mit you," said the man, yawning. "Rause!"

"Not till I get me notes back," said Patsy. He heard a small squeak; saw a door close stealthily in the rear. "He's in there!" shouted Patsy. He made a dash for the door.

But the bartender was too quick for him. Burly as he was, he took a nimble one-handed vault over the bar. He had an ugly-looking blackjack in his free hand.

"Oudt! Get oudt from mine place," he bellowed. "Du Gottverdammten Irisher!" Patsy made it just in time. The blackjack came down on top of one of the inswinging doors and splintered it. Patsy shuddered and ducked around the corner.

He walked the unaccustomed streets for hours. His heart wept for his familiar Irish village. He was lost and terrified. He was friendless and didn't know where to go. It was worse than being lost in a vast trackless forest. One could sit down and rest in a forest. There was no place on the street where he could sit down and rest.

In time, he came to a lonely side street and saw a man in white pushing a cart in which a broom and shovel were upended. He approached the white wing, cap in hand.

"Officer, could you be telling me, and me a greenhorn just landed," he said humbly, "how to get to this village?" He showed him the card.

"Sure, Greenie," said the obliging street cleaner. "Here's what you do." He gave him careful directions.

It took Patsy six hours, three horsecars, one ferry and miles of walking to get to Bushwick Avenue, Brooklyn. He stood at the bottom of the long stoop and took in the, to him, splendor of the three-story, parlor and basement, brownstone house with red geraniums in urns on the stoop railing posts. Patsy climbed the stoop. There was a white porcelain plate next the door. It had a black button in the center. Underneath it said: *Ring bell.* Patsy looked around but could find no rope to pull to ring a bell. He did the next best thing: He tapped on the etched-glass window of the vestibule door. After a while, a buxom wench opened the door, gave him one look and said:

"We don't want none."

From within the darkness of the house, Patsy heard the sweetest voice in the world say: "Who is it, Biddy?"

"A peddler, Miss Mary . . . some tinker's son," said Biddy.

"I'll attend to it."

She came out of the darkness to Patsy and his heart fell when he saw that the sweetest voice in the world belonged to, according to Patrick's standards, the plainest face and plainest figure in the world.

"I come from County Kilkenny," he began.

"Oh!" She clasped her hands and her face brightened up with the sweetest smile in the world. "You must be the new boy. Come in."

He followed her into the house, his heart sighing: *Oh, if God had only gone a little further after he made her voice and her smile!*

"Papa," she called, "the boy is here from Ireland."

Patsy stood on the Turkey-red carpet and looked around the dim room. The windows were hung with Brussels lace curtains and maroon velvet draperies tied back with golden cords, and green velvet portieres, hung from a fretwork arch that led into an alcove, were tied back to display a shiny upright piano with a velvet-covered stool. There were silver-framed photographs on the piano and a whatnot in a corner, its shelves filled with little "friendship" cups, and Boston ferns on the window ledges. And gilt chairs upholstered in pink and blue satin and a love seat. A big statue of a blackamoor was on the newel post of the stairs leading to the second floor. The blackamoor held a bowl over his head in which a gas light flickered. On the stair landing was a concave, oval, leaded, stained-glass window.

Patsy thought it was all beautiful . . . beautiful. He promised himself that he would have a house like that someday. *Until I get my own,* he thought, *I'll be content to live here.*

Moriarity came into the room and greeted him boomingly. Then he shouted for his wife. A timid little woman scuttled into the room.

"Missus, this is the new stable boy," he said. "Boy, this is your Missus." The Missus bobbed her head in a scared way and scuttled back into the shadows of the room.

"And me daughter, Mary." The plain girl gave Patsy her sweet smile. "American born," said Moriarity. It was obvious that he was proud of his daughter. "And she studied to be a teacher. This here is Biddy, the cook. She comes from County Down." He addressed Biddy.

"Biddy, me bird, Pathrick here is a fine-looking feller. Now don't you go making eyes at

35

him when the both of youse should be working.''

Patsy looked at the big-busted Biddy with aversion and she looked at him with distaste. *There's nothing there what I want,* thought Patsy.

''And afther, I'll introduce you to me two best girls, Jessie and Daisy,'' Mike said to Patsy. ''And now: Where's your satchel?''

''A young man took it off me. He said he worked for you and that you said he should.'' Patsy thought it best to say nothing about the two pounds.

''He took your satchel?''

''Yes. Me 'sack.''

''Are you standing there and telling me you was taken in by that old thrick?'' He laughed. ''Yah-ha-ha! Yah-ha-ha!''

The booming laugh scared The Missus. She threw up her hands in fright and scuttled from the room.

''Yah-ha-ha!'' laughed Mike. ''Wait'll I tell the boys down at headquarters.''

''Now, Papa, don't laugh,'' said Mary Moriarity. ''Remember the same thing happened to you when you came over. Only the man said he was your uncle's cousin. And he got your trunk. *And* all your money, too.''

Patsy gave her a grateful look. *Ah, she's kind,* he thought. *But then, 'tis the nature of plain women to be kind.*

''Har-umph!'' The Boss cleared his throat.

" 'Tis so. *Was* so. But sure 'twas only an old thrunk filled with rags. Mary, go below stairs with Biddy and see that she fixes a dish of hot supper for the new boy." The women left.

"And now Pathrick, me boy, I'll show you to your room." Patsy turned and went toward the stairs. "Not up there." The Boss laughed. "Across the yard. Folly me."

They had to go through the downstairs hall to get to the yard. Patsy heard Mary and Biddy talking in the kitchen.

Biddy was saying: "Hot dish, me foot! Cold dish! I'm not the one to cook after hours for inny greenhorn just landed."

"Now, Biddy," came Mary's gentle voice. "Don't call him that. You know you didn't like people to call you greenhorn when *you* came over five years ago."

Ah, she's the sweet girl, thought Patsy. *But plain. Ah, the pity of it!*

Patsy was introduced to the two mares, and shown a ladder which led to the loft above. "Your new home is up there. 'Tis small but you'll be as snug as a bug in a rug, ha-ha. Now get yourself a bit of supper and go to bed. I'll let you off work until tomorrow."

He climbed up the ladder and lit the lamp. He surveyed his kingdom. It was a small room with one window. It had a cot, a chair, a kitchen table with the lamp on it, and three nails in the wall for his clothes and towel.

'Tis barer than a convent cell, he thought.

37

And in America the horses do be living better than us honest immigrants. Was I born, now, to be a servant? No! Ah, he sighed, *the good Lord must have had it in for me, the way He sent me here.*

He fell asleep but woke up in the middle of the night. He woke up in a panic because he didn't know where he was. He walked lopsided across the room to find the lamp. *'Tis strange,* he thought, *the boat still rocking and did I not get off from it this morning?* He found the table and lit the lamp. He looked around the tiny room. *'Tis no dream,* he told himself. *I am here, alone, amongst strangers. I am without me mother and me girl and me friend, Rory-Boy.*

Too many things was done to me this day. And from now on, I'll make everyone who puts a finger to me life do penance for what has been done to me, to me, Patrick Dennis Moore.

Chapter Five

MIKE MORIARITY, called by all The Boss, was a stout, ruddy man with a big belly and big mustaches. He wore his pepper-and-salt hair parted in the middle with a thick lap on either side which looked like a pair of gray-and-black pigeons nesting on top of his head. He wore a black broadcloth suit with a white vest that looked as though it never had been spotless—even when new. A watch chain, the links big enough for a dog leash, bisected his belly. He was never without an up-tilted cigar in the corner of his mouth. Outdoors, he wore a square-crowned derby tilted over one eye to almost touch the tip of his up-tilted cigar. He looked like a caricature of a Tammany ward heeler.

He was a Tammany ward heeler.

Molly, his wife, known as The Missus, was a person soon overlooked. She was tiny, four feet ten, and weighed eighty pounds. She was forever frightened and put in her days scuttling back and forth, up and down the house.

Mary Moriarity, but for her kind ways, would have walked through life unnoted. Her face was plain. She was too tall for a woman and she lacked the curves that one looks for in a woman. One didn't notice her plainness at all when she spoke or smiled. But she was not given to talking much and she smiled rarely.

The two matched mares revolted Patsy. When he washed or curried them and the skin rippled beneath his hand, it gave him the creeps. He hated their coarse eyelashes. He wondered why they needed such big yellow teeth only for oats and hay. He was disgusted by their ankles, which seemed too thin to support the heavy bodies. And tears of indignity filled his eyes when the horse's rump before his face blotted out the light of the day as he stood there braiding red ribbon into a coarse-haired tail.

He hated the manure which he had to garner each day to deploy around the base of the snowball bushes in the yard because The Missus had told him, with fright in her face, that it must be done because the lumps were pure gold to the bushes and would make the flowers icy blue in color.

Each day, Patsy had to walk the horses four times around the block for exercise. He had to wear a bibbed apron, made of mattress ticking, while he walked the horses. How he hated to wear that apron!

The first day's walk was full of incident. Some

kids playing hookey from school followed him yelling: "Mick!" and "Greenhorn!" and "Why don't you button your dress in the back?" They got sick of that soon enough and went away.

An ambulance bore down on him. He had to get himself and the horses up on the sidewalk to avoid being run down. An intern or doctor leaned on the strap in the back. Patsy stared at the visored cap on top of a pompadour. He'd never seen a woman doctor before. Then a cop came along and gave him hell for standing on the sidewalk with two horses.

"Try that again," suggested the cop mildly, "and I'll run you in. You *and* the horses."

A street walker, off duty and returning from shopping, invited him up to her flat to see her birdie. He blushed raspberry red until he saw that she was actually carrying a box of freshly purchased birdseed.

She does be having a birdie in a cage after all, thought Patsy. *And may all the saints forgive me for thinking the other way.*

Then he had to stop while one of the mares obeyed a call of nature. He was shamed to death. A street cleaner appeared from nowhere with cart, broom and shovel.

"Good day to you, officer," said Patsy ingratiatingly.

"Son of a bitch!" said the street cleaner bitterly, as he started to clean up.

As Patsy led the horses away, he thought: *He meant the mare, for no man in the world could*

41

call me *that and live to tell it.*

He had other duties. He had to sweep the sidewalk and stoop and rake the yard daily. He put the filled garbage can at the curb at night and impaled the filled trash bag on a spike of the railing around the house. He beat the rugs and washed the windows and stretched the lace curtains on the frames. In short he had to obey The Missus' bidding and Biddy's whims.

The steamship man called on Patsy each payday and Patsy gave him two dollars, which the man marked in a little black book.

"Only fifty-eight dollars more," the collector had said after the first payment. "You'll be paid up in a year."

"I don't want to stay here a year," Patsy had told him. "I don't like it here. I want to go back to Ireland."

"No reason why you shouldn't—after two years."

"Two . . . ?"

"A year to pay off your passage here and a year to pay off your passage back."

Two years before he could go back or two years before he could send his mother passage money. No. He couldn't wait. He'd save every penny. . . . To that end, he got an empty cigar box from Van Clees, a young Dutch cigar maker from whom Patsy bought a penny clay pipe once in a while and a sack of tobacco. Patsy nailed the cover shut and cut a slit in the cover. He dropped his savings in the slit.

The savings accumulated very slowly. Patsy was not extravagant and his needs were few enough, but there was always something to buy. Aside from fifteen cents a week for clay pipes and tobacco, he had to pay ten cents twice a week for a shave at the barber's. He couldn't afford to buy a straight razor and honing strap. A haircut once a month cost twenty cents. A nickel went into the collection plate at Mass each Sunday. Then he needed socks and a union suit and another shirt and a Sunday tie and pomade for his hair. There was a beer or two of a Saturday night—not that he was a drinking man. But he liked the conviviality of the saloon where voices were raised in song and one could count on a grand fight starting up once in a while. But he did manage to save a dollar a week.

Mary asked him kindly had he heard from his mother. It was then he realized two months had gone by and he hadn't written. No, he said, he hadn't heard because he hadn't written. Yes, he could read and write but had never written a letter because at home everyone he knew was close by and letters weren't necessary. It was addressing the envelope that bothered him and the proper stamp.

That night she made him a present of a box of stationery and a penholder and a half-dozen penpoints and a bottle of ink. She had a stamped envelope addressed for him. He wrote that night.

He wrote his mother that it might be two years before he could send for her. He suggested she get in touch with the Liverpool sport and get passage and a job. He wrote: . . . *I have a fine apartment here* . . . He looked around his barren room. *God forgive me for lying,* he prayed.

He wrote that he was sending her an American dollar in the letter and . . . *The young lady of the house is stuck on me* . . . *She gave me a grand present.* . . .

He didn't believe, really, that Mary was stuck on him. He wrote it knowing his mother's tongue was tied in the middle and wagged at both ends and she'd be sure to tell Maggie Rose and the girl would be jealous and would write to him. A half page more of boasting, and the letter was finished.

He waited every day for a letter. Two months passed and he had given up hope of hearing from home, when one night Mary came down to the kitchen where he was eating supper with Biddy, and smilingly put a letter next his plate. He finished his supper in a hurry and went up to his room to read the letter. It was written by Bertie, the Broommaker.

Esteemed Son: Yours at hand and contents noted. Your one dollar received. I trust more to follow. I informed Miss Shawn of your new attachment. Miss Shawn requests that I tender you her congratulations. Miss Shawn requests me to inform you that she, also, has formed a new attachment.

I must decline with thanks your kind invitation to join you in America under the conditions you set forth. I have no wish to become a domestic for no gentlewoman of our family has ever gone into service. It is my desire to remain here in order to die where I was born and to sleep the eternal sleep at the side of my dear, departed husband, your father.

Pray extend my cordial greetings to your guide and mentor, M. Moriarity, Esquire. I remain your devoted mother, Elizabeth A. Moore. (Mrs.)

So she took it serious, thought Patsy, *and she thinks I have a girl and after I gave me promise . . . and now she won't come to me a-tall.* He put his head down on his arms and cried a little. He knew that the last link between him and Ireland had been broken. *Me mother don't want me now,* he wept, *but she wouldn't let Maggie Rose have me. And now me girl went and got another feller. . . .*

After a while, he wiped his eyes, busted open his bank and took out a half dollar. He went down to the saloon, had ten five-cent beers, two fights and ate most of the free lunch left over from noon. He felt much better afterward.

Mary, returning from the druggist's where she'd gone to buy a cake of castile soap with which to wash her hair, saw him go into the saloon. She surmised that the letter from home had not been a happy one. She decided to have a talk with him in the morning.

"Patrick," she said the next morning after the exchange of greetings, "you must be lonesome—a strange country, no relatives and you don't go out enough to make friends." Then, a little breathlessly, she made her suggestion. "Did you know there are places in Rockaway where Irish people go to dance? And many of the counties have their own dance hall. I know there's one for Galway and Donegal and Kerry. Perhaps there's one for Kilkenny. Why don't you go this Saturday, Patrick? You might meet somebody from home."

"I would, Miss Mary, but . . ."

"And get yourself some nice clothes."

"I would. Only . . ."

"Go to Batterman's or Gorman's. You can get clothes on time. Most working people do. So much down, so much a week. Give our name as reference."

"I will do so, Miss Mary, and I do be thanking you. . . ."

"Not at all, Patrick. You're too young to spend your evenings sitting in that little room."

He did as she suggested. He bought a straw hat for a dollar and bulldog-tip shoes that cost a cool two dollars, a candy-striped shirt and two celluloid collars and a made-up, snap-on polka-dot bow tie. His suit was dear: eight dollars. He got it just in time. The pants he'd worn steadily since leaving Ireland were almost transparent from wear.

"Them pants don't owe you nothing, Mister," said the salesman feelingly.

He dressed up the following Saturday evening and made a little sensation in the household. The Boss said: "When me stable boy dresses better than meself, one of us is got to go." Moriarity's idea of a joke.

Mary thought: *How very young he is! How good looking!*

Patrick tried the Irish dance halls out at Rockaway, but he met no one he liked—or disliked heartily enough—and he did spend a dollar-forty in one night, so he gave up that extravagance for good. Next, Mary talked him into attending night school, hoping he might make some friends there. He met one banty little Irish nick-named Mick Mack whom he liked to bully, but when the classes ended in June they saw each other no more.

Chapter Six

PATSY had been in America a year. His steamship passage was paid in full and he owed nothing more on his clothes. He had about thirty dollars saved. He'd heard from his mother twice in the year. Both letters told him his had been received and hoped more would follow. She wrote no news of Maggie Rose or of the people he knew; of the village or of herself. Both letters were copied from Bertie's book with no personal interpolations.

Patsy felt he ought to leave Moriarity and get a better job but he didn't know how to go about it. Then he reasoned that a new job might be worse than the old. Eventually, he decided it was better to put up with the drawbacks he had become used to than to take on unknown ones. Besides, in a way, he would have missed Mary. He was not at all in love with her but he had come to depend on her kindness and her understanding ways.

Also, Biddy was getting what he called

forward. She was the kind that, had he made advances to her, she'd have cracked his head open. But she was also the type who would crack his head open if he intimated that she wasn't worth making advances to.

She had him nudged into a corner one afternoon, trying to get him to agree with her that Teddy Roosevelt had false teeth. He thought otherwise but was on the point of agreeing with her in order to get away, when she suddenly dropped the argument and, in plain earthy words, made him a point-blank proposition.

Now Patrick Dennis was not one to refuse any bounty that came his way, but he liked his bounty young and fresh and softly yielding and not iron-bound like Biddy.

"I could not do so," he blurted out, "with you."

"So you think you could do better, eh?" she said ominously.

" 'Tis not that," he said placatingly, "but 'twould have to be with marrying."

God forgive the lie, he thought, *but what a grand, good way to get out of this sitcheeashun.*

"I got to marry you for *that?*" she gasped. "Why you're the last man I'd think of marrying."

"Who was asking you?" he said. "If I couldn't do better . . ."

"What'd you say?" she growled.

"Nothing," he said hastily. "And take me apology for it if I did. Sure and you'd make me

49

a fine wife, the way you work hard and the way you're healthy. . . ."

"Oh, Paddy, dear!" She fluttered her eyes.

"Only," he continued, "I would want a younger woman . . . not too young," he added hastily, afraid of insulting her again.

"Someone about Miss Mary's age?" she asked.

"I do not think about her that way—as me wife," he said.

"You think right," she said. "She'd never marry a stable boy."

"She could go farther and do worse," said Patsy, stung.

"Why, she wouldn't even *spit* on the likes of you!"

"She would so," cried Patsy indignantly.

The argument went on.

Because of Biddy's forever saying that Mary wouldn't spit on him and that he wasn't fit to clean her shoes and because Moriarity was always warning him not to get "idears" about his daughter, Patsy gave more and more thought to Mary.

I don't want her, he thought, *and the Lord knows she don't want me—and not because I'm a stable boy either. This is not the old country where the stable boy does not marry the lord's daughter. This is America, where 'tis the style, like Mick Mack would say, for the poor working man to marry the boss's daughter. Them books she gives me to read: All about poor boys what marries the rich boss's daughter and the poor boy then owns the factory when the old man croaks.* A thought struck him. *Did she ask me to read that book thinking that I'd get the hint, marry her and . . . Ah, no,* he decided; *she ain't tricky the way women is.*

Is she far above me like Biddy says? Sure, she has the grand education sitting in school till she was twenty studying to be a teacher. And meself? Six years of schooling I had. But did I not learn Latin good the way Father hit me on me head with his shillelagh (after Mass, to give him his due) when I didn't say it right when I was his altar boy?

She plays the piano to be sure. But do I not have the ear for music the way I can . . . the way I could, keep time to any tune was played the while I jigged?

She's rich and I'm poor. And that's the God's truth. But all her father's money couldn't buy for her what I do have for nothing: me youth. I'm twenty-one and she's twenty-seven. And that's old—old for a woman not yet married.

When I go walking, I could walk with a girl on each arm for the asking. But poor Miss Mary! Sure and she's never had a man make up to her. Then there is looks. She is sweet, but ah, she's plain in her face. So plain. And where is her shape? And me? I'd be lying to meself did I not tell meself I'm good looking and I'll say an Act of Contrition for me pride in me looks

51

before I sleep this night.

So, Patsy came to his conclusion. *She wouldn't be so bad off marrying me. But I will not think of it for do I not love Maggie Rose and I could never love another. And does she not wait for me with love? 'Tis a lie she has another feller. She could love no one else after me. And when I get me thousand dollars saved up, I'll go back. I'll tell her the waiting time is over and . . .*

And so he dreamed.

It was September of his second year in America. After supper now, Patsy sat on the stone bench in the paved areaway onto which the iron-grilled door of the basement dining room opened. He'd sit there and smoke an after-supper pipe, trying to put off the time when he'd have to go back to his miserable little room.

He watched the comings and goings of the people on the street and stared at the folk who climbed the step to ring Moriarity's bell. He wasn't at all interested. He was curious.

On Friday nights, many policemen, in and out of uniform, came to the door. The procedure was always the same. A cop rang the bell. Moriarity appeared and put out his hand. Instead of shaking it, the cop put something in it. The Boss put some of it back into the cop's hand and the cop went down the stoop, saluting another cop who was on the way up.

Eventually, his curiosity made him ask Biddy

what it was all about. She was appalled at his ignorance.

"And you living in the yard this year or more past and you don't know? Why 'tis graft, yes, it is, what The Boss is collecting. From the aitch houses. They can't run without paying. The madams pay the cops so the cops won't run them in. The cops pay our Boss so he won't snitch on them to the Big Cheese."

"And who is the Big Cheese?"

"The feller what takes half the graft The Boss collects from the cops what collects from the madams."

"Can't The Boss be arrested for that?"

"And who would arrest him?"

"A cop."

"They can't because all the cops is in on the graft, too, and who would arrest *them?*"

One October night, Patsy was sitting on the stone bench smoking his stub-stem clay pipe when he saw a big cop heft himself up the stoop. He was used to the cops coming but this was different. This was a cop coming on Wednesday night. The other cops came on Friday night.

The big cop pressed the button. Moriarity opened the door and put out his hand. Instead of putting something into it, the cop shook it warmly. The Boss, surprised, pulled his hand away and wiped it on his coat.

"Excuse me," said the cop. "I live in Brooklyn but me beat is in Manhattan."

Patsy was alerted. There was something about

53

that voice . . .

"What the hell are you doing here then, in my precinct? Go see the commissioner if you want a transfer."

"I came to see about . . ." Patsy lost the rest because the big cop's voice dropped to a whisper. But he was sure he heard his name mentioned. "And this is his address," concluded the cop in his normal voice. The Boss leaned down over the stoop.

"Boy?" Patsy looked up. The Boss waited. Patsy got to his feet. Still The Boss waited. Patsy took the pipe from his mouth. Then Moriarity spoke. "Patrick, the officer wants to see you. Take him to your room."

Patsy was up the ladder in a hurry. He lit the kerosene lamp while the big cop, with many a sigh and a wheeze, hefted himself up the ladder. The cop removed his helmet. There was that nimbus of red around his bald head. . . . The cop looked around for a place to sit. His feet hurt so. But there was only one chair in the room and he was too polite to take it without an invitation. Finally Patsy sat on the cot and the big man took the chair. He sighed in relief.

He introduced himself: "I'm the feller what licked you back in County Kilkenny nearly two years ago." Yes, Patsy had known it was Big Red. And what did he want of him now, Patsy wondered.

"I don't hold it against meself that I licked you. I thought it was right at the time. And I'm hoping that you'll let bygones be bygones being's everything turned out fine in the end.''

Patsy's heart leaped up. Everything turned out fine, Big Red said. Could that mean that Maggie Rose was in America now with her big brother and Big Red had come to ask Patsy to marry his sister? Yes. That's what he must have come for. And he'd marry Maggie Rose. Yes, he would!

''Yes. It all turned out fine for you and for me sister. You've got a good job and me baby sister . . .''

Eagerly, Patsy leaned forward and put his hand on Big Red's knee. He was so happy he could hardly speak. ''Maggie Rose! Where is she? How is she?''

''She's happy as a lark.'' He smiled tenderly. ''She's expecting.''

''Expecting? Expecting what?''

''Sure and you must have heard? She married a few months after you left.''

''Who . . . who married?'' croaked Patsy.

''Me sister. 'Twas from her husband I got your address.''

''What husband?''

''Hers. You know him. The feller what sold you the ticket to run away from me to America?'' Big Red laughed. ''He was quite a ketch, I hear, the way he came ten miles on his bicycle twice a week to court her.''

''He married her on me own wheel?'' said Patsy, bewildered. ''And the money given me for it stolen?''

55

"How's that?" asked Big Red, equally perplexed.

"The Liverpool sport?"

"I can't tell you what make 'twas."

"So she is married," said Patsy drearily.

"That she is. And happy, she writes me. Ah, I did you wrong," said Big Red humbly, "crossing the sea to come between you. Many's the Novena I did for it. Ach, why was we all against you? I was the worst. But me own mother did her best to make the trouble and your mother, God rest her soul, wouldn't listen to me. . . ."

"Me mother?" interrupted Patsy. "You said, 'God rest . . .'?"

That's how Patsy found out his mother had died. It was almost too much to bear. In a few minutes he knew he'd lost his Maggie Rose and his mother forever. Big Red kept talking, hoping to get him over the first shock.

He assured the boy his mother had not died alone. Her oldest boy, Neeley, who had gone to Australia before Patsy was born, had returned to her a few months before her death, Neeley's wife having died and his children long since scattered or married.

Patsy held in his grief. He didn't want Big Red to see him weep. When Patsy could hold back his grief no longer, he excused himself to Big Red, saying he needed to wash his face. He went down and washed in the horse trough. His tears mingled freely with the water from the tap. He thought as he wept:

Had I but stayed a while longer, he thought in anguish, *I could have held Maggie Rose to me and now with me mother gone, the way would have been clear for Maggie Rose and me. Not that I'd have me mother die. But if she had to go . . .*

He dried his face with the rough towel that had been issued him at the house and knelt before the trough to say his prayer for the dead. The horses shifted weight in the dark stable and made the straw rustle and Patsy was glad for the company of the sound. The big yellow cat weaved toward him, arched its back and leaned against his thigh for an instant, then sat close to him, lifted a paw and started to wash itself. Patsy felt less alone for the closeness of the cat.

Chapter Seven

AFTER Big Red left, Patsy went to a saloon to brood over a few beers. It was after midnight when he came home. He climbed up to his loft and threw himself on his cot.

Mary, standing at her window, saw him come home. She slipped out of the house in her dressing gown and climbed up the ladder. A horse whinnied. She paused halfway up the ladder afraid her father would hear. But all was calm. She called Patsy's name but he didn't answer. She went into the room. Patsy jumped up and lit the lamp. Mary blew it out. Patsy was in a panic.

"Miss Mary, please go," he said. "God help me if your father finds you in me bedroom so late in the night."

"Never mind my father," she said. "Patrick, please tell me all about it." He shook his head. "You've had bad news from Ireland." He said nothing. "Is it your mother?" He turned away from her.

"I am your friend, Patrick. Tell your friend your troubles. Don't hold them to yourself. A trouble shared is a trouble halved. Tell me, Patrick. It may help."

He broke down a little and started telling her. He spoke of his boyhood, his mother, Rory-Boy and Maggie Rose. He told of being whipped by Big Red and how he had sneaked out of Ireland and how his money had been stolen his first day in America. And then he told of his mother's death and Maggie Rose's marriage.

Her eyes were filled with tears all during his story.

"And now," he concluded, "me old life is gone and the new life I'm making . . . I mean the new life everyone is making for me is no good. I don't like nobody no more and I don't want nobody to like me."

"You don't mean that, Patrick. You say that because you've been so hurt; and so alone in a strange land."

"I mean it. I'm never going to give nothing to nobody and I'm going to take everything I can get from everybody."

She smiled at his boyish ultimatum. "Ah, no, Patrick," she said. "You could never live like that. Why, you're so young—so full of life. Everyone would like you so much if only you'd let people. . . ."

Suddenly, he broke down and wept piteously. She held out her arms in compassion.

"Come to me, Patrick dear," she said.

"Come to me."

She stood before him, her arms outstretched toward him. Her loose robe concealed the way she was straight up and down without curves. Her hair hung loose to her waist and the golden lamplight made her pass for pretty.

Because he was so lonesome and so starved for love, he went to her. She held him tightly and kept saying: "There now. There now." She was like a mother soothing a child. "There now," she said. He put his arms about her waist and she stroked his shoulder and said: "There now. Don't cry any more."

They held each other. But no matter how tightly they held each other, there was no blending. Her body stayed straight and stiff. It did not know how to relax against his.

He thought of the last time he had held Maggie Rose—how her little waist curved in and her thighs curved out. He remembered the evening. He had stood with one foot up on a stone wall and she had leaned against him. He remembered how his upraised thigh had fitted the curve of her waist and how the curve of his arm fitted all around her.

When a girl and a man fit together so grand, he thought, *sure God made them for each other. And why did I ever leave me own Maggie Rose?* He sighed.

And this good girl I'm holding in me arms now, he thought sadly, *we will never fit together.*

He was quiet and she thought he was

comforted. "I will leave you now," she said. She waited. He kissed her cheek. He held the lamp so that she could find her way down from his loft.

After she had slipped back into the house, he came down from his loft and stood in the yard. He leaned against the stable and smoked his pipe and thought of Mary—how good she was; how kind and understanding. He felt warm toward her. It was almost like love. Then his mood was broken. Biddy came out from behind a snowball bush.

"Ah, so," she said. "So me pretty man changed his mind about waiting for the marrying before he did—you know what."

"Go away, Biddy," he said wearily.

"That I won't till I've had me say."

He looked at her with aversion. Her hair was in a thick braid down her back and the end of it twitched and writhed around her backside like a black snake. She wore a crepe kimono and her flesh was unconfined beneath it. There was a continuous movement under the kimono as though something were boiling inside. Patsy winced.

I wonder do them things hurt her, he thought, *and them not being hoisted up and resting on top of the corset.*

"I seen youse," she said. "There I was sleeping and I heard this noise and what do I do but I wake up. First, I thought it was only the horses nooling around in the straw. Then I

61

looked up at your window and saw youse spooning against the lamplight.''

"Go back to bed," he said. He emptied his pipe by tapping it against the heel of his shoe. He stamped out the few live coals and turned to go back to his room. "Good night," he said.

"Listen!" she raised her voice. "I'm going to tell The Boss on you. On the both of youse."

"Do so," he whispered savagely, "and I'll tell The Boss on *you!* How you put in your Thursday night off by working in Madame Della's aitch house in Greenpoint."

She sucked in her breath and her face looked purple in the moonlight. " 'Tis a black lie," she choked out.

"I know it," he agreed. "But The Boss will take it for true. For is he not the one who likes to think the worst of everyone?"

"You'll see!" she threatened.

At breakfast next morning, Mary told her parents of the death of Patsy's mother.

"Is he an orphan then?" asked The Missus.

"Why not?" said Mike. "And we all got to go someday." He laved condensed milk over cooked ground horse's oats in a soup plate.

"Papa," said Mary, "Patrick's too good for the stable. He wasn't meant to be a servant. Couldn't you use your influence . . . pull . . . to get him better work?"

"Nothing doing," said her father. "I'll not

give meself the trouble of breaking in a new stable boy."

"At least, then, let him have that empty room on the top floor of the house. That stable room isn't fit for a man to live in."

"The next thing you know," he said jokingly, "you'll be wanting to marry him."

"I do," she said quietly. "And I will if he asks me."

"Yah-ha-ha! *Yah*-ha-ha!" laughed Mike. "You and the stable boy! That's rich. Ya-ha . . ."

Then something unprecedented happened. The Missus spoke up to The Boss! "I don't see nothing to laugh at," she said.

He put down his spoon with meticulous care. "What did you say, Missus?" he asked ominously.

"She's going on twenty-eight," said The Missus. "So far no one asked her to get married." (Mary winced.) "So I say if the boy wants to marry her, let him. She might not get no other chance."

"What did you say?" roared Mike, picking up his napkin ring as though to throw it at her.

The Missus jumped up so suddenly that her chair fell over backward. "Nothing," she whispered. "I didn't say nothing. Excuse me." She scuttled out of the room.

"See what you done?" Mike asked his daughter. "You and your loony talk at the table. Made your mother so nervous she couldn't eat."

"Excuse me, Papa," said Mary quietly. "I'm

almost late for my class." She left him alone with his now cold horse's oats.

Patsy was sweeping the sidewalk. The Boss peeped through the lace curtains and watched Mary as she stopped to talk to the stable boy. She seemed to be talking eagerly. He saw Patsy nod his head from time to time and he saw them smile at each other. She patted the boy's shoulder in farewell. He waved to her when she turned for a backward look.

Mike waited until Mary had turned the corner before he went down to deal with Patsy. He came up silently behind him and shouted: "You!" It pleased him when Patsy almost dropped his broom.

"Listen, you! You keep your place. Hear? Let me see you getting friendly with Miss Mary and you'll hear from me. Get me?"

"She wants to be me friend. 'Tis kind of her."

"I told you before: She's kind to everyone. Even the mongrel dogs on the street. And I tell you again: Don't get idears."

"What idears?"

"Like you think you're good enough to marry her."

"I do not have such an idear. But if I wanted to marry her and she wanted to marry me, whose business would it be? Only ours, being's we're both of age. But rest your mind. I'm not thinking of marrying."

"I'm glad to hear it," said Mike sarcastically.

"Because me daughter ain't thinking of marrying either—especially marrying a stable boy."

"I wasn't born a stable boy," said Patsy, quietly. "You made me one. And Mary . . ."

"*Miss* Mary," corrected Mike.

"Mary," continued Patsy evenly, "don't look on me as just a stable boy."

"Deary me, no," said Mike mincingly. "She *loves* you."

"Yes," said Patsy quietly.

"And you love her?"

Patsy hesitated before he answered. He said: "I'm attached to her."

"Attached to her! Attached, you say, Mister Pathrick Dennis Moore! And would it be that she's me only child and she and her husband would fall in for all of me property and money when me and The Missus dies have anything to do with this here attachment?"

"Yes," said Patsy. "If I have to put up with the likes of you for a father-in-law, by God, I'd deserve the property and the money."

"Get off me property," bellowed Mike. "Get the hell out of me house!"

"Stable," corrected Patsy.

"You're sacked! No recommendation. Pack up your rags and get!"

Patsy didn't pack up and he didn't "get," because the next day he and Mary were married by a clerk in City Hall.

Chapter Eight

THEY came home directly from City Hall. The Missus wept because there hadn't been a big church wedding with a Nuptial Mass. But Mary seemed very happy. From time to time, she looked at the wedding ring on her finger and smiled at Patsy. Patrick Dennis swaggered with his hands in his pockets and grinned at his father-in-law. Biddy stood listening behind a half-closed door with her mouth hanging open in amazement.

Mike Moriarity was the only one who didn't act normal. He acted as though he were thinking; as though he had been stricken speechless. His silence made his wife and daughter nervous.

"Won't you wish me luck, Papa?" said Mary.

"Let's see your papers," he said suddenly. Nervously but happily, she got her marriage certificate out of her reticule and give it to him. He examined it. "Ha!" he said. "So you wasn't married by a priest?"

"No."

"There wasn't time," began Patsy.

"And you came right home from City Hall?" asked Mike, ignoring Patsy.

"Of course, Papa."

"Good!" He gave an order to his wife. "Missus, get me hat and coat."

"Now, Michael," she started to say.

"Quiet!" he shouted.

"I mean," said The Missus timidly, "couldn't we have a glass of wine first? All of us? Kind of celebrate?"

"There'll be a celebration all right, later on," he said grimly. "But not what you think."

"Where you going now?" asked The Missus. Then she said: "Excuse me for asking."

"I'm going straight to Judge Cronin and get this marriage annulled."

"You can't!" wailed The Missus.

"Sure I can. Cronin owes me a favor."

"I mean they're married good."

"Oh, no, they ain't. Didn't you hear her say they came right back from City Hall without stopping anywheres?"

"But . . ."

"That means the marriage wasn't con . . . consa . . . . It wasn't consumed!" he said triumphantly. He rushed out of the house.

The Missus ran after him. "You can't, Michael," she panted as she caught up with him.

"Don't *you* tell me what to do."

"But what will she do with the baby?" wailed

The Missus. "And she not married?"

He stopped so suddenly that his Missus bumped into him. He grabbed her arm. "What baby?" he asked.

"Mary's and his."

"How do you know?"

"Biddy told me."

"How does *she* know?"

"She saw Mary up in his room. In her nightgown, Biddy said. And they was hugging and kissing . . ." The Missus blushed. ". . . and all. Biddy saw the whole thing."

"Why'n't she tell me?"

"Because she was afraid of Patrick. He said he'd kill her if she told. That's what she said to me anyways."

Slowly he walked back to the house with The Missus jogging along beside him. Arriving home, he gave her his hat and coat to hang up, and, without a word to anyone, he went into his den and locked the door. Alone there, he put his head down on his desk and wept.

He wept because all the plans he'd had for his daughter had come to nothing. When she was twenty, he had hoped she marry a young lawyer he knew who he thought had a wonderful future. But Mary had been too shy to encourage the young man. Now the young lawyer was Assistant District Attorney. Had a chance of being Governor someday. Moriarity had dreamed of saying, "Me son-in-law, the Governor . . ."

As the years went by, he was convinced she'd

never marry. Well, there were compensations in that, too. He could count on her to grow old devoted to him; to attend to his well-being if his wife died before him. That dream had gone now. And he wept for that.

But fundamentally he wept because he knew his daughter was sweet and good and honest. She was too good—much too good—for someone like Patrick Dennis Moore. That almost broke his heart.

They ate supper together. It was a sad wedding feast. No one knew what to say and everyone was apprehensive of Biddy, who served them with poor grace, banging the dishes down and muttering to herself.

After supper, they went upstairs to the parlor and sat in the chilly room. Mike sat in morose silence while Patsy and the two women tried to make conversation. The Missus asked Mary to play the piano. She requested "Over the Waves." Mary said her fingers were too stiff from the chill of the room. Then her father broke his silence and asked her to play "Molly Malone." Because she wished to ingratiate herself with him, she played a chorus of the ballad, then closed the piano.

They sat there. The evening wore on. The Missus dozed in her chair. Black shadows appeared under Mary's eyes. Patsy began yawning and got The Boss to yawning, too. No one wanted to be indelicate enough to suggest going to bed. Finally Patsy took charge of the situation. He got up, stretched his arms and yawned.

"I'm going to bed," he said. "I'm that tired." He held out his hand to his wife. "Come, Mary." Hand in hand they went to the door.

"Where are you taking her?" asked Mike.

"To me room," said Patsy. "Over the stable."

Mike stood up. "Me daughter wasn't raised to sleep in a stable," he said.

"Neither was my husband," said Mary.

"Michael," said The Missus timidly, "surely in this big house there is a room . . ."

"We'll sleep in my room," said Mary. The two women stood silent, waiting for Mike's outburst. He said nothing.

Patsy went to The Missus. "Good night, me sweet mother," he said. He kissed her cheek. The Missus beamed and gave him a fierce, loving hug.

"Good night," he said to Mike and held out his hand. Mike ignored it.

Mary kissed her mother, then went to her father, put her arms around his neck and rested her head on his chest.

"Oh, Papa," she said, "I'm so happy. Please don't spoil it for me."

Tenderly, he stroked his daughter's hair with one hand and held out his other hand to his son-in-law.

"Be good to this good girl," he said to Mary's husband.

Later, they were married by a priest. The Missus didn't want them to be married in the neighborhood parish. She said they were too well known and people would think it was "funny"—her daughter being married without a veil or bridesmaid or Nuptial Mass.

They were married in the adjoining parish of Williamsburg by Father Flynn, a priest newly come to the neighborhood. He was very nice to them.

The marriage disrupted the household. Biddy announced it was beneath her to wait on an ex-servant even if he had married The Boss's daughter. She turned in her notice and they had to break in a new servant girl. And The Missus and Mary decided it was not becoming for a member of the family to be a stable boy. Patsy agreed with them. Mike had to get a new stable boy and Patsy was released from his menial and odorous chores.

Mary lost her teaching job when she married. Married women were not permitted to teach in the public schools. Therefore, Mike had to support Patsy and Mary and pay a new stable boy in the bargain.

Patsy hung around the house all day smoking his pipe of clay and picking out "Chopsticks" with two fingers on the piano. He was very loving to Mary and courtly to his mother-in-law. Both women worshiped him.

The Missus bloomed under Patsy's attentions and she stopped scuttling for a while. He called her "Mother," which thrilled her. He stopped addressing Mike as "Sir." He called him "Hey, Boss!" which irritated Mike. Patsy got things out of Mike by using Mary's name. Mike referred to this process as "bleeding me white."

"Hey, Boss, me wife says . . ."

"You mean, me *daughter* says . . ."

"Me *wife* says I need a new suit. Me wife says I'm a disgrace to me fine father-in-law the way me backside is showing through me pants—they is that worn out. And the way me bare feet is on the ground for want of soles on me brogans. So . . ."

So Mike bought him new clothes. If Mary knew her husband was using her to get things from her father, she never said a word about it.

"Me wife . . ."

"Me daughter . . ."

"Me wife says I'm getting to be a reglar mully-cuddle the way I sit in the house day and night with only wimmen folks. 'Be like me father,' says me wife. 'Have the grand life like me dear father and he amongst the men all day.' "

"Me daughter don't talk that way."

"Them was her words. 'Take a night off once a week,' she says, 'and stand up to the bar with the boy-sis and have your schooner of cool beer. Or two.' "

So The Boss gave him a dollar once a week

for a night on the town.

One night, six months later, The Boss and his Missus were preparing for bed. She scuttled into the double brass bed and lay tight against the wall to displace as little space as possible. He sat down on the side of the bed to pull off his congress gaiter shoes. His weight made her bounce up and down once or twice. As usual he was complaining about his son-in-law.

(During the day, about the house and also in public, she seemed frightened of him and he never spoke to her without shouting or without sarcasm. But at night, in the privacy of the room and bed they had shared for thirty years, they turned into congenial companions.)

"Me patience is used up, Molly," he said. "Out he goes as soon as she has the baby."

"What baby, Micky?"

"Mary's. And," he added grudgingly, "his'n."

"Oh, they're not going to have a baby," she said brightly.

"But you *said.* You told *me* that Biddy told *you.* She told you that she saw them two nights before they was married. And they was intimate."

"Oh, Micky, you know what a liar Biddy always was."

He sat there aghast, holding a shoe in his hand. "So I've been thricked into this marriage! And that's how the durtee cuckoo got into me clean nest!"

"Say your rosary and come to bed, Micky."

"I got to find some way of getting him out of me house. But how?"

"You could get him a job and give them a house to live in. That's how."

"Hm. That's not a bad idear, Molly. I'll start thinking on it tomorrow." He got into bed. "Now where's me beads?"

"Under your pillow like always."

Moriarity pulled wires and cut red tape and bribed and blackmailed and got his son-in-law a job with the Department of Sanitation. He was asked whether he wanted his son-in-law on garbage collecting. He was tempted to say yes, but he knew he couldn't push Patsy that far. So he got him a job as street cleaner.

Then he gave his daughter and her husband a house of their very own to live in.

Among Mike's holdings was a two-family frame house in Williamsburg on what was then known as Ewen Street. Fifteen years before, Mike had bought it for five hundred down and a first mortgage of three hundred and a loan of two hundred. This was in the years when property was still cheap.

In those old days, the plumbing was an outhouse in the yard, people drew water from a community pump down the street, the lighting was from kerosene lamps and heating came from a cooking range in the kitchen and a "parlor" stove in the front room.

Recently gaslight and water had been installed

in the house. Mike had taken a small woodshed attached to the house and made it into a bathroom of sorts: a small tin tub boarded with wood and a toilet and wash bowl. Upstairs, a toilet had been put into a bedroom closet and a sink in the kitchen. Mike had paid off the two-hundred-dollar loan and then turned around and gotten a thousand-dollar mortgage on the "improved" house. The upstairs flat rented for fifteen a month and the downstairs for twenty. One half or the other was usually without tenants. Mike made no attempt to pay off the thousand-dollar mortgage. He simply paid the interest and kept "renewing" the mortgage. The taxes were still low. Since he put no money into improvements, the rent was a decent little profit on his original five-hundred-dollar investment.

This was the house he turned over to his daughter and her husband. He made a little speech when he turned over the deed ending up with: " 'Tis your very own, now."

The mortgage and the unrented upstairs apartment were their very own, too.

Mary got a woman in for a day to help her scrub and clean up the house. She had two hundred dollars saved from her teaching job and Patsy had nearly a hundred. They had the rooms upstairs and downstairs cheerfully papered and the woodwork painted. Mary was allowed to take the bedroom furniture from her room at home and she and Patsy bought what additional furniture was needed. She made muslin curtains for the windows and set up her hand-painted china plates on the shelf that ran the length of the kitchen wall.

She was able to rent the upstairs apartment soon after they had taken over the house. She made it very plain to Patsy that the rent was to be used entirely for taxes and mortgage interest *and* payments on the mortgage itself.

Mary liked her little home but Patsy didn't like it one bit. To Mary, it was a great adventure—creating a home of their own. Patsy liked the brownstone house on Bushwick Avenue much better. He liked that neighborhood and he had liked not working while living there with Mary. He hated his job. Nearly every evening, he visited his father-in-law and complained about everything. Now he referred to Mary as Moriarity's daughter rather than as his, Patsy's, wife.

" 'Tis a disgrace that your only daughter has to live in that cellar with a winder in it that you name a home. 'Tis a shame that a high-toned woman like your daughter has a husband who has to shovel horse manure all day to support her."

"Stop your bellyaching, me boy," said Moriarity. "Times is hard and men is out of work and banks is closing down. But let me tell you: I figured it out. The country is sound."

"I read that too," said Patsy. "In last night's *World*."

"They say there's a panic on," said Mike.

"But what's that to a man fixed like you? You got a house to live in. Nobody can take that away from you. You got a city job. Can't be sacked. You get your pension when you retire. And your wife gets a pension when you die."

"God forbid!" said Patsy. He waited but Mike didn't second the motion by an "amen" or by knocking on wood.

"Say! Did me daughter take her money out of the bank like I told her?"

"We took *our* money out. Yes."

"That's good because your bank closed this morning."

"We only had eight dollars in it. She, I mean, we, paid the interest and some of the taxes just last week and eight dollars was all was left. And you," asked Patsy shrewdly, "was you lucky enough to get all yours out before your bank closed up?"

"That I did. And in plenty of time, too."

"I bet it was more than eight dollars," suggested Patsy.

Wouldn't you like to know, thought Mike. He said: "Well, it wasn't a forchune, but enough, enough. It's safe under me mattress now. If anything happens to me, God forbid . . ."

He waited. Thought Patsy: *He didn't say "amen" for me when I said, "die, God forbid." So I'm not going to say it for him.*

"Tell The Missus . . ." continued Mike.

"You mean me new mother?" interrupted Patsy.

You bastard, breathed Mike under his breath. "Well, just tell her that the money is in a old sock under the mattress."

Stubbornly, Patsy went back to his complaining. "I still don't like to shovel manure —panic or no panic; pension or no pension."

"It won't be forever. Someday you will be superintent' and stand on the street in kid gloves making *other* men shovel manure. And sure, your house ain't no marble mansion. . . ."

"That can be said again," agreed Patsy.

"But 'tis only temporary against the time when you and me daughter get everything I own; me big house and me carriage and fine horses and all of me money. And it might be sooner than you or me think. Me old ticker ain't acting so good." He pressed his hand to his heart.

Patsy shivered because The Boss had not knocked wood when he spoke of his failing heart. Patsy had an impulse to knock wood for Moriarity. But he squelched it. *Let the bastid knock his own wood,* he decided.

Chapter Nine

THE way things turned out, Patsy and Mary were never to come into Mike's fortune. The reform party won the next election, and, true to its platform, the new administration started the Big Cleanup. The bright, new District Attorney polished up his armor, buckled himself into it and went out after the grafters crying, "Corruption! Corruption!" all the way. Little grafters ran for their holes. Medium-sized grafters, like Moriarity, couldn't find holes to hide in.

The Big Cheese saved his rind, that is, his skin, by turning state's evidence. Officious men came to Mike Moriarity's house and shook rattling papers in his face and attached everything he had: his house and furniture and stable and horses and carriage and even Mary's piano. Too late, Mike wished he had let Mary take it with her.

The men busted open the locked door of his desk and attached deeds, notes, stocks and bonds. They even attached a couple of bankbooks stamped *Account Canceled*. One reformer, a plainclothes man, found Mike's last withdrawal in an old sock under Mike's mattress. The sock held two thousand dollars in small bills. The reformer pocketed the money and neglected to give Mike a receipt. Probably he neglected to turn in the money, too.

The only things they couldn't touch were the house that Mike had deeded over to Mary and Patsy, and a paid-up life-insurance policy in The Missus' name.

Moriarity, along with a dozen others, was indicted. It was in all the papers.

Patsy, commenting on the indictment to Mary, said: "So I was never good enough for your father. So he always looked down on me. But *I'm* the one what's looking down on *him,* now. The thief!"

"Oh, Patrick," she said, tears coming to her eyes, "don't call him that."

He felt ashamed. *Why do I say things like that to her,* he thought. *I get no satisfaction out of it. It makes me feel like Jack the Ripper, or somebody.*

"There now, Mary," he said. "Who am I to talk? Did not one of me own relations steal a pig in Ireland? Yes."

She smiled through her tears and looked up at him with her hands clasped appealingly on her breast. "Did he, Patrick? Did he?"

"Sure," he said. "But he was a relation by

marriage only."

So Mike was indicted for graft and corruption. But he never stood trial. Just before the trial, he had a stroke and his "ticker" gave out.

It was nearly night when they got home from the funeral. Mary sat in the dark kitchen. Her face was pale and drawn. Patsy tried to find something comforting to say to her.

"After all, he was your father," he said.

"Yes."

"And he was good to you."

"Not always, Patrick. I remember—I must have been about ten years old—when I thought I didn't like him. I thought he wasn't nice to my mother and it seemed that he was always punishing me or scolding me.

"One night, I suppose he got free tickets somewhere, he took me over to Manhattan to hear a singer. I remember it was snowing and everything looked so beautiful. I had a little white muff and tippet with ermine tails. There was an old woman selling violets on the street. I remember the cold, sweet smell. He bought a bunch and pinned them to my muff. He gave the old woman a bill and he wouldn't take his change.

"He had a friend who had a high-class saloon. We sat in the ladies' back parlor, of course. My father introduced me to the man as though I were a grown-up lady. The man bowed as he shook my hand. He served me a big glass of lemonade on a silver tray. There was a tablespoon of claret in the lemonade to make it pink and a cherry on top. I thought it was wonderful. Papa and the man had a brandy together and talked about old times in Ireland.

"The man had left the door leading into the saloon open and I saw it all. The bar was beautiful! All the shining cut-glass decanters on the shelves with silver stoppers and glasses as thin as bubbles and that big mirror over the bar with a filigreed brass frame and oh, the chandelier with cut-glass crystals, or do they call them prisms? It was so beautiful with the gas lights in ruby bowls here and there. . . .

"Then we went to the concert. I don't remember now what the lady sang, except her encore song, 'The Last Rose of Summer.' I saw Papa take out his handkerchief and wipe his eyes.

"After the concert we were walking down to the cab stand and there was this little store still open. They sold trinkets and things. Papa took me in and told me to pick out a little bracelet or a locket. But there was a pair of side combs in the showcase. They were tortoiseshell and all full of rhinestones. I couldn't stop looking at them.

"Papa said, 'You know you're too little to wear them and they'll be out of style by the time you grow up. Now here's a nice little locket. It opens. . . .' But I couldn't take my eyes off the combs.

"Then Papa said: 'You *know* you can't wear them. What do you want them for?' I said I didn't know. Then he said: 'You want them just to *have* them, don't you?' I said yes, and he told the lady to wrap them up.

"I loved my father that night. I loved him so much I didn't know what to do.

"That was the only time he ever took me out. Well, there came times after that night when I felt I didn't like him very much. When I got that feeling, I'd go and take the combs out of the tissue paper and hold them and I'd feel the same love I felt that night when he took me to the concert."

After the funeral, The Missus took her insurance money and went to Boston to live out her days there with Henrietta, her widowed sister. Patsy was sorry to see her go. This contrary man really loved his mother-in-law.

"She's like me own mother was," Patsy told his wife. "She sees no fault in me."

Well before this time, Patrick Dennis Moore put away all his dreams and hopes. He hated his job but wouldn't dare give it up with no other work to be had. He was grudgingly grateful that he was working for the city and couldn't be laid off because times were hard. He realized, now, that he would always be a street cleaner. That was all he had to look forward to. He would always have to live in the shabby house on Ewen Street.

His last dream had died out when his mother-in-law went to live with her sister in Boston—instead of with him and Mary—and took all her insurance money with her.

Chapter Ten

MARY kept the upstairs rented and banked the rent money and used it throughout the years to keep the taxes and the interest on the mortgage paid up and sometimes she was able to pay a little on the principal. She was liked and respected on Ewen Street (which, for some reason, was now called Manhattan Avenue). The neighbors referred to her as "that refined schoolteacher what's married to that slob—*you* know. The street cleaner?"

Mary became friends with Father Flynn, the priest who had performed her marriage ceremony and never criticized her and Patsy for having a civil ceremony first. One time when his housekeeper took a week off to visit a married daughter in Albany, Mary went to the parish house every day and cooked the priest's food and laundered his collars and mended the torn lace on his alb. Thereafter, she visited him once in a while or he came to her home. They exchanged opinions on the news of the day and analyzed the rapid changes that were taking place that would eventually change the once dreamy village of Williamsburg into a city slum.

They had something in common in that both were strangers in the neighborhood, she having come from the prosperous and fashionable Bushwick section, and he from the Middle West.

Father Flynn had been born and reared in a small town in Minnesota. He had been educated in Midwestern schools. At college he had excelled in sports: football, baseball, basketball, hockey and especially skiing. He had been popular with faculty and classmates.

The time came, while he was still young, to put aside his dearly loved sports and his no less dearly loved contemporaries and, as an ordained priest, to take up his life and his work in an alien place. His Bishop had said: "You'll have your work cut out for you there." It was true, for it was a neighborhood of many nationalities.

Mary was of great help to Father Flynn. During her years of teaching public school, she'd had pupils of many nationalities and faiths. She had a general knowledge of the habits, temperaments and customs of various races and religions through her contact with her pupils. Father Flynn drew on her knowledge. He was grateful to her for it. It made his parish work somewhat simpler.

Although Mary loved her home and loved her husband, she wasn't happy in her marriage. She was unhappy because Patrick did not love her.

He was considerate toward her—as considerate as a person of his cynical nature could be—but he simply did not love her and she knew he never would. Withdrawn and sad after her father's disgrace and death, and lonesome after her mother had moved to Boston, she turned more and more to her church, where she always found comfort.

She went to Mass each morning and lit a candle daily to the Virgin Mary and prayed for a child.

Chapter Eleven

MARY and Patrick had been married nearly three and a half years when she gave birth to a daughter. She had a very hard time. It was a dry birth and she was in agonizing labor for two days. Her doctor told her not to have any more children. He told her that she wasn't built for childbearing.

His warning meant nothing to Mary at that time. She was so quietly and intensely happy. Father Flynn came to the nursing home to bless the baby and to pray for the mother's speedy recovery. He gave her a small medal of the Holy Child to pin to her baby's shirt. She said:

"I have something all of my own, Father. A child to love and to care for . . . a child who will grow to love me."

Patsy suggested that Mary name the child after her mother.

"That's nice of you, Patrick, but I don't want to call her Molly even if it is a nickname for Mary."

"Mary, then," he said. "There is no grander name."

"No."

"Me mother's name was Lizzie," he said tentatively. "Elizabeth's a good name."

"Patrick, I'd like to name her after the one who sort of brought us together."

"Biddy?" he asked horrified.

"Oh, no!" She smiled. "After that girl you liked so . . . you know, Margaret Rose? It's such a pretty name. And I'm so happy that I have a baby now that I want to give her the name as a present to you, sort of."

She saw his eyes flicker when she mentioned the name. She didn't know whether it was from surprise, pleasure, anger or memories.

"You will please yourself," he said brusquely.

"We'll have to get godparents," she said. "I don't know anyone and my few relatives are all in Boston. . . ."

"I know the very ones," he said. "Like your old man used to say, I know somebody what owes me a favor."

Patsy didn't ask Big Red to be the godfather. He ordered him to be. Big Red was touched and Lottie wept with joy at being a godmother.

The baby was christened Margaret Rose.

Big Red said the baby looked like his sister, then apologized, afraid he had hurt Mary's feelings. But she said she'd be proud if the baby looked like Big Red's sister, because she was sure his sister was very beautiful.

Patsy said the baby didn't look like anybody.

Mary invited them to come to the house and have a glass of sherry to celebrate. Big Red waited for Patsy to second the invitation. Patsy stood mute. Big Red, embarrassed, said, thank you, but they had to go home. Patsy said that was all right with him.

After they'd left, Mary said: "You never thanked him, Patrick."

"Why should I? He owes *me*. *I* don't owe *him*. He owes me—the way he can never make up to me for what he did to me."

"Remember that," she said a little bitterly, "the next time you go to confession—three years from now."

He felt a pang because it was the first time she'd ever spoken unkindly to him. He knew that she loved him. He had never responded to her love, nor even acknowledged it. But he liked to have it around—in escrow, as it were.

She has her baby, now, he thought. *And now she will take her love from me and give it all to the child.*

A few days after the baptism, a package for the baby arrived from The Missus. It was Mary's christening robe, slightly yellow with age. Attached to it was a five-dollar bill and a note. The Missus hoped the dress would get there in time for the christening, and she would have come to see her first grandchild, only Aunt Henrietta wasn't well and . . .

"Some family," sneered Patsy. "Wouldn't

take the trouble to come and see the only child of the only daughter."

"Now, Patrick," said Mary patiently. She knew Patsy was terribly disappointed that her mother hadn't come for a visit. She knew that he was very fond of The Missus.

For the first year of its life, the baby was called and referred to as "Baby." Mary waited for a nickname to evolve. Would it be "Maggie Rose" or "Pegeen" or "Magsie"?

In that neighborhood, few children were called by their baptismal names. The formal name appeared or was used only for diplomas and registration and things like that. Sometimes foreign-born parents had trouble pronouncing a name; sometimes the child nicknamed itself. A "Catherine" would be pronounced "Cat-rin," shortened to "Cat," then expanded to "Catty" and finally translated to "Pussy." "Elizabeth" went into "Lizziebet," to "Lizzie," to "Litty" (because the child couldn't pronounce the z's), and ended up "Lit." Long names were shortened and short names were lengthened. For instance, many an "Anna" ended up "Anna-la."

It was Patsy who accidentally gave the baby the name she'd always be known by. One night as he and Mary were preparing for bed, he looked at the big one-year-old baby who was sleeping sprawled sidewise across the bed.

"I don't get me sleep nights, no more," he

said. "This bed ain't big enough for the three of us. This baby now . . ." He paused, and then he gave her her name. ". . . This here Maggie, now, is big enough to have a bed of her own."

They got a crib for her. She cried the first night she slept away from her mother. Mary soothed her.

"There, baby, there!" The child bawled harder. "Hush," said Mary. "Hush, Maggie. Hush, Maggie, now." The child stopped crying, smiled blissfully, put her thumb into her mouth and went off to sleep.

She grew up healthy, happy and loving. She was full of mischief and cheerfully disobedient. The day long throughout the house it was:

"Maggie, now give me those scissors before you stab yourself."

"Maggie, now mind your father when he speaks to you."

"Maggie, now . . ."

And so she became known as Maggie-Now.

Chapter Twelve

MARY, never having had younger sisters or brothers, had no experience in bringing up a child. Her natural maternal feelings had been used in an organized way to handle thirty-odd children a day as a schoolteacher. She had a tendency, tempered by indulgent love, to regiment Maggie-Now. Mentally, she reached for a bell each morning to get the child started. She organized the child's day and was apt to give instructions as a schoolteacher would.

"We will take our little walk now."

"Eat your nice lunch, dear."

"What story shall we read tonight?"

"It's time for a certain good little girl to go to bed."

When Maggie-Now was three, Mary tried to teach her to read. Maggie-Now squirmed, itched, scratched, rolled her eyes and made spit bubbles. Mary had to give it up.

"She's intelligent," Mary told her husband, "but she won't sit still long enough to learn."

"She'll be on her behind long enough when she starts regular school," said Patsy. "Besides, why does she have to learn everything so quick? Why, she ain't housebroken yet and you expect her to read!"

"Don't you believe in education, Patrick?"

"No," he said. "I went as far as what amounts to the sixth grade in America. And where did it get me? Cleaning streets."

But Maggie-Now was very precocious in practical things—like work. Even as a toddler, she dusted while her mother swept, insisted on drying the dishes when her chin was but an inch above the sink drainboard, tried to make up a bed, and asked constantly when she could cook. Her reward for being good was permission to grind up left-over meat in the food chopper. Her punishment when naughty was the withdrawal of the privilege of grinding the morning coffee beans.

One day each summer, as she was growing up, her parents took her to the beach. Maggie-Now dearly loved the ocean. The ride in the open trolley was grand and the boarding of the Long Island train at Brooklyn Manor Station was a thrill. The high point of the journey was when the train went over water on a wooden trestle. Mary held the girl's arm tightly, admonishing her not to fall out, now.

"Maybe the trestle will break *this* time," said Maggie-Now hopefully, "and we'll all fall in the water."

"By God," said Patsy, "she *wants* it to break! She *wants* the train to fall in the water!"

"Sh!" said Mary.

Maggie-Now had no bathing suit. She grew so fast from year to year that it would have been a waste of money to buy one each year for just one day at the beach. Trying to follow her mother's admonition—not to be ashamed because nobody was looking—Maggie-Now undressed behind a big towel that her mother held around her like a limp barrel. She changed into a pair of outgrown pants and a worn-out dress in lieu of a bathing suit.

She ran whooping into the ocean and plunged into the first wave with a scream of delight. She held onto the rope and leaped and ducked and squatted to let the waves break over her head and howled in pretended terror (though flattered by the attention) when a big boy dived and grabbed her ankles and tried to duck her.

Mary and Patsy sat on the towel: she in her Sunday dress and hat, sitting primly with her gloved hands in her lap, and Patsy lolling on an elbow and, as was traditional with men, eying the women in their bathing suits, their legs in long, black lisle stockings and the ruffles of bloomers showing beneath knee-length skirts.

After an hour, Patsy went to the water's edge and induced Maggie-Now to come out. She changed back to her dry clothes inside the towel. Then they had their lunch which Mary had brought from home in a shoebox: ham bologna sandwiches, hard-boiled eggs, sweet buns and drinks, now warm, which Patsy had bought when they got off the train. There was a bottle of beer for Patsy, a celery tonic for Mary, and a bottle of cream soda for Maggie-Now.

After the lunch, Patsy announced that he would take a half hour's nap and then they would make a break for home to avoid the rush. Maggie-Now was given permission to walk up the beach and given strict orders not to take candy from anyone.

She ran up the beach, leaping over outstretched and sometimes intertwined legs. She stopped to stare frankly at a couple lying on the sand on their sides and looking into each other's eyes. Their faces were hardly an inch apart. The young man, discomfited by her staring, lifted his head.

"Get a gait on, kid," he said.

"What gate?" asked Maggie-Now.

"She don't get your drift," said the young woman languidly.

"Twenty-three, skidoo," said the young man.

"I getcha," said Maggie-Now, pleased that she could speak their lingo. "I'll beat it."

Going home on the Long Island, she sat between her parents and laved her hands in a paper bag of Rockaway sand.

"You know what?" she said. "I'm going to make a wish on the first star tonight. I'm going to wish that when I get big I'll have a house right by the water and listen to the waves when

I'm in bed nights. And in the daytime, I'll jump in any time I feel like it."

"I'll make a wish, too," said Mary. "I wish that all your wishes come true." Maggie-Now hugged her mother's arm.

Obscurely, Patsy felt left out. If he couldn't be in on their emotional closeness, the next best thing was to destroy it.

"People what lives by the water," he said, "always get rheumatism and their teeth fall out because they got to eat fish all the time."

"Oh, you gloomy Gus," said Maggie-Now.

"We do not use slang," said Mary.

"And we do not," said Patsy with bitter mimicry, "talk to our father that way, in the bargain."

Mary knew how he felt. She reached across and took the shoebox from his knees. It had Maggie-Now's wet bathing clothes in it.

"I'll hold it," said Mary. "It's leaking through on your good pants."

Not long after this, Mary told Pat that she was going to start Maggie-Now in parochial school in the fall.

"She ain't going to no Catholic school and that's settled," said Patsy.

"I've already enrolled her," said Mary.

"Unroll her, then."

"Now, Patrick . . ."

"That's me last word on the subject. She goes

to public school." He had nothing against the parochial school. He just liked to argue. He sat down to read the evening paper. Suddenly he jumped up with a great oath.

"I won't stand for it! By God! I won't stand for it!"

Mary thought he was referring to the school. "It's settled," she said firmly.

"What about Brooklyn?" he shouted.

"The school's in Brooklyn," she said, bewildered. "You know that."

"What the hell's the school got to do with it? Brooklyn ain't no longer a city. It says so in the paper. Now it's only a borough of New York City."

"Think how the people in New York feel. That used to be New York City. Now it's only the Borough of Manhattan. Anyhow, Patrick, you can't do a thing about it."

"Oh, no? I can take the kid out of parochial school."

"What good would that do?"

"It would let me have me own way for once." He got up, grabbed his hat and threw himself out of the house.

The saloon was so crowded Patsy could hardly get in. It was full of Irishmen bitterly cursing the annexation of Brooklyn by New York. They blamed it all on the British.

"And is it not the fault of England," shouted a burly man in a square-topped derby, "and she bragging how London is the biggest city in the world and that making New York jealous? And what does New York turn around and do? She steals Brooklyn and hitches it on to make *New York* the biggest city in the world."

"But there'll always be a Brooklyn!" rang out a voice in the crowd. This sentiment was loudly applauded and wildly cheered.

"Let's all drink to that!" yelled another man. They crowded up to the bar.

"What's yours?" the bartender asked Patsy.

"I ain't drinking to that damn foolishness," said Patsy.

"On the house," said the bartender.

"I'll have a double rye. With water on the side," added Patsy. The bartender gave him a beer.

All held their glasses aloft. "To Brooklyn!" said the bartender.

Before they could drink, another voice rang out. "Brooklyn go bragh!"

"Brooklyn go bragh!" shouted all the men in the saloon. And a couple of men passing on the street stopped to holler: "Brooklyn go bragh!"

Maggie-Now attended parochial school. To Mary's distress, her daughter was not the brightest one in the class. To Patsy's relief, she was not the dumbest one. She was down near the bottom of the average kids. But the teaching nuns liked her.

She got to school early and stayed late. She washed the blackboards and clapped the chalk dust out of the erasers and filled the inkwells. On Mondays, when the children had to bring pieces of broken glass to school to scrape ink spots off the floor, Maggie-Now showed up with a bagful of glass to supply the kids who had forgotten to bring their own. She spent her Saturdays collecting bottles and smashing them for that purpose.

Sometimes her mother let her take her lunch to school. Usually it was two bologna sandwiches. She always traded them for the three slices of dry bread a wispy girl brought for lunch, insisting that she hated meat and liked plain bread better. It wasn't that she was sorry for the girl or overly generous; she just liked to give things.

"She is a giver," sighed Sister Veronica to Sister Mary Joseph.

"She'll have a busy life, then," said Sister Mary Joseph dryly. "There are ten takers for one giver."

Regularly, each morning at ten and each afternoon at two, Maggie-Now's hand shot up in the air for permission to leave the room. This regularity irritated Sister Veronica. Once she frowned and said: "We had recess half an hour ago. Why didn't you attend to your needs then?"

"I did," said Maggie-Now frankly. "Now I got to 'tend to my horse." The class tittered.

"Watch your language, Margaret," said Sister Veronica sharply.

Out in the yard, Maggie-Now with many a "Whoa there," and a "Hold still, boy," untied an imaginary horse from an imaginary stake. Then she became the horse. She ran about the yard, galloping and prancing and snorting. Then she was a steeplechase horse taking imaginary hurdles. And lastly, not to neglect the humbler species, she was a junk-wagon horse in harness, straining to pull a load that must have weighed a hundred pounds. She was not above falling down in pretended exhaustion and death to give reality to her game.

She bounced back into the classroom, windblown, rosy and glowing. Although Sister Veronica frowned when she left, she always smiled when she returned.

She told Sister Mary Joseph: "She brings the smell of the wind back into the room with her." She pronounced *wind* to rhyme with *kind*.

"A pity you gave up writing poetry, Sister, when you took holy orders," said Sister Mary Joseph.

The rules of the order forbade any nun to walk abroad alone. She had to go with another nun or a lay person. The nuns liked children to go shopping with them. Maggie-Now was much in demand as an escort. When she turned up at the convent on a Saturday morning, the sisters pretended to quarrel over who'd get Maggie-Now. This thrilled the girl.

Sister Veronica needed new shoes. Maggie-Now went to the shoe store with her. She knelt down and helped the nun try on the shoes. She kneaded the leather over the toes and asked anxiously: "Are you *sure* they fit? Have you got room for all your toes?"

"You'll wear them out, child, before I have a chance to walk in them."

Sister Mary Joseph wore a wedding ring, as did the other nuns, because she was the bride of Christ. Through the years, the ring had become too tight. Maggie-Now escorted her to the jeweler's to have it sawed off.

Maggie-Now liked Sister Mary Joseph but was afraid of her because she said unexpected things. When Maggie-Now escorted Sister Veronica, she held the nun's hand and skipped along and chattered. With Sister Mary Joseph, she walked sedately—no hand holding, no skipping, no chatter. Maggie-Now had to stretch her legs to match the nun's long stride. They had been walking three blocks in complete silence when Sister said in an ordinary, conversational tone:

"What's your horse's name?"

The girl quivered and wondered how Sister knew. She gave her a quick look. The nun was staring straight ahead.

"What horse?" hedged Maggie-Now.

"The one you keep in the schoolyard."

"His name is Drummer."

The nun nodded.

Does that mean, thought Maggie-Now, *that it's a nice name? Or does it mean that she caught me?*

They walked another block in silence. Then Sister Mary Joseph said with her usual bluntness: "I used to play basketball when I was in high school."

"You never did!" said Maggie-Now in instinctive disbelief. "I mean," she gulped, "did you?"

"Why not?" said the nun crossly.

"I mean, I thought Sisters prayed all the time."

"Oh, we take a day off now and then to have a toothache or something. Just like other people."

"Nobody ever *told* me," said Maggie-Now.

"Margaret, are you afraid of me?"

"Not so much as I used to be." Maggie-Now smiled up at her.

When Mr. Freedman, the jeweler, began to saw on the ring, Maggie-Now threw her arms around the nun and buried her face in her habit.

"What's the matter, Margaret?"

"It goes all through me," shuddered the child.

"The finger, I will not take off," promised Mr. Freedman. "Only the ring."

"Take deep breaths, Margaret, and be brave," said Sister Mary Joseph, "and it will be over before you know it."

Chapter Thirteen

"MAMA, why don't we have relations like other people?"

"We do."

"Where?"

"Oh, Ireland. And you have a grandmother in Boston, you know."

"But why don't I have sisters and brothers and aunts and uncles and lots and lots of cousins like other girls do?"

"Maybe you will have a sister or brother someday. And we might go to Boston and try to find some cousins for you."

"When are we going to Boston?"

"Summer vacation, maybe. *If* you pass your catechism and make your first communion, and *if* you do your homework and get promoted."

"Chee! Other kids have relations without passing everything first."

"Don't say, 'Gee,' and I've told you that a kid is a baby goat and not a child."

"Sometimes you talk like Sister Veronica, Mama."

Mary sighed and smiled. "I suppose I do. Once a schoolteacher, always a schoolteacher."

"Well, it ain't every kid . . . girl . . . has a schoolteacher for a mama."

Maggie-Now waited patiently to be corrected on the "ain't." To her surprise, her mother didn't correct her, but hugged her instead.

Mary took ten dollars from the bank and to her surprise Patsy gave her ten dollars more for the Boston trip.

"Maybe you can talk your old lady into coming back to live with us."

"It's nice that you like my mother, Patrick," she said, "but it seems odd. It's not your way."

"She's never been against me."

"No one's against you, Patrick."

"Oh, no?" he said with a crooked smile.

"You are against yourself."

He raised two fingers in the air. "May I leave the room, *teacher*?" he said sarcastically.

They rode the day coach to Boston. To Maggie-Now it was like a trip to the moon. As they walked through the Boston streets, she said, surprised: "Why, they speak English!"

"What did you think they spoke?"

"Oh, Italian, Jewish, Latin."

"No. English is the language of America."

"Brooklyn's America. But Anastasia's father and mother speak Italian, there."

"Many old people speak foreign languages

because they came from foreign countries and never did learn English."

"What does Grandma speak?"

"English, of course."

"But you said she came from Ireland."

"They speak English there."

"Why don't they speak Irish?"

"Some do. They call it Gaelic. But most of them speak English with an Irish accent."

"What's a . . . an . . . accent?"

"The way people fix the words together when they speak and the different way they make the words sound."

"Mama, I guess you're the smartest lady in the whole world."

The Missus was a great disappointment to Maggie-Now. The girl's idea of a grandmother was a woman with a high stomach and a gingham apron tied about her waist, gray hair parted in the middle and steel-rimmed spectacles. She had this idea from a colored lithograph illustrating the poem "Over the river and through the woods, to grandmother's house we go." But Grandmother Moriarity wasn't like that at all. She was little and skinny and wore a black sateen dress and her hair was coal black and she wore it in curls on top of her head.

Henrietta was Grandmother's sister and Mother's aunt. Maggie-Now was instructed to call her "Aunt Henrietta." She didn't look like an aunt. A girl on Maggie-Now's block in Brooklyn had an aunt who was young and blonde and laughed a lot and smelled like sweet, sticky candy. Aunt Henrietta, now, was old and withered and smelled like a plant that was dead but still standing in the dirt of the flower pot.

She heard talk of Cousin Robbie, who was coming over that night. Robbie was Henrietta's son. Maggie-Now had seen a cousin in Brooklyn; he'd had shiny blond hair and wore a Norfolk suit with buckled knickerbockers, Buster Brown collar, Windsor tie, long black ribbed stockings and button shoes.

She'd been disillusioned about her grandmother and her aunt. She didn't expect Cousin Robbie to be wearing a Buster Brown collar. But did he have to show up bald-headed and fat and making jokes about his big stomach which he called a bay window?

He kissed Maggie-Now on the cheek. The kiss was like an exploded soap bubble. He handed her a square of blotting paper.

"I always give out blotting paper with my wet kisses," he said. He waited. No one laughed. "Oh, well," he sighed. "I'd do my rabbit trick for you if I had a rabbit." Maggie-Now giggled. He gave her a quarter and ignored her for the rest of the evening.

The three women and Robbie settled down to an evening of genealogy. "Let me see now," said Mary. "Pete married Liza . . ."

"No," said Robbie. "Pete died when he was three years old."

"I'm sorry."

"That's all right. That was thirty years ago. *Adam* married Liza. Let's see, Aunt Molly," he said to The Missus. "You married a Moriarity? Mike?" The Missus nodded. "I understand he died."

"Yes," agreed The Missus. "That was some time ago, God rest his soul."

"Whatever became of Roddy? Your wife's brother?" asked Mary.

"Oh, him," sniffed Robbie. "He married a girl, name of Katie Fogarty. I remember the name well because it was the same name he had. He was a Fogarty, too. Understand, they were not relations. They just had the same name. Well, sir, when they got the license, the clerk didn't want to give it to them. He said it was insects or something."

"What's that?" asked The Missus.

"Oh, the baby might be born funny," explained Robbie.

"How was the baby?" asked Aunt Henrietta.

"They never had one," said Robbie.

"What finally happened to Roddy?" asked Mary.

"He moved to Brooklyn, where people is more broadminded, and, for all I know, he might be dead or still living."

The saga of Roddy seemed dull to Maggie-Now. Lulled by the rise and fall of Robbie's voice, comforted by the warmth of the room and feeling safe surrounded by her mother, grandmother and aunt, she went into a half sleep. The conversation droned on. A word came up. A sharp word. A name. It kept piercing her drowsiness.

"Sheila!"

"No good," said Aunt Henrietta. Her voice was whippy and sharp, like a flyswatter coming down on a fly.

"It was just that she had hard luck," said Robbie.

"No good from the beginning, even if she was my granddaughter," swatted Aunt Henrietta. "Took after her mother." (Swat!) "Aggie was no good."

"Let the dead rest in peace," said Mary.

"She was pretty, so pretty," said Robbie. "The youngest, the prettiest of all my daughters."

Maggie-Now was awake but she feigned sleep, knowing that the grownups would talk in a way she couldn't understand if they knew she was listening.

"The way she was pretty was the ruin of her," said Robbie. "The boys were after her like bees after a honey flower by the time she was twelve." He sounded the way people sounded at funerals.

"She had a baby when she was fifteen," swatted Aunt Henrietta.

"She was married at the time," said Robbie with dignity.

"Seven months married," swatted back Aunt Henrietta.

"It was a premature baby."

"Like fun! Premature babies don't have fingernails. Rose did. Don't tell *me!*"

"In Brooklyn," said The Missus, "an awful lot of first babies are premature. The trolley cars shakes the houses and makes them nervous."

"Humpf!" said Aunt Henrietta.

"I remember," said Mary, "when Aggie brought Sheila to visit us in Brooklyn, once. I guess Sheila was six or seven. And my, was she pretty! Beautiful! I'd like to see her again."

"No, you wouldn't, Mary," said Robbie. "She looks bad and lives poor. Where her man is no one knows. He shows up from time to time, though. She lives in a slum. And believe me, a Boston slum is something. She takes in washing and Lord knows how many children she has."

"I'll go to see her before we leave Boston," said Mary.

"Not while you're staying in my house," said Aunt Henrietta.

"It's half my house," said The Missus, "and don't tell Mary what not to do or she'll do it, the way she got married when her father told her not to."

"Maybe it would be a good idea if she did go," said Aunt Henrietta. "Yes, go, Mary, and take your daughter so she sees what happens to a girl when she lets the fellers chase her. Not that you got to worry about *that*, Mary, the way she's so plain."

"She is not plain," said Mary. She put her arm around the child. "She's not pretty the way Sheila was with blond curls and dimples and pink cheeks. She's handsome! Look at those wide cheekbones and the way her chin comes to sort of a point. Why, she has a face like a heart."

Maggie-Now opened her eyes wide and stared hard into Aunt Henrietta's eyes, mutely daring her to contradict her mother.

"She's got tan eyes," said Aunt Henrietta.

"She has not!" said Mary. "She has golden eyes."

"Tan!" insisted the old woman.

"Now, Henrietta," said The Missus, "they're the same color yours were when you were young."

"She has golden eyes," conceded the old woman.

"I promised I'd find cousins for you, Maggie-Now, and I will," said Mary. "So be patient. Let me see." She consulted Robbie's directions on a slip of paper. "Turn right, go one block, no, three . . ." She lifted her veil because the chenille dots before her eyes made threes out of twos. "That's better. Two more blocks . . ."

They climbed up four flights of stairs. Mary knocked quietly on the door. It was flung open with a bang.

"Come in! Come in!" said a big woman. Her strong arms were bare to the shoulders.

The front of her apron was wet. Her tousled hair was half blond, half brown. Her face shone with sweat.

The room seemed to be boiling with life. A whole mob of children ran for cover when the visitors entered. They hid behind bundles of dirty wash standing on the floor and the smallest one burrowed into a loose pile of soiled clothes, half sorted, on the floor.

The window shades were up and the sun, full of dusty motes which seemed to quiver with life, poured in through the open windows. A network of filled clotheslines obscured the sky outside the windows. A breeze was blowing and the drying clothes billowed and collapsed and writhed and gyrated. The clothes seemed alive. There were bundles of dirty wash on the floor. The chairs were filled with clothes waiting to be ironed. A clothesline strung across the kitchen had freshly ironed shirts on it, and a bubbling boiler stood on the gas stove with the dirtiest of the wash boiling in it.

"Mary!" cried the big woman. She threw her arms around Mary and lifted her off the floor and swung her around. "Oh, Mary, I recognized you right away. You didn't change. You still look so sweet and so refined with your veil and gloves and all." Then she noticed Maggie-Now. "This yours?" she asked.

"Mine," said Mary. "We call her Maggie-Now."

"She's beautiful!" The big woman knelt

down and put her arms around the child.

"This is your cousin Sheila," said Mary.

Sheila!

Maggie-Now quivered in the woman's arms. Words she had heard when half asleep came back to her. "No good!" "No good from the beginning!" "No good like her mother before her!" Maggie-Now was confused. How could someone who was "no good" be so nice? Maybe this was another Sheila. But no. She heard her mother say:

"This is Cousin Robbie's girl. Aunt Henrietta is her grandmother. The mother of Aunt Henrietta and of my mother is her great grandmother and yours, too. That makes you cousins. There!"

"Do I have little cousins, too?" asked Maggie-Now.

"You certainly do," said Sheila. She called gently: "Come out, come out, wherever you are!" No response. Then she hollered: "Come out or I'll give it to you! Good!"

They came out of the dirty wash. There were four of them—all girls. The youngest was two, the next four, the third six and the oldest ten. Sheila lined them up, pulling a dirty sock out of the four-year-old's hair.

"Kids, this is your cousin Maggie-Now what came all the way from Brooklyn to see you."

The four girls and Maggie-Now stared solemnly at each other. The four-year-old was wearing a thumb guard. She pulled it off, took two good sucks on her thumb and replaced the guard.

All of the girls had tangled golden curls, heavenly blue eyes, dirty pink cheeks and dimples that went in and out like the first stars of night. They wore odds and ends of clothing which made them look like the illustrations of the children who had followed the Pied Piper of Hamelin.

"Oh, Sheila," said Mary, "they're pretty. So pretty the way you were. . . . I mean, there *you* stand, Sheila, four times over."

"Oh, go on, Mary, I was never as pretty as my kids. Anyhow, this is Rose, the oldest, this one is Violet, the thumb sucker is Daisy and Lily's the baby. She's two."

"What pretty names."

"I call them my bow-kay," said Sheila.

"Why, they've *all* got fingernails," said Maggie-Now clearly.

"Oh, Maggie-Now," moaned Mary.

"Oh, my sainted grandmother," laughed Sheila. "Will she ever let up on me? She told my father . . ."

To change the subject, Mary asked: "What are you going to call the next one?"

Sheila patted her rounding stomach. "Fern! To trim up my bow-kay." She nodded at Maggie-Now. "This the only one you got?"

"The only one."

"What's the matter? Did you marry a night watchman or something?" She prodded Mary with her elbow and laughed. Mary looked a little apprehensively at Maggie-Now. Sheila understood the look. "Listen, kids," she said, "why don't you go play with your cousin from Brooklyn so Cousin Mary and I can talk?"

The kids stood rigid except for Daisy, who removed her thumb guard and took three big sucks.

"Go on and play when I tell you," yelled Sheila, "or I'll give it to you. Good!"

Whooping like Comanches, the four kids dragged Maggie-Now away into the dirty wash. They bounced on the bundles and scattered the sorted clothes. They delved into the basket of wet clothing waiting to be hung on the line and belted each other with wet towels, screaming and laughing all the time while Mary and Sheila talked. Finally, they knocked over the ironing board with a sadiron upended on it. The iron missed Daisy by about an inch.

"Just for that," shouted Sheila, "you'll all get it!"

They lined up somberly. Then Sheila did a strange thing. She put her arm around Rose, gave her a walloping slap on the backside, and a kiss on the cheek at the same time. She did the same to the other three. They sobbed. And grinned slyly at each other at the same time, making the dimples come and go.

"My turn! My turn!" demanded Maggie-Now.

Sheila gave her the same, explaining to Mary: "I give 'em a slap and a kiss at the same so they know they're getting punished with no hard feelings."

Home again in Brooklyn, Maggie-Now remembered her "cousins." She spent her pennies on picture postcards to send to Boston. Her salutation was: "My dear Boston cousins." Her ending: "From your loving Brooklyn cousin." Sometimes she got a card back, always written by Sheila. "From cousin Sheila and all her flowers to the one rose, Maggie-Now."

A few months after their return, Mary had a letter from her mother saying that Sheila had given birth to her fifth child; a son. She had named him Joe.

"Why, oh why," wailed Maggie-Now, "didn't she ask me? I would have told her to call him Chris."

"Why Chris?" asked her mother.

"Chris is short for chris-san-thee . . . *you* know what flower I mean, Mama. Then he would have fitted in the bouquet."

Her next card had the salutation: "My dear Boston cousins and Joe."

Chapter Fourteen

THE growing years of Maggie-Now were not unhappy ones. She always had enough to eat, although the food was plain. She had warm clothes in winter even if they were not beautiful. She liked her school days although she didn't like to study. She loved the Sisters who taught her although they were very strict in their discipline.

She was well adjusted because she knew where she belonged in the social setup of her small world. She had a friend who had a hair ribbon for every day in the week. Maggie-Now had but two—one for Sunday, one for weekdays. On the other hand, another friend was too poor to have any hair ribbon. Her hair was tied back with a dirty shoestring. Maggie-Now was sorry she didn't have seven hair ribbons but she was glad she didn't have to use a shoestring to tie back her hair.

As she grew older, she gave some thought to poverty and riches. Her mother had asked her to read *Little Women,* explaining that it was a book about four girls who were very poor but happy just the same. Maggie-Now read the book and took issue with her mother.

"How can they be poor," she asked, "when they can waste hot potatoes to put in their muff. And I ain't . . . haven't a muff even. And then they have a servant and their father has money to go away on."

"To some people who are, say, used to three servants, to have only one servant is being poor. Poverty is relative."

The word "relative" puzzled Maggie-Now. How could "poor" be a relation, she wondered. She didn't probe further into the meaning of the word because she was anxious to go out to play. The word came up later, in another conversation.

One night, Father Flynn was paying a parish call and he, Mary, Pat and Maggie-Now sat in the kitchen having coffee. Mary, as always, was talking eagerly with the priest. He was one of the few people who made her articulate. Patsy was listening with outward respect because he had been brought up to respect priests, but he didn't believe a word Father Flynn was saying.

"I came from a small town," Father Flynn was saying. "Everyone seemed the same. No one was rich and no one starved. I had an idea, then, that poor people wore colorful rags and had rosy cheeks and danced all night to the music of a concertina. Those were my Francois Villon days.

Later, I thought poor people lived in cellars and had lice and lived on hard crusts of bread which they stole from each other. I was reading the Russian novelists in those days. Why, I was quite mature before I knew that poverty, like so many other things, was relative."

That word again, thought Maggie-Now.

The next day she asked her mother: "Why are some people rich and other people poor?"

"Yesterday, you wanted to know how big was the sky. And last week you wanted to know where the wind went when it stopped blowing down Ainslie Street."

"I mean like: Florry says we're poor. Bea thinks we're rich."

"Florry's father makes much more money than your father. Naturally, she thinks you're poorer than she is. But Beatrice's mother has to go out scrubbing for a dollar a day. Of course, she thinks that you, with a father who has a steady job, are richer than she is."

"It's all relations, then."

"Relations?" asked Mary, puzzled.

"Relations. But different than my Boston cousins are relations."

"Oh, you mean, *relative.* Yes, like everything else, I suppose it is relative."

"What's relative?"

"Oh, Maggie-Now! How high is the sky?"

"I asked first."

"Well, say a man has only one dollar in all the world. Somebody gives him a hundred

119

dollars. Another man has a hundred dollars. He's always had a hundred dollars. Someone gives him a dollar. He's just as poor as he was before. Now both men have one hundred and one dollars. But one is rich and one isn't. That's relative, I suppose."

"You're just *talking,* Mama. You're not *telling* me."

"To tell you the truth, I don't know how to tell you."

"Did you live in a rich house when you were a girl?"

"Oh, dear!" sighed Mary. "Well, people who lived in crowded tenements thought we had a rich house. But the Mayor's wife thought our house was poor compared to hers."

"What did *you* think, Mama?"

"I didn't think one way or the other," said Mary, trying not to get irritated by the incessant questioning. "I lived there."

"Why?"

"Don't be silly. I lived there because I was born there—because my parents lived there."

"Did you like it?"

"Of course. I didn't know about any other home, you see."

"Did that make it relative?"

"Oh, Maggie-Now, please stop. I'm getting *such* a headache."

"So'm I," admitted Maggie-Now.

Maggie-Now asked Sister Veronica what a rich home was and what was a poor home.

"A cell," said the nun, "with a cot in it and a chair and a nail on the wall on which to hang a shawl, is a rich home if our Holy Mother and our Blessed Lord are there. A grand home, with thick carpets and velvet curtains and a golden harp in the parlor, is a poor home if our Blessed Lord and our Holy Mother are denied there."

Maggie-Now asked her father: "Papa, did you have a rich home or a poor home when you were a boy back in Ireland?"

" 'Tis time you knew," he said, "how your poor father lived. It was a poor house. Poor. Poor. The poorest of the poor. A one-room sod shanty with a lean-to where me bed was and me bed a bag of straw. And the neighbor's starving pig sneaking in on cold nights and wanting to sleep with me for the warmth of it." The child laughed.

" 'Tis not to laugh at the way the slanty roof came down to the ground where me head lay and me bumping me head on it every time I moved in me sleep.

"And the black hole in the wall where the poor fire didn't keep us warm in winter but roasted us in summer when we cooked our food in it. And oh, the poor food! The small potatoes from the starving ground and the rough, black bread burned on the bottom, and an egg maybe once every two weeks, and our Christmas dinner, a hen, itself, tough, and she being too old to lay.

"And water from the well, and the well a cruel walk from the shanty on a cold winter's morning and the bucket too heavy for a skinny boy. And no toil . . . no plumbing in the house a-tall and we using the woods in back of our shanty."

"I betcha you were happy there, Papa."

"Happy, she says!" he commented bitterly. "I hated it and left without looking back once when the time came."

But he thought of how green the fields were in summer and the meadow flowers hidden in knee-deep grass and the lake that took its color from the sky or did the sky take *its* color from the lake? And the way the brown, dusty road to the village looked so lazy in the sun. He remembered the good nights in the tavern with the men liking the way he danced. His mind went to Rory-Boy in the great days when they had been true friends. He thought of his fiercely protective and possessive mother. And oh, the dear sweetness of his Maggie Rose! He thought of the idle, golden days of his youth and he wept in his heart.

God forgive the lie—me saying I hated it so, he prayed.

Remembering, he spoke with bitterness to his daughter; his darling's namesake. "Your mother was the one raised in a rich house. Tell her to take you over to Bushwick Avenue and show you the house. Tell her to show you the stable where your father laid his head nights. Look good at that rich house what should have been mine . . . ours . . . if that crook . . ."

Ah, he thought, *let the dead rest in peace even*

if he was a black'ard in life.

Walking over to the old house, Mary answered Maggie-Now's question: "Why didn't I take you there before? Because the house is so changed and it makes me sad."

Yes, it was changed. The rooms on either side of the stoop had been made into shops. The bay windows were now store windows. One was a hairdressing parlor with intricately coifed wax dummy heads in the window. The other window showed only a swan, pure, white and immobile and with each feather in place. The swan sat proudly on a bed of swansdown. A card, dangling by a brass chain suspended from the swan's beak, read: *Genuine Swansdown Filled Pillows.*

"Is it real?" breathed Maggie-Now.

"It was. Once. Now it's stuffed."

"Maybe it's still alive and they give it medicine to sit still."

"Now you know better."

The upstairs windows had a blank look. A card in one of them said: *Rooms.* The basement rooms had been converted. A swinging sign with a red seal informed people that a notary public was available there. A rooms-for-rent sign was attached to the notary's shingle.

Mary figured it out that the man who'd bought the house was the notary in the basement. He was squeezing every penny of revenue out of his investment. She wondered how many transients had slept in her white room since she had left. She sighed as she thought of her piano once standing in the room that now held sewing machines, bolts of ticking and bags of down.

The stable was now a separate property, divided from the big house by an iron picket fence. An unevenly painted sign over the barn door read: *Pheid & Son. Plumbers. Day & Night.* A broken toilet lay on its side in the yard. A man, Pheid himself, was uncrating a pair of double, soapstone washtubs. A boy, a few years older than Maggie-Now, was helping the man. The man looked up as Mary and Maggie-Now approached.

"Yes?" he asked.

"I used to live here when I was a girl," explained Mary.

"That so? Well, a Eyetalian owns the house now. But I own the shop."

"Is that so?"

"That sign: Pheid & Son? Well, this here is son. Son Pheid." He put his arm about the boy's shoulder. His pride was evident. "I'm breaking him in young. I believe in that," he said.

"I see," said Mary.

"Well, help yourself. Look around." He went back to his work.

"Where did Papa sleep?" asked Maggie-Now.

"Up there. That little window. Where the pipes are sticking out."

"Chee!"

"After we were married, we lived in the big

house, of course. For a little while, anyhow."

"Where is . . . are, all the snowball trees you said was always in the yard?"

"Someone cut them down, I suppose."

"I'm glad I never lived here."

"Why, Maggie-Now, don't say that. It was very nice before it was all cut up into rental property. It was good to live here long ago. It was cool and dark in the summer and bright and warm in the winter."

"Why did you all move away then, if it was so nice?"

"Well, your grandfather died."

"Why?"

"Oh, Maggie-Now! It was his time to die."

"Papa said he died from being scared."

"Your father didn't mean that."

Mary knew this was a logical time to tell her of her grandfather. But how could she tell the child that her grandfather had been a thief? But was he? The others who had stood trial had been exonerated. And politicians still kept on doing the same things.

No, I will not complicate her growing years by telling her. Patrick won't tell her since he hasn't so far. She may find out when she's grown up. By that time, his crimes—if crimes they were—will be softened; faded and far away.

"What *did* he die of then?" asked Maggie-Now.

"What we all die of in the end. His heart stopped beating."

"I'm glad . . . not that he died," amended Maggie-Now quickly. "I mean I'm glad I don't have to live *here*. I like our own house—where we live now. And I don't care if it's rich or poor."

I'm glad she's got that settled, thought Mary. *Maybe now she'll stop using that word "relative."*

"Of course," said Maggie-Now airily, "it's all relative."

Chapter Fifteen

IN the fifteen-odd years since Patrick Dennis Moore had landed in America, many changes had come about. The horsecars had given way to trolley cars. The completion of the subway, which changed into the elevated as soon as it crawled out onto the Williamsburg Bridge, did away with most of the East River ferries. Automobiles were no longer a curiosity, although some retarded kids still yelled, "Get a horse!" when one appeared, and all pedestrians were delighted when a car broke down. Most of the better stores had soldered off the gas pipes and put in electric lights. Some of the candy stores had phones in and you got your number by appealing to "Central." And some insane person went around the neighborhood saying he'd sat in a dark room somewhere and seen pictures that moved on a bed sheet. The ballad writers of the day started a new folklore by acknowledging the inventions in their creative work.

> Come, Josephine,
> In my flying machine . . .

And,

> . . . Lucille,
> In my merry Oldsmobile.

Also,

> Call me up some rainy afternoon,
> And we'll arrange for a quiet, little spoon.

Yes, there were changes. But Patsy never changed, except that he was getting too old to be called Patsy and the few people who had to speak to him called him Pat. He got to be sort of a character the way he smoked his stub-stemmed pipe upside down as he cleaned the streets. He smoked it that way so sparks wouldn't fly in his eyes on a windy day and to keep the tobacco dry on rainy days.

He became known as "Deef Pat" because he wouldn't get out of the way for anybody or anything. Motormen would stamp down on the gong, motorists would squeeze the rubber bulb of the horn or grind the klaxon, bicycle bells would tinkle hysterically; teamsters cursed him and pedestrians threatened to sue the city because he swept dust on them when they crossed the street. But he ignored them all, pretending not to hear, and he wouldn't move out of the way until he had finished the place he was cleaning.

People would say to each other: "He'll get run over yet."

The answer: "Let's hope so."

Sometimes on a still summer afternoon, when the German band played on one of his streets, he'd lean on his broom handle and listen a while. The band played a German song, a popular song of the day and, invariably, an Irish song. When the tune had a lilt, Pat's feet twitched inside his heavy work shoes and his mind made a dance pattern and he thought again of County Kilkenny.

One day, Maggie-Now happened to be with the group of children who followed the band from block to block. He watched his daughter waltz with another girl.

She's got them all beat, he thought with a flare of pride.

After the usual lugubrious "Blue Danube," the kids clustered around the musicians begging for "Rosie O'Grady." When the band complied, the kids made a circle and pushed Maggie-Now into the middle of it. As soon as she got the beat of the song, she went into a solo, soft-shoe clog. The pipe nearly fell out of Pat's mouth. He was that astonished.

Where does she get it from? he asked himself. *From meself,* he decided. *But who learned her?*

He watched her a while. *No, I couldn't do better meself.*

She lifted her skirts and the ruffles on her drawers showed. A couple of passing boys stopped, stared, whispered to each other and snickered. Pat threw his broom down and stalked over to the dancers. When Maggie-Now saw him, she gave him a big smile.

"Go on home," he said tersely.

She tossed her head, making her bangs bounce, put her hands on her hips and clogged away from him. He followed her around the circle, caught her and spanked her. He spanked her publicly before all her friends.

"That'll learn you," he said, "to show everything on the street."

She looked up at him, stricken. He had never hit her before. "Papa! You didn't kiss me when you hit me! You didn't kiss me like cousin Sheila! You meant it!"

"You betcha life I meant it and there's more where that come from."

He thought of Big Red—how he had said that and he wondered if Maggie-Now felt the same shame he had felt. He was sorry he had spanked her. He had never hit her before. Neither had her mother. She was not a bad girl. The spanking didn't hurt her, he assured himself. It was the public humiliation that hurt her. She ran home, weeping all the way.

The cornet player shook the spit out of his

horn. *"Du Heinzel Männchen!"* he sneered at Pat.

"Is that so? Well, Heinie, you go to your church and I'll go to mine." That was one of Pat's favorite retorts.

Maggie-Now changed toward her father. The sunny child had always chattered to him endlessly, never noticing that he made no answer. She had liked to tease him and had been quick to hug him warmly. She had never noticed that he took all her loving ways with indifference. She had so much emotional steam that she could go a long way on her own power without the encouragement of response.

She changed after the whipping. Now she was quiet and restrained in his presence. She spoke to him only to answer him. She gave him respect and obedience and nothing more. Secretly, Pat grieved. He felt that he had lost his child.

"Are you turning the girl against me?" he asked his wife.

"I would not do that, Patrick. You are her father and she needs you and loves you."

"She's still mulling over that spanking I gave her. I only gave her a tap or two but you'd think I licked her black and blue."

"But why in front of her friends?"

"She's got to learn," he mumbled.

"Did you learn anything by Timothy Shawn thrashing you? No. You'll hold that against him all the days of your life. Maggie-Now has some of your ways."

131

"Why don't you say my *bad* ways?"

She took his hand in both of hers. "I loved you for your ways. I never thought were they good ways or bad ways."

"Ah, Mary," he said, touched, and a moment tried to get born.

I could say I loved her, he thought. *And it would mean the world to her—my saying it. And I do love her in a kind of way. But I never said it before. Kinda late to start saying it now. I'd feel foolish . . . we'd both feel foolish. . . .*

The moment died stillborn.

He wanted the girl's affection back. To that end, he made plans to take her out on her birthday.

"I will give her a good time like your father gave you when he bought the combs. I'll give her the same good time according to me means and hope she'll remember it in the same way you did," said Pat to his wife.

No one sold violets on the Brooklyn streets. He bought her a pinwheel instead. When she ran ahead to make a wind to make it turn, he realized she was too big to play with a pinwheel.

Of course he didn't take her to a bar for a claret lemonade. There were no glamorous bars in the neighborhood and he'd be sure to be arrested if he brought a little girl into a saloon. There was no fine restaurant. They ate hot pastrami sandwiches and honey cake and drank tea from glasses in a Kosher Delicatessen & Lunchroom. The men ate with their hats on. Pat explained that was their religion. He took his hat off with the remark that they could go to their church and he'd go to his. The diners balled up their napkins and threw them on the floor when they were done. When Maggie-Now asked why, her father said they did that because they were very clean people. Maggie-Now thought that didn't seem clean. Oh, yes, her father told her. That was so the proprietor wouldn't serve the napkins again to later diners.

They went to the theater. They heard no prima donna raise a luscious voice in song. They went to The Folly and saw Marion Bent and Pat Rooney. And Rooney's waltz clog thrilled them more than the best soprano's aria.

Afterward, he took her to a novelty store and invited her to choose a present. She wanted a wood-burning set. There was a tie rack with an Indian chief's head in a war bonnet just waiting to be burned and an envelope of "jewels" to paste on the bonnet's headband. Pat wanted her to have a rhinestone brooch. Both things cost a dollar each. She didn't want a brooch. She wanted to burn wood. Pat said she would take the rhinestone brooch or nothing. She said she wanted nothing. He bought her the brooch anyway.

Yet it had been a happy evening and she held her father's hand all the way home and squeezed it happily from time to time, and once he squeezed back.

Chapter Sixteen

ONE night as they were eating supper (Maggie-Now was about twelve at the time), a handsome young man knocked on the door and was admitted to the kitchen. He was about twenty-three years old.

"Do you remember me, Mr. Moore?" The young man smiled engagingly. Patsy scratched his head, trying, trying to remember. The boy's face saddened. "Widdy."

"Oh! Big Red's boy. What do you want?"

"Mother sent me," said Widdy, turning his hat around in his hands. Then he seemed to lose the continuity of what he wanted to say. "I mean, you know Dad." He swallowed hard before he said: "God rest his soul . . ."

"No!" said Pat, putting his fork down. "No!"

"Mother said, I mean, Dad had no relations in America, except Mother and me and Grandmother. There's Gracie, too. We were going to get married in June, but now we'll have to wait a year out of respect."

Big Red had died in bed and had not been killed on the streets by hoodlums as Lottie had always feared. A blizzard had tied up the city. Big Red, like many another cop, had worked two days and two nights without rest. He had had a cold, and just when Lottie had thought he was getting well it turned into pneumonia.

Yes, Widdy's mother was bearing up well. There was pride mixed with her grief. Her Timmy had died an honored man, Widdy told them. His lieutenant would be one of the pallbearers, and Widdy supposed they hadn't heard, but Big Red had been promoted to sergeant a week before he took sick. Lottie had been so proud.

"So Mother said," concluded Widdy, "if you folks would come to the funeral . . . the Moores and the Shawns had been so close back in County Kilkenny . . . had almost become relations . . ."

Pat grieved. He didn't grieve for a friend; he grieved for a dear enemy. Although never a heavy drinker, he felt the need of going down to the saloon for a couple of beers.

"I lost the best enemy a man ever had," he told the bartender.

"That's the way it goes," said the bartender. He never flicked an eyelash. He was well used to hearing strange things from his customers.

Pat refused to go to the funeral, but he asked Mary to sew a black armband on his coat sleeve.

"But that's only for relatives, Patrick."

"And was he not a relative to me in a way, like the boy said? I'll wear it for a year."

Mary and Maggie-Now went to the funeral and went home afterward to Lottie's house. Mary fixed supper for them; Lottie, her aged mother, who was now living with her and Widdy, and Gracie, the pretty girl who was Widdy's fiancée. Maggie-Now helped briskly. Lottie, who hadn't seen her godchild since the christening, was much taken with her. She begged Mary to come again and bring the child.

The friendship grew. Mary looked forward to her visits with Lottie. Mary had not realized how still her life was. She was well liked in her neighborhood, but made no close friends because she was not gregarious. Her life was sort of somber: partly because she had a serious temperament and partly because her husband wasn't outgoing—he was not one to spread cheer and good will. If it wasn't for Maggie-Now . . .

Mary liked Lottie because Lottie made her laugh. She laughed at the things Lottie said and did. She relaxed in the great warmheartedness of Lottie. She listened sweetly and raptly to Lottie's reminiscences of Timmy, which always ended up: "And so we stayed sweethearts right up to the end."

To Maggie-Now, a visit to Lottie's was like a Christmas present. The flat was a treasure house to the child. She loved her godmother the way she loved everyone. She fetched and carried for

Lottie's old mother. She beamed on Lottie and ran her errands. She romped with Widdy and admired Gracie extravagantly. Once Widdy took her to an ice-cream parlor and treated her to a soda. He told her he had done so in order to have the first date with her. Maggie-Now began to think about growing up.

After Widdy married and went to live with his Gracie in Bay Ridge, Lottie didn't have too long a time to be lonesome. Maggie-Now slipped into her son's place. She started spending weekends with Lottie. Lottie fed her éclairs and cream puffs and neapolitans. She and Lottie did things together. They made Maggie-Now a peach-basket hat. They shopped in the dime store for the wire frame and cards of strips of braided straw and buckram. They trimmed it with bunches of tiny pink roses. Maggie-Now thought it was beautiful. Mary thought it was too mature for a child but she let her wear it to church just the same.

Lottie told her bit by bit about her father: his dancing days in County Kilkenny, his mother, his romance with Maggie Rose and how Timmy had gone to Ireland and licked him.

"Papa licked me once," said Maggie-Now. "Right on the street in front of everybody."

Lottie gave her a quick look but she was too good and too kind to question the girl. Then she told how the immigrant boy had been robbed. (All these things were new to Maggie-Now. Her father and mother had never told her these things.)

"There he stood," said Lottie dramatically, "a young boy in a strange country, full of dreams of the grand new life where all men is free and any poor man has the chancet of being a millionaire or president—whichever he likes best. And he thought this man was his friend, see? And he trusted him and the man robbed him and all the time he thought he was his friend."

"That was awful," said Maggie-Now. "Poor Papa!"

She told Maggie-Now what a wonderful heritage she had. She was not above exaggerating. To Lottie, the story was the thing—not the facts.

"Your grandmother was a great lady and she raised your mother to play the piano. And she played in concert halls and oh, my! How the people clapped!"

"Mama never told me . . ."

"She's not one to brag—your mother. And she painted things. Not like you paint a house, but pictures and on dishes. *You* know. And your grandfather: My, he was a man high up! He was the mayor of Bushwick Avenue or something like that. I forget. But he lost all his money and died."

"How did Mama meet Papa?" asked the girl, all agog.

"Now *that's* a story! Well, it was this way." She settled herself more comfortably in her chair, preparing for a long story. "Bring your chair closer, Mama," she shouted across the room. "You can't hear good over there.

"In the first place, your father was a very handsome man. He lived in the stable in your grandfather's yard. He didn't have to be a stable boy, mind you, but in America, everyone must start at the bottom. So, Mr. Moriarity, your grandfather, put him in with the horses to test him out. So . . ."

So Maggie-Now got to know a lot about her father. As she grew up, she came into a realization of how things that had happened to him in his young days had made him the man he was now. It cannot be said that her growing knowledge made her love her father more, but it made her understand him better.

And sometimes understanding is nearly as good as love because understanding makes forgiveness a more or less routine matter. Love makes forgiveness a great, tearing emotional thing.

Mary missed the child when she was away at Lottie's. The girl was the sum and total of her life. She loved her so much that she sacrificed her precious time with her because Maggie-Now was so happy with Lottie.

Pat didn't like it at all. He thought Maggie-Now was spending too much time at the home that Big Red had set up. *This Timothy Shawn,* he thought. *This Big Red: wherever he is, he's still reaching out to manhandle me life.*

He came home one Friday night from work to a quiet house. "Where's the girl?" he asked.

"Over to Lottie's."

"Again? I don't like the idear. Here I use meself up working to provide a home for her and she's never in it."

"It's hard for a man to understand, but a growing girl needs a woman friend. Maggie-Now's lucky to have Lottie."

"I don't see it. Why can't she be satisfied with her girl friends?"

"Maggie-Now has to know things," she said fumblingly. "I suppose she talks to the other girls but they don't know what Maggie-Now wants to know—needs to know. Now, Lottie is like a girl friend; she and Maggie-Now do things together like young girls. Yet, she can talk to Lottie like one woman to another. Well, I guess I'm not explaining it right."

"If you mean," he said bluntly, "that she's got to know where babies come from, you tell her. You're her mother."

She searched for words of explanation. Her thought was something about destruction of innocence. But she knew it would sound schoolteacherish. She said: "Maybe I could. Should. But the way I am . . . the way I was brought up, the way I carried her for nine months before she was born . . . the way when she was a baby she'd grab my thumb and look up at me so seriously . . . well, I guess I wouldn't know how to tell her. . . ."

"Well, does she have to *live* at Lottie's to find out what she would-a found out anyway in time?"

"That's not the only reason I like her to be friends with Lottie. We all have to die someday and . . ."

"That's news to me," he said.

"I mean, I don't think of dying. But like all mothers, I suppose, I worry, or did, about what would become of Maggie-Now if I died before she was grown up. Then I think that she'd have Lottie and I don't worry any more."

He had a flash of tenderness . . . or was it jealousy? "Think of me a little," he said. "What would become of me if you died?"

"Oh, Patrick!" she said. She clasped her hands and her eyes filled with happy, loving tears. "Would you miss me?"

He didn't want to say yes. That would be too embarrassing for him. It would be ridiculous to say no—churlish to say, I've grown used to you. He was sorry he had brought up the matter.

Chapter Seventeen

AFTER sixteen years, Mary was pregnant again. She had a feeling of awe about it. She was in her middle forties and had believed that the menopause had set in. She was quietly happy about it and a little frightened. She remembered the hard time she'd had when Maggie-Now was born; how the doctor had warned her afterward not to have another child. It would be dangerous, he had said. Mary, however, reasoned that a lot of advances had been made in obstetrics in the sixteen years since she had had her first child. Also she'd heard countless stories of women who'd had a hard time with the first child and very easy times with the second and third birth. All in all, she was pleased about it.

The neighbors watched the progress of the pregnancy with more concern than curiosity. They discussed it. It was a change-of-life baby, they admitted, and, yes, them kind what comes late in life is always the smartest ones. Yeah, he might grow up to be a great man but she'd be too old to care. Anyhow, was the consensus of thought, please God nothing should happen to her.

Maggie-Now talked over the baby with Lottie. "I thought Mama was—*you* know. Too old?"

"Good heavens, no! Lizzie Moore, your grandmother, was forty-five when she had your father. It runs in the family—to have a baby in middle age." Maggie-Now couldn't follow the reasoning. Lizzie Moore was not related by blood to Mary. How could Mary inherit the tendency to conceive in middle age from her? "And you, Maggie-Now: When you get married and if a baby don't come along right away, don't give up until you're fifty."

"I want lots of children," said Maggie-Now. "Lots and lots of them."

Lottie looked at Maggie-Now's ripe figure. The girl looked older than her sixteen years. She could pass for twenty and no one would challenge her age.

"Yes," said Lottie. "You'll have 'em. Only make sure you're married first."

Mary was four months pregnant. She went for her first examination to Doctor Scalani. When it was over, she asked: "Is everything all right?"

He waited a little too long before he said: "Yes."

"But at my age . . ." she fumbled with the buttons at the back of her dress.

"Turn around," he said. He buttoned up her dress.

"Tell me the truth, Doctor. Will I die?"

He unbuttoned a few buttons and buttoned them up again to gain time before he answered. "The first thing you must do," he said, "is to stop worrying. Doctor's orders. There! It's done." She turned around with a worried look on her face. He smiled at her. After a second, she smiled back.

"Come back in two weeks."

"I will. Good-by, Doctor. And thank you."

"Good-by, Mrs. Moore."

The doctor sat at his desk, tilted the chair back and put his fingers together. He gazed at his framed diploma hanging on the wall. He remembered a professor he had had in med school. He wished he could talk to him about an abortion in connection with his patient. He knew what his prof would say and what he, Doctor Scalani, would say.

He'd say: *Diagnosis clearly indicates that a therapeutic abortion is in order in the case of Mary Moore. How do I proceed?*

Two or more physicians must be in agreement with you after examination that the pregnancy should be terminated.

Would it be safe?

Under proper conditions, yes.

I could do it on my own.

Illegal, Scalani. Suppose you did abort and she died? Manslaughter.

But if I had acted in the best interest and post mortem indicated that death was inevitable, abortion or no abortion?

You may not go to jail, but you'd never be allowed to practice again.

The doctor heard the tinkle of the bell. Another patient? He sighed and went into his reception room. It wasn't a patient. It was his girl, Dodie.

She had been his mistress for ten years, and for ten years she had waited for him to marry her. He saw her but once a week, on a Sunday.

"I told you *never* to come to my office."

She said, "I know. But it seems so long to wait until Sunday to see you. And my period . . ."

"Oh, go away, Dodie. Please! I'll see you Sunday."

Lottie gave Maggie-Now instructions: "When your mother gets ready to go to the hospital, I want you to ring me up right away. Hear? Right away. I got a surprise for her I'm saving till the minute her labor starts. Did you ever telephone before?"

"No."

"Here's what you do: You go to a store where there's a phone. You ask Central to give you this number I wrote down. Then you put a nickel in the hole. Keep a nickel handy. When the candy-store man down by the corner says, hello, you say, Will you call Mrs. Timothy Shawn to the

145

phone? Any hour of the day or night he'll come and get me because I'm going to give him a dollar when you call up."

A few weeks later, Mary was awakened by the rupturing of the bag of waters. She was alone in the bed; Pat had taken to sleeping on the lounge in the front room during the past week because Mary was so big and twisted and turned all night trying to get into a comfortable position and she worried about keeping Pat awake.

Mary lay still awhile, knowing her time had come. *It will be hard, I know,* she thought. *It was hard when Maggie-Now . . . but when it was over and they put her in my arms, I forgot. I was so happy. It will be the same again. I'll forget the pain. I hope I have a son. Patrick would be pleased. He said he doesn't care but all men want a son. And won't Maggie-Now be happy. It's foolish of me to be afraid.*

But she found she was trembling. She got up and changed the linen on the bed, then she went to wake her daughter. She looked down on her. In sleep, the girl's face still had the lineaments of childhood. She grasped the girl's bare forearm gently, because, even though Maggie-Now didn't have red hair, she had the skin that went with red hair and she bruised easily.

"Wake up, dear. I have to go to the hospital."

Maggie-Now was awake instantly. She threw her clothes on. "I'll go wake up Papa."

"No, let him sleep a while longer. It's going to

146

be hard on him anyhow and I want to put it off as long as possible. No use both of us suffering." She thought of the girl. "I know you don't mind helping me. But your father's different."

Maggie-Now put her arms around her mother. "Don't go to the hospital, Mama. Have the baby home where I can take care of you."

"It's better that I go to the hospital." Doctor Scalani had told her it was necessary in case of surgery. "Now you get the buns and a morning paper for your father to take his mind off things and stop at Doctor Scalani's first and tell him."

Maggie-Now tapped at the doctor's door. The shade was down. It shot up a second after her knock. He was in his pajamas and the couch where he had been sleeping was rumpled with sheets and blanket. He assured Maggie-Now that he'd be at the hospital waiting for her mother. He shut the door and pulled the shade down again.

He took a brand-new shirt from a drawer. Dodie had made it for him as a Christmas present. He buttoned it up. The sleeves were a little long. He put sleeve garters on to pull up the sleeves. Dodie had made the garters for him as a birthday gift. He fastened on a stiff collar with a gold collar button that Dodie had given him when they first started going together. He knotted on a black knit tie also made by Dodie for some anniversary or other. He put on the best of his two suits. It was the first time he had ever treated one of his patients at the hospital and he wanted to look nice and make a good impression on the nurses and doctors.

It was very early in the morning and the bakery was still closed but Mrs. Luthlen was carrying buns from the back and putting them in the showcase. But she opened the door for Maggie-Now. The girl told her about her mother and asked for ten cents' worth of sugar buns. The woman filled a bag to overflowing with buns hot from the oven. She pushed Maggie-Now's dime back.

"On a day like this, I can treat a good customer. Tell your mama I'll be thinking of her. And let me know, Maggie-Now."

She put a penny on the newsstand and picked up a *Journal* and went into the candy store and asked to use the telephone. She got the number and shouted through the mouthpiece that she had to speak to Mrs. Timothy Shawn. It took hours, it seemed, before Lottie answered.

"Aunt Lottie! Aunt Lottie! Can you hear me?"

"Don't holler, girlie, I ain't deef—yet." Maggie-Now told her the news. She wanted details but Maggie-Now didn't have any to tell. "Well, listen good, Maggie-Now. Gracie—*you* know, Widdy's? Well she gave birth to twins three weeks and two days ago. I've been saving it as a surprise for your mother. I know she's nervous so I thought if she finds out just before how little and skinny Gracie is and how she was

148

in labor only two hours, it might make her feel better. You tell her what I said, hear? About how skinny Gracie is and only two hours . . . and she was up the third day."

"What's their names, Aunt Lottie?"

"Well, I'll tell you," said Lottie.

Maggie-Now groaned. She knew Lottie. She knew Lottie would string out the story. Maggie-Now was nervous. She was afraid her mother would have the baby while she was phoning. "They're here with me right now," said Lottie. "Widdy and Gracie went over to Manhattan last night and didn't . . ."

"Please, Aunt Lottie, what's their names? Mama will ask me."

"Well, I wanted to name them Timmy and Jimmy. I think that's cunning, don't you?"

"Is that their names?"

"Wait. Widdy wanted to call them Ike and Mike. *You* know. Because they look alike?"

"I haven't got much time, Aunt Lottie."

"Well, Father Shaley got insulted about Mike and Ike. He said he wouldn't christen them that. Oh, my! He gave Widdy Hail Columbia."

"I'll call you up later, Aunt Lottie."

"Wait! Do you know what they finally named them?"

"Put another coin in the slot, please," droned the operator.

"I got to go, Aunt Lottie."

"Wait! They finally named one *De Witt* and the other *Clinton.*"

"Put another coin . . ."

"Good-by, Aunt Lottie."

"Listen! Tell your mother not to be brave. Tell her to give in and holler. You don't holler, they think it don't hurt. They don't do nothing. Tell her to holler. . . ."

The phone went dead. Maggie-Now was sweating and the warm buns were crushed out of shape because she had held the bag so tight against her. When she got home, her father was up and dressed. Her mother was very nervous and Pat had been trying to calm her down.

"If you'd only stop telling me it's going to be all right . . . If you'd only stop talking," she said. Maggie-Now was astonished. She had always known her mother as kind and considerate. She'd never heard her speak that way. "Where have you been so long?" she asked Maggie-Now fretfully.

"I promised to call up Aunt Lottie because she had a surprise for you. Gracie and Widdy had twins."

Mary's face smoothed out. She smiled and sat down. "Oh, isn't that nice!"

"She said to tell you that you know how skinny and nervous Gracie is and Gracie had an easy time. In labor only two hours, Aunt Lottie said."

"Did she say that?"

"Yes, and she was out of bed in three days."

"My, that makes me feel better. What did they name them?"

"De Witt and Clinton," said Maggie-Now. Mary smiled again.

"That Big Red," burst out Pat. "That Timothy Shawn. Still butting in. Here," he said to Maggie-Now, "I been trying to quiet down your mother since you went to the store. She won't listen to me. But let her hear about Big Red's grandchildren . . ."

"That's all right, Patrick," said Mary absently. She patted his arm and then began giving nervous instructions as she put her hat on.

"Keep the house up, Maggie-Now, so that it's nice and clean when I come back with the baby. And see that your father has a hot supper when he comes home. . . . Oh, Maggie, how could I get along without you! And make your father's coffee strong in the morning. And Sunday, go over and see Lottie. And keep off the streets while I'm away."

"Oh, Mama, now . . ."

"And Patrick," continued Mary in an offhand way, "I want you to deed over this house to Maggie-Now when she marries."

"We'll talk about that when the time comes," he said.

She held his arm in a tight clutch. "Promise me, Patrick!"

"I will do so, Mary," he said.

"You heard your father, Maggie-Now?"

"Yes, Mama."

"Remember. He promised."

She gave the girl a little black bankbook.

"When the tenants pay the rent, put the money in the bank. It must be saved for taxes and interest."

"I know, Mama."

Mary started to put her gloves on and a pain caught her. She dropped her gloves and held on to the back of a chair. They watched for an agonizing moment.

"There!" said Mary. "That was the first one." Maggie-Now put her gloves on for her. Mary looked around vaguely. "I didn't get all the ironing done," she fretted.

"Now, Mama, I'll finish it," said Maggie-Now. "Don't worry about a thing. I'll take good care of Papa and the house will be shining clean for you when you come back."

Mary started trembling violently when she walked into the hospital. It was gloomy and smelled of sickness. The downstairs windows were barred. People stood in line before a nurse's desk waiting to be admitted or treated. Mary was told to sit on a bench along the wall until her turn came. She sat between her husband and her daughter. Pat sat with his head down, his hands holding his hat between his knees. Maggie-Now pulled her mother's arm through hers and held it tightly.

The nurse finished filling out an old man's card. She tapped on a bell and an orderly came to take him to a ward. The old man was weeping.

"I will never come out alive," he wept. "No

one ever comes out of here alive."

This was almost true. The poor people were terrified of the hospital and few entered unless they were at death's door. So it was logical that few came out alive.

They kept Mary waiting there because there were so many emergency cases that had to be handled immediately. Childbirth was considered routine—not an emergency. The old man's weeping had unnerved Mary. She had a sharp pain and when it had passed she said:

"Patrick. Do something. Please do something!" her voice was hysterical.

Pat jumped to his feet and shouted: "Where's that damned doctor?"

An efficient, middle-aged nun, the steel bows of her eyeglasses making ridges in her fleshy cheeks on account of the tightness of her coif, was passing through the room. She turned and scowled and was about to rebuke Pat when Doctor Scalani came into the room.

He looked neat and efficient and almost handsome. Even Mary looked at him in surprise. He was so different from the last time she had seen him. He spoke authoritatively to the desk nurse. Mary was admitted immediately. A nurse came with a wheelchair to take her away. Doctor Scalani told Maggie-Now and her father to go home. He said he'd let them know. . . .

At the start of Mary's third day in labor, Doctor Scalani realized his life's ambition as a doctor.

He was given a consultant—a very important consultant indeed—the chief of staff of the hospital, who examined Doctor Scalani's patient and gave him every professional courtesy, which made Doctor Scalani feel good. It was a brief consultation and they were in agreement.

If labor continued to term, they agreed, the baby would be born dead. But there was a slight chance that the mother would live. If they intervened and took the baby from her, the child would live but the mother, in her weakened condition, would die.

So, according to the dictates of the religion, they saved the baby and let the mother die.

She knew she was going to die. She didn't review her whole life as it is said one does at such a time. She had no last word of wisdom or conclusion drawn from living, no great truth to articulate before she died. She had no thought save for her new-born son. There was a great aching place where the child had been torn from her body. The milk was beginning to fill her breasts. Like a primitive creature, she whimpered for her young and wanted to crawl to it. She begged the nurse to get the child and put it to her breast. The nurse concealed her horror with professional briskness.

"After a while," she said brightly. "After we've rested a bit. Then we'll bring our baby in." The nurse ran out in the corridor looking for Doctor Scalani. She found him. She said:

"She wants to nurse her baby. Isn't that awful?"

"Let her," he said.

"But to let a live, healthy baby nurse from a dying mother! It gives me the creeps."

"Let her have her baby. That's an order."

"Is it?" She tossed her head. "You're just an outside doctor. I don't have to take orders from you."

He grabbed her arm and held it tight enough to make her wince. He spoke, putting a space between each word. "I am the doctor on the case. I am giving you an order. Nurse, take the baby to the patient."

"Yes, Doctor," she said.

There wasn't much time. They sent Maggie-Now to her first. "Just act natural," said Doctor Scalani. "That's always best."

There was a screen around Mary's bed. Maggie-Now's eyes widened in fear when she saw her mother's waxy-looking face. "Mama!" she said. "Oh, Mama!" She started to babble to avoid sobbing. "I got all the ironing done, Mama. And Papa ate everything I cooked. And I put new shelf paper . . ." Mary heard nothing of what she said.

"The baby," whispered Mary. She tried to pull the blanket away from his face and couldn't. Maggie-Now pulled it back.

"Oh, isn't he tiny," exclaimed the girl. "Isn't he cute!"

"Take him up," whispered Mary.

"What?"

"Pick him up."

Maggie-Now put the baby in the crook of her left arm. Instinctively, she held him correctly. His head, not much bigger than an orange, rested against her breast and went up and down a little with the beating of her heart. She put her outspread right hand under his little backside.

"Why he *fits*, Mama," said Maggie-Now in surprise. "He fits to me just right!"

"Margaret Rose!" Mary tried to smile. "You're such a good girl, Maggie-Now," she whispered. Then she was quiet for so long that Maggie-Now thought she was sleeping. Maggie-Now started to croon to the baby. Mary opened her eyes then.

"Listen," she whispered. "Do what I say. His bottle . . . the doctor will tell you. Wash eyes, boric acid. Warm sweet oil on head till soft place closes. Keep band on till cord drops off. Boil diapers so no rash . . . Things you don't know, ask . . . ask Lottie or neighbor with children. Ask . . ."

Maggie-Now started to cry. Mary drew on some last strength. Her voice was almost normal. "Don't cry," she said. "I might have to stay here a few weeks. Then I'll be home. Until then . . ."

The lie was the last sin of her life.

A nurse appeared with Patrick Dennis. "Only one visitor at a time," she said cheerfully.

"Wait for me downstairs, would you, Maggie-Now," said Pat. "I don't want to go home alone."

The girl put the baby back in her mother's arms. She kissed her mother and went downstairs to wait for her father.

Pat looked strange. He'd had his hair cut, his suit pressed, his shoes shined and he smelled of bay rum. He too had been told to act natural. He tried to act natural and succeeded in acting like a stranger. He sat next to her bed.

Dear God, he prayed, *give me another chance. Don't let her die. I'll do better. I'll be good to her. I swear it!*

Her lips moved. She was trying to say "Patrick."

"Well, Mary," he said heartily. "I see we got a boy. Now I'll have somebody to go hunting and fishing with." (He'd never fished or hunted in his life but he thought men were supposed to say that when they had a new son.)

She turned her face to him. He looked away because the deep caverns in her cheeks and the black hollows under her eyes frightened him. He talked:

"Me vacation's coming up about the time you get out of here. And I tell you what! We never went nowheres before on me vacation but this time we'll go to the country. You know. The Catskills? Good country air—sure and 'twill put you on your feet again. And them fresh eggs off the chickens every day and them vegetables . . ."

She looked at him with a fixed stare and her eyes flooded with tears which ran down either side of her face. He put his hand on hers but withdrew it without meaning to when he felt how hot and dry her hand was.

"Oh, Patrick," she whispered hoarsely. "In all our years you never told me . . ."

"No, I never told you, Mary. But I do."

No, he had never told her that he loved her and now he knew he *did* love her. He felt he should say the word "love" now. It was a simple word, easily said, but he couldn't say it. In some obscure way, he felt it would make him a stranger to her.

"But I do, Mary, and you know it. I don't have to say it. Me and you . . . we was never ones to say things like that to each other because we never started out that way. But I do. I do."

"It's too late," she whispered, weeping.

"That's no way to talk," he said with false heartiness. "Why, you'll bury us all."

It wasn't the right thing to say but that's the way he was used to talking. *If I talk different,* he thought, *she'll know that I know she's going to die.*

Mother Ursula, the head of all nurses, lay nurses and nursing sisters, came in. She put her hand on Pat's shoulder and pressed it. He stood up.

"Was the child christened?" he asked.

"This morning," said Mother Ursula. "Right

158

after he was born. He was named Dennis Patrick.''

"My wife?'' he asked.

"Father Flynn will stay with her.''

Pat understood. He got his hat from under the chair and leaned over Mary. He pressed his cool cheek to her dry cheek.

"I love you, Mary,'' he whispered.

He bumped into the screen as he went out. Mother Ursula straightened it.

A very young nun came in with a basin of water and a towel. She washed Mary's face and hands and feet. Another nun brought in a small table covered with a linen napkin and set up two beeswax candles on it. She placed a crucifix between the candles. She arranged a tumbler of water and a saucer of fine salt on the table. She added a cruet of oil and a piece of cotton. Mother Ursula lit the candles.

Father Flynn came inside the screen carrying the Host. The three nuns genuflected and withdrew. Father Flynn knelt down by the bed with his ear to Mary's lips and she made her last confession. He absolved her from her sins and gave her Extreme Unction. When all was over, she made a harsh sound of fear. He understood. He took her hand.

"My child,'' he said, "my friend. Have no fear. I'll stay with you. I'll stay with you all the time that's left.''

But the terror grew in her. She didn't want to die! She didn't want to die! Her hand clutched the sheet and she made little moans. A nurse looked in and flew down to the office to get Doctor Scalani. He came after a while with a hypodermic needle poised in his hand.

Father Flynn shook his head. "No," he said.

"Obviously, she's suffering," said the doctor. "This will help."

"As long as one can suffer, one is living. Let her live and suffer until life is gone."

The doctor could have said what he had said to the nurse: "I am the doctor on the case." But he knew Father Flynn would say: "I am the priest." The priest took precedence at death. To show he was in accord with the priest, the doctor pressed the plunger of his needle and let the liquid squirt out on the floor.

She was past talking now and her terror grew. Her face seemed like a grotesque mask with a twisted mouth. Father Flynn spoke quietly to her but he couldn't get to her. He prayed.

Then the baby cried. Concern mixed with her terror. The baby was lying in the crook of her arm and she tried to tighten her arm to bring the baby nearer. Her other hand plucked futilely at the drawstring of her nightdress. She stared at the priest and her face went into distortions as she tried to communicate with him.

He guessed what she wanted to say. "You want me to turn my head away?" Her face straightened out and she waited. "I'll help you, my child, and I'll keep my eyes shut."

He felt for her arm with his eyes shut, and

folded it around the baby. Gently, he pushed the baby toward its mother's breast. He put her other arm across the child, placing the palm of her hand at the back of the baby's head. He pulled the sheet up over her exposed breast.

When he opened his eyes, he saw that the terror had left her face and her distorted mouth had relaxed. The peace was beginning to come. He sat down to stay with her to the end as he had assured her. He waited and he prayed while he waited.

And soon his waiting was ended. He undid her arms and took the child from them.

He walked down the hospital corridor carrying the child. A nurse with briskly tapping heels walked past him and smiled back over her shoulder.

"Nursery's down the corridor, Father," she said. "First turn to the right."

"I know," he said.

Chapter Eighteen

MOLLY MORIARITY had been unable to come to the funeral. She had nursed Aunt Henrietta through her final illness. Molly herself was frail and failing and the news of her only child's death had prostrated her. Cousin Robbie came down from Boston to represent Mary's kin.

Mary had been insured for enough to provide a simple burial and to buy a grave. Cousin Robbie had instructions from The Missus; Mary could be buried with her father provided the money Pat saved on the grave would be used to pay off the balance of the loan on the house. Pat agreed. So the little house was freed.

Before he left, Cousin Robbie said: "Aunt Molly said she'd be glad to take the children but on account of her poor health . . . and she's too old . . . But my girl, Sheila, said she'd be tickled to death to have them. With six of her own, she said, two more won't make much difference. Maggie-Now would be a help and you could send so much a week for board. . . ."

"I'll keep me children with me," said Pat. "Maggie-Now knows how to run the house and she'll look after the boy."

"She's young. She shouldn't be tied down with a baby. Maybe she wants to live her own life."

"Me mother was tied down with two children when she was Maggie-Now's age and it didn't harm her. The girl is strong and healthy."

"The responsibility . . ."

"It will keep her out of trouble. She'll know the work of a home and a baby. She won't be so anxious to marry the first clown what comes along."

"She's not going to have much fun."

"And is that any of your business?"

"No, Patrick," said Cousin Robbie slowly. "It's none of my business."

Maggie-Now had to leave school, of course.

She didn't mind at all. She was not the studious or bookish type. She missed her school friends and the nuns who were her teachers. Otherwise she was glad to be done with school. When she dropped school her girl friends tried to continue to include her in their activities but it couldn't work out because Maggie-Now was tied down with a house and a baby.

The few boys she knew, had taken walks with and joked around with, drifted away. Maggie-Now seemed a woman all of a sudden and it made a boy feel "funny" to see a girl with

163

whom he had romped in Cooper's Park just weeks ago now trundling a baby carriage through that same park.

Her friends now were more mature: Lottie, of course, and a neighbor or two who had helped her out with the baby at first.

The shopkeepers, for the most part, liked her. They admired her courage and wished her well. Mr. Van Clees, the Dutch cigar maker, whom Maggie-Now saw twice a week when she bought her father's clay pipes and tobacco, became her friend. He took almost a paternal interest in the baby boy.

She cared for the baby and ran the house for her father. Her arrangements with him were simple. He gave her two dollars to buy groceries. When the money was gone, she asked for more. He always said: "What'd you do with the last two dollars I gave you?" She always answered: "I spent it." Then he gave her another two dollars.

She collected the rent and put the money in the bank. Once a year she went down to Borough Hall to pay the taxes. She had expected her father to handle that but he had said: "Since you're going to be the owner someday, *you* learn to handle property." Sometimes there was a *little* surplus in the bank after taxes. Other times the surplus melted away when the rooms were tenantless.

Maggie-Now was a natural-born mother. She washed the baby and fed him and changed his diapers and had him out in the air for a couple of hours each day. When he started to walk and was knowing enough to get into mischief, she took a true mother's privilege and spanked him—but always with a kiss as Sheila had done with her children.

Like a mother, she thought Denny was exceptionally handsome and she enjoyed the admiring looks given him when she took him out in his buggy. She wanted nice clothes for him, but when she asked her father's permission to use some of the surplus rent money to buy them, he refused, saying the money must be saved for hard times—for his old age. "When you're married to a man in business for himself you'll have everything you need, while me, who slaved me life away for me children, will be sitting and starving in a hallroom in me old age."

Because she wanted pin money of her own and because time sometimes hung heavy on her hands, she, as the expression went in the neighborhood, "took in piecework." She "turned" kid gloves. They were made in a factory in Greenpoint and sewn wrong side out on machines. She took bundles of them home to turn right side out. She got twenty cents a hundred pair and made two or three dollars a week in her odd hours.

When she got bored with the gloves, she went to a shoe factory and got bundles of bronze leather slipper vamps and sewed cut bronze beads on a design stamped on the vamp. She liked the work and got satisfaction out of her neat stitches.

Bronze slippers went out of style and she "made beads." These were necklaces of tiny white beads with yellow or blue daisies at intervals—much like Indian beadwork. She worked with five threaded needles simultaneously and enjoyed the emergence of the daisy design.

She considered herself fortunate to be able to earn a few dollars a week without leaving her home. She used the money to buy nice things for the baby and, once in a while, an item of clothing for herself.

Each time she bought a new bonnet for Denny or a new pair of rompers, she brought him over to Mr. Van Clees's store to show him off.

"Hello, liddle mudder," was his greeting. "How goes it, hey?"

"Fine."

Then he'd ask questions about the baby—how much did he weigh now, did he cry a lot and did he eat good. He was astonished at each answer: He weighs all that? My! Never cries and eats *everything?* My! A wonder of a boy! A wonder!

"And do you miss your school, Miss Maggie?"

"Yes. The sisters and the girls. But I sure don't miss all that homework."

He gave Denny a little blue candle on his first birthday. ("In case'n you have a birthday cake for him, Miss Maggie.") He gave him two on his second birthday and started a tradition.

Once Maggie-Now, thanking him, said: "Oh, Mr. Van Clees, *you* should be Denny's godfather."

"That I could not be, Miss Maggie. I ain't a Catholic."

"But I see you at Mass every Sunday. Used to, anyhow."

"I go by the Catholic church because it's nearer as my church. But I ain't a Catholic."

"I see," said Maggie-Now. But she didn't see at all.

Chapter Nineteen

MR. VAN CLEES had a friend, August (Gus) Vernacht who came to America from the old country. Gus, a woodcarver, spent many an evening in Van Clees's store, carving out a chess set. While Gus carved, the friends discussed many things.

They spoke of Maggie-Now. What life did she have, they asked each other, tied down by taking care of her brother and catering to her father's wants? And she so young.

"By golly," said Gus, "I will take her by my Ahn-nee and my woman minds the boy and Maggie-Now goes down on the street and fun has with the boys and girls."

Gus invited Maggie-Now to his house and she said she'd love to go, but first she must ask her father.

Her father said, "Nothin' doing. You ain't goin' out nights and get bad ways from people what I don't know."

"Oh, everybody knows what nice people they

are," said Maggie-Now. "I'll be safe. Anyhow, I'm nearly eighteen and I know what I'm doing."

"Yeh? The House of the Good Shepherd is full-a girls, eighteen, what knew what they were doing," he said darkly.

"What house?"

"Where they put wayward girls."

"I'm not wayward."

"Things happen before you know it," he said mysteriously.

He had a clutch of fear. She *was* growing up. She looked mature for her age. Why, he had started courting Maggie Rose when she had been a year younger than Maggie-Now. It had been the girl's virtue and her mother's nosiness and not his inclination that had kept Maggie Rose virginal.

But that was nearly twenty-five years ago, he consoled himself. *Things is different now. Girls that young don't keep steady company nowadays.*

Still there is things she should know. Mary, why did you have to die when the girl needs a mother so bad to tell her things? I can't tell her.

No, he couldn't. As with many fathers, the thought of sex in his daughter's life was abhorrent to him. He couldn't stand the thought of any male lusting after her.

For the first time, he worried about his daughter. He knew that in some ways the congested neighborhood was a jungle where men

169

preyed on girls: innocent girls, susceptible girls and willing girls. He knew of the narrow, trash-filled back alleys, the dark cellars, tenement rooftops cluttered with chimney pots, vacant stores where doors could be forced . . . he knew all of these places where men took young girls for their purposes.

He had thought his daughter was safe in the home and where else did she go? To the store and sometimes to Lottie's house. But was she safe? This man who invited her to his home to meet his wife: Maybe he didn't have a wife; maybe that was a comeon. Something else came to his mind.

A month before, the upstairs had been rented to a mother and father who worked and their son, about twenty, who didn't have a job and loafed around the house all day. After they had examined the empty rooms and had announced when they'd move in, the woman had commented on the fact that Pat's daughter was young to be married and have a two-year-old baby.

"She ain't married," said Pat.

The woman exchanged a surprised look with her husband and their son grinned.

"That's why the baby has her maiden name for his last name."

"He has *my* name. He's *my* son. His mother died in childbirth."

"I see. Well, that's all right." She exchanged another look with her husband.

Pat wondered how many men, strangers to the neighborhood—newcomers—believed that Maggie-Now had an illegitimate son. Did those kinds of men think she was available? He recalled the fellow upstairs—how he had been standing on the stoop one time when Maggie-Now had gone out to the store and how the young man had looked after her as she walked down the block.

He was angry with his daughter because she made him concerned about her and spoiled the even tenor of his days. So he shouted at her, not realizing that she couldn't know what he had been thinking: "And I don't want you making free with that loafer upstairs, either."

"Papa! Where'd you ever get the idea . . ." She stopped abruptly. She had had some contact with the boy upstairs.

A week ago, he'd come to the door and asked politely if the upstairs tenants had the privilege of the yard. She said they did and she let him go through her rooms because there was no other way to reach the yard. He explained that he wanted to get a little tan. He pulled his shirt off in the yard and bounced a ball against the wooden fence. She watched him through the kitchen window, admiring his manly torso and wishing she could go out and play handball with him.

She decided he must never walk through their rooms again. Suppose her father came back during the day for some reason or other and he found the young man in the kitchen! He wouldn't accept any explanation she could make. Thereafter, she kept her door locked when she was in the house alone with Denny and didn't answer when he knocked.

One evening in the time between after supper and dark, she was sitting on the stoop with Denny. She was restless. She dreaded the evening ahead. She'd put Denny to bed and then what? She'd walk about the house looking for something to do to kill the long evening. She and her father seldom conversed with each other at any length. She was not an avid reader and what was there to do but go to bed?

She didn't want to go to bed. She wanted to be out walking these summer nights with some girls her own age. She wanted to laugh and exchange confidences. She wanted some boy to call for her and take her for a walk; treat her to a soda. She wanted to ride on an open car to Coney Island with a bunch of boys and girls and laugh with the girls at the way the boys cut up. She wanted to ride side saddle on a merry-go-round horse with a nice young man standing at her side, his arm about her waist, pretending he had to hold her so's she wouldn't fall off. She closed her eyes and dreamed the scene: The blend of merry-go-round music and the voices of barkers and the hum of talking voices and laughter and the sound of the sea. The smells mixed of hot corn and cotton candy and candied apples on a stick and over all the heavy salt smell of the sea. And the breeze and the motion of the merry-go-round making her hair blow back and the delicious reaching out for a grasp at the gold ring and the nice-looking young man looking up to smile at her and his arm tightening automatically about her waist when the horse went up . . .

That was her sudden dream. She closed her eyes to see the reality. She got up at seven each morning to get breakfast for her father. She did the housework. The rooms were few and the furnishings sparse. She had it neat and shining in an hour. She drew out her shopping as long as she could. The storekeepers were her only social contacts. At ten, save for getting a simple lunch for herself and the baby and preparing a simple supper for the three of them, her work was done. The long day and evening stretched out interminably.

She washed her hair and filed her nails and washed clothes that were already clean and pressed things that needed no pressing and did piecework when she could get it. On nice days she wheeled Denny to the park, first walking down the block and asking the neighbor women if they would let her take a preschool child along as long as she had Denny anyhow. She usually took three or four small children to the park with her.

But all this wasn't enough. She was strong and healthy and vital and full of energy. She wanted to work hard. She wanted to go to places. She wanted friends her own age. She wanted to talk and laugh with young people. She wanted to work in a factory; she wanted to work in a store measuring cloth or wrapping up dishes. Most of all, she wanted to "go out."

She thought of Annie Vernacht. When Gus had told her about his Annie, Maggie-Now had thought how wonderful it would be to be friends with Annie; to have someone pour her a cup of coffee, cut her a piece of cake. And Gus had said Annie would mind Denny. . . . Maggie-Now had planned that, for each hour Annie would mind Denny while she, Maggie-Now, went out, Maggie-Now would mind Annie's children three hours to pay back.

But her father didn't want her to visit the Vernachts. And that was that.

The young man from upstairs clattered down the stoop. He touched the brim of his hat and said it was a pleasant evening. She agreed, turning her head away as she spoke in case her father was watching from the window.

As she put Denny to bed, she made up her mind. She would go and visit Annie Vernacht and she wouldn't tell her father.

The following Sunday afternoon, she dressed Denny in his nicest rompers, slicked down his hair, dressed herself up and told her father she was going out and would be home in time to cook his supper. He grunted without looking up from the paper he was reading.

"Come in! Come in!" boomed Gus. "This is my Ahn-nee." He grabbed his hat. "I go now by Jan's cigar store and leave the ladies to talk lady talk." He left.

Annie was hospitable but bewildered. Gus, like many another man before him, had forgotten to tell his wife he had invited Maggie-Now for a visit. In fact, he had forgotten to tell her anything at all about the girl.

Annie smiled. Maggie-Now smiled. "Sit down," invited Annie.

The room was neat, warm and peaceful. The boy, Jamesie, leaned against his mother's knee. The baby, Theresa, slept in her mother's arms. Another baby, soon to come, lay quietly in the womb.

Dennis struggled to get out of his sister's arms. "Can I put him down?" asked Maggie-Now.

"Sure, sure."

She put Denny on the floor. He staggered around frantically for a few seconds, then crawled under the table and composed himself for sleep. He slept during the entire visit.

"What's her name?" asked Jamesie.

"Sh!" said Annie. Smiling at Maggie-Now, she said: "I am Annie."

The girl smiled back. "I know."

"And you?" Gus had forgotten to tell his wife the girl's name.

"I'm Margaret Moore. *You* know. Maggie-Now?"

Again they exchanged smiles. The girl sat with her hands in her lap waiting for the friendship to begin. Annie wished there was some tactful way in which she could ask the young girl what was the object of the visit. Annie cleared her throat.

"You are young to be a mother."

"Oh, he's my brother. My mother died when he was born."

"I think maybe I saw her on the street. Some ladies was telling me about her baby coming. Your father: He is the street sweeper?"

"Yes. Street cleaner. He's home," she added.

"He's got good work. Steady. My man, he makes the rocking chairs."

"I know. Mr. Van Clees told me."

"Ah, that Jan!" Annie smiled mysteriously.

Maggie-Now, half child, half woman, wondered: *Will she ask me if I'd like her to mind Denny sometime, like Mr. Vernacht said, so I can go out by myself sometime?*

Annie thought: *What must I say to her now?*

Annie was good and kind but inarticulate and shy. If Gus had only thought to tell her about Maggie-Now! She would have been so happy to take the girl into her heart and her warmth. Gus would have denied that he had forgotten to tell his wife all about Maggie-Now. It was that they had so much wordless and perfect understanding together that he thought somehow Annie knew as much about Maggie-Now as he did. Annie sat there trying to draw on this unspoken understanding. The most she could get was that something was expected of her; that Gus had prepared the girl for something and the girl now expected it. But what?

"Did Gus say I should do something?" she asked gently.

Maggie-Now's face flushed with embarrassment. So Gus had said nothing to his Annie and she, Maggie-Now, had come there so brash expecting . . .

"No," she said. "Nothing."

There was a little more forced conversation and then Maggie-Now prepared to leave. The good-bys were effusive because both were ill at ease and the good-bys were something they could get their teeth into.

"You come again when you can stay longer," said Annie.

"And you come to my house some afternoon," said Maggie-Now. "I'll make coffee."

Annie did not return the visit. Some weeks later, Maggie-Now saw Gus in the cigar store and told him she hoped Annie would come for a cup of coffee sometime.

"Ahn-nee, she don't go out now," he explained. "The baby comes soon. But you come by our house."

"I will," said Maggie-Now. But she didn't. And Annie never did come to see her.

Van Clees told Maggie-Now when Annie's baby, a boy, was born. He had been named Albert August. Maggie-Now gave Mr. Van Clees a pair of booties to give to Gus to give Annie.

She gave a verbal message: She would come to see Annie and the baby as soon as Annie got over the ordeal of birth. Annie sent a message by Gus, who gave it to Van Clees, who gave it to Maggie-Now: Annie would come and visit Maggie-Now as soon as she got on her feet.

They never did get together. However, whenever Gus saw the girl he said: "Ahn-nee sends best regards." Maggie-Now always said: "Likewise."

One day the cigar store was closed. There was a sign in the window: *Closed on Account of Death in the Family*.

Gus Vernacht had not been a relative of Van Clees but the cigar maker had borrowed the sign from the baker who had bought it two years ago when his wife's father died. Van Clees could not cross out *In the Family* and print in *Of Friend* because the baker wanted it back. He thought he might have to use it again. He had a lot of relatives.

About Gus: It was nothing you could put your finger on; nothing you could anticipate. He went to bed one night as usual and didn't wake up the next morning. Doctor Scalani said: "Heart!" and charged a dollar. The neighbors gave what comfort they could to Annie.

"Such a good man," said one.

"Yeah, the best ones are the first to go," said another.

"Sure. The bums, they hang on."

"Well, if he had to go," was the general opinion, "it's better he went in his sleep. That way, he never knew a thing about it."

Chapter Twenty

MAGGIE-NOW let a year go by without seeing Annie. Denny came down with the measles and the Board of Health put a quarantine sign on the door. While Denny was convalescing, Pat, to his great shame, caught the measles from Denny. Pat had never been sick before and he carried on as though he were in the last stages of leprosy. He called for the priest and demanded the last rites of the church. Father Flynn said he didn't give Extreme Unction for measles. But he heard his confession and gave him communion and sat at Pat's bedside for an hour lecturing him on his sins and his conduct.

"That's right," said Pat, aggrieved, "take advantage of a man sick and flat on his back."

"As an ordained priest," said Father Flynn, "I have to be patient with you. But as private citizen Joseph Flynn, I'd enjoy punching you in the nose."

Pat looked at him with interest and felt a glow. *Sure, he is a man after all,* thought Pat, *and worthy of me hate.*

During that year, Annie had moved away; somewhere on Dekalb Avenue, Van Clees said. He could go right up to the house, he said, but he couldn't tell her the number. The next time he'd write it down and Maggie-Now could go and visit poor Annie.

Something happened to Maggie-Now about this time and it drove all thoughts of Annie and of nearly everything else out of Maggie-Now's mind.

She was sitting in the yard one afternoon with Denny. She had washed her hair and was drying it in the sun. It hung loose almost to her waist. She sat in a camp chair and watched Denny try to dig holes in the cementlike ground with a tablespoon. She heard her kitchen door open and close. To her consternation, the young man from upstairs came into the yard! She'd forgotten to lock the front door. He greeted her, said, "Hello buster," to Denny, who stared at him, and pulled off his shirt. He started hand batting the ball against the wooden fence, running back and forth. He stopped as suddenly as he had begun and threw himself on the ground next her chair. He leaned his head against her knee, panting from his exertions. She was fascinated and revolted. His curly hair was sweaty and she felt his hot face against her knee through her thin summer dress. She pulled her knee away.

"We got a hard-to-get girlie here," he said.

"I got to go in now," she said inanely.

"Suits me," he said. "What are we going to do about the kid?"

She started to get up. He put his arms around her legs. "Stop that!" she said sharply.

"Just as you say." He clasped his arms around his knees. She stood there a moment, feeling foolish. "Come, Denny, we're going in the house now," she said.

"Listen," said the fellow from upstairs, "a couple friends of mine are throwing a party tonight. How about it?"

"How about what?"

"Would you like to go?"

"Thank you. But my father wouldn't let me."

"Tell him you're spending the night with a girl friend. I'll sneak you in the house before he wakes up."

"My father wouldn't let me go out with you. Not with any feller."

"He must have let you out once," he said. He winked toward Denny.

"You go in the house first," she said. "And go right upstairs to your own house, so I can go in."

"Now listen, kid, I'm wise. I know my way around. Sure, sure. You palm the kid off as your brother. Well, that's all right by me. So you made a mistake once. Well, we all make mistakes. That's why they put rubbers on lead pencils."

"But he is *so* my brother. Aren't you, Denny?"

"Mama?" murmured Denny. He held the spoon out to her.

"That's the ticket, buster," said the young man. "Spoon. We'll do a little spooning first . . ." Maggie-Now started to tremble. He put his arms around her.

"Let me go!" she said, trying not to scream on account of the neighbors. He kissed her.

"You . . . you . . ." she searched for a word. "You slob!" She was frantic with anger and with fear that a neighbor might be watching from a window. "I'll tell my father what you said. And he'll kill you."

He surrendered suddenly. "Okay, then. Only you can't blame a feller for trying. You know how it is. You been there."

She pulled Denny up and ran into the house. She slammed the door and locked it. She locked the front-room door. The young man pounded on the kitchen door.

"Hey! How am I gonna get in to go upstairs?"

"Go jump over the fence!" she shouted.

He did. It wasn't a very high fence. She heard him come in through the street door. He went up the stairs whistling.

She didn't leave the house for a week she was so frightened and ashamed. She thought that any man she might encounter on the street would think as the boy upstairs thought: that she was no good and had had a baby without being married. She sent a neighbor's little girl to the store for her groceries and aired Denny in the back yard. She sat close to the house so the boy upstairs couldn't see her without leaning far out the window. And always she worried about the boy upstairs. She didn't tell her father as she had threatened. She knew he would say: It's your fault. You must have encouraged him.

The time came when her father ran out of tobacco and busted the last of his clay pipes. He told her to go to Van Clees. She said she didn't want to go; she was no longer a child and it didn't look right for a young lady to go into a man's cigar store.

Pat went and came home in a rage. Van Clees had inquired about Maggie-Now and told Pat of Gus and Annie and how much Annie had enjoyed her visit and Van Clees said he hoped Maggie-Now would go to Annie's new home to see her. He gave Pat the address on a slip of paper and Pat tore it up and threw the scraps at Van Clees and said he'd take his trade elsewhere. Van Clees said bluntly that there was no profit in clay pipes. He carried them only to accommodate people he liked.

"And you are one people I don't like," he said in conclusion.

Pat took it all out on Maggie-Now. She listened at first with astonishment and then with weariness. She saw her father with new eyes. How wrong he was, she thought, talking about the Vernachts as though they were white slavers when she herself knew they were kind and gentle. Before this time, the girl had always believed that her father was right—not fair, but essentially right. Now she doubted a lot of the things that her father had told her.

She was certain, now, that she couldn't tell him about the boy upstairs. He'd never believe her story. He'd have his own version of the incident and it would be lurid and poor Maggie-Now would be made to be at fault.

She was too wholesome of temperament and too resilient to brood too long. When she got tired of staying in the house and being afraid of the boy upstairs, she went out again and stopped being afraid.

Let people think what they want, she decided. *They can't be arrested for thinking. And I can walk around with a sign on my back which says: This is my baby brother and not my son. And as for the feller upstairs . . . he just better stay out of my way, that's all.*

The young man was removed from her life. The people upstairs defaulted in their rent and Pat went up to see about it.

"Being's your daughter won't let my son go in the yard, we're not going to pay the rent," said the tenant.

"The roof is for the people upstairs and the yard for the people downstairs," said Pat.

"The roof is slanty," argued the tenant. "Nobody can sit on it."

"Pay the rent or move out."

"We'll move out."

"You can't move out unless you pay up the rent."

"We can't stay; we can't move. Make up your mind," sneered the tenant.

The tenants cut this Gordian knot by moving and not paying the rent. They got the iceman to move their furniture in his pushcart. Maggie-Now sent a little boy to where Pat was working. Pat came running, clutching his broom in his hand.

Pat started to pull a marble-topped bureau off the cart. He figured that was the same value as the rent owed. The tenant called the cop on the beat. The cop judiciously listened to both sides, holding his nightstick in his hands behind his back and swinging it between his legs. When Pat and the tenant had done, the cop gave his verdict.

"I got no use for landlords," was his opening statement.

He handed down his opinion at length. He thought it was "funny" that a man working for the city could own his own home. He cited his own experience. He'd been on the force twenty years making good pay and *he* couldn't afford to own his own home. There was something fishy. . . . In short, he found for the tenant.

The iceman moved off with bells jangling and furniture swaying on the cart. Pat followed him with brandished broom. He was going to follow the cart to the new residence, and badger his ex-tenants from there.

"Make him stop follying our furniture," ordered the tenant.

"I got me rights," said Pat. "I'm not follying anything. I'm walking back to me work and the pushcart is in front of me."

Pat kept walking. The cop put his chin in his hand and squeezed it—thinking. There was nothing in rules and regulations about a man walking to work. . . .

"Ain't you gonna do nothing?" inquired the tenant.

The pushcart and Pat rounded the corner. The cop solved the problem. "There's nothing I can do. He's off my beat now."

The Italian iceman stopped. "Look wall-yo," he said to Pat. "I know how is. Me, I on your side. I give you address new place. You don't walk so far."

Pat thought that was a good idea. The Italian gave him a fake address.

Thus the feller who gave Maggie-Now her first kiss was gone forever. From now on, he'd be nothing but a lifetime memory.

She took Denny to see Van Clees on his third birthday. It took the good man a few minutes to recognize her. She had grown tall in the year and now was quite buxom for her nineteen years. He was pleased to see her and delighted with Denny. He had three small blue candles for him.

He told her about Annie; she'd moved again, to Flushing Avenue, the other side of Broadway;

a very poor neighborhood. The two younger children went to nursery school or the day nursery as it was called and Jamesie—such a good boy, said Van Clees—ran the house while the mother worked.

"Yes, she works now," sighed Van Clees. "In the five-ten store on Broadway. Now she gives the best years of her life up for making open sandwiches." He sighed again.

Maggie-Now went over to the dime store. It was lunch time and she had to wait for a seat. Eventually, she got one. Annie came and set down a plate of food in front of a girl sitting next to her. Maggie-Now smiled and said, "Remember me?"

Annie looked at her and said, "I'll get to you in a second, miss." Annie went and got change for a customer.

She don't know me, thought Maggie-Now sadly. *She just don't know me.*

A waitress came and said, "What's yours?"

"I don't believe I'm hungry. Thank you." Maggie-Now got up and went home.

Chapter Twenty-One

WHEN Maggie-Now was a child, her mother used to take her to the cemetery on Decoration Day, to plant a geranium on Michael Moriarity's grave.

She remembered how she had enjoyed the trip in the open trolley car, how it was like going to the country. And the way the warm summer air smelled like buckwheat honey and warm dust. And that wonderful woman whose husband was buried near Moriarity's grave. What was her name again? Yes. Mrs. Schondle. She and Maggie-Now's mother became once-a-year friends.

Maggie-Now stopped going to the cemetery when her mother died. She couldn't go anywhere because she had to take care of the baby.

When Denny reached the age of five, his sister thought he ought to go to the cemetery with her.

Denny gave her a hard time. He demanded to sit on the front seat of the trolley. Only he didn't sit. He jumped up and down and kept telling the motorman how to drive the trolley.

"He's only five years old," apologized Maggie-Now.

"God help me if he was six," said the motorman.

Before going into the cemetery, Maggie-Now stopped at an outdoor flower stand to buy a geranium for her mother's grave. She told Denny that he could plant it. He didn't want to. He wanted to plant a flag on his grandfather's grave.

"Flags are only for soldiers, Denny."

"Grampa was a soldier."

"No, he wasn't."

"He told me he was a soldier."

"Why you never even saw him."

"I want a flag anyhow."

She bought him a little flag.

Mrs. Schondle was at the cemetery. She wore the same battered black hat draped with black widow veils that she had worn five years ago. And after five years, she still remembered Maggie-Now and hobbled over to greet her. "I ain't seen you since you was that high," she said. "But I know'd you right away."

They hugged each other and Maggie-Now said, "I have never forgotten you. And here is my brother."

"That one sticking the flag in the grave?"

"That's right. Denny, come say hello to the lady."

"Will she give me a penny, then?"

"Shame on you, Denny!"

"That's all right," said Mrs. Schondle. She rummaged in her handbag and gave him a penny.

"Now what do you say?" said his sister.

He said, "Hello."

Maggie-Now planted the flower and the friends prayed together and talked a while. When it was time to leave, Denny pulled up the flag.

"You're supposed to leave it there, Denny."

"Grampa said he didn't want it."

"What would you do, Mrs. Schondle, with a boy like that?"

Mrs. Schondle knew what *she'd* do but she was too polite to say so.

Yet . . .

The next year, Mrs. Schondle did not walk over to greet them. The Schondle grave looked raw and was mounded. Maggie-Now walked over to the grave. Yes. Fresh carving . . . a winter date . . . *Elsie Schondle, beloved wife* . . . Maggie-Now sat on the ground next the grave and wept. It wasn't that she had been so close to Mrs. Schondle. It was because while Mrs. Schondle was alive, a little bit of Maggie-Now's mother had still lived.

The boy, Denny, came to her, knelt down by her side and put his arms around her neck.

It was an evening after supper. Denny was on the floor shooting marbles. Maggie-Now was reading *Laddie,* a book that had just come into the library. Patrick Dennis had read the evening paper. Now he was digesting the news.

We'll never get in it, he thought. *Wilson will keep us out of war. If we did get in, though, I wouldn't have to go—a man of forty-six with two children to support without a mother. I say let them kill each other over there. They're all a bunch of foreigners anyhow. Why should we butt in?*

He looked at his son. *By the time he gets big,* he decided, *war will be a thing of the past. Maggie-Now. If she was a boy, she'd have to go if there was a war. But there won't be. The worst thing that could happen to her is some no-good man will come along . . .*

He looked at his daughter. She had put aside her book and was on the floor helping Denny with his houses. She was twenty-one now and well formed.

She's a woman, now, he thought, *and it's just a question of time when she'll marry and leave the home. The boy will start school soon and he'll grow up quick, and before you know it he'll be out of the house, too, and I'll be left all alone in me old days.*

He sat there and wondered what life would have been like were he friends with his children. He had to admit he had his lonely times. He would have liked to be one with them instead of the outsider who came home every night and lived there, yet had no part in their secret lives. He wished now that he had started to gain Maggie-Now's love and friendship when she was a little girl. Encouraged her to confide in him; brought her home little surprises and made her laugh in delight in the way of children.

In the warm, comfortable room with his children nearby, he was cold and lonely. Maybe it wasn't too late. Maybe he could yet make friends with them.

I've never mistreated them, he thought. *I've given them a home and they have plenty of food and I watch that nothing bad happens to them. But why then does the boy stop laughing or talking or whatever he's doing when I come home nights?*

"Denny," said Maggie-Now. "It's time for bed."

"Maggie-Now," said Pat, "after the boy goes to bed, sit down with your father and we'll talk things over."

A look of alarm came over her face. "What did I do?" she asked. "Was it the supper? I know the potatoes weren't mashed good because Denny kept bothering me. . . ."

"No, no. I mean . . ."

"Is it my dress? I didn't take money to buy a new one. This is an old one. I dyed it and put a new collar on."

"No. I just want to talk to you."

"About what, Papa?"

"Nothing. Anything. Just talk."

"Is something the matter? Something I can fix up? Just tell me what and I'll try."

"Never mind," he said. "Never mind. I just thought we could say things. I could say something and then you could say something."

"Say what things, Papa?"

"Well, like I'd say: 'Denny's got red hair and nobody in me family or your mother's family had red hair. Only Timmy Shawn and he was no relation.' Then you could say . . . ."

"Denny can't help it that he's got red hair. And he's a good boy just the same."

"I didn't say he wasn't," shouted Pat, now exasperated.

He sighed and got his hat and went down to the corner saloon for a beer. He had more than one.

"You know," he told the bartender, "I once had two of the nicest children a man ever had and I lost them."

"That's the way it goes," said the bartender.

Chapter Twenty-Two

MAGGIE-NOW was twenty-two. She was restless and lonely and needed young friends. Of course, she had old friends. Father Flynn was a friend but she was too awed by him ever to have the easy but respectful friendship her mother had had with the priest. Then there was good Mr. Van Clees and some of the storekeepers and neighbors who were her good friends, but they were all older than Maggie-Now. She longed for friends of her own age and generation.

Of course, there was always Lottie, but as Maggie-Now grew to womanhood she saw less and less of Lottie. The twins were living with Lottie now. Widdy, believing America's entry into the war was imminent and being afraid he wouldn't be drafted (because he had a wife and two children), enlisted in the navy. Gracie turned the twins over to Lottie and got a job and a room down near the Brooklyn Navy Yard. She liked to see the ships come in. Widdy might be on one of them.

Lottie had her hands full. Her mother was old and senile and needed constant care as did the twins. But she loved the twins dearly and supported them and her mother and herself on Timmy's pension. Lottie told Maggie-Now it was hard, sometimes, to make the pension "reach."

Maggie-Now did not enjoy poor Lottie's company as much as she used to. Lottie's life was standing still, and when Maggie-Now was with her the girl felt that her life too had been frozen, as far as Lottie was concerned, in the year of Timmy's death.

Lottie still told the same old stories about Big Red and Patsy Dennis and Kilkenny and the thrashing and Margaret Rose and the Moriaritys. Maggie-Now was tired of the old stories and she was irritated that Lottie's world was fixed in those olden times and that she expected Maggie-Now's to be fixed in the same times.

Claude Bassett drifted into Williamsburg, Brooklyn. Nobody knew where he came from because he didn't say. He was tall and good-looking but a little too thin. He had a closely clipped small mustache and he wore pants and coat that didn't match, which made him very conspicuous in a neighborhood where men wore pants, coat and vest all made of the same material. He smoked cigarettes, which made him suspect in a community where men smoked cigars or pipes or chewed tobacco.

His speech was precise English on the

academic or even literary side. This was a strange affectation or was it a sort of defense? After he warmed up to a person or began to feel at ease with someone, his English was just as colloquial as the next man's.

He had what appeared to be another mannerism. When one spoke to him, he listened intently for a moment, then cocked his head sharply sidewise. This gave the impression that he didn't want to miss one precious word of what the person was saying. It was very flattering—especially to women. They felt that he hung on to every word they said.

As a matter of fact, he had a punctured eardrum which made him deaf in his left ear. Therefore, the habit of the sharp turn of his right ear to the speaker, in order to enable him to hear better. He cocked his head more for women than for men because men spoke louder and he didn't have to strain to hear.

He would have been surprised to know that he was under observation as he walked the streets. He thought he moved about unnoticed in that strange, teeming, yet quiet neighborhood with its old-law tenements and new walk-up apartment houses and slanted-roof houses dating back to pre-Revolutionary times wedged in between the larger buildings. He would have been surprised to know that Williamsburg, along with Greenpoint, Flushing and Maspeth, still retained the customs and way of thinking of the small town. And he was a newcomer in a small town.

Maggie-Now first saw him in Van Clees's store when she went to buy tobacco for her father. Claude Bassett had some placards under one arm and a burning cigarette in his other hand. He was talking earnestly to Van Clees in a very educated voice and Van Clees was answering with a flat, uneducated "No." Claude gave Maggie-Now a quick appraising look when she walked in and then continued urging something on Van Clees.

Maggie-Now gathered that the young man was trying to rent Van Clees's store in the evenings for a week. She heard him mention "school." Van Clees said "No," looking with distaste the while at the cigarette in the man's hand. Ingratiatingly, the man asked something about a card in the window and it was "No" again. Maggie-Now felt sorry for the man. She wished she could tell him he'd get nothing from Van Clees while he held a cigarette, the way Van Clees hated cigarette smokers.

Later, Maggie-Now saw his placard in a grocery-store window. It announced a free course in salesmanship. "Earn twenty dollars a week in your spare time. Nothing to buy and etc. etc." Classes were to start the following Monday and the place where instructions would be given was written in ink at the bottom of the placard.

Schools were always cropping up in the neighborhood. Someone was always setting one up in a parlor, a loft, a basement or a too-long-vacant store which could be rented for a song. Self-styled teachers gave lessons in tatting, tattooing, singing, dancing, juggling—everything. There were lessons in marcel waving and in how to sit and stand and breathe; how to make hair grow, how to get rid of hair growth, how to develop your bust and how to grow mushrooms in the cellar.

So many teachers who knew these things and couldn't get rich by knowing them thought they could get rich by telling other people how to do them. Those who took lessons or courses dreamed of being headliners in vaudeville like those other Brooklyn boys, Van and Schenck, or a dancer like Irene Castle, or getting to be Miss Flatbush with a developed bust or being in a carnival to exhibit hair that grew in waves down to the ankles like the Seven Sutherland Sisters on the hair-tonic bottle.

No teacher became rich; no pupil's dream came true. All that teacher or pupil garnered was a little gleam of hope for a while. None of the schools lasted long; a week or two or, at the most, a month. But they brought a little interest and excitement to the community.

Maggie-Now decided to attend the classes. One, she was interested in making twenty dollars a week in her spare time. Two, she was anxious to get out, be with other people; and, three (she didn't fool herself at all), she wanted to see more of Claude Bassett.

The school was an upstairs dentist's waiting room on Grand Street. The dentist didn't practice nights and the waiting room just stood there and the dentist thought he might make a dollar or two out of it.

The little room was crowded when Maggie-Now arrived. There were about a dozen women there and four men. The women ranged in ages from eighteen to forty. The men were nearer middle age and one was quite old. There weren't enough seats. Five women sat on a wicker settee meant for three. The others were two to a chair. They sat slightly sidewise, turned a little away from each other. They looked like Siamese twins joined at the hip. The men sat on the floor. They looked awkward and ill at ease.

The scent of Djer Kiss and Quelque Fleurs talcum powder and of Pussy Willow face powder and of sachet powder that smelled like sweet, warm candy filled the room. This scent was interlarded with the acrid medicinal smell belonging to dentists' offices.

I'm the only one, thought Maggie-Now ruefully, *without cologne on.*

The women for the most part wore cheap georgette waists, transparent enough for the camisole, beaded with pink or blue baby ribbon, to show through, or crepe de Chine waists and long, tight skirts with wide, cinching belts. They wore beads and pearl button earrings and dime-store bracelets which filled the air with jingle-jangle.

Their hair was arranged in the styles of the day: spit curls or dips or an iron marcel wave. The youngest girl, being the most daring, had a Dutch cut. She thought it made her look like Irene Castle. All seemed to have the same makeup—faces powdered dead white with two coats on the nose, painfully plucked eyebrows and mouths painted to look like baby rosebuds.

Why, it's like a party, or a dance, decided Maggie-Now, *the way everybody's so dressed up. They didn't come here to learn anything,* she thought derisively. *They came to get a man! Listen to me,* she chided herself. *As if I didn't come here for the same thing!*

"Good evening," said Claude Bassett, who was sitting behind a small table on which were piled a dozen books.

I know her, he thought. *I've known her for a long time. But who is she?* He smiled at Maggie-Now.

She smiled back. *He's trying to place me,* she thought. *He doesn't remember he saw me in the store.*

"I'll fetch you a chair," he said to Maggie-Now.

"She gets personal service yet," whispered one girl to another.

He went into the dentist's lavatory and brought out a three-legged stool. They stood a second, the stool between them, and looked steadily at each other.

She sat apart from the rest on the low stool. Claude's eyes roved over the others but always came back to rest on her. She wore a plainly made, russet-colored dress. It was high in the neck and had long sleeves and a full skirt. Her thick, straight, dark brown hair was in two braids wound around her head. He thought her mouth was too wide but then he realized it was not foreshortened by lipstick. In fact, she wore no makeup and no ornaments.

She's as wholesome, he thought, *as an apple on an Indian-summer afternoon.*

She felt his interest. *Oh, why,* she moaned, *didn't I wear my blue dress with the lace collar and cuffs and my rhinestone necklace and a hat, and I must put lipstick on hereafter so my mouth don't look so big.*

He stood up and tapped the edge of the table with his pencil. The jingle-jangle of the bracelets stopped suddenly and the waves of scent seemed to settle in the room like a fog.

"This is a course in salesmanship. Salesmanship is the art of using friendly persuasion to induce people to buy merchandise that they are quite certain they do not want." He paused. The "class" looked stunned. This unnerved him. He didn't know it was their way of paying absolute attention. He continued. "To sell, one must have a product and," he paused, "personality." He looked at Maggie-Now.

"This is our product." He picked up one of the small books. "This is *The Book of Everything.*"

There was a rustle among the girls and a perfumed murmur of *"Every*thing?"

"Everything," he said firmly.

From somewhere, he got a stack of matted colored lithographs. He held one up. "It tells you how to set a table for guests." The picture showed a table with a lace cloth and candles and American beauty roses and silver and crystal with a turkey on a platter and champagne in a cooler. "How to fix a stopped-up sink." He showed a picture of a naked sink. "How to dress a baby." They saw a pink and blue and golden cherub in a lace-bedecked bassinette. "How to clean wallpaper . . ."

Then he showed them the pictures as transferred to the book. There was some disappointment. In the book, the illustrations were two by four inches and in black and white.

After extolling the book and illustrations, he went into the sales approach. "The best time to approach the prospect is after dinner when he is relaxed and in a mellow mood." One of the men raised his hand. "Question?" asked Claude Bassett.

"I work in the afternoon," said the man.

"He means after *supper,*" explained one of the other men.

"Of course," said Claude. "Thank you." He continued. "After supper, then. You hold the book in the crook of your arm . . . so. You ring the bell or knock on the door and greet the prospect with a pleasant smile. Your approach is: 'I am . . .' " He looked at Maggie-Now. "What's your name?" he asked.

"Me?" she said.

"Please."

"Margaret Moore."

Now, he thought, *I know how she looks, I know the sound of her voice and I know her name.*

"You smile, then, and say: 'I am Margaret Moore. I live down the block a way and I came over to see how you folks are getting along.' Allow the prospect to talk, and then, as if by the way, mention the book. . . ."

The hour dragged on. Two of the men sitting on the floor played a surreptitious game of odds-and-evens with their fingers. The old man was sound asleep, legs spread out, back against the wall and snoring in rhythm to the rise and fall of Claude's voice. The fourth man sat with his chin in his hand staring moodily at the pattern of the oil-cloth covering the floor. Maggie-Now sat with her hands loosely clasped in her lap with a serene half smile on her lips. The other girls leaned forward tensely, staring at Claude, not hearing a word he said, but trying subconsciously to project themselves as desirable females to the attractive male.

At last, Claude got to the heart of the matter: making money. He told them that the first lesson was free. There would be four more at a quarter a lesson. At the end of that time, each would be given a certificate and a copy of *The Book of*

Everything, free. They would then go forth and sell the book for two dollars. With that money, they'd get two books from him at the salesman's price of one dollar per copy. They'd sell these and buy four; sell those, buy eight . . . sixteen . . . thirty-two . . . sixty-four . . . And so on into infinity, it seemed. And all for an initial investment of one dollar and a little spare time!

Maggie-Now recalled the time in her childhood when she had tried pyramiding her capital. She had a weekly allowance of five cents. Wishing merely to double her money, she bought ten pretzels from the cellar pretzel baker at the wholesale price of two for a cent. She borrowed her mother's market basket, stuck a stick in the end, put the pretzels on the stick and sold the ten that afternoon in Cooper's Park.

It seemed easy to double her money again. The next day after school, she bought twenty pretzels and managed to sell them although she had to stay out longer. The next day was Saturday. She debated whether to take her profit and quit or go on. She bought forty pretzels. She sold two. Then the rains came. It rained three days. The pretzels got soggy and Maggie-Now lost not only her profit but her initial investment of five cents. In addition, her father had been angry and made her eat most of the pretzels in lieu of bread, for almost a week. Remembering, she laughed aloud.

Claude looked up quickly. "You are amused, Miss Moore?" he asked.

"No. I was just remembering the pretzels."

"The *what?*" he asked, astonished. He tilted his head sharply to hear better.

"The pretzels." (Only she pronounced it the Brooklyn way—bretzels.)

He threw his head back and burst into laughter. The men laughed. The girls stirred and the room was full of jingle-jangle and disturbed layers of perfume.

One of the men said: "She's full of life."

Another answered. "Yeah. I wish my wife . . ." He put away the disloyal thought. "Anyway, my wife's a hard worker."

The other girls relaxed their tense attitude of sweet attentiveness. They knew they had lost. This Miss Margaret Moore had captured the handsome teacher's interest and attention. They whispered to each other under the laughter of the men.

"I wouldn't be found dead in a tacky dress like hers."

"I bet she made it herself."

"Yeah. Without a pattrin, too."

"And that old-time hair comb she's got!"

"I *couldn't* be forward like her. I'd sooner die an old maid."

Claude tapped for silence. "All who wish to continue, please remain to register."

It seemed that everyone tried to get out of the door at once. When the smoke had settled—that is, when the waves of scent stopped swirling and the jingle-jangle died away—there were five people left behind: three women, the old man and Maggie-Now.

Oh, well, thought one of the women, *maybe the old man has a nice son I can get to meet.*

Another, about thirty with graying hair, thought: *He might have a brother . . . a little younger.*

The third one wiped her glasses and thought: *It's hard for a decent girl to get a chance to meet a decent man—any man. Just the same, though, it's better to sit here nights than to sit alone in that hall room of mine.*

Maggie-Now registered last, after the others had left. She wrote her name slowly and carefully because she knew he was watching her and she wanted to write nicely.

Watching, he thought: *Beautiful hands. Strong, shapely, capable and thank God she doesn't file her nails to a point like so many women do.*

Why, oh why, she thought, *didn't I take time to file my nails and buff them? My hands must look just awful to him.*

"Thank you," he said, when she returned his leaky fountain pen, the point toward herself, as the nuns had taught her to do.

He gave her a slow smile. She grinned back. He stood up and took a deep breath. "Tell me about the pretzels," he said.

"I'll put the stool away first," she said.

She carried it into the dentist's lavatory. She looked at herself in the mirror. She was surprised she looked the same as before because she felt that some great change had taken place in her during the evening.

She searched her mirrored face and thought how queer it was that she didn't know him at all and yet had that feeling that she had known him always. And how natural and right it seemed that they were alone together in this place—sort of like keeping house.

She straightened the hanging mirror. She noticed some spilled face powder on the basin's ledge and wiped it off with a piece of toilet paper. She pulled the roller towel down until a clean place showed up. Lastly, she put the seat down on the toilet. The cubicle looked neater that way. She gave the place a last searching look before she left it.

There! she told herself with satisfaction.

She went back into the waiting room and told him about the pretzels. She straightened the room as she talked. He'd put the magazines back on the little table. (They had been put on the floor to make room for his copies of *The Book of Everything*.) The magazines were piled helter skelter. She interrupted her story to cluck, "Tsch! Tsch!" while she stacked the magazines neatly.

I hope she's not a doily straightener, he thought. *If she is, I'll break her of it.*

"So I had twenty cents . . ." she went on with her story. She started to push the settee back to the wall.

"No, no," he protested. "You stand there and look pale and helpless while I move it."

"Helpless?" she asked, puzzled.

No sense of humor, he told himself.

". . . Then you bought forty pretzels."

"And it rained . . ."

Under the settee, she found an orange powder puff lying in a little nimbus of face powder that had shaken off when the puff dropped to the floor. She threw it into the wastebasket. He fished it out and put it in his pocket.

"Have to get rid of it," he said "Compromising. Dr. Cohen may be married."

So may you, she thought.

As if divining her thought, he said: "But I'm not."

First she looked startled, then relieved. She finished the pretzel story. He tucked his books and pictures under his arm. They stood at the door ready to leave. She looked around the room lingeringly as some women are prone to do when they leave a room which belongs to them and which they had attended to.

"Now I'll wind the cat and chuck out the clock," he said.

"What?" she asked, puzzled.

Serious minded. I warn you, Bassett, he admonished himself, *she's not one to like joking.*

"Nothing," he replied. "A poor joke. Something out of my childhood."

With her finger extended toward the switch plate, she paused. She had seen the dentist's mezuzah higher up on the door frame. Something out of her childhood . . .

Ida was a friend. Maggie-Now was in Ida's kitchen, visiting just before supper. There were the candles on the table and the kitchen smelled of chicken soup and baked fish. Ida's father came in from work. He closed the door, turned and touched the mezuzah with two fingers.

"Why did he do that?" asked Maggie-Now in a whisper. The father overheard and answered.

"So we shouldn't forget," he said. "This is a mezuzah. It holds the prayer." Then he intoned: "Hear, oh Israel! The Lord our God is one Lord . . .

"The prayer is here. I touch it and I remember. In the old times the prayer was written on the posts of the house. It was the Hebrew law." He quoted: *"And thou shall write them upon the posts of thy house."*

"But we move away all the time—we Jews. We own no house posts to write the prayer on. The mezuzah is the post—the house post that we carry with us when we move."

If Mama were here now, she thought, *she'd say, "And they touch the mezuzah the way we dip our fingers in holy water."*

He noticed her abstraction. "Tell me," he said.

"As you said: It's something I remembered out of my childhood." Outside in the hall, she said: "It's funny, but tonight seems to be the night for remembering things of when I was a little child."

He was about to say that was because she was sorting out her past and putting it away because she had no need of it now that her future was starting. Instead, he said as they went down the stairs: "I don't believe you were ever a little girl."

"Oh, yes. I was," she said somberly. "And for a long time, too."

I told you before, he reminded himself. *She is a serious woman. And very literal, too.*

Down on the street, she held out her hand and said: "Good night, Mr. Bassett. I enjoyed the lesson."

"I have to go past your house on my way home, and if I may, I'd like to walk with you."

"I would like you to walk with me," she said frankly.

"Thank you. Now where do you live?"

"But you said . . ."

I warned you, Bassett . . .

"Anyhow, we turn at the next corner and then it's three blocks."

"Thank you, Miss Moore. It *is* Miss, isn't it?" he asked suddenly.

"It's 'Miss' all right," she said.

"All the men around here must be stupid or blind."

"Oh, no."

"Yes. Else you would have been snatched up

211

long ago by one of them and put away in cotton wool."

"You mean, marry me?" she said in her frank way. "No. No one ever asked me. You see, I have a brother and some people think he's my son. (He's just started in school.) My mother died when he was born. I brought him up. I mean, new people coming to the neighborhood think he's my child and . . ." She thought briefly of the yard and the boy from upstairs. "Anyway, a man wouldn't want to marry a girl and take her brother, too." She sighed. "Another thing: My father's strict. He wouldn't let me go out with anyone."

"I'd like to meet your father and shake his hand."

"*My* father?" She was astonished. "But why?"

"For beating off all the boys and men. For keeping you locked up. I mean for keeping you safe for me."

He's kind of flip, she thought critically, pleased that she had found a flaw in him. *I'm glad I found that out so I don't fall in love with him so quick.*

Again, as if reading her mind, he said: "You think I'm flippant, don't you?"

"Flip . . . flippant . . . ?"

"Don't you?" he persisted.

"I don't know what to think," she said honestly. "I never knew anyone like you before. I don't know whether you're serious or making fun of me."

"Of you? Never!" he said earnestly. "Really, I'm a serious person. Or so I like to believe. I say things lightly. I mean, I say light things. I've traveled around a lot, met many people, got to know none of them well and got into the way of saying things quickly and lightly . . . no time to really get to know anyone enough to be sincere . . . that takes a little time . . ."

"You must have traveled a lot."

He gave her a quick look. He decided she wasn't being sarcastic. She wouldn't know how.

"Quite a lot," he said. "And you?"

"I've never been out of Brooklyn, except . . ."

"San Francisco," he said dreamily. "Cincinnati . . . Chicago, Boston . . ."

". . . except once. When I went to Boston."

"I'm crazy about big cities. Denver . . . a mile nearer the sky than other cities . . ."

Suddenly she knew they weren't in tune with each other. He was in a world of his own. She shivered. *Someone's walking over my grave,* she thought.

She stopped walking and he, talking, walked on ahead, not knowing he was alone.

"Good night," she called ahead to him.

He whirled around and came back to her. "What happened?"

"I'm home."

"What's the matter with me? Could you overlook my rudeness?"

"There is nothing to overlook. And it was

interesting . . . about the cities."

"But you weren't interested."

"A person must say they are, anyhow. To be polite. But I'm not really. I like Brooklyn and . . . anyway, I have to go in now."

"Not yet. Not yet," he said. He grasped her arms as she stood on the step above him and he spoke rapidly as though time was short. "I wanted to tell you—I need to tell you so many things."

He spoke fast and breathlessly. "I want to tell you about the way you smell of good soap and fresh-washed, dried-in-the-sun clothes, and . . ."

"Oh, that's only castile soap," she said. "It's cheap. They have blocks of it in the drugstore and you ask for a nickel's worth and they cut off a slice."

"Your good healthy hair smell. And I wanted to tell you how much I like your beautifully simple dress."

"I know it's plain but I made it myself. I make all my dresses the same way because it's the only pattern I can figure out."

"And the classic simplicity of your hair style."

She started to feel uncomfortable. She thought he was making fun of her.

"I know it's old-fashioned. But my hair's so thick and stubborn, I can't make it curl like other girls do."

"If you don't stop belittling yourself, I'm going to call you my little Chinee."

"Chinee? Why?"

"Because, in China, when you compliment someone on, say, a lovely jewel, he'll say it has a flaw in it. Admire a Ming vase and you'll be told it has a crack in it."

"Why do they do that?"

"It's their way of being modest."

She was about to ask whether he'd been in China. She decided against it, fearing he'd start talking of far-off places and she would lose him again.

I'm silly, she thought. *Here I'm afraid of losing him. When did I ever have him? He's just someone I met only a few hours ago.*

"Who's modest? I just happen to know that my dress is not in style. That's all."

"It is always in style. A girl in a Portugal village wore one like it a hundred years ago. Tonight in London, a duchess is wearing one like yours. Only of white satin.

"And those shining braids wound around your head: So Ruth wore her hair, perhaps, when she stood in the alien corn. . . . And Narcissa Whitman . . ."

"Who?"

"They opened up the Oregon Trail—she and her husband, Marcus. The Oregon trail . . ." He waited, his head turned as though straining to hear something from far away.

"You say nice things," she said. "But I know I'm behind the times. I can tell by the way the other girls look at me."

"You are not of any time, past, present or

time to come. You are of all time. You are forever."

Maggie-Now squirmed a bit. She felt uncomfortable. She thought his talk was sort of fancy. Did he mean all those things? Or did he just like to talk to fill in time?

She was a combination of child and woman. At sixteen, she had been a mature woman with a woman's grave responsibilities. At twenty-two, she was yet a child waiting to come into her maturity. She waited for the new thing which was just around the corner; she clung to a few modest dreams. The woman and child in her walked side by side. In a way, she knew, as the saying goes, all about life. Conversely, she knew nothing about it. But she believed in so much. She didn't love all the people she knew but she believed implicitly that they were as they seemed to be. Her father presented himself as unkind and unloving. She believed he *was* unkind and unloving. That's the way it was and she accepted him and loved him as a child should love a parent.

She believed that Mr. Van Clees tried to put his hand on the life of everyone he knew. Sure, that made him intrusive and tiresome sometimes. But it was in the open. He did not try to be otherwise than he was. She liked him and believed what he said.

She believed that Lottie and Timmy had been sweethearts all their life because Lottie told her so. She believed Annie was kind and good because Gus and Van Clees had told her so. She took it all on faith.

Now came the first intimations of maturity. This man—holding her arms and looking up at her: Was he to be believed? Was he speaking true? Did he mean all he said? Or did he talk one way and think another. He spoke as people spoke in books. Was that natural with him? Was that natural with him or was it something he put on like a coat? How could she know? In her characteristic way, she decided the only way to know was to ask him.

"Mr. Bassett . . ."

"My name is Claude and I hereby serve notice," he said severely, "that I will not be called 'Claudie.' "

"You want me to call you by your first name?"

"I do."

Why, she thought, *didn't he just say, Call me Claude?*

"I couldn't," she said. "Not yet. I don't know you long and *Mr. Bassett* is strange to me. *Claude* would be even more strange." She paused. "What I started to say: Do you mean everything you say to me?"

"Why not?"

"I could understand better," she said a bit timidly, "if you'd say yes or no."

"Margaret," he said sincerely. "I do. Oh, I use too many words, perhaps. I talk too much. But you see, it's so long since I had someone to

217

really talk to. But I mean what I say. Believe me, please."

"I'm glad you do," she said, "because the way you talk to me—you make me feel like a princess or something. And it's a wonderful feeling."

"Thank you."

"Good night."

"Where you been?" asked her father.

"Now, Papa," she said patiently, "after all, I'm over twenty-one."

"I know how old you are. But I don't know where you been."

"Good night, Papa." She moved toward her bedroom door.

"Listen," he said to hold her, "did you use up all the house money yet?"

"I don't know," she said. She went into her bedroom.

She acts funny, he thought. *Like she's sick. Could it be she met a man—was out with him? And she, what don't know nothing about men—what bastids they are? I wonder does she know what she should know? She must. Lottie or somebody must-a told her.* He was relieved, then characteristically, he became angry. *Sure and they told her. They couldn't wait. Damn married wimmen—always blabbing. Always disthroying innocence.*

Suddenly he felt old. This made him angry, too. He didn't want to be old or *feel* old. But if he had to be or even *feel* old, he wasn't going to work any more.

By God, he vowed, *I'll go out on pension. That's what I'll do. The old man will stay home all day. I'll get in her way,* he thought with satisfaction. *That'll fix her. That'll fix everybody.* He felt more cheerful.

He took down from the shelf the broken-spout teapot in which Maggie-Now kept the household money. There was only twenty-eight cents in it. He stuffed two dirty dollar bills in the teapot and put it back on the shelf. He changed his mind, took it down again and brought it over to the table. He removed the bills and smoothed them out on the table. After a little hesitation, he took another bill from his pocket. He put the three bills side by side on the table where Maggie-Now would see them the first thing in the morning. He put the teapot on top of them so they wouldn't blow away.

After Maggie-Now went into her house, Claude walked over to Lorimer Street to catch a streetcar. There was none in sight so he went into a bakery and got two doughnuts. He stood on the corner and ate them while he waited for a car. A newsboy turned the corner calling:

"Extra! Extra! Read all about it. The President asks for war!"

Claude beckoned to the boy. "Don't you know that according to books and stories you should call *Wuxtry* and not *Extra?*" he said.

The boy said "Huh?" and backed off staring at Claude as if he were a freak.

I thought she *had no sense of humor,* thought Claude. *But* nobody *seems to in Brooklyn.*

He bought a paper. The extra announced that President Wilson had spoken before Congress that night at eight-thirty and had asked for a declaration of war. Claude felt a tingle of excitement.

War! he thought.

He looked at the books and posters he was carrying, with revulsion. *What am I doing with this nonsense?* he asked himself.

Chapter Twenty-Three

ONLY Maggie-Now, three women and the old man showed up for class the next night. Maggie-Now wore her blue dress with the lace collar and cuffs and the new hat she had bought for the coming Easter Sunday. She smiled widely at Claude when she came in. She put her quarter on the table as the others had done. He looked up and frowned. Her heart sank. She thought perhaps he was offended that she had put a quarter down. He frowned, however, because he didn't like her to wear a hat. It made her seem like a stranger.

The three girls were sitting on the settee, leaving the old man sitting alone in the middle of the room. Maggie-Now felt sorry for him. She took the chair next to him. Claude Bassett arranged the five quarters in a row, then in a circle. Finally, as if coming to a definite decision about them, he piled them one on top of the other. He stood up.

"I appreciate more than I can say your

willingness to come here again but . . . ."

He announced that the course would be discontinued. The enrollment, while interested, was small and there was the rent on the classroom and he smiled and said he didn't believe anyone would be interested in *The Book of Everything*. War was inevitable . . . he had decided to enlist. . . . He spoke at length.

Maggie-Now thought: *I'll never see him again!* She envisioned him lying on the field of battle; torn, bleeding and dying. She shuddered.

"The money will be refunded, of course."

There was a chorus of objections.

"No."

"I don't want my quarter back."

"You should get something for your time."

"You will have to pay the rent for these two nights," said Maggie-Now.

Everyone was friendly now and they spoke back and forth. The girl who lived alone in a hall bedroom took off her glasses and wiped them and put them in her lap. She had a suggestion. A sort of organization or club was badly needed in the neighborhood—a place where people could get together and meet other people and just talk and maybe serve refreshments . . .

"I mean," she said, "couldn't we just keep on meeting here nights and just sit around and talk; read books, say, and talk about them? I mean, it would be worth a quarter a night to me," she said defiantly, "just to have someplace to go to."

There was a hush. The other women looked away from this girl, ashamed that one of them would display her loneliness so nakedly.

"I don't see any harm in asking," she said. She put her glasses back on.

"That is a fine suggestion," said Claude. "Nothing would please me more, but . . ."

Again he spoke of America at war and the uncertainty of war years. They sat around for the rest of the hour discussing the war—touching vaguely on the changes it would make in the community and so on.

At the end of the hour, he tried to give each his quarter back. There was great indignation at the idea on the part of the three girls. Maggie-Now and the old man did not press the matter one way or the other. Finally Claude said he'd keep the quarters if each would accept a copy of *The Book of Everything* in return. The three girls accepted enthusiastically. They wanted their copies autographed. Claude obliged. His inscriptions were flowery, which was the way the girls wanted them:

In memory of a brief encounter . . .
With gratitude for pleasant hours . . .
With the hope that we shall meet again . . .

When Maggie-Now held out her book for autographing, he said: "Later." The old man said he didn't want a book. "I'd sooner have my quarter back," he said. Claude gave him his quarter *and* a copy of the book inscribed simply: *In friendship.*

After Maggie-Now and Claude had straightened up the room, turned out the lights and gone down the stairs, they found the three girls standing on the sidewalk comparing inscriptions.

"That was real swell of you, Mr. Bassett," said one.

"That's nice of you," he answered.

"It was a real pleasant evening," said another.

"The pleasure was surely mine," he said.

"I still think . . ." began the girl with the glasses.

"And I agree with you," he said.

"Good night, good night," they said singly and in chorus. They withdrew a little, waiting for Maggie-Now to join them. Claude took Maggie-Now's hand and drew her arm through his.

"Good night, ladies," he said.

"Good night, girls," said Maggie-Now.

The girls walked down the street discussing Maggie-Now.

"Ain't she got the luck?"

"It's not that she's classy or anything."

"Old-fashioned, if you ask me."

"Whatever he *sees* in her . . ."

"I know what he sees in her. She's got one of them big busts and some men like that. *You* know. Puts them in mind of their mother?"

Going down the street, Maggie-Now turned to

wave to them. They waved back and made their smiles friendly.

"Take your hat off," said Claude.

"My hat? Why?" asked Maggie-Now.

"Here." He removed it and handed it to her. "You should never wear a hat."

"Where'll I put it?"

"Carry it."

"Like this?"

"In the hand away from me. You can swing it now and again as we walk, if you like."

"I thought it was a pretty hat," she said sadly. She stared at it. It was made of soft straw with a wide brim, flat crown and a band of velvet.

"It is a pretty hat. Very pretty. And you rushed out today and bought it to wear tonight." She hung her head because it was true. "It's a pretty thing to carry," he said. "And nothing looks prettier than a woman with lovely hair holding her pretty hat as she walks. Now don't hold it between us. The outside hand I said." She changed. Again he took her hand and drew her arm through his.

They walked slowly in step and she remembered to swing her hat a little from time to time. They walked without talking, savoring the warm night and the wind from the west. (He broke the silence to tell her the wind was from the west and she, having always taken the wind for granted, was pleased to know it was from the west.)

They walked past a saloon with door open to the warm night. The drinkers were discussing the impending war.

"I got nothing against the Germans theirselves," said a man, "I figure they're yumen like everybody else. It's the Goddamned Kaiser. . . ."

Claude and Maggie-Now smiled at each other. Children played on the streets, calling to each other in muted voices (because night-time street playing was a privilege not to be abused), while their parents sat on the stoop or in chairs lined up before closed stores. And there was music. An opened tenement window, a victrola playing a recording of Lee Morse singing and her Blue Grass Boys helping out. Oh, her husky voice . . .

This is me, thought Maggie-Now, *walking so. With him on such a night as this. I can't believe it's me—that this is really happening to me. This is something I'll remember all my life.*

After a while they talked. That is, she did all the talking that night. He wanted to know everything about her life; especially her childhood—her mother, brother, father and grandfather. He prodded her with questions and drew her out and she spoke freely as if dictating an honest autobiography. As she had everything else, she had taken her childhood for granted. But as she noted his delighted and interested reactions, her childhood seemed very wonderful all of a sudden.

He laughed in delight when she told him how

she had always wanted cousins and how her mother had found Sheila and her bouquet in Boston, and he grinned when she told of her father spanking her publicly for dancing on the street, and he pressed her arm very tight when she told of how Sister Mary Joseph had to have the wedding ring sawed off and how she, Maggie-Now, had felt about it. He blew his nose very hard after she told how her mother had told her to pick up the new-born baby. . . .

After she had finished that story, he lifted her hand, which was resting so lightly on his forearm, and kissed it. Then she was much embarrassed, though pleased, and she said she had talked too much and that they had walked past her house and she'd really have to go in because her father . . .

"You don't have to go in yet," he said. "It's only a little after nine."

"No, I don't. But it's better that I do."

She knew her father would be waiting and he'd fuss and scold and maybe take the extra dollar out of the teapot. *But,* she decided, *he'll complain whether I come in at nine or at twelve. I might as well stay out.*

"Please?" he asked.

"All right," she said. "After all, I'm almost twenty-three."

"And I'm thirty. Where shall we walk?"

"Where do you live?"

"At the Bedford Y."

"I'll walk you home."

"Good! Then I'll walk *you* home."

He urged her to tell him more about the years of her growing up. She demurred at first, saying it wasn't interesting and that he was asking just to be polite. Besides, she said, she'd like to know something about *his* childhood.

"No," he said. "I want to know all about you. I want to walk every step of the way with you through your childhood so that I'll know you from the beginning of your life."

She told him all she could remember (excepting the boy upstairs who had kissed her). They walked to the Bedford Y.M.C.A. and back to her house and it was nearly midnight. She stood on the bottom step of her stoop and looked down at him and smiled.

"So you see," she said, "my childhood wasn't much of anything. The beach once a year, the cemetery on Decoration Day, a trip to Boston, the few girl friends I had—the few people I knew. Church, school, home and parents. And that's all."

"Ah, my little Chinee," he said, "again belittling something that was quite wonderful. You don't know how wonderful. . . . Oh, how you take everything for granted. Why, one thing! Even the sewing of beads on slippers for pin money . . ."

"I forgot I told you that," she interrupted. "That was kind of silly."

"Stop it!" he said. "Nothing was silly. It was all part of the wonder of a girl growing up into a woman."

He told her how moved he had been at her stories and how amused, too. He spoke ecstatically about the wonder of her childhood.

What's so wonderful, she thought. *Wasn't he ever a child?*

After a while, she saw it a little through his eyes and she was strangely disturbed. It was as though he had lived her childhood but on a more wonderful plane than she had. She felt, vaguely, that she had given away her childhood that night. She had given it to him or he had taken it from her, and made it into something wonderful. In a way, her life was his now.

A light came on in the window. "My father," she whispered, and trembled a little bit.

He grasped her arms as she stood above him. "Tomorrow night," he whispered. "I'll come by for you. Eight o'clock. I want to meet your father."

"Yes, yes," she whispered nervously. She scuttled into the house.

"Out again," was her father's greeting.

"Yes," she said.

"You was out last night, too."

"I know."

"I suppose you're going out tomorrow night."

"I am."

"Well, you ain't," he said flatly.

"I'm over twenty-one . . ." she began.

"Age's got nothing to do with it because I'm going out tomorrow night and somebody's got to stay with the boy."

"I'll ask the tenant upstairs. Mrs. Heahly? She'll keep an eye on Denny while you slip out for a beer."

"I ain't going out for no beer. I'm going *out*. I have a friend. For once I'd like to spend an evening with her."

"*Her?* You mean another woman?" Maggie-Now was shocked and indignant. "All these years you've gone out with some woman and enjoyed yourself while I . . ." her voice broke as though she were going to cry, ". . . while I, a young girl growing up, who should have been out with boys and girls my own age, stayed home and cooked and washed and cleaned and took care of the baby?" She paused. When she spoke again, her voice was steady.

"Ah, no, Papa," she said gently. "You couldn't. You couldn't after having been married to Mama."

"Your mother, God rest her soul, was a good woman. The best there ever was. But she's been gone from me these seven years or nearly, and, well, a man's a man."

"Then a man should love and marry in love. Otherwise, a man is no better than an animal."

"Where'd you hear that nonsense?"

"Father Flynn said so. He had this special sermon for young people."

"And what would he be knowing about it the way he prays and fasts all the time?" Suddenly he had one of his rages. "How dast he!" he

230

shouted. "Talk about such things to them what is innocent or should be? I'll get him fired. . . ."

"Priests can't be fired."

"Well then, defrocked . . . unfrocked. Something. At least transferred. I'll talk to the bishop."

"Now, Papa, you stop it. He said nothing out of the way. He is a good man and you know it. Look how good he was to Mama. You forget."

"It is true," he said. "He was good to your mother."

"And he is to *every*body. Oh, Papa," she sighed, "when I was sixteen, you never thought of me as a child. You let me handle a grown-up woman's job. And now that I am a grown-up woman, you're trying to pretend I'm a child. Papa, you must face it. I'm going to live my own life from now on."

He had to think out an answer to that. *This man she just met: He's putting her up to it. I bet he's been giving her a lot of blarney and making her feel like she's somebody. Now I must watch me step,* he planned craftily. *Be nice to her like I know how everything is. 'Twould be the same like throwing her in his waiting arms was I strict with her now.*

"You are right, girl dear. You're a child no longer. You're a fine figger of a woman and you can thank the good food I worked me life away to get the money to buy for you that made you the fine woman what you are."

"No. It wasn't the food." She turned her wide

smile on him. "Because you're a fine figger of a man yourself, Papa, and to hear you tell it, you were brought up on hard, little potatoes and chicken only once a year on Christmas and that tough, too, back in Kilkenny."

That's me girl, he thought with pride. *Smart as a whip. Like meself.*

He said: "Don't be changing the subject on me. Sure and you're a grown woman and it's right and healthy that you want a man of your own. And do I not want grandchilthren round me knees in me old days?"

And so I do! he thought with surprise. *Or am I talking meself into it?*

" 'Tisn't that I'm not willing to give you up but I don't want you to throw yourself away on the first man what says, 'Ah there,' to you. Remember, he's not the only pebble on the beach."

"Who wants a pebble?"

"You know what I mean. There's always another streetcar coming along."

"You'd never let me look for a pebble on the beach or stand on a corner to wait for the next car and you know it."

"You know what I mean, Maggie dear. Me thoughts don't always come out in the right words. But I have only your good in me mind." Then very offhand, in order to conceal his craftiness, he said: "Now here's what we'll do: You bring the young man . . . ."

"What young man?"

"Now, now," he said roguishly, "*I* know. Bring him around to meet your father, like the decent girl what you are, and I'll size him up and tell you whether he's good enough for you."

"Oh, Papa! Even if he was the Sheik of Araby, you still would say he wasn't good enough."

"Listen!" he yelled, forgetting to be diplomatic. "Child, girl, woman—whatever you are, don't give your father none of your sass."

She didn't answer. She went out to the kitchen and noisily filled the kettle with water. He followed her.

"Hear me?"

"Oh, Papa, stop annoying me, do," she said. Whenever her speech sounded Irishy, he knew it was a sign that she was going to lose her temper.

"I'll say no more," he said with quiet dignity. But he did. And he said it loudly. "But you're not going out tomorrow night!" He hurried out and into his own bedroom before she could answer. He wanted the last word.

The long walk had made her hungry. She thought of Claude as she made coffee and cut some of the supper's pot roast for a sandwich. She thought of the way he talked to her—the way he listened, with that quick turn of his head when she spoke, and how it made everything she said seem so wonderful and important. She thought how different her father was from Claude.

She wondered where people got the idea that

girls were inclined to marry men who were like their father. Sure, she loved her father and she'd feel bad if anything ever happened to him. But she was in love with Claude because he was so very different from her father.

"Mama? I mean, Maggie-Now?" The little boy, in pajamas, stood in the doorway.

"I thought you were asleep this good while, Denny."

"I was. But now I'm awake."

"Hungry?" He nodded. "Come on then. Sit down. I'll get you ginger snaps and milk."

His eyes strayed from his milk and crackers to her hot sandwich and rested there longingly.

"Can I have some of that?"

"No. It's too heavy to eat late at night."

"You're eating it."

"Never mind, now."

"Just a taste?"

"Just a taste, then. No more." She gave him a fork. He ate from one end of the sandwich, she from the other. "Do your crayon work?"

"This afternoon. You saw me. You forgot," he said reproachfully.

"That's right. You did. Well, what did you do tonight, then?"

"Me and Papa played checkers."

"Who won?"

"Papa. I let him."

"Now why did you do that?"

"Because he won't play with me if he don't win."

"If you are winning, you shouldn't back up like that."

"Oh, I don't care if I don't win."

"You should care. You shouldn't do anything if you *don't* care. Drink your milk."

"You drink half with me."

"I've got coffee."

"I helped you eat half your sandwich. Now you gotta help me drink my milk."

"Oh, all right." She poured half his milk into her coffee cup.

"Maggie-Now, if you ever get married, would he be my father?"

"Your father?"

"*You* know. Like you're my mother, only you're my sister?"

"What's the matter with you, Denny?"

"Would he?"

"Let's see: If I was ever lucky enough to get married, why, my husband would be your brother-in-law. Why did you ask?"

"Because Papa told me you were going to get married, he guessed. He said he guessed you knew a man, now. But he said I shouldn't tell you what he said."

"And you shouldn't tell, then, if he asked you not to." She paused. "What else did Papa say?"

"He told me to tell you that you shouldn't get married and leave me here alone. And leave Papa alone, too."

"Oh, he did, did he?" she said grimly.

"But don't tell I told because he said not to tell you."

"Do you know what a tattletale is?"

"Sure. But you ain't going away like Papa said, are you?"

"No." She put an arm around his shoulder. "I'll stay with you until you get old enough to find some nice girl to take my place. Okay?" He nodded. "And if I ever have to leave here before then, I'll take you with me."

"And Papa, too?"

"No. Papa's a big man and can look out for himself. But don't tell him I said that, hear?" She knew full well he would tell their father the next morning.

"And now, bed! And don't beg because you can't stay up any longer."

"I want more milk first. You drank half of mine."

"Oh, no, you don't. You had your chance with the milk. Come on, now. I'll put you away for what's left of the night."

She tucked him in. He tried to prolong her stay. "Do I hafta have a blanket?"

"Yes."

"But it's hot out."

"It's warm now. But it will get cool towards morning."

"What time will it get cool?"

"Four o'clock."

"How do you know?"

"Now stop it! I'm not going to get tricked

236

into a long conversation with you."

"I want the light on, then."

"No!"

"Then I hafta have a drink of water."

"*No!* Good gosh, Denny, it's one o'clock in the morning. Now shut up!" She smiled and kissed him.

About to turn out the light, she gave her usual housewife's last look around the room, trying to imagine what it would look like if she were a stranger seeing it for the first time. It wasn't a room, really. It was a corridor with a window. It was an oblong partitioned off from Maggie-Now's room. There was space only for Denny's cot and a small dresser.

He had tacked a Dartmouth pennant to the wall. Then there was a dirty baseball with a strip of bicycle tape covering a tear in the horsehide and one of Maggie-Now's good sauce dishes, holding a dozen blue clay marbles. His glass shooters were gone and she surmised that he'd played a bad game that day.

There was the inevitable ball of tin foil. Like other kids, he garnered discarded cigarette packages and gum wrappers, the foil of which he added to the ball. When it got as big as a baseball and twice as heavy, it was believed that any junkman would give you a dollar for it. To make sure it would be heavy enough, Denny had placed an iron washer in the core of it.

He was making a rubber ball, too. It started with a wad of paper and every rubber band he could get was stretched and wound tightly around it. It went slowly. He'd been working on it for months and it was only the size of a golf ball. He persisted because he knew if it ever got to be the size of a regular ball, it would be the bouncingest ball in the whole world.

On an impulse, Maggie-Now picked it up and bounced it. It hit the ceiling on the rebound. She scrambled after it awkwardly, her hands cupped to catch it before it bounced again. She missed it and had to chase a couple of more bounces. Denny giggled into his pillow.

"That's enough out of you," threatened Maggie-Now. "If you don't go to sleep . . ."

A newly-made slingshot on the dresser caught her eye. The kids called it a beanshooter. It was made of a crotched twig which she suspected was broken off a tree in the park when nobody was looking, two strips of rubber and a square of fine supple leather. She felt the leather.

"Oh, no!" she moaned. "Oh, no!"

She picked up his shoes and, as she had feared, the tongue of one of them had been cut off and used in the slingshot.

"Oh, Denny," she said despairingly, "what did you do to your good shoes?"

"Don't start no conversations with me," he said, afraid of a scolding, "because I'm sleeping like you told me."

When she put his shoes away under his cot, she saw his sled there where he liked to keep it until it snowed again. But now it was spring.

Soon it would be kite-flying time and he'd get sticks and tie them together into a sort of rhomboid and paste a sheet from the colored comics of the *Journal* over the frame and tease her for rags which he'd tear into strips and knot together for a tail, and hint for two cents to buy a ball of cord to fly it.

Maybe I'll buy him a ready-made box kite this year. It would be nice if we could afford to get him a two-wheel bike, but . . . Maybe there'll be some money for a catcher's mitt. Oh, well, Papa can get him a new baseball, at least. Still and all, he seems content with what he has or makes or gets on his own. He has what the other boys have. If he had less, he'd be sad. If he had more, he wouldn't fit in with the other boys. Anyway, he seems satisfied.

She smiled toward her mother's photograph and said aloud: "*You* know. It's relative?"

"What-cha say?" asked Denny sleepily.

"Nothing. I'm going to turn the light out now." She did so.

"Don't close the door all the way, Mama."

"Afraid?"

"Naw."

"I'll leave it open anyway. For air," she added tactfully.

Preparing for bed, she thought: *Funny that something that makes me so very happy makes Denny so sad and worried and Papa so mad and worried. Papa,* she thought scornfully, *who makes believe he's got another woman! As if he could've kept it a secret all these years if he did have one! Still and all . . .*

Gratefully she settled into bed and started to recall dreamily her whole wonderful evening with Claude; what he said, what she said—how he had looked when he spoke to her and the wonderful nuances of the silences made by the pauses in the conversation.

But she was so tired from the long walk— so used up emotionally from her father's antagonism and her brother's concern—that she fell fast asleep in the middle of savoring all over again the thrill when he had tucked her arm into his.

Chapter Twenty-Four

THE next morning, when Maggie-Now went to the baker's for the morning buns, the neighborhood seemed to be in a state of excitement. Since President Wilson had addressed Congress, wild rumors had been flying around. Some said war had already been declared; others, that it was merely a question of hours before it would be declared. Somebody said that Hamburg Avenue was going to be renamed Wilson Avenue.

She passed some men waiting for a streetcar to take them to work. One said his wife had kept him up half the night urging him to change his name from Schmidt to Smith. Mr. Schmidt told the others that the way he looked at it he was an American citizen, no matter what his name was, but his wife thought no one would give him a job with a German name like that. Another man said that as soon as the war started the bosses would get down on their knees begging men to work no matter what their names were.

Maggie-Now bought a morning paper. She set it next her father's coffee cup and told him of the talk of war being declared. He merely grunted and told her that just the same he was going out that night; war or no war.

Maggie-Now spent the day in an ecstasy of preparation. She pressed the last of her three dresses, a summery, flowered print made like her other two. She got out her last summer's white pumps and cleaned them. She bought a cake of geranium-scented soap and washed her hair with it. She rinsed her hair in lemon juice and water and sat out in the sun to dry it.

Later in the day, she took a bath with the scented soap. She lathered and rinsed, lathered and rinsed until her skin was almost stiff. She dried herself and dusted all over with Mennen's Violet Baby Talcum Powder. She braided her hair, pinned it up and buffed her fingernails.

When she had dressed, she went upstairs to see the tenant about keeping an eye on Denny in case her father carried through his threat to spend the evening with his mythical (as Maggie-Now firmly believed) woman friend.

There was an understanding that landlords did not make friends with tenants, especially when both occupied the same house. It was considered right that a tenant should not be burdened with social obligations toward the landlord. The tenant should be free to come and go. Also, friendship would weaken the landlord's right to request prompt payment of rent and his privileg-

of making it uncomfortable for the tenant when he defaulted in paying the rent.

Maggie-Now knew that by asking a favor of the tenant she was giving up her right to dun Mrs. Heahly for last month's unpaid rent. She was willing to risk this, however, rather than possibly miss out on her evening with Claude.

Maggie-Now felt uncomfortable and turned her head away when she saw the look of apprehension on Mrs. Heahly's face.

"Come in," said Mrs. Heahly, not meaning it.

"For a moment," said Maggie-Now.

"Sit down?"

"No, thank you."

"Somebody looks very nice today," said Mrs. Heahly with an ingratiating smile.

The poor thing's trying to get on my good side, thought Maggie-Now. She sighed. *It's hard to be a landlord.*

"About being late with the rent," said Mrs. Heahly brightly. "Never fear. You'll get it. My husband's working steady now, but we had some extra expenses, and . . ."

"I didn't come about that. I came up to ask you for a favor."

"Any time! Any time!" said Mrs. Heahly eagerly. "If I can do anything for you . . ."

"I'm going out tonight and my father might step out a few minutes while I'm gone. If you could kind of keep an eye on my brother . . ."

"Glad to, Miss Moore. Glad to."

"You don't have to do anything. Just in case

there's a fire or he gets sick."

"Sure! Sure!" The woman's relief at not being dunned for the rent was pathetically obvious.

Yet, after Maggie-Now left, Mrs. Heahly justified herself. *I don't mind her father getting it in the neck, the rip, telling me to go soak my head the time I told him the toilet was out of order. But it's a dirty trick to pull on the girl. She's halfway nice.* Mrs. Heahly sighed. *Ah, well, you can't make a deposit on a new flat and pay rent on the old one at the same time. Then there's the cost of moving in the bargain.*

By the time she had it all thought out, she was indignant. She figured that the landlord owed her more than she owed him.

Maggie-Now had supper ready ahead of time and, of course, Pat took this special night to be late. Maggie-Now was sure he was doing it on purpose because he knew she was going out and he wanted to make her so nervous that she wouldn't enjoy herself.

When he got home, however, she saw that he had a reason for being late. He had been to the barber's for a shave and haircut. He smelled of bay rum, hair tonic and Danderine. Maggie-Now's heart sank.

He wasn't fooling then, she thought, *when he said he was going out.* She tossed her head. *Well, I wasn't fooling either.*

He smelled the soap and talcum powder and the scent of lemon juice coming from her healthy hair. He noticed that she was dressed with unusual care.

So, he thought, *I can talk meself deef, dumb and blind and she'll trot out all the same.*

"We're getting in the war after all," he announced. He went into the bathroom to wash his hands.

The bathroom was no more than a windowless closet. The tub was a shallow scoop of white-painted tin enclosed in an oblong box of zinc. Had it had a lid, it would have looked like a coffin for a shrimp of a man. The closed quarters smelled strongly of scented soap, talcum powder, wet hair and wet towels. The painted walls were still wet from steam. It was hardly the place or setting for Sybaritic rites of the bath and the voluptuous longings engendered thereby. But Pat feared the worst.

He thought: *She must be serious about the bastid whoever he is. An she's out to get him. Then what's to become of me in me old days,* he worried, *and her married and away and me left to die alone in a furnished room?*

As they sat down to supper, he said: "Who's been taking a bath, now?"

"Me," said Maggie-Now.

He fixed her with his eye and spoke slowly with hidden meaning: "Don't you think you're going a little too far—taking a bath in the middle of the day?"

She saw Denny jerk his head to stare at her. "Eat," she said. "The both of you, before it gets cold."

They were eating in complete but scented silence when a low voice came through the keyhole. "Are you all right in there?" asked the voice. Denny looked scared and Pat dropped his fork.

"That's only the lady upstairs minding Denny," she whispered. She raised her voice. "Thank you, Mrs. Heahly, but we're not gone yet," she said.

"Excuse me," breathed the voice.

So she fixed it! She fixed it so I got to go out. But where, Pat thought in despair, *am I going to go?*

Maggie-Now bribed Denny to help her wash the dishes by giving him a nickel for a glass shooter. Pat went into his room to change from uniform to Sunday suit. Maggie-Now went into her room to primp a little. After the dishes were done, Denny sat in the kitchen to do his homework. It wasn't exactly homework—there was no school during Holy Week. It was "review work," one crayon picture each night to keep the kids out of mischief.

Maggie-Now and her father came out of their rooms simultaneously and went into the front room. He sat at one window, she at the other.

"We're getting in the war, now," he said.

"You said that before, Papa."

"Anything that important you can say twice."

"That's right," she agreed.

He read his paper and she watched for Claude. She started to get nervous. "Papa, i you're going out, go."

"When I get good and ready."

"Look, Papa. I asked the tenant the favor of keeping an eye on Denny. That means I threw away my chance to push her about the back rent. So, since it's going to cost, take advantage. I *want* you to go out. I fixed it up."

Sure she wants me out, he thought, *so's she can have him in here.* He said: "Don't you go putting me out of me own home. First I want to see what kind of gink is coming for you."

She had feared he had that in mind. He and Claude couldn't meet. They just *couldn't!* Her father would insult him and throw him out and she'd never see Claude again! Now it was a quarter to eight. She was so nervous she had to do *something.* She went out into the kitchen to talk to Denny.

"Denny, if you feel like buying your marble now, I'll walk to the corner with you."

The boy was willing. Pat was relieved when he saw them leave the house together. *Taking the boy with her,* he thought. *I guess she can't be so serious about the man, then. Anyways, there won't be no spooning. Not with a wet blanket of a boy along.*

He relaxed. He took off his pinching shoes and his chafing celluloid collar and removed the brass collar button that had already branded his Adam's apple with a green circle. He unbuttoned his vest and put his feet up on a chair.

A man, he told himself, stretching luxuriously,

is a fool to go out sporting of a night when he's got a clean, decent home to sit in. Ah, yes.

Then Denny came back.

"Where's your sister?" asked Pat.

"Don' know."

"Did she go off with a man?"

"Don't know."

"What do you know, hah?"

"I know she went with me to buy my marble and then she said I should go home because you ain't going out and you would be lonesome."

"So I ain't going out, she thinks!"

He buttoned his vest and with many a sigh he put his shoes back on. The tarnishing collar button was put back into place and the restricting collar and tie. He went for his hat.

"I'm gonna be here alone," said Denny.

"I'll tend to that," said Pat. He went out into the hall and bellowed up the stairs: "Hey!"

Mrs. Heahly opened her door and hollered back down: "Hay is for horses."

"Don't forget to mind me kid," he said, "like me daughter told you."

"Mind your own kid," she answered.

"Yeah? And you put that back rent in me hand first thing in the morning."

"Yeah? And you go to hell," she said, and slammed her door.

He walked down to the saloon feeling pleased with himself. *That'll learn her not to get snotty with me,* he told himself smugly.

Denny wasn't afraid to stay in the house

alone. He just didn't like it. He went out and sat on the stoop. He told himself that he wasn't lonesome, yet he wished some boy would come along so they could talk about his new marble. A woman came by and asked: "What class are you in?"

"One B," he said.

"That's nice," she said and went on her way.

Denny was not an introspective child but he couldn't help wondering why people always asked him what class he was in, and his sister and father were always asking him, how's school, and, did he do his homework. Why did people think he had no other life than school?

Gloomily, Pat watched the bartender shave the foam from the small beer he'd ordered. With no preamble at all, he started in on his troubles.

"You raise a kid. Work like a dog. Do without things yourself to give her things. Then she gets big. And just when she could be a help—pay back the old man—what happens? She goes loony over the first gink what comes her way."

"That's the way it goes," said the bartender, giving the bar a ritual wipe.

"That all you got to say about it?" asked Pat.

"What do you want for a nickel beer?" said the bartender. "The Gettysburg Address?"

"I had to earn that nickel for that beer, I'll have you know," said Pat.

"Well, you better earn a dime for the same

next week. Maybe fifteen cents. Beer's going up now that we're getting in the war.''

"War or no war, sooner than pay fifteen cents, I'll go without me beer," said Pat.

"You'll go without it pretty soon whether you want to or not. This here prohibition is going through someday and then, good-by, Charlie.''

The only other customer further down the bar now entered the conversation. "It's a God-damned shame," he said. "That's all *I* got to say.''

"Another county heard from," sneered Pat, and he tried to wither him with a look. But the man was at the other end of the bar and the saloon was dimly lighted. In lieu of the look, he raised his voice.

"Yeah, and I suppose you went down and enlisted today, hey?''

"Me?" called back the stranger. "Why I'm fifty-two if I'm a day.''

"Who asked you your age?" said Pat.

"Nobody.''

"Who you calling nobody?" asked Pat, itching for a fight.

"Nobody.''

"Dry up, then," said Pat.

I feel I know him from someplace, brooded the stranger, staring down into his beer.

Walking home, Pat had the same feeling. *I must-a seen him someplace before,* he thought. *But where?*

Denny saw his father turn the corner. He

scuttled back into the house and did his crayon work all over again so he wouldn't have to go to bed right away.

Claude and Maggie-Now were walking arm in arm. "I'm disappointed," he said. "I had hoped to meet your father."

"I thought it wasn't the right time. . . ."

"I see." He sounded offended.

"I mean, he's not used to the idea that I . . . I . . ."

"That I . . . you and I . . ." He didn't finish because, startlingly enough, she was blushing. "You haven't told me much about your father, excepting that he was born in Kilkenny."

"There's not much that I know about his childhood. Anyhow, I talked too much last night."

"Oh, no! No, it was wonderful—every word of it. I'd like to hear it all over again. You see," he said simply, "I never had a childhood with parents and a home and relatives and stores to go to and penny candies and a sled in winter. No, I never had the things you had."

"Please tell me how it was," she said impulsively. "I'd like to know more about you."

"There is nothing to tell—nothing to know," he said harshly.

"Excuse me," she said humbly.

His face cleared and he smiled. "Oh, someday, when we're old and sitting by the fire and it's snowing outside, I'll tell you everything."

"I will wait," she said shyly.

He looked at her strangely. After a while he said: "In the meantime, I'll take your childhood for my own and your Brooklyn and all your friends, too, your brother, your father, your Aunt Lottie . . ." Suddenly, he said: "Take me to see her."

"She lives way over in East New York. Some night next week . . . I'd have to send her a card first."

"I may not be here next week."

Her heart fell. *He didn't mean it,* she thought sadly, *about us getting old with each other. I must try not to believe everything he . . . anybody says.*

"Maybe," she said tentatively, "you'd like to see the house where my grandfather lived—where my mother was brought up?"

Enthusiastically, he told her that was exactly what he wanted to do.

It hadn't changed much since Maggie-Now was a little girl. The white swan, now gray from dust, still sat placidly in the showcase. Claude visualized the house as it must have been in the nineties. He admired the fine, wrought-iron grillwork of the basement door and house railing.

"Yes, like New Orleans homes," he said.

"Then you've been *there,* too," she murmured.

The stable plumbing shop was more up-to-date

now. Showcase windows hid the lines of the stable. A new auto truck stood in the yard. The sign over the door, *Pheid & Son. Plumbers. Day & Night,* was now framed in electric bulbs.

A young man came out of the store and walked toward them. "That's 'And Son,' I believe," whispered Claude.

The young man smiled at Maggie-Now and said, "Yes?" inquiringly, as his father had done twelve years ago.

Claude answered. To Maggie-Now's distress, he used his academic voice on the young man. "May we be permitted to browse around?"

Young Pheid looked at him with distaste. "How's that again?" he asked.

"My grandparents . . . my mother used to live here," explained Maggie-Now.

"No kidding!" said young Pheid, smiling at her.

"My grandfather owned this property."

"Kolinski, the notary?"

"No. His name was Moriarity. Michael Moriarity."

"Hey, Pop," the young man called back to the store. "Did you know a Moriarity?"

"Moriarity?"

"Yeah. Moriarity."

The name was sounded back and forth and, for a breath, Mike Moriarity seemed to *be* again.

"Naw," said Pop Pheid, and the breath was gone. "Sorry," he added.

"That's all right," she said. "We just want to look around."

He said what he had said many years ago to her mother: "Help yourself." Pop and Son went back into the store.

"There used to be a hedge of snowball bushes, Mother said, along here."

"Snowball . . . ?"

"Some people call them hydrangea, I guess. Mother loved them so."

Walking back home, she told him how her father had lived in the stable loft when he first came from Ireland and how he had hated the horses.

"The more I hear about your father," he said, "the more I want to know him."

"You wouldn't like him."

"I'm sure I would. If for no other reason than that you like him."

"Oh, I don't like him."

"You don't?" he asked, astonished.

"I suppose I love him, though."

"How can you love without liking?"

"I don't know. But he's my father and a child should love its father."

"I see. You love him because he loved your mother."

"No. Because my mother loved him."

They said good night on her stoop. He turned his head away to tell her he couldn't see her the next night; he'd be busy. And she turned her head away to say that was all right.

This is the end of it, she thought. *I'll never see him again.*

But, he told her, he might be able to make it Friday night if that was all right with her. She told him that would be fine. And she thought: *He's trying to let me down easy. I know I'll never see him again.*

"Good night," he said.

"Good-by," she whispered. She turned and went into the house.

Her father was standing by the window. He let the curtain fall back into place when she came in. Maggie-Now knew he'd seen them together and she was dully surprised that he hadn't come out and made a fuss.

"I seen him! I seen him," said Pat exultantly, "the little bit of a man what you think is in love with you."

"Oh, Papa," she cried out, "he isn't, he isn't. No one is in love with me."

He felt her despair and was jubilant, thinking it was all over—her friendship with the man. Perversely, however, he was indignant that the man wasn't in love with her.

"He's not worth your little finger," he said.

She looked at him, waiting for the quick retort to come into her mind. It didn't come. She said: "I'll get you up early tomorrow so you can go to six o'clock Mass before work."

"What for?"

"Because tomorrow's Holy Thursday."

"It's enough to go on Sunday," he mumbled.

255

"Once in a while," he added.

Sadly, Maggie-Now prepared for bed, convinced that she'd never see Claude again. *I should have been more careful,* she thought, *watched myself more and not told him everything about myself and I shouldn't have shown so plain how much I liked him.*

She couldn't get Pat up the next morning to go to Mass. He said his back hurt. She and Denny went to the eight o'clock Mass. When Pat came home that night, he noticed with relief that there were no wet towels, no steamy bathroom or scent of soap and powder. And she had cooked his favorite supper: breaded veal cutlets, mashed potatoes, stewed tomatoes thickened with a slice of rye bread, and an open-faced apple cake from the baker's. Also the coffee was good and strong the way he liked it.

Ah, the good girl, thought Pat. *She's making it up to me the way she tormented me by going out with that feller. Sure and she had a fight with the little man and sensible girl what she is, she gave him the gate. Now she's glad she's got a father to fall back on.*

He had a feeling of well-being. It made him generous. "Have another piece of cake, Denny," he said.

"You took the last piece already," said Denny.

Pat shoved his piece of cake over to Denny. "Have it, do," he said. "I ain't touched it yet." He turned to Maggie-Now. "Girl, dear, being's

256

tomorrow is Good Friday, I'll go to Mass."

"I'll try to get you up early," she said without interest.

"You don't need to. I'll go to the eight o'clock with you and Denny."

"You'll be late for work."

"Half an hour. I'll make it up Saturday afternoon. The way I look at it," he said, "a family should stick together; go to church together."

"Ah, Papa!" she said, and gave him her wide smile.

Chapter Twenty-Five

THE church was crowded for the eight o'clock Mass. Workingmen stood in the back: the letter carrier, bag slung over shoulder, pausing in his rounds to attend Mass; the uniformed cop deserting his beat for ten minutes; Pat among them in his street cleaner's uniform, and others. Few missed Mass that Good Friday.

After lunch, Maggie-Now took Denny shopping with her to buy the fish and vegetables for supper and the huckleberry pie; and dye and eggs for colored Easter eggs. The streets seemed unusually crowded and people moved about slowly or stood silently in groups as though waiting for something to happen. She heard one man ask another what had happened.

The man said: "They say we're in the war." He shrugged. "But I don't know. You hear all kinds of things nowadays."

Within the hour, the extras were on the streets. The word "War" was in black letters six inches high.

"War!" read Denny, proud that that was another three-letter word he could read.

There it was. President Wilson had signed the declaration of war at 1:13 P.M., Good Friday, April 6, 1917. The President had made a statement: "America has found herself."

The people of the neighborhood were one with each other as they were always when there was a blizzard or a great fire, a child raped and murdered by a fiend in the neighborhood or some other great catastrophe. People spoke to each other without formality or preamble.

"War is terrible," said a woman, a stranger to Maggie-Now.

"Yes," agreed Maggie-Now.

"But it's more terrible when it starts on our Lord's Day, Good Friday. And the time one-thirteen. That's unlucky and it makes it more terrible."

"War by itself," said another stranger, "is terrible, no matter what."

Maggie-Now and the first woman agreed.

Later in the afternoon, there was proof positive that America was at war. The kids in the street had already invented a war game. Maggie-Now and Denny watched from the front window. Three boys, about Denny's age, had their sawed-off-broomstick shinny sticks aimed at the enemy. They stood in a row. The "enemy" was a little kid of three, his sodden, baby-wet diaper hanging out the legs of his manly little pants. They had placed an upsidedown white enameled child's chamber pot on his head for a Hun's helmet.

"Bang, bang, bang," they shouted. The little kid stood there, bewildered.

"You're supposed to be dead," yelled a kid.

"Fall down, you Goddamn bologna," said another kid.

And the little kid stood there and cried and baby-wet his diaper some more.

"Can I go out and play?" asked Denny.

"No!" said Maggie-Now.

"Why?"

"Because I say so," she said sharply.

"*Why* do you say so?"

"Because," she said more gently, "this is the day our Lord died and it's not right to play such games on this day." She pulled down the shades.

Pat was relieved that night when he came home from work (full of theories about the war which he was anxious to give voice to) to smell fish frying. She wasn't going out, then!

For no woman in her right mind, he thought, *would go out to meet her sweetheart smelling of frying fish.*

He also smelled the incense she had burning in a tin jar lid on the stove. He assumed it was some religious observance. (His wife used to burn incense on special religious days.) He would have been upset had he known she was burning it to take the fish smell out of her hair.

Maggie-Now was going out to meet Claude. Her strong feeling that she'd never see him again had changed to a stronger feeling that she would see him again. The declaration of war had something to do with it. Also, the candle she had burned in church that morning. She dressed after supper.

"So you're going out again," he said.

"Yes."

"What about the boy?"

"He is your son, Papa. You should look after him once in a while."

After she had left, Pat prepared to go out, too. He wanted to talk about the war to somebody. Denny followed him from the bathroom where he washed, to the bedroom where he changed his clothes.

"Why are you follying me around?" he asked.

"Because I don't want to be left," said Denny.

Standing before the mirror, struggling with his collar, with Denny standing next to him, Pat examined his son's face in the mirror. Again, he wondered where the boy got his red hair from. There had been no red heads in the Moore or Moriarity family. Timothy Shawn had had red hair. It occurred to Pat that maybe a hundred or so years ago, back in Ireland, a Moore had married or mated with a Shawn and the red hair had worked through to Denny. Somehow, the thought pleased Pat.

I'd be proud, he thought, *if the boy grew up to be half the man that Timmy Shawn, the bastid, God rest his soul, was.*

He turned around and looked directly at the child. The boy didn't have the light lashes that usually went with red hair. He had dark lashes like his mother and he had his mother's eyes, too.

He thought of Mary with the baby in her arms; how he had said he'd always wanted a son to go hunting and fishing with. He had a small moment of prescience.

When I'm a very old man, he thought, *I'll remember how the little boy wanted to be with me this night and I'll cry me heart out and wish I was young again so I could stay with the little boy. So I will grieve when I am old.*

But tonight I am *younger and I don't want to stay with the little boy. I want to talk to men about the war.*

He compromised. "You can come along when I go out," he said.

The boy looked up at him and put his hands together in ecstasy and smiled the way Mary used to smile at Pat when he said or did something nice. Pat's heart turned over a little.

Walking down the street, the boy slipped his hand into his father's and said: "I like to go out with you."

The man felt a drop of moisture in the corner of one eye and felt a second of anguish. *Why does he always give in? If he'd only tell me to go to hell! Then I'd know what to do. First I'd beat the be-Jesus out of him for talking that way to his father. Then I'd be proud of him for standing up to his old man and not taking no guff from me or nobody.*

They came to a candy store. Pat said: "Here's five pennies. You go in and buy whatever you want. And look around. See if there's anything you want for Easter. Not more than a quarter, hear? And maybe I'll buy it for you." The boy gave him what Pat called "that Mary look"—a look of gratitude and happiness combined. "And wait for me here."

Pat asked for a short beer. The bartender said maybe he'd like to think it over. A small beer now cost a dime and would cost fifteen next week. On account of the war, explained the bartender.

The saloon was crowded. There was a lot of loud talk; they talked loudly about the war and much louder about beer going up a nickel a glass. The little fellow that Pat was sure he had seen someplace was in the center of a group of men, waving his glass of beer and giving his version of the outbreak of war. Pat made his way over to the man.

"I thought you'd be in uniform by now," he sneered. To Pat's surprise, the little man shook his hand.

"The honor you did me," said the stranger, "yourself saying I should enlist and me what'll never see fifty again. You gave me me youth back. Do you not remember me, Pathrick, your old friend from night-school days?"

Pat knew it was Mick Mack, *for,* he thought,

who else in all the world would take an insult for a compliment.

"Ah, you've changed," said Mick Mack.

"Not as much as you," said Pat, "the bad way you look, I didn't recognize you."

"And I didn't recognize you, Pathrick, the grand way you look after all these years."

Mick Mack's story was soon told. He had sustained a back injury when a big truck had run into his trolley car and, after years of litigation, the truck company had settled fifteen dollars a week on him for life. His wife was dead and his children all married. He didn't see much of them. In his own words, they had no room for the old man. But he was happy, he insisted, with his fifteen dollars a week and the room and board he got at the home of a grand widder woman for ten dollars a week.

"She owns her own house," he said, "on Schaeffer Street, just off Bushwick Avenue. She runs a hat store for ladies in the basement and upstairs is the boarders. And, oh, the grand table she sets! Her husband," he continued, "rest his soul, even though I never laid eyes on him, left the widder well fixed with the house in her name, and, I wouldn't be surprised, a bit of money to go with it, and she with a darlen shape in the bargain."

"And I wouldn't put it past the likes of yourself," said Pat, "to look at her darlen shape and get idears."

"Ah, no. 'Tis her cooking has won me heart.

Do you come and eat Easter Day dinner with me, Pathrick. Only thirty-five cents for outsiders."

"No," said Pat. "Home I eat for nothing. And eat good, too."

"I'll treat," said Mick Mack. "Friendship, to me, is more than money."

"I'll eat with you then," said Pat. "Not that I want to, but because I'm sorry for a miserable little man, the likes of you, having to pay to have someone eat with him."

"Ah, you talk so mean," said the beaming Mick Mack, "because you don't want me to find out the goodness what is in you."

"Miss me?" asked Claude.

"Yes."

"That's the way it should be," he said, tucking her arm into his. "I am taking you to dinner tonight."

"That's nice." She was pleased. He didn't ask and she didn't tell him she'd already had her evening meal.

He took her to an upstairs chop suey restaurant on the corner of Broadway and Flushing Avenue. After they were seated, they made an agreement not to discuss the war.

"Let us talk only of ourselves," he said. "Our time together may be shorter than we know. Now: Will you have beef or pork chop suey?"

"Could I have something else?" she asked.

"You see, I've never eaten Chinese food before and . . ."

"Start on something familiar, then. You like eggs?"

"Oh, yes."

The Chinese waiter was at their table. He had come silently. "Yiss?" he inquired.

"Shrimp eggs foo yung for the lady and pork chop suey for me."

"Yiss."

The waiter brought a pot of tea and two little bowls. "Oh, how beautiful," she exclaimed, admiring the bone-white china with its larkspur-blue Chinese markings. "And this!" She ran her hand over the raffia-wrapped handle of the teapot and smiled across the table at him.

He picked up one of the little bowls and looked at the bottom. "Yes. Made in China. The Orient." He smiled back at her and her smile widened. *"All the Orient is in your smile,"* he half spoke, half sang.

"There's Egypt in your dreamy eyes," she quoted.

"That's a bold thing to tell a man," he said.

"No. I mean, that's the name of the song you started to sing."

"We have our song, then," he said. "Will you pour the tea?"

Thrilled, she filled his bowl and her own. "Sugar?" she asked, arching her eyebrows as she had seen an actress, Jerry Morley, do at the Lyceum in a play where Jerry had poured tea.

He grinned. "No sugar."

"I don't take sugar, either," she said.

"Good. We have the same habits. We'll have no trouble getting along."

"It's such good tea," she said.

"I don't know whether it's good or not. But it's wonderful because we're drinking it together." After the third bowlful, he sighed, leaned back and relaxed. "All we need is a fire on the hearth and a cat purring on the rug. Do you like cats, Margaret?"

"I don't know. I never had a cat."

"We'll have a cat, maybe two," he said. "You'll love them."

She set her bowl down because her hands were trembling. *Now,* she thought, *he'll say, we'll have a cat when we set up our own home after we marry.*

He said: "Ever see a Manx cat?"

"What kind of cat is that?"

"They have no tails. They're very common in Scotland. Scotland! Have you ever been . . ."

"No," she interrupted. "I've never been to Scotland." He laughed.

The waiter brought the food. She stared admiringly at the nicely arranged, steaming mound on Claude's plate. She said the obvious thing: "My, that looks good!"

Now! he wondered. *Will she say I'll give you some of mine and you give me some of yours?* He detested women who wanted to share food in restaurants. He tried her out.

"How about I give you some of this and you give me some of yours?"

"You can have some of mine," she said, "there's such a lot of it. But I don't want any chop suey."

Perversely then, he wanted her to share his food. "Please?" he asked.

"I can't. Because it's Friday."

"What does Friday have to do . . ."

"I can't eat meat on Friday, especially Good Friday."

"And why not?"

"My religion . . ."

"Of course! How could I be so stupid? Please don't hold it against me." He reached over and put his hand on hers.

So he's not Catholic, sighed Maggie-Now to herself. *Even if he did want me, that's another thing—religion—in the way.*

"I'd like to go to service with you," he said.

"Service? Oh, Mass. There's high Mass Sunday. Easter high Mass is very beautiful. Even outsiders," she said bravely, "think so."

"I'll think so too, my little Chinee," he said. "I want to share it with you. I want to share everything with you." Again, he leaned across the table to put his hand on her arm.

She saw the waiter coming with the dessert and, as many women do, she changed the subject, feeling that talk should be casual in the presence of a waiter.

"It's sprinkling outside," she said.

"An April shower," he said.

"We'll stay here and drink tea," he said. "And talk. Maybe the rain will let up." He ordered another pot of tea. "I have about two days left," he said, "and I'd like to spend them with you. Could I spend tomorrow at your home?"

She looked so stricken his heart went out to her. He knew she was thinking of her father. He made it a little easier for her.

"Could we ride out to the cemetery?"

"Cemetery?" She was astonished. "But why . . . ?"

"It sounded so wonderful when you told me how your mother took you there and how you took your brother. . . ."

"Well, it's not Decoration Day, but I guess we could go just the same." He laughed. "Only, I'd have to take Denny."

"I wouldn't think of going if he didn't come along," he said gallantly. She gave him her wide smile for that. "And tomorrow night?" he asked tentatively.

"Well, I always go to see Aunt Lottie on Easter eve. To bring Easter baskets to the twins, but . . ."

"Would you," he asked eagerly, "would you take me?"

"I would like to," she said.

The rain continued. They were the only guests left in the restaurant. The waiter started to mop the floor and they left. They walked home in the rain. He put his arm around her waist, holding her close to his side as they walked, saying that one side of her, at least, wouldn't get wet. She thought that was a very nice way to walk.

When she got home, Denny was sitting on the floor with a shiny, new humming top. "Why aren't you in bed, Denny?" she asked with a frown. Denny and his father exchanged understanding looks.

"He's still up because I asked him to keep me company."

"Where'd you get that pretty top?" she asked.

"Papa bought it for me. For Easter."

"Ah, Papa!" she said. She put her hand on his shoulder in a gesture of affection. She was pleased that he'd been nice to Denny and relieved that he hadn't started the usual argument about her going out that night.

"By the way," said Pat casually. "Don't count on me for Easter dinner. I'm going to have Easter dinner with me friend."

Maggie-Now's heart leaped a little. *I can have Claude here for dinner,* she told herself joyously.

"I hope you won't mind," he said with stiff formality.

"No, Papa. I'm glad you have a friend," she said sincerely.

Chapter Twenty-Six

ON the way to the cemetery, Claude didn't ask Denny how old he was; what grade he was in; whether he liked school and what he wanted to be when he got big—stock questions that adults usually ask children when they're trying to get acquainted. He drew out Denny about kite making and he listened with sincere interest. He told Denny how the Chinese made kites; the lacquered sticks and the gold and silver paper and the symbols painted on them; turquoise, jade green and Chinese red. And the kite itself in the shape of a dragon, perhaps, and the tail, intricately made of twisted paper to look like a dragon's tail. The trolley ride seemed all too short to Denny and to Maggie-Now, too.

She bought a red geranium and the man said the price had gone up. It was fifty cents now and he confided that the price would go up to a dollar on Decoration Day. On account of the war, he said.

Claude insisted on buying a hothouse

hydrangea. It cost a dollar and a half and Maggie-Now told him it was too dear, but Claude said, since her mother had loved them so, he wanted to plant one on her grave.

"Margaret," he said, as they walked through the cemetery, "do you believe that when someone dies, he dies altogether?"

"Yes," she said. "Except the soul."

"What is the soul?"

"What goes to heaven when you die," said Denny. "Brother Bernard said so."

"That's his catechism teacher," explained Maggie-Now.

"What do you think the soul is, Margaret?"

"I suppose it's the something that stays or *is* after someone dies. The soul of him is around. It's the kind of stamp he made on whatever he did and thought and the way he lived; things that sort of stay after he dies. And it is what goes to heaven, too, like Denny said."

"Do you believe that a person ever lived before in another time, a hundred or so years ago, maybe?"

"Oh, no."

"Have you ever turned a corner in a strange neighborhood and come on a street that you'd never seen before and had the feeling that you'd been there before? In another life?"

"No. I walk around only in my own neighborhood and I know all the streets and they never are strange to me. No, I never had that feeling."

"Some people believe," he said, "that a person comes back to live in some other form after death."

"Like what?" she asked.

"Like these hydrangeas: You told me your mother loved hydrangeas. Wouldn't it make you happy if you knew she lived again as one of these plants?"

"I couldn't say," said Maggie-Now, disturbed and ill at ease. "No. I wouldn't like it. You wouldn't want to be a flower, would you?"

"Not a flower. A bird."

"A bird?" blurted out Denny in astonishment. Maggie-Now pressed his shoulder hard, meaning he was not to laugh.

"But why?" she asked.

"Because a bird is free . . . free. He flies over the sea and over the land."

"In winter," said Denny, "chippies come in our yard and Maggie-Now throws out bread crumbs for them."

"No, not a sparrow; not a small bird. A great gray and white sea gull. I saw some when I crossed over on the Staten Island ferry some weeks ago. That kind of bird, Denny."

The talk was making Maggie-Now uneasy and uncomfortable. She was relieved when Denny ran ahead and shouted: "Here it is! I found the grave all by myself."

Claude read the graven names aloud. "Michael Moriarity; a powerful name." He paused and breathed, "Mary Moore. The sound of it is like a sigh in the valley on a gray autumn day.''

Maggie-Now's eyes misted over because she thought that was such a beautiful thing to say. But Denny backed off and looked at Claude with suspicion. He liked Claude when he talked about kites and things like that. But he wasn't sure of liking him when he talked about being a bird and how somebody's name sounded.

They had the traditional pot cheese and chives for lunch and Denny had his usual hot dog and strawberry soda. The waiter asked Claude wouldn't he like a glass of beer with his pot cheese and Claude said, no, as if he were astonished that anyone would ask him to drink beer. This pleased Maggie-Now. She thought that, at least, he wasn't a drinking man. She invited him to Sunday dinner at her home. His acceptance was humbly grateful.

With flattering courtesy, he consulted Denny. ''Is it all right with you, Denny?''

''Sure,'' said Denny. He was so overwhelmed at being asked that he forgot about Claude wanting to be a bird when he was dead.

They went up the stairs, Denny carrying the Easter baskets for the twins. Maggie-Now tapped on Lottie's door.

''Who is it?'' called out Lottie.

''Me. Maggie-Now, and Denny.''

''And a friend!'' called out Claude.

There was a living silence before Lottie called

out: "Just a minute, please."

There were hurried thumpings and bumpings behind the closed door. Maggie-Now knew that Lottie was furiously straightening out the room for "company."

"I guess I should have dropped her a card," whispered Maggie-Now. "But I thought she'd expect me. Denny and I always come over Easter eve with the baskets."

A slightly disheveled Lottie opened the door cautiously, stared frankly at Claude and said, "Come in." She embraced Maggie-Now warmly, gave Denny a kiss on a reluctantly offered cheek, smiled at Claude and said: "I'm their Aunt Lottie."

"Aunt Lottie," said Maggie-Now, "let me introduce Mr. Bassett."

Claude took Lottie's hand and bowed a little bit too much over it. "This is a pleasure I've been looking forward to for a long time," he said.

Maggie-Now was dismayed. Claude was using his "educated" English and Maggie-Now knew that Lottie would think he was putting on airs. She saw that Lottie, expecting the traditional "Pleased to meet you," was taken aback by Claude's little speech.

Lottie replied with the traditional, "Likewise," and then felt foolish because her reply didn't fit. She had *not* looked forward to the pleasure of meeting him because she hadn't even known he *lived* until a few moments ago.

"These are for the twins," said Denny, handing Lottie the two baskets.

"What a shame," she said. "They're not here. Last night," she explained to Maggie-Now, "on account of the war starting, Gracie dreamed Widdy was killed on the battleship and she said the children would be all she had if Widdy died so she took them back." Courteously, she included Claude in her explanation. "You see, Mr. Bassett, Denny and my twin grandsons were born just a few weeks apart."

"Really?" he said.

She thought he sounded doubtful. She said, "Yes," emphatically.

"How's your mother?" asked Maggie-Now.

"Mama fell asleep while she was eating her supper so I put her to bed. All she eats now is mashed potatoes and a glass of port wine the doctor says she can have." She turned to Claude. "My mother is ninety-two, you know."

"Really?" he asked.

"Well, she *is*," said Lottie.

"Can I show him the album, Aunt Lottie?" asked Denny.

"Sure, go ahead, Denny." Again she addressed Claude. "Mr. Shawn, Timmy, my late husband . . ." she waited. He waited, knowing something was expected of him, but what?

"God rest his soul," said Maggie-Now.

". . . gave it to me," continued Lottie, "on our fifth anniversary. He wrote on the card: 'To my sweetheart.' He always called me sweetheart.''

"Is that so!" He opened the album and cocked his ear to listen to the tinkling music. "Why, this is charming," he said.

Lottie looked at him strangely. She turned to Maggie-Now. "Come in the kitchen with me a minute. I want to show you something." To Claude, she said: "Excuse us?"

"Certainly." He stood up.

"Stay sitting," said Lottie.

Out in the kitchen, Lottie spoke in a tense, hurried whisper.

"Who is he?"

"Claude Bass . . ."

"I know his name but who *is* he?"

"Someone I met last Monday."

"What does he do?"

"Oh, different things."

"What does he work at?"

"Different things."

"Where does he come from?"

"Different places."

"Where?"

"I don't know, Aunt Lottie."

"Is he got parents?"

"I don't know. He never said and I never asked."

"He ain't Catholic."

"I never asked. . . ."

"I *know*. Because he didn't say 'Rest his soul' when I mentioned Timmy's name. Look! I'm your godmother and it's my place to see that you don't marry outside your religion."

"You don't like him, do you, Aunt Lottie?"

"No."

"Why?"

"Because he's not like Timmy. Oh, Maggie-Now, dear," said Lottie, "what do you see in him?"

"Everything. Like when he talks . . . the things he says make me feel like a princess."

"And the things Timmy *did* for me made me feel like a queen. Like the way he'd lift my washboiler on the stove. Your man would only look at it and say, 'Interesting, ain't it?' "

"Oh, Aunt Lottie, if you knew how much I loved him, you wouldn't run him down so."

"Why do you love him?"

"Because he *needs* me so," said Maggie-Now.

"Famous last words," said Lottie cynically.

"The way Uncle Timmy needed you, Aunt Lottie."

"Timmy didn't need nobody. *I needed him.*"

Maggie-Now hung her head. She was saddened because the godmother she loved didn't love the man she loved. "He asked to go to Mass with me tomorrow," she said hopefully.

"Sure! Sure! Them smooth talkers will do anything before marriage and nothing after. Well, I tell you this, Maggie-Now, it's my place to see that you don't marry him. And you *won't* marry him. I had my say, now, and I guess we better go back. He might think we're talking about him."

As they came out of the kitchen, Lottie talked

loudly and brightly as though continuing the kitchen conversation. "I just wanted you to look at it and tell me if I paid too much for that wash wringer."

Claude was not fooled. He stood at the mantelpiece, holding the china pug dog with the china nursing puppies, and looked at Maggie-Now appealingly. Her heart went out to him.

"My Timmy . . ." said Lottie. And waited.

"God rest his soul," said Maggie-Now, looking intently at Claude and hoping he'd understand that he was expected to say that, too. But poor Claude only looked bewildered.

"Thanks," said Lottie pointedly. She continued, ". . . gave me that pug dog on our first wedding anniversary."

"It's an amusing little thing," he said.

Maggie-Now moaned inwardly. *Why,* she thought, *can't he talk plain to her the way he talks to me? I know what he means—that it's cute in a way that makes you smile. But Lottie thinks he means that he thinks its comical.*

Indeed she did. She snatched the dog from him and held it to her breast. "I was going to give it to Maggie-Now when she got married. Yes, I was *going* to give it to her." Her intonation said plainly that she wouldn't *think* of giving it to her *now.*

It was an uncomfortable visit. Claude kept saying the wrong things—as far as Lottie was concerned—and his habit of cocking his head to hear better, a habit that usually endeared him to women, made Lottie nervous.

It was time to go and Lottie gave Denny the Easter basket she had prepared for him. It was large and elaborate.

"Oh, Lottie! You shouldn't have," protested Maggie-Now.

"Why not? You give two and I only give one back so it should be bigger. Like it, Denny?" He nodded. "Well, what do I get for it?" He gave her a big hug.

"Well, Mr. Bassett, it was nice to meet you," said Lottie. "And come again when you can stay longer." She didn't mean it, but that was the right thing to say.

Going home on the trolley, Claude said: "I'm sorry she doesn't like me—your Aunt Lottie."

Maggie-Now thought of saying, *But she does. It's just her way.* But she was too honest to say it. She said: "Lottie's not used to strangers. She'll like you after a while. When she knows you better."

"But I like you, *now,*" said Denny.

Claude placed the little boy's hand on his palm. When he saw how little the hand was and how vulnerable it looked, Claude put his other hand over it protectively. He held the child's hand so and said: "Thank you, Denny." There was a little break in his voice. "I'll always remember that."

Chapter Twenty-Seven

LIKE many people with limited amounts of money to spend, Maggie-Now thoroughly enjoyed the spending of it. She loved to shop, especially for food. She loved to see things in great abundance: a basket of tomatoes, a bin of potatoes, a thick stalk of bananas or a huge side of beef. She was one of those women who like to touch things; she picked out onions one by one to drop into the bag the greengrocer held for her. She picked up muskmelons to hold and to smell before she bought. She picked up objects in stores and held them a second before she replaced them; ran her palm over dress goods in the bolt.

Shopping for food was a daily pleasure but shopping for Easter dinner for Claude Bassett had been pure ecstasy. She had taken Denny along with her, as soon as they got back from the cemetery and before she went to Lottie's.

She had wanted the traditional ham for Easter but prices were up to twenty-two cents a pound on account of the big demand. She decided on marinated leg of lamb. Her usual butcher had lamb but it was twenty-two cents a pound and Maggie-Now thought that was too dear.

"Last week it was eighteen cents a pound," she said.

"It's gone up because we're in the war," he said.

She didn't see how being in the war for twenty-four hours would affect the price of meat he had had in his icebox for two weeks, but she said nothing. Another woman in the store said: "Pst!" Maggie-Now went to her.

"Go by Winer's, near Lorimer Street," she whispered. "He's got lamb for seventeen cents."

"What goes on there, hah?" called out the butcher suspiciously from behind the counter.

"Nothing, nothing," said the woman hurriedly. (She owed him money.)

Maggie-Now went to Winer's but there was a catch in it. It was seventeen a pound if one bought the whole leg; nineteen a pound for half. Also it wasn't lamb; it was mutton. Maggie-Now felt a thrill. She liked mutton better than lamb but the butcher mustn't know or the price might go up. She hesitated and he said eighteen a pound if she'd take the shank end. That was the end she'd intended to buy but she was crafty.

"Let me see it first," she said.

He brought out the leg of mutton and threw it on the block. Maggie-Now fell in love with it at first sight. "All right," she said.

"How much?"

"About four pounds and cut off the bone end for soup." It was done and she was happy.

While the butcher was sawing away, Denny worked his way behind the counter and watched the butcher. "Denny!" called Maggie-Now reproachfully.

"Leave him," said the butcher. "Maybe he'll be a butcher when he gets big." Maggie-Now must have made a little grimace for he said: "But maybe you'd sooner he was President?"

"I wouldn't mind," said Maggie-Now.

"Listen, lady. How many Presidents is there? Just one. But how many butchers? A couple thousand. He's got more chance of being a butcher than President." He wrapped up the meat and gave Denny a slice of liverwurst.

She bought a few pounds of small, new potatoes with curls of red skin peeling off, a bunch of green spring onions, the smallest carrots she could find and a sliver of Roquefort cheese.

She put the mutton in a big bowl with sweet oil, pickle vinegar, salt, pepper and a bay leaf, and left it to marinate overnight in the icebox.

The next morning, Easter Sunday, Pat got dressed up and left soon after breakfast with the information that he wouldn't be home until the evening. In a flurry of excitement Maggie-Now put up her dinner so it could cook while she was at Mass.

She took the mutton from the bowl, wiped it

dry and braised it in hot bacon drippings until it was a golden brown. She transferred it to her big, heavy iron pot, added five peppercorns, salt, a new bay leaf and a cup of water. She let it boil up, put the heavy lid on and turned the heat down to simmering.

She fixed a simple salad in her old, warped, wooden salad bowl: chopped lettuce, grated onion, slivers of green pepper, crumbs of Roquefort cheese and olive oil and vinegar dressing with seasonings and a pinch of sugar.

At ten o'clock, Denny, all washed and pressed, left for the children's Mass. Maggie-Now dressed herself carefully, wishing she had a new dress but pleased that she had the new hat she had bought that week. Just before eleven, she put the potatoes and carrots (which she had scrubbed earlier) into the pot, added the peeled onions, let the whole thing boil up once more, and then put the heat down to simmer. It would be done to a tender turn when they got back from church.

She wet the cork of a bottle of oil of cloves that her father used for his toothaches, and touched the cork to each hand (in case her hands still smelled like onions), and rubbed until the pungent scent was somewhat faint and smelled a little like spicy carnations. She took a fresh handkerchief from the box where it had rested all week on a bag of orrisroot, and was ready for her church and her Claude.

He was waiting outside the church. She

thought he looked handsome in his freshly pressed suit and shined shoes. He had a package and a book under his arm. The children's Mass was just getting out and Denny ran over to say hello. Claude asked Denny to take the package and book home.

"And don't open the package to look," said Maggie-Now.

"I won't," he promised.

"And nobody's home so don't go near the stove, hear?"

"I never go near the stove."

"Promise me plain."

"I won't go near the stove."

He walked down the street, holding the package up to his ear and shaking it.

"Margaret," whispered Claude as they entered the church, "how will I know what to do?"

"Do whatever I do," she whispered back.

They remained after the Mass was over because Claude wanted to examine the Stations of the Cross and see the details of the altars. He watched fondly while she knelt before the statue of Saint Anthony, lit a candle and bowed her head briefly. She stood up and smiled at him.

"Why did you do that?" he asked.

"For my intention."

"What was your intention?"

"I can't tell you." She couldn't tell him that she had prayed to the saint, asking him to intercede for her in gaining Claude's love.

Father Flynn was standing outside the church

in cassock and biretta, enjoying the spring air and anticipating the goodness of the Easter dinner that would break his long fast. He greeted Maggie-Now and looked sharply at Claude.

"Father," she said, "I want to introduce Mr. Bassett. Claude Bassett." To Claude, she said: "This is Father Flynn."

Claude started to extend his hand, then drew it back. He didn't know whether to bow, genuflect or shake hands. The priest noticed his confusion and reached out and grasped Claude's hand. Claude didn't know whether to address him as Father, Reverend or Mister. He decided on "sir."

"How do you do, sir."

"I am pleased to know you," said the priest.

Father Flynn watched them go down the street. *So she's found her man,* he mused. *And his faith isn't the same as hers.* He sighed deeply.

Denny was sitting on the stoop with the packages because the door was locked and he couldn't get in. Denny was disappointed when Claude took the package and book from him. He had thought he'd say: *Keep the package, a present for you.*

When they entered the house, Claude said what thousands of men were saying all over the country at that same time: "Something smells good."

And women were answering: "I hope it tastes good," or "Why shouldn't it smell good?

spent the whole morning cooking it." But Maggie-Now said: "Oh, it's nothing. Just some meat and potatoes."

He followed her out into the kitchen, informing her that he was the type who peered into pots to see what was cooking. He told her it was the most beautiful kitchen he'd ever seen.

She looked around the large room, wondering whatever another person could see in it. There was the plate shelf running around the walls with her mother's hand-painted china plates leaning against the wall. The wooden bowls for the morning oatmeal stood on the shelf and her blue willowware dishes. The cups hung by hooks from the bottom of the shelf.

"Reminds me of the kitchens in Devon," he said. "They have blue willowware with the cups hung up like that."

"Oh, those," she said. "Everybody around here has dishes like these. You get them for trading stamps. It's such a common pattern."

"Is it, my little Chinee?" he asked.

The conversation bored Denny. He went out to the front room and sat on the lounge next to the package, sweating out the time until Claude should either open it himself or give it to him, Denny.

Maggie-Now was chattering away in the kitchen. "I like those dishes, though. Lots of women keep them in dish closets but I like them where I can look at them. The way some people like to look at books."

While she was talking, she thickened the gravy with flour and stirred in a teaspoon of grated horseradish. On each of three plates she placed a thick slice of mutton, three of the small new potatoes with their skins flaking off, a couple of soft but intact baby carrots and a ladleful of soft, almost transparent, tiny onions. She gave the mutton a thick coating of the pungent gravy and called Denny to the table. Before she sat down, she set the wooden bowl full of salad in the middle of the table.

She watched anxiously as Claude took his first bite of the mutton. "Venison!" he announced.

"No," she said. "Just mutton."

"No, my little Chinee. Venison or something better."

She flushed with pleasure.

Denny, feeling the oneness between them, and feeling left out in the cold, pushed his plate away. This had his hoped-for result. He got his sister's attention away from Claude.

"Now what?" she asked.

"I'm not hungry," he answered.

"Eat!" said his sister.

"But I don't like it."

"Eat it anyhow." She explained to Claude: "He's been eating eggs from his Easter basket, that's why he's not hungry."

"Just two," Denny mumbled.

But he ate everything on his plate. So did Claude and so did Maggie-Now. Claude had some gravy left on his plate. He looked over the table, wondering why there was no bread and butter.

"This wonderful gravy," he said, "cries out for a piece of bread to sop it up with." Denny opened his mouth to say something.

"Don't tell him, Denny," said Maggie-Now sharply.

"Tell me what?" he asked smiling.

"About the dessert," she said. "It's supposed to be a surprise. Do you want more gravy?" Yes, he did. She poured a ladleful on his plate and gave him a spoon. "Please use this for the gravy," she said graciously.

"Denny, will you grind the coffee while I go and get the dessert?"

"Okay."

"Denny," said Claude, "I'll give you a nickel if you'll let *me* grind the coffee." The deal was consummated.

Maggie-Now almost ran the two blocks to the Jewish delicatessen. The bread wagon was just leaving. Inside the store, Mrs. Fine was arranging the warm round mounds in the showcase.

"You come just in time," she told Maggie-Now. "Only now did the breads come. Still warm. Half a loaf like always?"

"Like always," smiled Maggie-Now.

The woman wrapped the half in a clean rag. "So it should stay warm for you," she said kindly.

Maggie-Now went to the dairy next door.

Three tubs of butter lying on the side faced the customers across the counter. The vats were labeled: *Good, Better* and *Best.*

"A half pound of the best sweet butter," said Maggie-Now. The man lifted the glass door and picked up the wooden paddle. "And all in one piece," she added. "No crumbs!"

He faced her, hands on hips. "No crumbs! No crumbs, she says! So I'm magic and can cut exact-tle one half pound! Sure! Well, look on bottom the tub. Look on all the pieces from people what don't want crumbs. Them," he said dramatically, "them pieces is my profits."

"My bread's getting cold," she said.

He put the wedge of butter on the scale. His hand trembled as he did so because he feared the worst. His fear was justified. The wedge weighed an ounce over the half pound. He hit the side of his head with the flat of his hand.

"My profit! My profit!" he cried out. "Now I must cut off my profit and throw it on the floor of the tub!"

"Oh, I'll take the whole thing," she said.

"Don't do me no favors," he said bitterly as he wrapped the butter.

She made the coffee very strong and heated a saucepan of milk and served it half coffee, half hot milk. She brought the still-warm bread to the table and stood before Claude holding it in her hands.

"Ceres!" he said.

"I guess you'll think it's funny—bread and

butter for dessert," she said.

"No, my little Chinee, I think it's a very nice idea."

"We always have it for Sunday dessert because it's better than any pie I could bake or cake I could buy."

He stood up. "It's wonderful, Margaret. Beautiful bread. Nice to look at and it smells so good. It's nice to the touch and will be nice to the taste. Like good wine, it appeals to all the senses except sound."

"Listen!" she said. She pressed her forefinger on the eggshell-thin but crisp crust. An inch of the crust collapsed into flakes with a sound like a small sigh.

"The clink of touched glasses that gives sound to good wine," he said.

"Can I have a piece now?" asked Denny.

She cut the bread. She watched while Claude broke off an edge and spread it thinly with butter.

"Let me do it for you," she said. She took his slice and spread the whole thing thickly with the good butter. "That way, it's dessert," she said. "Eat it all in one piece."

He took a bite. "Wonderful! Wonderful!" he said. "It deserves to be brought to the table under a glass dome like pheasants and mushrooms."

They're starting up that dumb talk again, thought Denny resentfully.

He decided to make a diversion. He folded his

buttered bread in half and defiantly plunged it into his cup of coffee and milk.

"Denny!" cried out Maggie-Now. "Where are your table manners?"

Claude put his hand on the boy's arm. "Thank you, Denny," he said. "You opened the way for me to do exactly the same thing." He dipped *his* bread into his coffee.

"What can I do with you, the both of you?" said Maggie-Now in pretended despair.

"Nothing. Just smile and put up with us."

She gave him her big smile. "You make everything seem so special," she told him.

"Ah, no, Margaret. *You* do. You're the one. You make the simple ordinary things of life seem good and new and wonderful. You put a shine on life."

Denny couldn't stand any more. "When you go," he said to Claude, "don't forget your package. It's on the lounge in the front room."

"Denny!" she said, horrified at the broad hint.

"What's the matter with me?" exclaimed Claude. "I forgot to give you the little present I got for you." He got up from the table. "Come on, Denny." To Maggie-Now, he said. "I hereby give notice that I'm not the type of man who helps with the dishes."

"And I give notice," she said, "that I can't stand a man fussing around my kitchen."

The package contained an Easter gift for Denny, a beautiful little kite made of paper-thin silk as transparent as a bubble, with a dragon design picked out in gold thread. The sticks were thin bamboo, lacquered black, and the tail was of jade-green and turquoise-blue strips of paper. Maggie-Now said it was too beautiful to fly and that it ought to be framed and hung on the wall. Of course Denny had to go right out and fly it.

Left alone in the house with Claude, Maggie-Now worried. Suppose her father came home and found her alone in the house with Claude! She suggested that they take a walk. But he begged to be allowed to sit and talk with her for a while.

He told her how much he'd enjoyed the dinner—how much it had meant to him that she'd let him share for a while a part of her family life. He spoke of Denny with fondness and understanding and seemed genuinely disappointed that her father hadn't been with them. After that, he fell silent. She stole a look at him and saw a muscle twitching in his cheek.

She thought: *He's trying to figure out a way to ask me something important.*

"Margaret," he said. "About religion."

"Yes?" There was a faint warning bell in her mind.

"The services this morning . . ."

"Yes? You mean the Mass?"

"The Mass, then. It was wonderfully beautiful with the pageantry and the chanting and the glorious Latin. A revealing experience to me. The stately progress of the ritual . . ."

"High Mass is always like that," she said, uncomfortable because he used words like "pageantry" and "chanting" and "ritual"—words that nice outsiders used when they spoke of a Mass.

"Do you understand it?" he asked.

"Not all of it."

"Aren't you curious about the things you don't understand?"

"Why, no. I believe. I don't have to understand."

"How can you believe without understanding?"

"Oh, I believe that my heart beats and that I breathe, but I don't understand a thing about how those things happen. Well, let me say it this way: I believe without understanding it—but I *know* that when the priest elevates the Host, the wine changes into the blood of Christ and the bread into His body."

"But you can't explain it."

"No. A convert might be able to explain it. They're the ones who understand every small thing about the Catholic religion. I don't know why."

"Do you know any converts?"

"No. Yes, I do. She never *said* she was a convert, but I *know* she is."

"How do you know?"

"By the way she talks."

"How does she talk?"

"Well, she lives down the block and

sometimes I walk home from church with her and this lady will tell me how she went to confession the night before and what penance she got and how she went to bed early so that she wouldn't forget and take a drink of water after midnight. Then she'll say she *took* communion. (I always say, I *received*.) And she'll talk a long time about how wonderful she feels after confession and communion."

"Don't you feel wonderful afterward?"

"I've been going to confession and communion ever since I was six; before I could read. It's . . . it's always been there—the feeling about it. I never think that I have to talk about my penance or my receiving."

"Perhaps she's more talkative than you, Margaret."

"Oh, I talk enough," acknowledged Maggie-Now. "It's just that we talk *different* about our faith."

"She may be different from you—the kind of woman who likes to analyze everything."

Maggie-Now thought that over. "No," she decided. "She only talks that way about the faith. Not about other things." She paused while she searched her mind for an illustration. "Like, well, she lives down the block and she washes her hair like I do; she sits in the yard on a nice day and lets the sun dry it and then she brushes it and braids it like I do. But all she says is, 'Well, I washed my hair today.' And I say, 'So did I.' And that's all. She doesn't tell me how much the soap costs and what time it was and how she felt and how her hair felt and how it's a good thing to wash your hair once a week. Because she's *used* to washing her hair—the way *I'm* used to being a Catholic.''

"Margaret, have you ever thought what it would be like to have another religion? A simple one where the minister doesn't wear robes, and lives like other men with a wife and children, and understands people's problems because he has the same problems, and who conducts the service in clear English and everything is clear and understandable?''

"Why, no. I've never thought about how it would be to have a different faith.''

"Why not?''

"Well, I was born white. I never sit around and think how it would be if I had been born a colored person. I'm a woman. I never think about how it would be to be a man.''

"You take your religion for granted, then.''

"I guess I can't explain. I can only *know*.''

"Tell me this, Margaret. No, don't tell me if you don't want to.''

"I don't mind. What?''

"Understand: I'm not asking you all these questions because I'm curious but because I'm very interested.''

"Oh, that's all right,'' she said.

"Don't you think having to make confession is an invasion of privacy?''

"Oh, no,'' she said with a half laugh.

"Everybody has sins. Mine are no different from other people's. When Father Flynn asks me exactly how many times I told a lie in the week, I never think it's . . . what did you call it?"

"Invasion of your privacy."

"No. I never think that. He's supposed to ask."

"Now, Margaret, you're a Catholic."

"I know." She smiled.

"Now that's all right for you. But if you had a child, maybe he wouldn't want to be a Catholic. Don't you think he ought to be allowed to choose his own religion when he's old enough?"

She was so astonished for a moment that she couldn't answer. Then she said: "Before a child is born, is it allowed to decide whether it will be a boy or a girl? When it wants its first nourishment do you let it starve until it's old enough to decide whether it wants milk or beer? Do you keep him without a name until he's old enough to pick out one for himself? When he's six years old do you let him decide whether he wants to go to school or not? No. You give him milk, you give him a name, you send him to school and you give him a faith."

"I see." He got up and walked to the window and stood there looking out.

"Couldn't we talk about something else?" she asked timidly.

"Just one thing more, Margaret, and then we'll never talk about it again as long as we both shall live." He asked the question very carefully. "If you were in love with a Protestant, would you give up your religion to marry him?"

"I wouldn't have to. We could . . . I mean, a person could marry a Protestant with a Catholic ceremony. But he'd have to say that he wouldn't interfere with her religion and that their children would be brought up in the Catholic faith."

"But the next morning she'd expect him to go see the priest and be converted."

"Oh, no," she said quickly. "It's not as easy as that. It takes a long time. You have to have the faith."

"How do you mean?"

"I don't know the words to explain it. If you have it, you just *know* it."

"Margaret, look at me." She got up and went to him and looked clearly and truly into his eyes. "Do you love me?"

"Yes," she said simply.

"Could you, if we married, take my religion and bring up our children in my religion? Could you?" She shook her head dumbly. "Couldn't you love me enough to do that?"

"I could want to," she said, "and I could say I would and mean it when I said it. And I could try very hard. But inside, I couldn't change."

"Like you couldn't change into a Negro or change into a man."

"You wouldn't like me, would you," she asked beseechingly, "if I was any other way than the way I am?"

"I don't suppose I would," he said in an offhand way.

She knew it was all over. She had a feeling of numbness.

"Would you like some coffee?" she asked timidly.

"No, thank you." His tone was brusque.

They talked a little while longer about the war and rising prices and the coming of prohibition, and his language was academic and strained the way it was when he spoke to strangers.

After a while, he thanked her politely for the nice dinner and expressed regret that he hadn't met her father. He said good-by and left without making arrangements for another meeting. She stood at the window and watched him until he was out of sight. Only then did she notice that he had forgotten his book. It was lying on the lounge. She picked it up. It was *The Book of Everything*. She opened it. On the flyleaf he had written:

To Margaret, with love, Claude.

She cried, then.

Chapter Twenty-Eight

SHE knew he wouldn't come back. Yet, she thought that if she admitted the fact and suffered over it she would, paradoxically, be rewarded by his return. So she bathed and dressed carefully each afternoon, and, after supper, she sat at the window and waited. Pat often sat with her and spoke enthusiastically of Mrs. O'Crawley, Mick Mack's landlady, who was trim and tidy and forty-two and owned property. He was lyrical about the Easter dinner she'd served: baked ham with pineapple slices and candied sweet potatoes and creamed onions and peach shortcake.

"All home-cooked, you understand," he said. "No bakery stuff and nothing out of a can. And why can't we have candied sweet potatoes sometime?"

Maggie-Now said yes, and no, and that's nice, not really listening to him but making the sounds of interest and companionship. Evidently, Denny hadn't told him that Claude had been there for

Easter dinner, for Pat made no comment.

Although Maggie-Now had not forbidden Denny to tell of Claude's visit, he probably found it expedient to say nothing on account of the kite. It was broken the next day and Denny said his father had broken it, but under pressure Denny admitted that he himself had broken it.

"Why did you lie, then?" she asked.

"Because I didn't want to get scolded."

"Oh, Denny," she sighed, "you mustn't lie. If it was broken by accident, I'd feel sorry along with you, but if you broke it on purpose, you deserve a scolding and should be man enough to take it."

She worried a little bit about Denny. He was inclined to take the easy way out of things. He never faced up to any of his small problems; he never made a protest when he was wronged and he was learning that a quick lie was the easiest way out of a tight spot.

Maybe he needs more love and more understanding, she thought. *I love him and I try to understand him. But maybe there are some things that only a man can understand about a boy. He can't look to Papa for much. Papa treats him like somebody that's visiting here. But Claude, now . . .*

Yes, Claude.

The weeks passed and no word from him. She wrote a careful little letter, thanking him for *The Book of Everything,* and addressed it to the Y.M.C.A. and timidly wrote a small *Please*

Forward on the envelope. It came back stamped *Address Unknown.*

She tried to convince herself that he had enlisted or been drafted. (She knew he had been anxious to get into the war.) And maybe he had been shipped overseas right away and now was someplace where he couldn't write to her. But in her heart she knew that he'd find a way to get in touch with her if he wanted to.

The hours of her knowing him, five evenings and two afternoons, had changed her whole life. She was no longer content to be her father's housekeeper and her brother's mother. She'd had a glimpse of another way of life; a full, rich, woman's life. She had known for a bit of time the wonder of unspoken understanding with another soul, the delight of perfect companionship and the happiness of exchanging thoughts (and no thought had been too trivial or silly to exchange) with a sympathetic being. And woven throughout all this had been the golden anticipation of physical love to come.

He seemed to like everything about me, she told herself, *not enough to want me for all of his life. He thought my religion was beautiful at first, but not beautiful enough to let it be. Should I have gone against it for him? Love is so scarce and so hard to find, especially the love I have for him. Wouldn't it have been better to give up my church for the sake of love, marriage and children? After all, Protestants are Christians, too. I told him I couldn't do it. But if I had tried—tried hard! Maybe . . .*

She sighed because now she had another sin to confess to Father Flynn—the sin of *thinking* of giving up her faith.

Now Father Flynn will know, she thought. *And he won't like him. Aunt Lottie doesn't like him; Mr. Van Clees doesn't like him. And Papa. He doesn't know what Claude's religion is and he never spoke to him but he doesn't like him anyhow.*

If they only knew him the way I know him, they would love him too.

She needed so much to have someone to talk to—some understanding woman. *Oh, if Mama were only still here,* she grieved. *She would understand how it is with me. And she'd say something to make me feel better.*

About this time, she had a card from Lottie, asking why she'd stayed away so long and saying that Mama was failing and asked for her, Maggie-Now, a lot.

Maggie-Now brought a jar of jellied chicken broth over for Lottie's mother. Lottie was touched and greeted Maggie-Now tenderly. She asked about Claude. Maggie-Now told her that Claude was gone and had not written. Lottie's face showed satisfaction at the news and concern for Maggie-Now's sadness.

"It's all for the best, Maggie-Now, dear," said Lottie.

"Not the best for me," said Maggie-Now. "But I guess it couldn't be. He was a

Protestant. . . ."

"Oh, I had nothing against his religion," said Lottie quickly. "I just thought he wasn't good enough for you."

"But you said that as my godmother you couldn't let me marry a Protestant."

"I thought it over after. Sure you could, if he got converted. And sometimes converts are more religious than those born in the faith."

"I don't think he'd ever have turned."

"He would if you went about it right. Like some night, if you was alone with him, all you'd have to do is put your arms around him and kiss him hard. *You* know. And you could ask him while he was under the influence if he'd turn for you. And he would."

"No, he's not that kind. Anyhow, I wouldn't want to trick anybody. . . . Aunt Lottie, tell me. Would you have married Uncle Timmy if he hadn't been a Catholic?"

"Oh, that reminds me of something funny," said Lottie. "When Timmy and me was keeping company, he knew I was a Catholic but I didn't know what he was. I thought he *must* be—being's he was Irish and a cop—but I wasn't sure and I didn't like to ask. So I asked Mama, *you* know, just to find out how she felt about it. I said, 'Mama, should I marry Timmy even if he ain't Catholic?' And you know what Mama said?"

"What did she say?"

"She said I shouldn't let religion interfere with

love, being's I was thirty years old already. So Timmy gave me the ring and we set the day. So I asked him what church he wanted to be married in and he said St. Thomas-iss. And I said right out, 'That's a Catholic church,' and he said, 'Sure,' So I came out with it. I said:

" 'Are you a Catholic?'

" 'Sure,' he said.

"So I got all choked up and started to cry and I said: 'Oh, Timmy, why didn't you tell me before?' You know what he said?"

"No."

"He said, 'You never asked me.' " She smiled a tender smile of memory and said fondly: "That Timmy!"

"But would you have married him if he *wasn't* a Catholic?"

"But I told you he *was.*"

"But for the sake of argument . . ."

"No argument. He *was.*"

"But your mother was willing to let you marry a Protestant."

"Oh, she was just talking."

Maggie-Now sighed. *She doesn't even know what I'm talking about,* thought Maggie-Now.

But Lottie knew. "That's too bad that you had to fall in love with him," she said.

"I know," said Maggie-Now.

"How long did you know him. Maggie-Now?"

"Just a week, Aunt Lottie."

"Only a week? You'll forget him."

"If I only could!"

"Don't worry. You will in time."

"Do you *really* think so, Aunt Lottie?"

"No, I don't. That's just something to say because there's nothing else to say."

Chapter Twenty-Nine

APRIL went into May and the lilac bush in Father Flynn's yard came into bloom and it was Decoration Day again. Then it was June. And all the days of that spring, Maggie-Now sat by the window each evening after supper, and waited. But he never came by. She stood at the window watching for the letter carrier, but there was never a letter from Claude.

She lived on hope; persuaded herself that he was in the army and overseas in a trench and unable to get a letter out. As the weeks passed, she assured herself that there had been no differences between them; that the disscussion of religion had been merely a friendly debate and she had been wrong to get so serious about the whole thing.

I shouldn't have said that about the woman, the convert and about her hair washing. Maybe he was thinking of becoming a convert and he thought I made fun of converts. And that silly talk about asking a baby whether he wanted beer or milk. Men don't like women to be too serious but they don't like them to be silly either.

She lived on hope and became a little thin and drawn-looking on this diet. She took little pleasure in shopping for and preparing food and less in eating it. She had to work very hard (for instance, painting and papering the upstairs apartment after the Heahlys moved out) so she'd be tired enough to sleep at night.

She stopped in at the church every other day or so and lit a candle at the altar of the Blessed Mother, beseeching her to intercede with her Son to keep Claude safe wherever he was.

She no longer enjoyed conversations with the storekeepers. It wasn't enough for one to sell a bag of salt. He had to explain how necessary salt was. (One had said: "If you have nothing but salt, bread and water, still you can live.") In a dim, inarticulate way, she had realized that the selling of stuff was the all of most storekeepers' lives and they had to round out their lives by giving background and interest to everything they sold. Before Claude left, she had enjoyed their home-made philosophy, but now it irritated her.

Talk, talk, talk, she thought. *All about nothing. What do I care? I don't want to know how it is with them and I don't want anybody to know how it is with me.*

But they knew; more than she thought they did. Van Clees knew. He had seen her pass his store arm in arm with Claude and had

308

noticed the way they looked at each other when they spoke. When she came into the store, he sometimes adroitly inserted Claude's name into the conversation to see her expression.

"And your friend Mr. Bassett, how does he do?"

Her face fell into sad lines as she said: "I never hear from him. He's in the war, I guess."

"Ah, so?" he said. He waited, hoping she would confide in him. But she didn't.

And so he left her, he thought. *And she's in love with him and he's a no-good with a fancy name what smokes cigarettes. She is a good girl and she should find some good man to take care of her. But she would not know how to let anybody take care of her because she is so that she must take care of others and she wants that man because she wants to take care of him like he was a baby.*

"Gott damn!" he said aloud. Interested in analyzing Maggie-Now, he had ruined a cigar in the making.

Her father knew how it was with her; that is, he knew according to his way. *So she lost the man what she thinks she loves. I lost the girl what I knew I loved. I got over it. I didn't die. She'll get over it and she won't die. She'll meet another man someday and forget that first one.*

Did you forget? he asked himself.

What has that got to do with it? he answered himself. *I'm stubborn and she ain't.*

Father Flynn knew how it was with Maggie-

Now. In the dark confessional, she had told her sins to him; the sin of carnal pleasure she'd known when a man pressed her arm against his side; the sin of almost hating her father; defying him and lying to him because he was against her happiness; the sin of thinking for a second of giving up her faith. She had confessed and had done penance.

Theoretically, a sinner kneeling in the dark confessional was anonymous, only a soul seeking expiation of sin. But Father Flynn knew the timbre of her voice; the clean smell of soap and water and starched clothes that he associated with her. He knew she suffered. He knew she needed comfort.

He felt, however, that he could not approach her and say in effect: "Considering the confessions you've made to me in recent weeks . . ." No. But he waited for her to come to him for guidance.

Weeks passed. Finally Father Flynn requested Maggie-Now to come to the parish house. Father Flynn was in his garden when Maggie-Now called, and Mrs. Harrigan, his aged and bitter housekeeper, took her through the house into the yard.

Maggie-Now admired the lilac bush. The only other growing thing in the "garden" was a piece of ivy climbing the board fence.

"That's from a rooted slip your mother gave me many years ago," he told Maggie-Now. "I had hoped it would cover the whole fence in time but it grows slowly."

"You'd get more ivy and quicker if you made slips."

She explained. He went into the house for a paring knife and they cut off a dozen shoots and Maggie-Now said she'd take them home and keep them in water and when they formed roots she'd plant them back in his yard. He seemed pleased. Mrs. Harrigan came out with two glasses of iced tea on a tray.

"Because it's a warm day," explained the priest.

They sat on a castoff park bench half under the lilac bush. Father Flynn had salvaged it from the junk pile, repaired it and given it a fresh coat of green paint each spring. Maggie-Now said it was a very nice bench. Father Flynn agreed but added that it was rather uncomfortable. They sipped the tea.

"Tell me, Margaret," he said, "how are things with you?"

"Fine," she said.

"What about your future?"

She looked startled. "I'd like to get a job but I have to wait until fall, when Denny goes back to school."

"Life goes on, Margaret. Perhaps you think there is little of interest in life for you now. That is wrong. You are needed by more than one person in the world, you know."

He waited, giving her an opportunity to speak of her unhappiness. She said, "That's all right,

Father," meaning: Do not trouble yourself about me.

"I asked you here, Margaret, because I need your help."

"Yes, Father."

"I've fixed up the basement of the church as a sort of recreation room. Someone was kind enough to donate a pianola, and Mr. Rummel, the undertaker, donated a dozen folding chairs. I thought we could have Thursday-night socials. So many of our boys are going into the services, and a little send-off party . . . Young people getting together to sing—talk. Some modest refreshment. I want you to take charge of this for me," he said.

"I will be pleased to," she answered.

When they had finished the tea, he took the two wedges of squeezed lemon and buried them at the base of the lilac bush. He knelt in the dirt and gestured with his trowel.

"That's to make the soil acid. I heard lilacs like an acid soil. But I bury my breakfast eggshells here, too. Just in case they like a calcium soil." He got up and brushed the soil from his knees. "Ah, Margaret," he said, "I had hoped you'd talk to me."

She knew he meant talk about Claude and her unhappiness. "I know," she said. "But there's nothing to talk about . . . now."

Maggie-Now canvassed the neighborhood and found three unmarried Catholic girls who said they'd be tickled to death to do their bit for their country by entertaining young men about to be drafted. By agreement, the girls were at the place first in order to welcome the young men.

The church basement was warm, tidy and softly lighted. Church supplies were stored on shelves: tins of French incense, grosses of beeswax votive candles; pads of marriage certificates and birth certificates. There was a brand-new iron for baking communion wafers.

(Nuns from a nearby convent baked the communion wafers and delivered them each Saturday. But at the time of the great blizzard the nuns hadn't been able to get through the drifts and Father Flynn had had to use stale wafers for the few communicants who fought their way to Mass. He had, after that, obtained the iron and the recipe so that in case of another blizzard he could bake the wafers himself.)

There were many garden implements: spade, hoe, shovel and rake—too many for one lilac bush, thought Maggie-Now critically—and, looking lost and out of place, a pair of skis standing in the corner.

The four young men came together—to give each other nerve, one of them explained. The girls tittered. They introduced themselves. One of the young men was the son of Pheid, the plumber. He was introduced as Son Pheid.

"Call me And Son for short," he said.

This called for some merriment which the young people prolonged as long as possible because they didn't know what to do next. Father Flynn heard the laughter in his house next to the church, and was pleased. *It keeps them off the street,* thought the kindly priest. (Although they were all too old to hang out on the streets now.)

Father Flynn was in a quandary. If he went over to the basement to greet them, he might cast a pall over the evening. If he didn't go, they might think he wasn't interested, or worse, might feel they were without supervision and free to carouse.

He went over, said good evening, announced that coffee and doughnuts would be served at nine o'clock, gravely instructed everyone to have a good time, and left.

The donor of the pianola had donated but one roll with it: "The Oceana Roll." They played it four times because each feller wanted a turn at pumping the piano. They were sick of that song and were at a loss about what to do next when one of the boys, named Charlie, which they pronounced Cholly, said he could play by ear.

"Give us a tune, Cholly. Give us a tune," they urged.

He was willing. "They laughed at me when I sat down to play," he said. Everybody thought that was a very comical remark.

He threw the lever that changed the pianola into a piano. He sounded a few mellow chords and played the chorus of "When You Were Sweet Sixteen." When he played the chords preliminary to going into the verse, the other three fellers put their heads together and sang in fairly close harmony.

And even though we're drifting down life's
   stream apart,
Your face I still can see in dream's domain.

The tender little song put everybody in a misty mood. After it had been repeated several times, the boys urged the girls to sing. They sang "I Wonder Who's Kissing Her Now." They refused to be coaxed into an encore and the party started to die away.

Cholly, the piano player, who had evolved into the social leader of the evening, said: "What's the idear standing around like a bunch of deadheads? Let's get some life in the party." He struck up the ragtime rhythm tune of the day: "Everybody's Doing It!"

"Sh-h-h!" hissed the girls in horror.

"Listen, Cholly," said Son Pheid, "don't you think that tune's a little out of place here with the church right upstairs?"

"Just as you say," said Cholly agreeably. "How about a little reminiscing, then?" All agreed that that would be grand.

He played a medley of sentimental songs, old and new, and the girls stood in a loose semicircle with their arms about each other's waists and swayed in time to the music and hummed or sang the tunes, and the boys stood with their heads touching and sounded "bum, bum," from time to time for accent, and finally Cholly went into "There's Egypt in Your Dreamy Eyes," and Maggie-Now sang the song in her heart:

And you stole my heart, with your cunning art . . .

She closed her eyes and swayed and hummed and thought of Claude. She was filled with a delicious sadness and the sadness pleased her and she thought it was almost better than being happy. When she opened her eyes, she saw that Son Pheid was staring at her.

Why, that's the girl, he was remembering, *who came over to the shop that night with that feller. . . .*

Maggie-Now pretended he was Claude and gave Son Pheid a big smile. He smiled back and one girl whispered to another: "Oh-oh!"

After a while, Cholly ran out of reminiscing and they pumped out "The Oceana Roll" again. At nine, there was a tactful tap at the door. Father Flynn gave Maggie-Now a tray on which were mugs of coffee and a plate of doughnuts. He handed it over as though it were contraband and backed away into the night.

They stood around nibbling daintily on the doughnuts and sipping the coffee until Cholly said: "Look, folks, I'm just an ordinary, everyday slob with no manners so I'm going to dunk my sinker."

That broke the ice. Everybody laughed and dunked and agreed that that was the only way to eat a doughnut.

One of the girls, bolder than the others, said: "Cholly, you're a regular card."

"My mother thanks you," said Cholly. "My father thanks you . . ."

"He's a whole *deck,*" said Son Pheid in an aside to Maggie-Now. She smiled at him and he smiled back.

They washed the mugs and the plate in the washtub. There was no towel to dry the dishes so Son Pheid gave up his clean handkerchief, which was carefully planted in his breast pocket and folded into a miniature three-picket fence, to do the job. Maggie-Now said, "Who wants to take the tray back to the priest's house?" and Son Pheid said he would. But, he said, he didn't know the way and Miss Moore would have to go with him. The other fellers winked at each other and the girls giggled.

The two hurried across the yard, talking in whispers. Since the house was dark, they decided to leave tray and dishes on the back stoop. Maggie-Now whispered that they ought to say thanks, at least. Son Pheid took one of his printed cards from his pocket: *Pheid & Son. Plumbers. Day & Night,* and wrote "Thanks" on the back of it while Maggie-Now held a lighted match. He put the card on the tray.

When they got back, the other fellers leered and said: "Ah-*hah!*" in a certain way and

Cholly said: "We thought you two went to China."

"Go fly a kite," said Son Pheid in an exaggerated, bored tone of voice.

They folded the undertaker's chairs and stacked them against the wall. Maggie-Now took the key from her pocketbook to lock the door. As a matter of course, Son Pheid took the key from her, locked the door, and, as he returned the key, he asked could he walk her home. She said he could.

They grouped on the sidewalk to make their farewells. All agreed they had had a wonderful time and all the girls thanked Cholly for his wonderful piano playing.

"Any time," said Cholly graciously. "And listen," he went on, "being's that us fellers just been drafted . . ."

"Maybe you were drafted," said Son Pheid, "but I was selected."

"Greetings!" said one of the other fellers and the girls laughed.

"Anyways," continued Cholly, "being's we might get killed or something, it's only right that we get kissed good-by."

Well, what could good, patriotic girls do in a situation like that? They did it. Each boy received a kiss on the cheek from each girl. Now it happened that Father Flynn was sitting at the window in his dark living room and telling his beads. He had heard the talk and seen the boys getting kissed. He worried.

Was I too liberal, he asked himself, *leaving them alone in the cellar for two hours?*

Walking home, Son Pheid said: "I expect to get sent to Camp Upton any day now. I'd like to take in a good show before I leave. Would you go with me, providing I can get tickets for Saturday night?"

"Why I would love to, Mr. Pheid," she said.

"Look," he blurted out. "It's not my fault and I can't help it, but everybody calls me Sonny."

She laughed and said: "And they call me Maggie-Now and I can't help it either."

"So long for a while, Maggie-Now."

"So long, Sonny."

He kissed her and, to her surprise, she liked it.

After the show he asked her if she'd care for some chop suey. She thought of Claude and felt a pang. She said she didn't care for chop suey, so they had butter cakes and coffee at Child's. Going home on the B.M.T., he told her he had been going with a girl but she liked a feller who could spend a lot of money on her, and the way it was with him, he was partners with his father and he got room and board and pocket money, but all the profits went back in the business. And Sonny said he thought that was all right seeing that he would get the business after his father died, but the girl found another feller who had more money to spend on her and that was that, he said.

"Are you going with anyone?" he asked.

"Not any more," she said.

"We're both in the clear, then," he said.

He told her he was going to camp Tuesday and he had to spend Monday night with his family but couldn't they do something together on Sunday? She told him she had to go and see her godmother but it would be a short visit. He suggested picking her up there and they could have a soda or something. Arrangements were made. She received his good-night kiss, which she had looked forward to, with a sensation of pleasure.

Lottie, her conscience bothering her a little because she had been so outspoken in her dislike of Claude, treated Sonny most cordially and insisted that he stay a while. She made him sit in Timmy's chair.

He sat down, leaned back and looked around. "My, it's nice here, isn't it, Maggie-Now?"

"I love this room," said Maggie-Now.

"Timmy always liked it so," said Lottie.

"Your son?" he asked.

"My husband. He passed away some years ago."

"God rest his soul," said Sonny.

"I'll show you his picture."

The album tinkled out its little tune when she opened it. "Say! Do that again," he said. She opened and closed it several times. "That's a dandy picture album."

"Timmy gave it to me on our anniversary.

Here's a picture of the two of us taken just before we was married.''

He looked at the picture and looked at her. "You haven't changed," he said. An old-rose flush came to her faded cheeks. She showed him a picture of Tim in his uniform. "Your husband must have been quite a man," he said.

"Oh, he was! Didn't Maggie-Now tell you about my Timmy?"

"I haven't know Mr. Pheid very long," said Maggie-Now. Sonny looked around the room.

"Looking for an ashtray?" asked Lottie.

"I'm looking for this Mister Pheid."

Maggie-Now laughed. "I mean Sonny," she said.

"Well, *I'll* tell you about Timmy," said Lottie.

To Maggie-Now, the story seemed interminable. She had heard it a hundred times, it seemed. Also she was a little annoyed with Lottie, who had been so cool toward Claude and now was so warm toward Sonny.

Eventually, Lottie concluded her story with the inevitable: "And we was sweethearts until the end."

Sonny was moved by the story. "You were a lucky woman, Mrs. Shawn," he said.

"Don't I know it!"

He touched her hand briefly and said: "And he was a very lucky man."

Quick tears came to Lottie's tired eyes. She rubbed the tears out with her fingers. "Thank you, Sonny." she said. She turned to Maggie-Now. "Come in the kitchen with me. I want to show you something. Excuse us?" she asked Sonny.

"Certainly." He didn't get up. He was looking through the album.

In the kitchen, Lottie whispered: "Where'd you meet him?"

"Church social. But I knew who he was, though. He and his father have a plumbing shop together."

"Will he get the business when his father dies?"

"I guess so."

"He's just the right man for you, Maggie-Now."

Maggie-Now thought of Claude and sighed.

"You're still thinking of that other one, ain't you?"

"Always," said Maggie-Now.

"Listen. He was all right for one springtime of your life—the way he looked at you and the things he must-a said to you. He gave you something nice to remember from time to time as you grow old. And that's all he should be: a memory.

"But for the long haul . . . marriage, a home, children, being supported . . . someone to get old with, Sonny's the one."

"What makes you think he'd want me?"

"He does. Or he will. Don't be foolish. Hang on to him."

When they got back into the living room, Sonny was standing at the mantelpiece. He grinned and said: "Well, ladies, will I do?"

Maggie-Now couldn't help but laugh. But she was embarrassed when Lottie went to him, put her hands on his arms, looked up at him and said: "You'll do."

Maybe Sonny was embarrassed, too. He looked away from Maggie-Now and pointed to the china pug dog on the mantelpiece. "I was looking at this," he said. "Can I see it?" (He meant, could he pick it up.)

"Sure. Go 'head," said Lottie.

He examined it admiringly. "Say, it's a little dandy," he said. "Just a little dandy."

"My Timmy give it to me for a anniversary present. He loved it, too. He used to stand there, just like you, and hold it and say: 'Look at the little buggers getting theirs!' "

Sonny let out a roar of laughter. "Sh!" said Lottie. "Mama's sleeping."

But Mama had awakened. She called out querulously from the bedroom: "Timmy? That you, Timmy?"

"It's all right, Mama," called out Lottie. There was a little silence. The old lady mumbled and evidently went back to sleep.

With awed voice, Lottie said to Maggie-Now, "Mama thought it was Timmy laughing." She stared at Sonny. "Yes," she said, "come to think of it, in many ways, he reminds me of Timmy."

With a little shock, Maggie-Now told herself: *Yes. He does! But how? Why?* She wondered. *He doesn't look like Uncle Timmy.*

"Anyhow," Lottie went on, "when Maggie-Now gets married, I'm going to give her that little dog for a wedding present."

"I better be careful then, not to break it." He replaced it carefully on the mantelpiece.

Sonny took Maggie-Now home. "I'd ask you in," she said, "only . . ."

"I know how it is," he said. "My pop's the same. My sister used to go with Cholly. *You* know, the piano player? She couldn't bring him in the house. Pop always passed some remark. He had nothing against Cholly, but he passed these remarks. She always had to meet Cholly on the corner."

In a way, thought Maggie-Now, *it's a relief to be with someone of your own kind, who knows how things are and who doesn't keep saying he'd like to meet your father.*

"Look, Maggie-Now," he said, "if I write to you, will you write back?"

"I'd be so glad to, Sonny."

"Good-by, then." He put his arms about her tightly and kissed her urgently.

"Don't," she murmured.

"Just a long good-by kiss, Maggie-Now?"

"Please don't," she said.

"It wouldn't go further than that. I'm not that kind of a guy."

"I know, Sonny."

She submitted to the embrace, wishing Sonny were Claude and unhappy because she felt that she was disloyal to the one she loved and would always love, even though she never saw him again.

Chapter Thirty

HE wrote once a week. His first letter was a detailed account of the weather of Camp Upton. Her answer was a detailed account of the weather of Brooklyn. In his next letter he gave her a detailed account of the meals served at camp. She wrote back how dear everything was getting and how, now, three people could hardly eat on a dollar a day.

Next he wrote, asking her for a picture of herself. *All the fellows here have pictures to hang up. . . .* She went down to Batterman's and had a cabinet picture made of herself. She thought it was a good picture. She inscribed it: "To Sonny, from Margaret Rose." (She thought the fellers might laugh if she wrote "Maggie-Now.") A few weeks later, he sent her a snapshot of himself in his lima-bean pants and rolled puttees and campaign hat straight over his eyes and cradling his rifle in his arms. He was looking straight into the camera. He looked like exactly what he was: a good, honest, straightforward, ordinary boy. She showed Lottie the snapshot when she visited her.

"His face is a open book," said Lottie.

Yes, thought Maggie-Now, *and his life is an open book.*

She knew all about him: she knew his father, she knew what their business was, what their background was. She knew where he lived and where he had come from. She knew of his sister and his brothers and the girl he used to go with. She knew he had graduated from Boys' High and that he was a Catholic.

She knew nothing about Claude.

Yet . . .

Sonny wrote, after he'd been in the army for two months, that his next letter might come from a different address.

> I can't tell you anymore than that, but if I come back all in one piece, will you be my girl?

She was touched. *Be my* girl was tantamount to saying: *Become engaged to me and we'll marry . . .*

She found it hard writing an answering letter. She was a fairly direct person and it was always easier to say yes or no rather than maybe. But now she couldn't say yes, and she didn't want to say no.

> Any girl would be proud to be your girl,

she wrote. (But she couldn't write: *I'll be proud to be your girl.*)

I'll see,

she wrote, meaning she'd think it over. (She couldn't write: *I've made up my mind.*)
His answer came three weeks later.

I'm tickled to death you didn't say no. I'll wait and I'll keep my fingers crossed.

The letter came from overseas.
She looked forward to getting Sonny's letters and she enjoyed answering them. He kept pressing her for a decision.

. . . we'll be moving up soon and it would mean a lot to me if I knew . . . [And] P.S. If you run into Father Flynn, tell him our chaplain, Father Newsome, said he went to college with him and I forgot to say, don't worry if you don't hear from me in some time.

She started to worry immediately. As soon as she'd finished reading the letter, she went to church and lit a candle and prayed for his safety. She saw Father Flynn outside the church and told him about the chaplain.
A longing, faraway look came to Father Flynn's face as he said: "Oh, yes. Freddy! The

best end the school ever had. It seems so long ago."

He told her how pleased he was with the Thursday-night socials in the church basement. Sometimes there were as many as twenty young people attending. He told her he had ten new player rolls for the pianola.

"I went from door to door begging for rolls old and new," he said.

"But, Father, we were going to appoint a committee to go out and get donations. . . ."

"I couldn't wait that long. I got so sick and tired of hearing 'The Oceana Roll.' " He paused. "I've heard there was some criticism about using the church basement for the socials. I've heard that some of our parishioners are against them."

"There are always a few people against things," she said. "But *I* heard that people think they're a good thing. They bring young people together."

He looked at the letter in her hand. "Yes, they do, don't they, Margaret?" There was a twinkle in his eye. He put two fingers on the letter as though blessing the sender. "He's a good boy, Margaret."

"Yes, he is, Father. But . . ."

He remembered the way she had looked at Claude that Easter morning when they came out of the church.

"He is a good man," he said firmly. "Pray to our Holy Mother for guidance."

"Yes, Father."

She prayed long and hard and sincerely and then wrote to Sonny. She wrote: *Maybe* . . .

It was some weeks before she got his answer.

Chapter Thirty-One

WAR is a terrible thing, people kept telling each other, but just the same, they admitted, it sure made things exciting for the people at home. There was work for all and salaries were high and luxuries were available to all. The conservative haberdashery on Grand Street was forced to stock men's silk shirts for the first time in its long history. Workmen bought them.

Before the war, women had worked as factory hands, store clerks, waitresses, telephone operators, typists, cashiers, housemaids and so forth. Those with more specialized training could put their names on waiting lists for teachers, librarians, nurses, private secretaries, and wait around for an opening.

Now, most all jobs were open to them. They worked as trolley-car conductors, operated elevators, drew beer, worked milk delivery routes, replaced men in the post offices, wore cute uniforms and worked down at the Brooklyn Navy Yard and were called yeomanettes. Men stopped giving them their seats in the subways.

They wore pants. Since pants made expressly for women were not available, they wore their brothers' pants. They discarded high shoes and wore oxfords with spats. They invaded barbershops and had their hair cut short. They stopped pinching their cheeks to make them red. They used rouge. They took to smoking cigarettes. Like men, they argued over politics. The time was drawing near when they'd be allowed to go to the polls to vote.

In short, they were freed at last and they had a hell of a time.

The war was good for real estate, too. The "Rooms for Rent" signs disappeared from the windows and prospective tenants gave landlords a "bonus" for first chance on a vacant flat. People who lived in hall bedrooms now could afford a flat; flat renters moved to apartments and apartment dwellers moved to little houses out on the Island that they could buy for so little down and so much time to pay, small additional charge for built-in breakfast nooks.

Landlady Maggie-Now Moore profited. The contentious Heahlys had moved away, owing thirty dollars back rent, leaving a broken-back chair and a gentleman roomer in the hall bedroom. Maggie-Now had believed the woman's story that the man was a brother-in-law who was "staying" with them for a while because his wife had just "passed away."

The gentleman didn't move away with the

Heahlys because he had paid two months' advance rent on the hall room. No, he wasn't a relative of theirs, he told Maggie-Now, but it was true that his wife had died recently. She left a two-year-old son, he said, who had been placed in a "home," and he paid the home five dollars a week, until he remarried. Yes, there was a widow, he confided to Maggie-Now; they'd marry after the decent interval of a year from his wife's death. He was marrying again so his child could have a home and mother.

Oh, if he'd only let me keep the baby here, instead of that place, until he married. I'd be so happy to have that baby, she thought.

I wish I had the nerve, he thought, *to ask her to board the boy for five dollars a week. I could have him every night and she's so nice. . . .*

But he didn't ask and she didn't ask.

He continued renting the room for ten dollars a month and Maggie-Now rented the rest of the place to an eager family who paid twenty-five dollars a month rent for it. Now she collected thirty-five dollars a month rent, instead of fifteen. Taxes remained the same and the surplus in the bank account grew.

She used some of the money for herself. She bought a sheer georgette crepe blouse and a lacy camisole to show through and a tight skirt and high-heeled slippers. She wore silk stockings now, instead of lisle.

She still ran the Thursday-night church socials. She was popular with the boys—someone always

333

walked her home. The girls liked her, too. Some of the girls had their hair bobbed. They urged Maggie-Now to have hers cut.

"Why don't you get a Castle clip, Maggie?" they urged her.

In her mind, she heard Claude say: *The classic simplicity of your hair style* . . .

"You'd look like Irene Castle, wouldn't she, girls, with those high cheekbones and all?"

Said Gina Pheid, Sonny's sister, who took almost a relative's interest in Maggie-Now: "You could be a model with your face."

"It's only a face," said Maggie-Now.

Little Chinee. She remembered his voice. Remembering still made her feel a little sad but it didn't hurt much any more.

She mentioned getting her hair cut to Lottie.

"Don't," said Lottie, horrified. "Don't cut your hair off."

"Why not, Aunt Lottie? All the girls are doing it. It would be easier to manage."

"Listen, if a woman ain't got hair, what *has* she got?" asked Lottie.

Maggie-Now decided against bobbing it.

Pat settled into the routine of taking his Sunday dinners at Mrs. O'Crawley's boardinghouse. She had three regular men who roomed and boarded there and a few transients like Pat. She had been married and widowed twice. Her first husband left a thousand dollars in insurance. She never did get around to telling her second husband

334

about that. Her second husband died and left her two thousand dollars in insurance and the narrow house.

She converted the basement dining room into a millinery shop. (She made all the hats she sold.) She took in three somewhat elderly men as boarders. They lived upstairs. She had no children, no relatives. When she started the venture, her friends advised her to take in women boarders; they said "people would talk" if she took in men. She said, "Let them." She took in the men. She didn't want women boarders because she said they washed their pants in the sink and asked for hot tea in the middle of the night when they had cramps.

She cast an eye on Pat. He was fairly young, worked for the city. His widow would get a pension when he died. That was almost as good as insurance.

Pat cast an eye on her real estate. He asked her if the house was hers, free and clear, and she asked him, coyly, wouldn't he like to know! She didn't tell him, though.

Pat took an interest in her house. He asked Mick Mack how much he paid for room and board and he multiplied that by three and thought, thirty dollars a week wasn't a bad income plus what she got from making and selling hats. Although a lazy man, he went to the trouble of doing some odd-job repairs around her house, saying: "We don't want the place to run down, do we?"

She said: "No, I don't."

He brought Denny around once, for Sunday dinner. He knew Maggie-Now loved children dearly, and his wife had loved children. He though Mrs. O'Crawley felt the same way.

"Denny," he said, "how'd you like Mrs. O'Crawley for a mother?"

Denny sized her up and decided he wouldn't like her for a mother. He said: "I don't care."

Pat said: "Mrs. O'Crawley, how'd you like a son like Denny?"

Mrs. O'Crawley had nothing against children. She just didn't like them. "He seems like a nice boy," she said. "If you like children."

Pat thought it best to postpone his courting until he could think of a better angle. He nurtured his bitter friendship with Mick Mack. They spent the long summer and early autumn afternoons and evenings in footless arguments.

"If I didn't have two kids to support," said Pat, "I'd go and enlist."

"And sure, you're the one would wipe out the Germans in no time a-tall," said his admirer.

"The Germans?" asked Pat, astonished. "Why, I'd enlist in the *German* army."

"What for? You ain't German."

"I'd enlist in the German army just the same to lick hell out of the English."

"What do you want to lick them for?"

"Because of what they done to Parnell."

"What did they do to Parnell?" asked Mick Mack in all innocence.

"You don't know?" asked Pat, shocked.

"I was a boy in Dublin at the time."

"You ignorant mick!" Mick Mack looked hurt but he said nothing. "And you call yourself a man," sneered Pat aching for a fight.

"And I *am* so," said Mick Mack with unexpected dignity.

"Not if you take all this guff offa me," said Pat.

"I take it," said the little fellow quietly, "because you're my friend all the same."

"And sure, you're the one is hard up for a friend, then," said Pat. "Taking all the guff from me."

" 'Tis better," said Mick Mack, "to have a mean friend than no friend a-tall."

Summer went into fall. Denny went back to school. Pat went to his superintendent and asked how soon could he retire on pension. He'd put in more than twenty-five years cleaning streets and Pat thought that was more than enough.

"Men are dying in the trenches," said the super, "so that men like you can live."

"Live to shovel up horse manure," mumbled Pat.

"And you want to quit! Come around again sucking for retirement and I'll put you on the ashcan detail and you can retire after five years with a hernia. Now get out of here!"

Maggie-Now had a long letter from Sonny.

There was talk, he wrote, of the fellows getting out of the trenches by Christmas. He asked her to marry him. He wrote he'd like to settle down and raise a family. He'd written to his folks and his father wrote he'd give him half the profits of the business. And his mother and sister and brothers were crazy about her, Maggie-Now, he wrote.

She made up her mind. *I want children, lots of them, and a home for them. Sonny would be a good father, a good provider, a good husband, like Uncle Timmy was. Of course, he wouldn't sit around and talk. He'd have his bowling nights and his lodge meeting and one night a week to play cards with the boys and maybe fishing at Canarsie like other men do. I'd be lonesome the first year, then I'd have the children and my life would be full. I like him. I respect him. I'm proud that everyone thinks so well of him. And that must add up to love—if not now, someday. At least he wants me. It's nice to be wanted. And I want a husband. I want children. I don't want to wait. . . .*

She made up her mind to marry him and she felt at peace after her decision.

Then she heard from Claude Bassett!

Chapter Thirty-Two

HER father, as always, intercepted the postman on the stoop. Pat was leaving for work. She saw the postman hand him a card. She saw her father's face tighten as he read the message and she *knew!* She came out on the stoop and held out her hand. Pat made no move to give her the card. She took it from him. The message was simple:

Dear M: Wait for me. I'm coming back.
Love, C. B.

Her face went radiant. She pressed the card to her breast and smiled up at her father. "Oh, Papa!" she said happily.

"Where'd it come from?" he asked in a thick voice.

"You smudged the postmark with your thumb," she cried out. "Now I'll never know. Oh, Papa!"

"What about that plumber?" he asked.

"What plumber?"

"If you got to throw yourself away, throw yourself away on the plumber, not that damn Claude Bastid."

"Bassett," she corrected him. Then she gasped. "How do you know about Sonny Pheid?"

"I got ways of finding out things what people think they're hiding from me."

"Papa! You read my letters in my top drawer!"

"If you don't want people to read them, don't leave them, then, where people can find them." He left for work.

She sat at the kitchen table and gloated over the card. She thought his handwriting was beautiful; like engraving on a wedding announcement. She smiled fondly at the picture: mountains and sky and river bathed in rose light. The title said: *Western Sunset.*

She erased the smudge with a moistened eraser but the postmark got erased along with the smudge. She looked at the crumbs and thought sadly that now she'd never know what city it had been mailed from.

And he'll never tell me either, she thought.

Even though she had no idea when he'd be back, she started getting ready for him. She washed her hair and was so happy she hadn't had it bobbed because she felt that *he* wouldn't like it.

She held the card and pressed it to her cheek,

thinking: *His hand rested on it when he wrote it. He pressed the stamp down with his fingers.* She envisaged him standing at a mailbox in some strange city, reading the card once more before he dropped it in the slot.

After she had braided and pinned up her hair, she sat down and wrote to Sonny.

. . . honored. But I must tell you there is someone else and . . .

She thought of writing: *I hope we can still be friends,* but she discarded the idea immediately. She knew they couldn't be friends. It had to be love between them or nothing.

But I wish I could keep him as a friend, she thought sadly. *Someone to talk to, to smile at, to like—the way I talk, smile at and like Father Flynn and Mr. Van Clees.*

His answer came. She read it through her tears.

. . . so, like we say in France, Ah Reservoir. But honest, Maggie-Now, dear, I wish you all the luck in the world. . . .

She put this last letter with his other letters and his picture, and tied them up with a piece of blue baby ribbon from a discarded petticoat, and put the little packet in the box with her mother's rhinestone combs.

Sonny never wrote again. She missed getting his letters.

Chapter Thirty-Three

IN November, Maggie-Now got a job as night ticket seller in a neighborhood movie house. When Pat went out nights, Denny sat in the back row of the theater and watched the movies. He liked his sister's job fine.

Maggie-Now earned twenty dollars a week and saved most of it. She *knew* Claude was coming back and she *knew* they'd be married and she wanted to buy a dress for her wedding and some household things for their home. She liked selling tickets and chatting with the customers. When the weather got cold (there was no heat in the ticket booth), she brought a filled hot-water bottle from home, took her shoes off and rested her stockinged feet on the hot bottle. That kept her warm all evening.

The Sunday after Thanksgiving, it started to snow as evening came on. When Maggie-Now closed her booth at ten o'clock, the streets had a covering of snow. She looked in on her father. He was rolled up in his blankets and snoring warmly. She checked on Denny. His blankets were on the floor and he slept with his knees drawn up to his chin and his arms wrapped around his chest. She covered him securely, leaving only his head exposed. His head still looked like a baby's head: tender and vulnerable.

She looked down at him and thought: *I want all my children to look like Claude, except the next-to-last one. I want him to look like Denny, and the last one of all I want to look like me.*

She undressed but didn't feel like going to bed. She put her Navaho-blanket bathrobe over her warm flannel nightgown and got into her felt bedroom slippers. She went into the kitchen and made herself a cup of tea. After she'd had the tea, she banked the fire in the kitchen range, got her hairbrush and sat by the window in the front room to brush her hair. The room was comfortable. There was still some fire left in the parlor stove.

That's one thing you can say for Papa, she thought. *He does keep the fires up. I hope the snow doesn't get too deep. How he hates to shovel snow! He'll go on sick leave if it's deep and I'll have to go down to the section office and lie and say he's sick and the super will say, like always, sure he's sick—sick of working, and whoever is standing around will laugh. . . .*

She wanted him to go to work the next day because she planned to start making a new green challis dress to wear for Claude's return and she didn't want him hanging around the house. He'd spoil her pleasure in the making of the dress by making remarks like:

"Another new dress?"

"Closet's full of dresses already."

"Think money grows on trees?"

And she'd say, "Oh, Papa!"

She smiled and decided she wouldn't let her father bother her if he were home the next day. *I'll just think of Claude,* she decided, *and how happy I am because he's coming back.*

She brushed her hair and watched the soundless movement of the snow coming down and her brush strokes took the down rhythm of the falling snow. She looked at the flames flickering behind the isinglass panes of the stove door. She recalled her wonderful delight, as a child, at seeing the fire glow through the isinglass.

What a pity, she thought, *that you get used to things and never see them again the way you saw them for the first time.*

She braided her hair, one braid over each shoulder, and tied the ends with rubber bands so the braids wouldn't unravel in the night. She leaned forward, idly swinging the brush between her knees, grateful for the warmth of the fire and aware of the quiet beauty of the night, and she had a feeling of peace and blessed relief; the kind of humble and thankful relief that comes to an anxious parent when a sick child's terrifyingly high temperature starts dropping back to normal.

The fire died down, the room started to get cold and reluctantly she decided to go to bed. She checked the front door to see if it was locked and noticed that the snow had drifted against the doorsill outside. She got the broom and swept it away before her as she went out on the stoop. She stood in the cleared place, hands resting on the broom handle, and absorbed the snowy night.

Silent night, beautiful night, and for such a little time. Tomorrow the loveliness would be ugliness. The snow, with all the debris of the street beneath it, would be shoveled into hummocks at the curb. It would thaw a little, freeze a little and be veined with chimney soot and decorated with bits of dirty paper frozen into it and dogs would urinate against the peaks and leave behind dirty, mustard-colored patches.

Even now, the lovely baby-blanket look of the snow was being defiled by a man walking down the middle of the street and leaving dirty holes where his feet had stepped. Maggie-Now thought he must be crazy—he was wearing neither hat nor overcoat.

Suddenly, in her breast, where she judged her heart to be, something clicked out of place and then clicked back. She dropped the broom and ran down the street in her nightgown, bathrobe and felt slippers. She threw herself with such force at the hatless man that she all but knocked him off his feet.

"What took you so long?" she asked, as

though he had merely gone to the store.

"Margaret!" he said. "Oh, Margaret! Here."
He tried to give her the lumpy, sodden paper bag
he was carrying, but she was shaking him by the
shoulders the way a mother shakes a stubborn
child. The bottom fell out of the damp bag and
two naked chickens fell in the snow and lay
there, breast to breast.

"What's that?" she asked, startled.

"I thought you could cook them and we could
have a sort of late supper."

"Oh, Claude!" She laughed and then she
started to cry.

"Don't, Margaret! Don't!" He kissed her
gently. "You knew I'd come back, didn't you?"

"Yes," she sobbed. "And you'll never go
away again, will you?" She waited. He stood
silent. "Will you!" she insisted.

Typically, he wouldn't say yes, he wouldn't
say no. He said: "But I *did* come back, didn't
I?"

"Yes," she whispered.

He got a soggy handkerchief from his pocket
and tried to wipe the mixed tears and snow from
her face. He succeeded only in spreading the
wetness.

"You waited for me, Margaret, didn't you?
Because you knew I'd come back."

She thought of Sonny for a second, then said
"Yes, I waited. I waited all the time."

They stood on that quiet, empty street
holding each other tightly, and the snow fell on

them and flakes lingered briefly in the interstices of her braids.

He said: "You'll catch pneumonia."

Simultaneously, she said: "You'll get pneumonia."

They walked toward the house. He carried the chickens by their feet in one hand, and put his other arm about her waist.

"After your father spanked you for dancing in the street, did you give up dancing for good?"

"In a way. You see . . ."

And they resumed talking where they had left off seven months ago.

She installed him in the kitchen and closed the door so her father wouldn't hear and wake up. She punched up the fire in the kitchen range, threw in some slivers of wood and some fresh coal and added half an inch of kerosene measured into an empty tomato can. The fire took hold. She put on a kettleful of water for coffee and put the chickens in the roasting pan.

"I won't bother making stuffing," she whispered. "It'll take them two hours to get done as it is."

She made him take off his worn, wet shoes and socks and she put them in the warming oven to dry. She helped him off with his wet coat and her heart contracted as she touched him and knew that he had no undershirt under his thin top shirt.

In the darkness of his bedroom, the sound of the coffee grinder penetrated Pat's sleep.

Morning already, he thought, *and still dark out. Must be raining. Oh, God what a life,* he moaned, *having to get up every morning.* He pulled his pants on over his long woolen drawers which he used for pajamas. He opened the door to his son's room and called out ringingly: "School!" Hysterically, Denny threw all the bedclothes on the floor, tied himself into a fetus knot, and went back to sleep.

Claude and Maggie-Now talked in whispers as he knelt before her, took off her sodden felt bedroom slippers and dried her feet with a clean dish towel.

Suddenly, her father was in the doorway. "*What* the hell's going on here?" he asked, more astonished than angry.

"You see, it's snowing out," she started to explain, "and . . ."

"And who the hell are you?" he asked Claude. "And what the hell are you doing with her feet in the middle of the night?"

"Why, I'm *drying* them," said Claude.

"Papa," said Maggie-Now formally, "I'd like to introduce you to Mr. Bassett."

"Get up, Mr. Bassett," said Pat. "I'll not hit a man and him on his knees before me."

Claude stood up. Pat balled his hand into a fist and stepped back for leverage to throw a punch. Claude picked Pat's fist out of the air and pried it open. He fitted his palm into Pat's to form a handshake. Claude narrowed his eyes and started to press Pat's hand slowly and strongly. Pat all but cried out in his pain. He was sure that every bone in his hand was broken.

Holy Mother, thought Pat. *He looks like a sissy but he's got the strength of a murtherin' bastid.*

"I've been looking forward for a long time to meeting you, old sir," said Claude in his best educated accent.

. . . a murtherin' educated *bastid,* amended Pat to himself.

"I hope we will be friends, old sir," said Claude, releasing Pat's hand after one more bone-crushing squeeze.

Pat let his hand hang by his side, using all his will power not to flex the fingers to feel if they were still intact. His face burned at the idea of being called "old sir." He didn't think he was old.

"Get him out of here!" he yelled at his daughter.

Claude said, "Margaret, go change into dry clothes and give me a chance to get to know your father."

Maggie-Now said, "All right," and left.

"Sit down, old sir," said Claude.

"You telling *me* to sit down in me own house?" gasped Pat.

"Sit down," said Claude wearily. "Life is too short for this nonsense. Get done with the sparring. Hang up your gloves. Your daughter and I are going to marry. You might as well get used to me because you'll have to put up with me until you die."

"I'll bury *you* first," said Pat bitterly.

"That may well be. But while you're waiting to do so, let's be amiable. It's easier on the liver."

Pat felt a flash of interest. This man might well be an enemy worthy of him. Mick Mack always turned the other cheek and Timmy had not been a consistent enemy. He'd beat up a man and then weep in contrition. But this Claude Bassett: Pat knew he would fight to a draw. He decided to test him with what he knew to be a sure-fire insult.

"Why ain't you in uniform, you slacker?" he asked Claude.

"I was weighed in the balance and one of my ears was found wanting."

"A real man," said Pat disparagingly, "woulda pucked me in the nose for calling him a slacker."

"So?" said Claude. "Old sir, I had hoped we could be friends, on account of Margaret. But if it's a lifelong enemy that you want, I'll try to be worthy of your Irish spleen."

"Why can't you talk like a man?" said Pat irritably. "All them Goddamned educated words!"

Claude put his hands in his pockets and stretched out his legs under the table. He smiled at Pat. "You're enjoying this, aren't you?" he said.

Pat was so confounded by this remark that he

had nothing to say. Maggie-Now came in dressed and poured boiling water over the coffee Claude had ground. They spoke in incomplete sentences to each other as if they had been living together for many years. Pat couldn't stand it.

"Now that you're dressed," he told her, "pack your things and get out. And take him with you."

"Now, Papa," she said with a little laugh, "pack in what?"

"Now, now, old sir," said Claude. "You wouldn't put your wonderful daughter out on a night like this—in all that snow."

"She can stay," muttered Pat. "But," he turned to Maggie-Now and shouted, "get this man out of my house!"

"*My* house!" said Maggie-Now sharply. "Mama said you were to give it to me when I married." She went to Claude and put her hand on his shoulder. "Now, Papa, you stop being so mean. This is my man and I want him." Claude took her hand and pressed it to his cheek. "And if we all can be friends together, I'll be glad. If we can't, I'll feel bad, but I'll do what I want to anyway. I'm over twenty-one and I don't owe you anything, Papa. Except love. And that's because you're my father."

By God, he thought in sincere admiration, *she's got spunk! She stood up to me for once.* Then, he felt that he had lost the old Maggie-Now. From now on, he knew where he stood with her. He felt terribly alone. *Where,* he cried

351

in his heart, *is me mother who would have died for me? Me wife who loved me so? Timmy who licked me but all the time knew how it was with me? Where is the little girl what held my hand so tight when we walked down the street?* He wept in his heart.

"Margaret," he heard Claude say gently, "you mustn't speak so sharply to your father."

"Me daughter can speak to me any damn way she wants," said Pat belligerently.

Maggie-Now went to him and patted his head. "That's all right, Papa. You have a cup of coffee with us and then you get your sleep; you've got to work tomorrow. Claude and I will talk a while and have something to eat, then he'll go and tomorrow we'll all sit down together and talk things over."

At first, he refused the coffee. Then he reasoned that, after all, he'd paid for the coffee and the milk and the sugar and he might as well drink it. He had three cups. He cast about in his mind for something to say that would make Claude angry but wouldn't make Maggie-Now angry. He thought he had it. Jealousy! He cleared his throat.

"Maggie-Now, dear, did you hear from Son Pheid lately?" he said.

"Who?" asked Maggie-Now. "Oh, Sonny! No," she said.

"He's a plumber," said Pat to Claude. "In business for himself."

"That so?" commented Claude politely. He

turned to Maggie-Now. "You didn't tell me," he said, "whether you lost interest in dancing after that or . . ."

I got to think of some way, thought Pat desperately. *I can't beat hell out of him because he's younger and stronger than me. I got to lick him with me mind. I can't throw him out. She'll go with him. She's that loony about him. Yes, she'd go with him and that's just what he wants. Then he could have her without marrying her and that's what he's working for. He's not the marrying kind. I know them kind. Well, I'll think of something. You can catch more flies with sugar than with vinegar,* he concluded vaguely.

He got up and scratched his ribs. "Like Maggie-Now said, I'm a working man and I got to get me sleep."

Claude stood up. "Oh, I'm sorry," he said, "but I got to talking with Margaret and . . ."

"That's all right," said Pat. "Good night, all."

"Good night, Papa," she said.

"Good night, old sir."

"Good night," Pat paused, "old son." He stood in the doorway. "I wish I wasn't such a light sleeper," he said with a significant look at Claude. He went to his room, leaving the kitchen door ajar.

Claude went over and closed the door. He came back to Maggie-Now. "How soon can we get married?"

She straightened the cup in her saucer before she said: "You know I'm a Catholic."

"No!" he said in mock surprise.

"But I told you," she said seriously.

"I was joking," he said.

"I didn't really know. . . ."

"Ah, Margaret, you know so much about so many things and so little about so many things. Now: When can we be married?"

"In a month—five weeks. I'd have to ask Father Flynn."

"Do you love me?"

"Yes."

"How much?"

"There's no measure. I loved you when I first met you in the dentist's office, I guess. I loved you when you left, even though I thought you'd never come back. And if I had married someone else, I still would have loved you somewhere in the back of my mind. When you sent that card and told me to wait for you, I thought everything was all right, even though I was a Catholic."

"Don't belittle your religion, my little Chinee. It's a grand faith. But could you love me enough to give it up?"

He saw her hand on the table tremble. She put it in her lap. She lowered her head and he saw her face work in anguish.

Look at me, he told himself scornfully, *a vagabond. That's classy for bum. What have I got to give her? Nothing. I know how she is about her religion. What difference does it make? No faith means anything to me. So I ask her to give it up. Why? Just to own all of her? To prove I'm a man?*

But he had to go through with it. "Will you, Margaret?" Silence. "Will you give up your religion for me?" No answer. "Please say you will. I need you to say it."

"I will," she said finally.

"Thank you, Margaret." A pause. "But you don't mean it, do you?"

"No," she whispered. Then she burst out: "Why did you make me say it? How could I fix my mind to mean it? Is it a crime to be a Catholic?"

She put her head down on her folded arms on the table and wept. She cried noisily and her whole body shook. He went to the door to see if it was tightly shut. He didn't want her father to hear. Then he went to her, pulled her to her feet and put his arms around her.

"Why, I wouldn't have you give up your faith for me. I only wanted to hear you say, just once, that you would." She sobbed louder. "There, Margaret, there! Stop crying. There, Margaret, there!" He stroked her hair. "There, there, Margaret now. There, Maggie. There, Maggie-Now.

"Listen! You got me around to calling you Maggie-Now. And you can call me Claudy, if you want to." She shook her head and continued sobbing. He shook her roughly. "Stop it, you little fool. Don't you know that I'm anxious to marry you in the Catholic faith? And you know why?" She held back a sob to listen. "Because there's no divorce in the Catholic Church. I want my marriage to be that way: no divorce. After we're married awhile, you'll find out I'm nothing but a bum and you'll want to divorce me. But you won't be able to. And I'll have you safe for always. Now dry your eyes and tell me how to go about things."

She wiped her eyes. "You'll have to see Father Flynn. He'll give you instructions. I'll make an appointment for you and I think the chickens are done now."

He couldn't help it. He started to laugh. He laughed until he was weak.

"What's the matter?" she asked.

"You," he said. "You're the matter. Oh, Margaret! Oh, Maggie-Now, my practical love!"

Maggie-Now's sobs had not penetrated Pat's sleep, but Claude's laughter had. Pat turned over and muttered, "Bastid."

They mended the fire, made more coffee and ate the roasted chicken with bread and butter while they discussed plans for their marriage. Maggie-Now wanted to know where they would live.

"Here," he said, "if it's all right."

"But the neighborhood's so rundown. . . ."

"I love this neighborhood."

"And this house is so old. . . ."

356

"It's wonderful! It's a safe place—it's a *home.*"

"But Papa lives here. . . ."

"I *like* your father," he said. "He has his own special kind of integrity. I'll get a good job and pay all the expenses. Your father will be our guest."

"Papa would pay something for himself and Denny."

"I wouldn't let him.

"To think," said Claude happily, "me—who never had anything; who never had anyone! And now I'll have a wife and a father and a young brother and a home life. All this to come to me!"

Maggie-Now had a flash of intuition. "You were brought up in an orphans' home, then." She saw his eyes flicker but he wouldn't say yes and he wouldn't say no. But she knew it was true. "I wish you'd tell me . . ."

"There is a little to tell. I was a boy, I grew up and got a fairly good education and I turned into a wanderer. You could call me a tramp, except that I worked my way around."

"But there must have been things that happened to you—someone that you got to know real well. . . ."

"Do you mean, have I got a past?"

"I guess so."

"*You* are my past. My past, my present and my future. I am making my past now. And it is a good one. Twenty years from now, maybe, someone will ask me about my past and I'll say: 'My past started one Easter week in Brooklyn where I met a girl named Margaret Rose Moore, only everybody called her Maggie-Now.' "

Chapter Thirty-Four

SOME men don't like to work; they duck work as long as they can. When conscience or need drives them to work, they're apt to pick the hardest work available, probably as penance or to prove they *can* do hard work. Claude took a temporary job shoveling snow for the city.

The snow was a curse to many but a blessing to jobless men and to children. Even in this war year, with so many men in the services and well-paid, wartime jobs for nearly all, there were still men available for snow shoveling: men too old or too young to have steady jobs, college boys wanting to pick up a few dollars, and drifters.

In one of the far-flung neighborhoods of Brooklyn, there was a sanitation boss who had seemingly been born just to hire college men to shovel snow. Henny Clynne had come up from the ranks. He had started as sweeper and by taking civil service exams over and over until he finally passed, and by pull, he got to be superintendent and gained the power, along with his other duties, of hiring and firing college men. He liked to hire college men for snow shoveling because he couldn't stand the sight of any man who had gone to college. When Claude applied for work, Henny looked him over and considered him a prize.

"What college you from?" he asked Claude.

Claude fixed his stare at the bottom of Henny's left ear and said: "The college of hard knocks."

"Don't get wise with me," snarled Henry. "Though I don't blame you for being ashamed to admit you went to college. But you can't fool me. I can tell a college man a mile off."

"That's interesting, sir," said Claude. Henny was getting nervous at Claude staring at his ear lobe. He moved his head. Claude refocused his stare.

"Yep, I can tell by your shoes. A honest, hard-working man don't wear thin shoes with thin soles. I always say, let me see a man's shoes and I'll tell you what he is."

"That's very clever, sir."

"I know you're a college graduate. Come on, now. What college?"

"Shall we say, Oxford?" said Claude.

"Where's Oxford?"

"In Mississippi."

"So you went to college! Born with a silver spoon in your mouth. And you end up begging me for work; hard work, mind you. Dirty work. Now take me," he went on complacently.

"Never went to school more than three years in me whole life. Would you believe it to look at me?"

"Oh, no, sir!"

"I learned meself everything I know and I know plenty. I came to this country thirty years ago—a ignorant mick with me trunk on me back. I didn't know *nothing*. And look at me today!"

"My!" breathed Claude admiringly. He thrust his head forward to take a closer look at Henny's ear lobe.

"What's-a matter?" asked Henny.

"Nothing."

"You wait here, now, till I interview them other rah-rah boys."

Henny separated the wheat from the chaff. Then he lined up the wheat, gave them instructions, handed out shovels and marched them to their work area. He went back to his office, which was a rented store, and examined his left ear in the lavatory mirror.

For a minute, there, he thought, *the way that feller was looking at me, I thought there was a louse or something crawling around me ear.*

The men had been working two hours when Henny showed up for the morning pep talk. He chose to address his communal remarks to Claude.

"Shovel it up, college boy. Shovel it up! We ain't here to pick daisies, you know." Some of the men stopped working and leaned on their shovels. Henny was waiting for this. "I see that the coach called time out. That gives us a chance to give out with the old razz-a-ma-tazz, fellers." He took a cheer leader's stance and chanted: "Raw-raw-raw! Raw-raw-raw! Shovel it up, shovel it up, raw-raw-raw!"

One shoveler guffawed, one grinned, another turned his head to spit, some looked astonished, some looked sheepish and Claude stared at Henny's left ear lobe. He stared until Henny scratched it, then Claude resumed piling up the snow.

A small crowd had gathered to enjoy Henny's show—mostly old men with nothing to do and marketing mothers with small children.

"Those men went to college," said a mother to her small son.

"How can you tell, Missus?" asked a garrulous old man who had overheard the remark.

"Because some ain't got overcoats and because Mr. Clynne said so."

"So they went to college," mused the old man.

"Yeah."

"And what does that prove, Missus?"

"I didn't say it proved anything. I just said what was a fac'. They went to college."

Late that afternoon, dead tired, but with earned money in his pocket, Claude went to keep the appointment with Father Flynn that Maggie-Now had made for him. He was glad, at the priest's invitation, to sink into a worn, brown-leather Morris chair.

Claude was surprised that the priest's living room looked like any room in a comfortable house. He had expected it to look a little like a small church. The wintry, lemon-colored sun slanted in through a window and shone through a clear glass decanter, half full of sauterne (the gift of a parishioner). It made a pale golden shadow on the polished wood of the table. There was a rack of pipes on the desk (each pipe a loving gift), and a humidor of tobacco supplied by Van Clees.

The room smelled good—of coffee simmering in the kitchen, of mellow, burning tobacco, and the warm, ironing smell of freshly laundered linen. He saw stunted boughs of a bare bush outlined outside a window. He knew it was the priest's treasure, the lilac bush. Maggie-Now had told him about it.

Father Flynn knew the purpose of Claude's visit. After a few preliminary remarks about the weather, the state of the world and the war, and after both had agreed that the boys wouldn't be out of the trenches by Christmas, Father Flynn filled his pipe, lit it and settled back in his chair.

"I understand," he said, "that you wish to marry Margaret and have agreed with her to a Catholic marriage ceremony."

"Yes, sir."

"What is your faith?"

"Oh, I'm a Christian at large," said Claude airily. Too late, he realized he'd said the wrong thing. He saw the priest's kindly expression go stern and he waited apprehensively for the priest's reply.

"If I asked your political affiliation, no doubt you'd say you were a citizen at large. Is that correct?" He saw Claude shift his eyes. "I mean," said Father Flynn, trying again, "what is your denomination?"

"I'm not a Jew, if that's what you're getting at," said Claude.

"That statement," said Father Flynn, coldly minting each word, "should be made with humility and not with arrogance."

"Sorry," mumbled Claude.

"For our Lord was a Jew," said the priest.

Father Flynn thought: *As an ordained priest, I must love, understand and forgive him. But as private citizen Joseph Flynn, I can't stand the sight of him. God forgive me.*

Thought Claude: *He hates me, the way her father and her godmother hate me. The way everyone who loves her hates me.*

"What was your parents' religion?"

"I don't know."

"*You,* a non-Catholic, have come to *me,*" said Father Flynn sharply, "to plead for the privilege of marrying a Catholic. I will refuse you that privilege unless . . ."

"I do not know who my parents were," said Claude quietly.

Father Flynn put his pipe down very carefully. He put his finger tips together, leaned back in his chair and waited. He waited. He waited a long time.

Finally, he urged: "Yes, my son?"

"I was brought up in a nondenominational institution. A very good one. Someone paid for me. I was given a good education. Someone paid for it."

"I see," said the priest. And he *did* see. He understood now why Claude was the way he was.

"Have you told Margaret?"

"No. I have told no one in the world, except you."

"Tell her."

"If I choose not to tell her, will you tell her?"

"As a priest, I cannot violate a confession. As a man, I will not violate a confidence."

"Thank you, sir."

"Father," prompted the priest.

"Father," said Claude.

"But tell her, my son. She is worthy of knowing it."

"I think she knows," said Claude.

Claude had a feeling of immense peace. He felt a great warmth toward the priest; almost a feeling of tenderness.

That's why he wanders, thought the priest. *He goes to a new place, thinking there he will find a bit of the piece that's missing from his life.*

They talked further. Claude said he would like

to be converted to Catholicism. Father Flynn said he couldn't become a Catholic merely by requesting it. He'd have to take instructions, learn the history and theology of the church. It would take time.

"And there is the question of faith. It cannot be taught you, you cannot have it by announcing that you have it. It must come from something within you. There is no formula. You will *know* when you have it. Only then can you become a Catholic."

"How soon?" asked Claude. "For Margaret's sake. I want to be one with her in all things."

"To some, faith comes soon and to others, late. And to many, it never comes at all."

It was dark in the room now. The housekeeper came in to turn on the lights. She spoke bitterly and said she couldn't keep Father's supper warm much longer. It was drying up. Father Flynn apologized and asked her indulgence five minutes longer. He stood in some fear of his housekeeper. She left the room muttering.

"I always have a glass of sauterne before my supper," said the priest. "Will you join me?"

Claude said he would. He stood up when the priest did. He was relieved that, for once, someone didn't say: "Keep seated."

The street seemed cold and lonely after the warmth of the priest's living room. Claude went to a bakery lunchroom and had several cups of coffee and a couple of doughnuts. He was tired to death. The day before he had traveled through miles of snow to get to Maggie-Now. He had sat up most of the night talking to her and had put in a hard day shoveling snow.

He didn't know how long he had been in the lunchroom. A stout woman was shaking him awake.

"You can't sleep here, Mister. Go home."

He made his way to the movie theater where Maggie-Now was working. She gave a gasp of pity when he loomed up before her outside the glass enclosure. He looked so tired and bedraggled. She gave him a ticket and told him to wait inside for her; she'd be through in an hour and would fix a hot supper for him.

He stumbled into the theater and collapsed in a backrow seat. He slept soundly through the most controversial part of *The Birth of a Nation*.

Chapter Thirty-Five

IN spite of all Pat's efforts to lick Claude with his "mind," plans for the marriage went forward. Pat had come to the conclusion that Claude was an ex-convict, else why was he so reticent about his past? He knew his daughter would not marry an ex-convict. But how to get Claude to admit it?

Pat, knowing how most men babble when they are drunk, took him to a saloon to get him drunk. Claude spent the evening staring into his untouched shot glass of rye. He wouldn't drink; he wouldn't talk. Pat drank too much and he was the one who talked. He told Claude the complete story of his life and, when he had finished, he told it all over again with variations. Then he got sick and Claude had to take him to the men's room and hold his forehead while he retched. Claude took him home, gave him a Bromo-Seltzer and put him to bed.

In order to be with Maggie-Now in the afternoon, Claude got a job as night clerk in a downtown Brooklyn hotel. He wouldn't say what hotel except that it *wasn't* the St. George. Maggie-Now asked no questions but Pat had to know. Claude wouldn't name the hotel but Pat got this much out of him: that it was a small family hotel catering to permanent guests, mostly elderly couples who had just enough money to keep out of the poorhouse.

From this explanation, Pat concluded that the place was a brothel, else why should Claude go to so much trouble to throw him off the track by assuring him that the place was so respectable? Now if Maggie-Now had proof that Claude was a procurer . . .

He decided to let Claude compromise himself. He took him aside and asked how about their having a fling together. He hinted that Claude would be a long time married, and . . .

"Maybe you can dig up two 'skirts' for us from that hotel where you work and get us a couple of rooms there and I'll bring along a bottle of Four Star Hennessy and we'll have ourselfs a high old time."

Claude looked at him with distaste and said: "Aren't you a bit along in years for that sort of thing, old sir?"

After the banns had been read for the first time, Pat came to another conclusion: that the marriage was inevitable; that there was no way to stop it now. He went on to his next project: the house. He knew Claude wanted to live there.

"How much will he pay?" he asked Maggie-Now.

"How do you mean, Papa?"

"I'll rent him the downstairs for twenty-five a month and you can have me big bedroom and I'll take your bit of a one. Of course, I'll pay for me share of the food and the boy's."

"Now, Papa, must we go all through that again? Mama said I was to get the house when I married. You promised."

"It was one of them promises no man has to keep."

"Oh, shame, Papa. Shame. Grandpapa gave it to Mama in the first place. It was never yours."

"Ha! Me deed says: To Patrick Dennis Moore ate us."

"And you know what *Et Ux* means?"

"Sure. *All His,*" he ventured, figuring that she didn't know what it meant either.

"It means *And Wife.* I know that much Latin anyhow. If you give the house to me after I marry, even if you don't want Claude to have it, the deed would have to be in his name."

"Over me dead body!"

"All right, Papa. I won't fight with you over it. I'll get the house anyway—after you die."

"Knock wood when you say that," he shouted.

"I will not!" she shouted back. "I don't want to live here anyhow. What kind of a married life would I have and you always making trouble? We'll get an apartment."

"Do so. 'Tis right married people live alone."
She got her hat. "Where are you going?"

"I'm going out to rent an apartment."

"Who's going to cook me meals? Who's going to look after the boy?"

"I'll find you a housekeeper, Papa. Maybe Father Flynn's housekeeper knows somebody . . ."

"How much will it cost?"

"A very old lady will work for fifteen a month and room and board. Only you have to give her so much every week for groceries—not a dollar whenever you feel like it."

He did some mental arithmetic; then he started to negotiate: He'd give her the upstairs rent free for the rest of her life, provided she continued keeping house for him. She declined. The downstairs, then; same conditions. She said no. They reached no agreement. Maggie-Now went out to look for an apartment.

When the banns were read for the second time, Pat made a deal. Because, and only because, he'd promised her mother, he told Maggie-Now, he would turn over the house to her. There were provisions. The house was hers for her lifetime only; after that, it went to Denny; she was to continue keeping house for him and Denny; he was to have the upstairs hall bedroom as his own to occupy or to rent out—he to receive said rent.

"But why do you want to own a hall bedroom, Papa?"

"Because I just got to end up with *something* out of this."

She agreed. He had the deed made over to her right away. She suggested he wait until she and Claude married.

"It would be a nice wedding present," she said.

"I don't want it to be *Et Ux*," he said.

Claude helped her move Pat's furniture to the upstairs room. They painted the walls and ceiling of Pat's old room, which would now be theirs, and Maggie-Now made new, rose-sprigged, ruffled dimity curtains. She bought a new bed and dresser for the room that would be hers and Claude's, and a taffeta, green bedspread. She decorated the bed with half a dozen tiny, heart-shaped lace pillows and two French dolls with their legs knotted. This was the fashion of the time. Claude raised his eyebrows when he saw the decorated bed.

"I guess you think it's tacky or something, but all my life I wanted heart-shaped lace pillows. I *like* that stuff on my bed."

"*Our* bed," he said.

"That's right, Claude, and I'll put the stuff away after we're married."

"Oh, leave it, Margaret. Just so there's room for a husband."

She was ecstatically happy during those waiting weeks, but sometimes the thought of Lottie diluted her happiness. She put off telling Lottie about her coming marriage as long as she could because she knew Lottie would rave. She did.

"A fool! That's what you are, a fool! Marrying this nobody when you could have had a man like Timmy; you could have married Sonny. Who is this Claude anyway? What do you know about him? He might be a jailbird; he might be already married to someone in Jersey. What do you see in him?"

"I love him so."

"You love the grand way he talks to you. And more shame to you. Are you not used to grand talkers and you coming from the Irish who is the grandest talkers of all?"

"But you'll come to my wedding anyhow, won't you, Aunt Lottie?"

"No!"

"Please! Since Mama died, you've been my mother. I want my mother to come to my wedding to wish me luck."

"I use' to think of you as my daughter. Now I'm glad you ain't because I' rather see a daughter of mine in her casket than married to a man like him." Maggie-Now broke down and sobbed. Lottie wasn't moved an inch by her tears. "Go on and cry," she said bitterly. "Get use' to crying. You'll shed many a tear after you're married to him."

Pat went to Mass with Maggie-Now and Claude the Sunday when the banns were read for the last time. He half closed his eyes and the church seemed like the little church in Ireland.

He heard the same names he had heard in that little church; his beloved's name and his: Margaret Rose Moore. He half expected that a burly man some pews ahead would turn around and it would be Timmy.

He sat with his head bowed, wringing his hands in anguish between his knees. *Oh, if only I was a boy again, back in Ireland,* he mourned. *I'd marry me Maggie Rose and gladly. And I wouldn't care what Henny, the Hermit, sang about me. I'd work from morning to night cutting peat, and when they'd call me a bog trotter, I'd only laugh. 'Twould be heaven to live in a one-room sod shanty and sleep on a bit of straw on the floor and eat the small, hard potatoes that I planted meself and, yes, take a licking every day of me life from Timmy and never complain. Anything . . . anything! If I was only young again! Anything, if only I was young again!*

Chapter Thirty-Six

MAGGIE-NOW was married in the new green challis dress she'd made; new hat, new shoes, new white gloves and a winter coat that had been new five years ago. She carried a bunch of baby bronze chrysanthemums. She came out of the priest's house on Claude's arm and two lines of people had made a path for them from the house to the curb. They were friends, neighbors, acquaintances, curious people and children.

Bride and groom walked down the path. She nodded to strangers, waved to friends and kissed the children. Claude bowed from side to side like a visiting dignitary. Aunt Lottie was at the end of the path.

"You came to my wedding after all!" Maggie-Now hugged her.

"What made you think I wouldn't?"

Lottie congratulated Claude and said sternly, but with a smile: "Take good care of her or you'll hear from me."

"If I ever mistreat her in any way," said

375

Claude, "I hope you will take an aunt's privilege and spank me."

Lottie frowned. She thought his little speech was affected. *He puts on too much,* was the way she described it to herself. Claude may have felt her aversion for he put his arms about her and pressed his cheek to Lottie's.

"I hope you will like me in time," he murmured. "You're such a grand, sweet lady."

Something stirred in Lottie. *I don't like him for a nickel,* she thought. *And I never will. But I can see now what she sees in him.*

She gave Maggie-Now a wrapped gift, said no, she couldn't come to the house for a cup of coffee, because she had stopped going out socially ever since Timmy passed away. Maggie-Now watched her go down the street.

Bride and groom walked home arm-in-arm. Children playing on the street ran up to her, looked up at her, said, "Hello, Maggie," walked a bit with them and dropped out. Other children took their place. Maggie-Now gave each one a flower. A woman with her arms hugging her sides against the cold came out on a stoop and called: "Luck, Maggie." A woman in an upstairs flat tapped on the window and, when she got Maggie-Now's attention, blew her a kiss. Maggie-Now blew one back.

At home, a little party had been arranged. Guests stood in a line behind the parlor table, on which were a bottle of port wine, glasses and a wedding cake. There were a miniature bride and groom on top. The groom looked like Charlie Chaplin. Pat stood at the head of the line. Next to him was a tiny, trim woman with a chenille-dotted veil stretched taut across her face, taut kid gloves and coat buttoned tautly about her waist. At her side stood a little grinning gnome of a man with two rows of perfect white teeth. Then there was Mr. Van Clees. Maggie-Now was ecstatic about the cake.

"Who got it?" she asked.

"He did," said the taut lady, indicating Pat.

"She made him," said the little gnome, indicating the taut lady.

Pat made the introductions. "This here," he said, "is me friend, Mrs. O'Crawley, the lady what I eat with, Sundays." The lady bowed graciously and the newlyweds bowed back. "And this is Mick Mack," said Pat indifferently.

The little man grinned up at Maggie-Now and said: "He is my friend from night-school days."

"Where are your manners?" said Maggie-Now sharply

The beam left his face. *By God,* he thought, *she's just like her old man!*

"Don't you know," continued Maggie-Now, "that you're supposed to kiss the bride? Shame on you!"

The beam came back. Mick Mack put his arms about her waist. He stood on tiptoe but was only able to reach her neck. He put a smacking kiss on it.

Maggie-Now greeted Van Clees. He lifted her

hand and kissed it. "Just so you should be happy, is all," he said. She thanked him.

There was the ceremony of cutting the cake which everyone tried to make hilarious by all talking at once in a notched-up tone of voice. They drank to the bride and groom in port wine. They drank to the future; they drank to each other. A boy rushed in from the corner candy store with a phone message from the manager of the movie house: that, as a wedding gift, he would not dock Maggie-Now for the night off for her honeymoon. Maggie-Now gave the boy a piece of cake.

"Give the boy a nickel, Papa," she said.

"Give the boy a nickel, Claude," said Pat. Claude complied.

There was the presenting of and the ritual of opening the wedding presents. Mrs. O'Crawley led off with what she called: "Just a little something. Not much." It was a fine linen handkerchief with tatted edges. The bride proclaimed it "Lovely!" Mick Mack gave her a small pottery bowl filled with hardened cement into which were stuck six pink paper roses. Maggie-Now claimed it was exactly what she had always wanted.

Father Flynn dropped in and accepted a glass of wine. He declined the cake but asked for a piece to take to his housekeeper. She was in one of her dish-banging moods, he said, and the cake might get her out of it. He didn't stay long. He blessed the bridal couple before he left.

Mrs. O'Crawley, who was "up" on wedding procedure, suggested that it was time that the bride change into her going-away outfit. Maggie-Now looked surprised. She had no going-away outfit. Her wedding outfit was the whole thing. But she said yes, it was time to get ready.

She opened Lottie's present in the privacy of her room. She smiled tenderly at the china pug dog and the nursing puppies. She didn't like it for what it was, but she loved it for what it meant. Her father came into the room.

"What's that you got?" he asked.

"From Aunt Lottie." Impulsively, she thrust it into his hands. "Here, Papa. Hold it!"

"What for?" He scowled at the thing.

"Because I remember Timmy standing by the mantelpiece and holding it. And Aunt Lottie. Claude held it, too." *And,* she thought, *so did Sonny.* "Everyone I love has held it. I want you to hold it too."

He held it for the count of three and then put it on the dresser. "Trash!" he announced. "Giving away second-hand junk for a wedding present."

"Now, Papa!"

"I got a present for you," he said. "I didn't want to show off in front of the company and make them ashamed of the cheap presents what they gave you, so I give it to you in private." He gave her a twenty-dollar gold piece.

"Oh. Papa! Papa!" She put her arms around

him and squeezed him. He suffered the embrace.

"Don't lose it," he said, "because them gold pieces is hard to get. And don't let *him* spend it either." After which gracious presentation speech, he left to rejoin the company.

Maggie-Now checked the contents of the little red leather suitcase Claude had given her as a wedding present. It held a new white nightgown, a new white woolen robe, new white bedroom slippers, a change of lingerie and her toilet articles. She tucked the gold piece in the toe of her slipper and at the last second decided to take the pug dog with her. She thought Claude might be pleased with Lottie's gift. She snapped the case shut, put on her hat and coat and went out to say good-by to her friends.

She looked around for Denny. Only then did she recall that she hadn't seen him since the ceremony. She went to his room. He was sitting on the middle of his cot.

"Denny, why didn't you come out for a piece of cake?"

"I don't like cake."

"Why, you *love* cake."

"Today, I don't. Where you going?"

"Away with Claude for a little while."

"I want to go with you."

She knelt down and put her arms around him. "I'll be back tomorrow."

"No, you won't. You just say that so I won't cry."

"I promise. And I'll bring you a nice present."

"But I'd sooner go with you."

"Not this time, Denny, dear. Now come out and see the company."

"I don't want to."

"Why?"

"Because I don't *like* to."

She got to her feet and spoke a bit sharply. "It makes no difference whether you like to or not. There are certain things that you *have* to do. You can't always run away and hide. Come on, now." He went into the living room with her.

She kissed everyone good-by, her father last of all. "Say something nice to Claude, Papa," she whispered.

"Not while he's above ground." Pat didn't bother to whisper, either.

"Please?" she begged.

Grudgingly, Pat extended his hand to Claude. He tried for words. He wanted to say something to Claude that would please Maggie-Now and yet not be something nice. Eventually he came up with the words spoken to him more than twenty-five years ago by Mary's father.

"Be good to this good girl," he said.

"I promise," said Claude, "not to beat her more than once a day."

The bastid, thought Pat. *Why couldn't I a-thought of that remark twenty-five years ago?*

They scrambled down the stoop in approved newlywed fashion, ducking their heads correctly to avoid being spattered with the conventional rice, which Mrs. O'Crawley had thought to bring with her. Hand in hand, they ran to the corner to get a trolley and, arriving there out of breath, had to wait fifteen minutes for a car to come along.

Claude had two surprises for his bride: the wedding supper and the hotel where they'd spend their one-night honeymoon. He took her to Gage and Tollner for the supper and Maggie-Now couldn't get over how beautiful it was; the wonderful food and the exquisite service. When the headwaiter presented them with a split of champagne, compliments of the management, she was so delighted that she stuttered when she tried to speak. She took a sip of champagne.

"I love it!" she said. "It's so *good*."

"That's strange," he said. "Champagne is an acquired taste. Like olives."

"I love olives, too." Then she cried out in exaggerated happiness; "I love everything in the whole world!"

When the waiter appeared before them with the tray of French pastries, she was lost. "What will I do? What will I do?" she moaned. "They are all so beautiful. No matter which one I take, I'll be sorry that I didn't take some other one."

"I'll choose for you," he said. He had not one, but two pastries put on her plate.

She was about to eat a pastry the way she ate her breakfast bun: out of hand. But she saw Claude pick up a short fork to eat his with and she followed suit.

"Do you mean to say," she asked, "that there are people in the world who eat like this every day?"

"You ain't seen nothing, yet," he said in an inept Al Jolson imitation. "Wait until I take you over to the Chambord in Manhattan. Wait until I take you to Antoine's down in New Orleans for a New Year's Eve supper."

"It couldn't possibly be better," she said flatly, "than this place right here in Brooklyn."

He had reserved a room for them at the St. George Hotel. She had never been in a hotel before. She was so awed that she spoke in whispers.

"Do you mean to say," she whispered, "that you take wages for working in this beautiful place?"

He laughed. "Good Lord, I don't work here. I work in a mean, grubby . . ." He broke off to show her the register. "Look!" In a careful, beautiful hand, he wrote: *Mr. and Mrs. Claude Bassett, Manhattan Avenue, Brooklyn, N.Y.*

Tears of happiness came to her eyes. "It looks so real," she said. "Like forever," she whispered.

"It is, my Margaret. It is," he said.

She babbled happily about the beauty and luxury of their room. She was awed by the huge, gleaming bathroom. She would have spent hours joyously examining each piece of furniture and each bathroom fixture, but he cut her short.

"It's been a long day," he said, "and you

must be tired. I know I am. So . . . ."

Faint pink colored her cheeks. "All right," she agreed. She took her little suitcase and went into the bathroom.

She took a bath, using her geranium-scented soap, and dusted herself with Mennen's talcum powder. She got into her new white nightgown and robe and slippers. She took her hairbrush and went back into the other room. He was sprawled out in an armchair but he got up when she entered the room. She stood in front of the dresser mirror and brushed her hair.

"You look like a bride," he said with a smile.

"I *am* a bride," she said seriously. He took his hat from the closet shelf. "Going out?" she asked, surprised.

"Margaret," he said, "you want children, don't you?"

"Oh, yes," she said eagerly. "Lots of children. Why?"

He turned his hat twice around in his hands before he answered. "Wouldn't you like to wait a year or so? Give us a chance to know each other better; get used to each other . . . have some fun? You're still so young."

She turned to face him, her brush stilled and suspended over her head. "But, Claude! I want a child right away."

He put his hat back on the shelf.

He bathed and got into his new blue pajamas. He buttoned up the frogs and examined himself in the door mirror. He didn't like the way he looked. He put the pajama coat inside the pants and pulled the string tighter. He thought that looked worse. He pulled the coat out again. He took a pair of military brushes from a leather case: Maggie-Now's wedding gift to him. He wet his hair and started to brush it. He brushed and brushed and brushed. Finally, he had to admit to himself that he was stalling for time.

I must be very careful, he thought. *She's never been with a man. I must be careful not to frighten her. Not to disgust her. She will remember this night all of her life. I must not let it be a bad night to remember.* He made plans. *I'll walk around the room and fix the shades and look out the window and say easy things like all the stars are out tonight. I'll hang up my clothes and maybe sit on the bed and get her to talking about, say, the church socials, and when she's relaxed and drowsy . . .*

When he felt he could put it off no longer, he entered the bedroom with trepidation. She was sitting up in bed in her modest white nightgown and a braid over each shoulder.

When she saw him, she smiled, stretched out both arms to him and said: "Come to me."

Chapter Thirty-Seven

"IT ain't a home no more," complained Pat. "It's the Long Island Railroad Depot where people come and go all hours. It's a short-order lunchroom where they throw food at you, and," he concluded vaguely, "that's where all me money goes."

It wasn't as bad as he said, even though all didn't sit down to meals at the same time and all didn't sleep at the same time. Claude came home from work as Pat and Denny were leaving the house in the morning. Claude and Maggie-Now had breakfast together, then she pulled down the bedroom shades and they went to bed together. She got up in time to fix Denny's noon lunch and didn't go back to bed. She put in the afternoon attending to her household duties.

Claude got up at six and had supper with Maggie-Now and Denny. Pat got home for his supper just as they had finished theirs. (This gave him the idea that he was served leftovers.) Maggie-Now left for work at seven and Claude didn't have to leave until nine. He spent the two hours talking with Pat; that is, listening to Pat talk, and helping Denny with his homework.

Weekends were different on account of Pat or Denny being home, and Maggie-Now couldn't go to bed with her husband. Pat complained bitterly that all ought to eat one meal together at least once a week. Since the Sunday-noon dinner was the only time in the week when this could happen, contrary Pat chose to eat that meal at Mrs. O'Crawley's house.

There was no religious friction. Claude stayed up Sundays to go to eight o'clock Mass with Maggie-Now. He got up an hour earlier Saturday evenings to escort Maggie-Now to church for her weekly confession. He waited outside for her or else sat quietly in a back pew. When Maggie-Now apologized for having fish each Friday instead of meat, he said he liked fish and that they ought to have it twice a week. Denny was to make his First Communion that spring and Claude helped him memorize his catechism. Lottie's old mother died in February and Claude gave up an afternoon of sleep to go to the funeral with his wife. He told her how much he had been moved by the great and somber beauty of the Requiem Mass.

"I'm waiting the day," confided Pat to Mick Mack over a beer, "when he'll show up in his real colors. He's too good to be true, the bastid."

"Yeah, like me own son-in-laws," agreed the little man. "Bastids *and* sonsabitches, all of them!" (He didn't really believe that. He just wanted to be in sympathy with Pat.)

"*That* I can believe," said Pat coldly, "seeing the father-in-law what they got."

It was inevitable that changes came about. For one thing, Claude stopped going to Mass. "I'll wait until I'm accepted in the church as a convert," he told Maggie-Now. "It's not right to go merely as an outsider; a spectator."

He asked her jokingly why she went to confession *every* week; how in the world could she accumulate so many sins in a week? She said she went weekly because she was used to it, she guessed. He smiled and said that was hardly an intelligent reason, was it? After that, she didn't wake him up to escort her to the church. She went to confession alone.

He no longer sat with Pat and Denny when she left for her work. He went with her and either stood in the booth and talked to her or else went directly to the hotel where he worked. "I can sit in the lobby and read," he explained, "until it's time to go on duty."

She surmised that Claude no longer spent the evenings with Pat because her father asked too many questions. She recalled a shred of conversation between them she'd overheard.

"How'd you come to get such a name like Claude?" asked Pat.

When Claude answered, Maggie-Now noted he spoke in that academic way which meant he was coldly angry. He said: "Shall we say I had a romantic mother?" (*Too romantic,* he thought bitterly.) "And she got the name out of a Victorian novel?"

"I bet you know how you got your last name, though," persisted Pat. "I guess your father's name was Bassett."

"Your enunciation, old sir," said Claude icily, is a little less than perfect. For your information there is no 't' or 'd' sound in the middle of the name Bassett."

"Yeah? And for your information," countered Pat, "there ain't all the time a 'old' in front of that word 'sir' neither. Especially when a man is still in his forties."

It was a morning in late March. They were in bed together with the shades pulled down to shut out the daylight. He was holding her and caressing her and talking about nothing in the broken-sentence, murmuring way of one who is content. Gently, she put his hand away from her.

"Why?" he asked.

"I can't," she said. "It's My Time."

"What time?"

"*You* know."

Sure he knew. But he liked to tease her. He knew she had a queer distaste for the medical words of the woman cycle, such as "menstruate," "pregnancy" and "menopause." She substituted euphemisms for these terms: "My Time," "With Child," and "The Change." He liked to try to get her to say the medical words by pretending he didn't understand *her* words.

"I'm so disappointed," she said.

"*You're* disappointed! What about me?" he asked in pretended anger.

Suddenly, she was weeping. *Why can't I ever remember,* he thought, *that she takes everything so literally?*

"I didn't mean it, darling. I'm not mad. Of course, I know you can't. It's all right. It's only for a few days. I can wait." Then, hoping to change her tears to laughter, he said sternly: "Only the next time see that it happens on a weekend whan I can't have you anyhow."

"It's not that," she sobbed.

He put his arms about her and said, "Then tell me what it is, love."

"It's . . . it's . . ." she sobbed, "that I'm not going to have a baby. This is the second time since we married that I'm not going to have a baby." He gave a spurt of laughter. "Don't laugh," she said piteously.

"But you're so funny, my little Chinee. Most women cry their eyes out when they *miss* a period. You cry when you *don't.*"

"Because I *want* a baby. Because I *need* a baby so bad." She continued to weep as though she never would stop.

He petted her as he would a child. "There, Margaret! There, Maggie-Now, dear; my own dear, good girl. Don't cry. A baby takes time. I mean when a girl has been a good girl before her marriage, she doesn't get pregnant right away. Now: When you're all over this period, we'll try again. And this time, I'll put my mind on it."

This made her giggle through her sobs and soon she had stopped crying. After a while he said: "Since you can't sleep with me, would you brush-talk me to sleep, dear one?"

Often when he couldn't sleep, he liked her to brush her hair and talk to him about her childhood. So now she took her hair down, got her brush and sat on the bed facing him. She started brushing her hair.

"All right. Now! What do you want me to talk about?" she asked in her practical way. He howled with laughter. "What did I say that struck you so funny?" she asked indignantly.

"Nothing. Only you're such a *practical* darling; such a dear little thing with your no sense of humor; your *dear* no sense of humor."

"Anyhow, what do you want me to talk about?"

"Tell me about the nun and the hair and the bird's nest."

"Well . . ." She started to brush her hair with slow, rhythmic strokes. "When I was a little girl, Sister Veronica said: 'When you cut your hair, put the cuttings in the yard so the birds can use them in building their nests.' So I had bangs and

Mama used to cut them every time she washed my hair. So I told Mama to wash my hair first before she cut my bangs. You see, I wanted the birds to have clean hair for their nests. . . ."

Watching the up-and-down motion of the brush, listening to the rise and fall of her voice acted like a hypnotic. Soon his eyes were closed and he slept peacefully. She looked down on his face with love. With her forefinger poised an inch above his face, she traced the outlines. In this way, she conjured up the way he must have looked as a little boy.

He is so cold to the outside world, she thought. *And so different when he's alone with me. Oh, if only everyone knew him the way I know him . . .*

The next day, he was gone.

Chapter Thirty-Eight

THE next morning was one of those rare ones that come sometimes in early March when you had made up your mind that the long winter would *never* end. Sunshine burnished the hummocks of frozen slush in the gutters and there was a warm breeze.

Claude was late getting home from work that morning. Denny was leaving for school and still Claude hadn't come home. Maggie-Now went out on the stoop with Denny to see if Claude was coming. She sniffed the air. It smelled like freshly watered flowers. A breeze lifted a tendril of her hair and let it drop back against her cheek. She shivered in sensual delight. It felt like a lover's touch.

"Yes," she murmured.

"What?" asked Denny.

"It's a south wind."

"How do you know."

"Because it's coming from South Brooklyn."

"Kin I stay home from school then?"

"I should say not! Get going." She gave him an affectionate whack on the backside to propel him on his way.

She put Claude's slowly frying bacon on the back of the stove. She put his rolls in the warming oven and threw the warming coffee away; she'd make fresh when he came in. She told herself that, because it was such an unexpectedly wonderful day, he was walking part way before he took the trolley. She knew how excited he was about all weathers.

When he comes home, she thought, *we'll lie in bed and talk about what a wonderful day it is before we . . .*

The day wore on slowly and she began to believe that he wasn't coming home. She wished and wished that she knew what hotel he worked at. Why didn't she make him put the address in a sealed envelope and let her assure him that she wouldn't open it ever except in a terrible emergency?

From time to time, as she went about her routine household duties, a whinnying sound came from her—like an animal in pain. And while she was washing Denny's lunch dishes, her throat got dry suddenly and tightened up and an ugly sound came from her: like an "ugh" when one is kicked suddenly in the stomach. She leaned way over and put her forehead down on the sink and sobbed loudly and hoarsely until she was exhausted. She went about her housework with violent tremblings in her stomach. *If I was going to have a baby now,* she thought, *I'd lose it.* And she started to cry again, knowing she was not going to have a baby and Claude would never come back and there never could be another man. . . .

What did I say to him? What did I do? Was it Papa? Denny? Was it the house? That we could never be in bed together all night like other husbands and wives and all we had was a few hours in the morning? Come back, come back, darling, she prayed, *and we'll have our own home . . . even if it's only one room somewhere.* . . .

Then she got the idea that he had died where he worked or was deathly sick and they didn't know where he lived because he never told people things like that. She washed her face with shaking hands and got her hat on. She was halfway to the trolley stop when she remembered that she didn't know where he worked and could not go to get him if he was sick.

Denny came home from school. "I got nought in arithmetic today," he announced, "and I got double homework."

"Do it!"

"I want to go out and play first."

"Do your homework!" she screamed.

"It's too hard. You got to help me."

"Let me alone!" she screamed.

This frightened the boy. "I'm going to get Claude," he said. He went to the bedroom.

"Claude's not here," she said.

"Where'd he go?" She didn't answer. She went into her room. Denny went out on the street.

The three of them sat down to a haphazard supper that night. "Hey, Papa," said Denny importantly, "Claude went away."

Pat put his fork down. "So," he said. "So. Three months was all he could stand, hey? Well, if he thinks I'm going to support his wife . . ." Maggie-Now pushed her plate away and ran into her bedroom and closed the door. "What did I say?" asked Pat of Denny. He sounded genuinely bewildered.

Maggie-Now lay on her bed in the darkness. She did not know how long she had been there. The house was quiet. She heard someone knock on the door. She jumped up, thinking it was news of Claude, but it was only a boy with a message from the movie-theater manager. It was seven-thirty and the manager wanted to know why she was late.

"Tell him I'm sick," she said. "Tell him I'm sick. I can't come to work tonight."

She went into the kitchen to clear the table and wash the dishes. She saw Denny's books still strapped up and knew he had not yet done his homework. She looked in his bedroom. He wasn't there. She surmised he had gone out with his father.

Her father came in at eight-thirty. "Where's Denny?" she asked.

"Why? Ain't he home?"

"I thought he was with you."

"Well, he ain't."

Without bothering to put on her coat, she ran out into the night, which had turned cold after the warm day, looking for her brother. She found him at last, three blocks away. There was a corner candy store with a newsstand outside. Denny, with two bigger boys, stood just around the corner. As she waited to cross the street, she saw a man pick up a paper, throw down some coins and go on his way. One of the bigger boys, quick as a flash, darted out, snatched the coins and went back to the others. As she crossed the street, she saw another man take a paper and put down the money. She reached the stand in time to see Denny duck around and grab the pennies.

When he saw her, he was petrified with fright. She grasped his wrist tightly, held his clenched hand over the newsstand and hammered at his hand until he opened it and the pennies dropped back on the papers. The other kids ran away. She dragged him home. He cried all the way.

When she remembered the episode afterward, she was always glad that the candy-store man had been too busy with customers to notice what had been going on outside his store. He was a mean man and would not have hesitated at all to call the police.

Pat offered cruel reasons for why Claude had left her. All the reasons were to Claude's discredit. From time to time, Denny asked when

Claude was coming home. There was talk in the neighborhood. One woman spoke to her bluntly.

"I don't see your husband around no more."

"No," said Maggie-Now.

Others, more considerate, said nothing to her but discussed it with others. "He was never no good in the first place," was the verdict, "and she's well rid of the dirty, black Pratt-ess-stant."

One woman said to a neighbor: "Now I'm just as broad-minded as the next one. But there's always two sides to every story and I'd sure like to hear *his* side. The way *I* look at it, a man just don't get up and leave his wife for nothing."

Maggie-Now endured the gossip, real or imagined, and it neither added to, took from, nor diverted her from her grief.

On her monthly visit to Lottie, she had to tell her Claude had gone. Lottie waited a long time before she spoke. "You know what I think about him," she said. "But that's got nothing to do with the way you feel. I won't run him down. You get enough of that from your father. But tell me this: Before you married him and you had known for sure that he would leave you, would you have married him anyhow?"

"Yes," whispered Maggie-Now.

"Well, so in a way, you bought it and now you have to pay for it. Still and all, that don't make it easier. I felt the same way, almost, when Timmy left me that time to go back to Ireland. I thought maybe he wouldn't come back and then I thought, anyways, I was lucky that I had him

398

for the time I did have him even if he never came back.''

But I had a child, she thought. *And where is her child? Her children? She can't marry again while he lives. Not in our religion. I don't wish him any hard luck. God forgive me, but . . .*

Spring came. Denny made his First Holy Communion. Father Flynn catechised him.

"Who made the world?"

"God made the world."

"Who is God?"

Denny was letter perfect, not missing a single answer. Father Flynn was surprised and pleased. Maggie-Now had told him that Denny did badly in school.

"You did fine, Dennis. Didn't miss a single question."

"Claude learned me . . ."

"Taught you . . ."

"Yeah. Every day Claude made me say the answers."

Father Flynn was pleased about that and felt a degree of warmth toward Claude.

Maggie-Now went to the First Holy Communion Mass and was proud of her brother. She thought of how moved Claude would have been at the beautiful ritual and how they would have talked about it afterward.

It started to be summer and Denny came home trembling the last day of school to tell his sister he'd been left back: a terrible disgrace in the neighborhood.

"Don't tell Papa," he begged.

"He must know and you must tell him yourself."

"He'll whip me."

"Yes, he will. What's a spanking? It will take your mind off being left back. And remember: You'll have a little boy someday and you'll spank him too, if he gets left back."

"Will you hold my hand when I tell him?"

"Yes."

Hand in hand, they confronted their father. "Papa, Denny has something to tell you."

"What?"

"Tell him, Denny."

"I got left back." Denny crowded closer to his sister.

To their surprise, the unpredictable man sided with his son. First, he said they gave Denny too much homework for the second grade. Next he put the blame on Claude.

"I don't wonder," he said, "I knew it would happen the way that bastid filled the boy's head up with all that stuff about South America and them grouchies on the pampies or peepees or whatever the hell they was, instead-a helping the boy with his A,B, Abs."

Pat, in his element because he had a chance to abuse Claude, ranted and raved and was indignant at Claude to such an extent that Denny began to feel that he had accomplished something admirable in not being promoted to the next grade. But Maggie-Now made Denny go to summer school all the same.

Missing Claude was still a dull ache to her. Sometimes she had a tiny flash of resentment toward him. Usually, it was when her Time came. *If only he had left me With Child,* she thought, *it wouldn't be so hard for me to keep going. And,* she thought further, *it's a terrible thing when a woman never slept with a man before and then she gets used to sleeping with one man and then he goes away. That's the hardest thing of all.*

And summer became fall and fall started to change into winter and suddenly the war was over.

It was the Armistice and people poured out of their stores and houses and walked up and down the street with a jigging, up-and-down walk and hollered across the street to each other that the war was over. And kids ganged up and looted the stores. Most shopkeepers locked up for the day, but the candy-store man, who had two sons in the service and was deliriously happy that the war was over and that his boys would come home safe and sound, got a barrel and emptied the contents of his store into it and lugged it out onto the sidewalk and threw handfuls of candy into the air and laughed as the little children tumbled over each other scrambling for it. Then some big boys came along, kicked over the barrel, chased the man back into his store, chased the little kids away and gathered up the candy.

Not all the people of the neighborhood were out on the streets, though. Lots of older ones went to church to give thanks. And in some houses, where there was a gold star in the window, the people stayed home and pulled the shades down as though it were night.

That was the false Armistice.

When the real one came through on November 11, an impromptu block party was organized that night. A band got itself together: a fellow with a cornet, a girl with a violin, a middle-aged German, taken on sufferance because he played the concertina, and a high-school kid with a drum. Two benign cops, one at each end of the block, closed the block to traffic so that there could be dancing in the street.

There were a few men in uniforms. They were from nearby camps. Some were home on furlough, others on short leave, and a few were just A.W.O.L. They danced with their own girls or with pick-ups. There were some sailors, those who did paper work down at the Brooklyn Navy Yard, and they had their own girls. You could always tell a sailor's girl. She wore pants, a lace blouse, very high-heeled shoes, rhinestone earrings and had a shingle hair-cut. Just the same, there were more girls than men and the surplus girls danced with each other.

Maggie-Now stood on the sidewalk with Denny to watch. From time to time, someone started a song in competition to the band.

Though the army is in clover,

sang out a voice, and everybody else sang the next line:

'Twas the navy brought them over.

And everybody agreed songfully in the punch line that the navy would bring them back.

Maggie-Now saw Sonny's sister dance by with Cholly. "Look!" called out Gina. She pointed to the chevron on Cholly's sleeve. "Private first class!" she called out proudly.

Cholly whirled Gina around so he could talk to Maggie-Now over Gina's shoulder. "I fought and I fought," he hollered, "but I had to go anyhow."

"Yeah," said a soldier, evidently a buddy of Cholly's. "Yeah! He fought a good clean war up there at Yaphank."

Someone started to sing: *You're in the army now.* There were cries of "Shut up!" and "Drop dead!" and "You should live so long!"

The next time Gina danced around, Maggie-Now called out: "How's Sonny?"

"As if you cared," said Gina bitterly.

Maggie-Now waited until Gina danced around again. "I ask as a friend," she shouted above the noise.

Gina made Cholly pause and they stood,

swaying to the rhythm of "There Are Smiles," while she answered Maggie-Now. "Strange as it may seem to you, *Mrs. Bassett,* he's just fine."

"Meow!" said Cholly, and they danced away.

"It's late, Denny," said Maggie-Now. "Let's go home."

Then it was Thanksgiving again, and soon after that Maggie-Now lost her job. The manager of the movie house told her that the veterans were coming home and needed jobs and it was only right that he give her job to a guy who was willing and ready to die to make The World Safe for Democracy. Maggie-Now agreed that she felt the same way.

"Yeah," said the manager, "they fought for the privilege of eating apple pie and watching the Dodgers play ball. And the least we can do . . ."

"That's right," agreed Maggie-Now.

She wasn't worried. She had fifteen hundred dollars in the bank saved from her salary and the rent from the rooms upstairs. If Claude came back . . . *if,* and if he didn't get work right away, there was enough money to go on for a while without her father getting nasty about finances.

It was December. There wasn't much snow. One day it did snow real hard but it changed to rain. Then it snowed again a little and for three days it snowed on and off. Maggie-Now did not believe that Claude would come back. What did she have to go on? True, he had come back last winter, but then he had been free to go away in the first place. He had come back because he wanted to marry her then. But now . . .

Still, she waited for him, pretending. . . . Each night at ten, she dressed warmly and went out on the streets, walking for blocks in the direction he had come from the year before. Then she'd go home, prepare for bed, put on her white robe, go out and sit at the window, brushing her hair, and wait. No, she didn't expect him to come back, but the waiting for him, the pretending that he might come back, gave her a kind of surcease.

One night she was out walking. The snow had been around for days now and she told herself there was no rule that he would come back with the snow. She heard her name spoken in his voice but there was no one on the street. *I'm getting queer,* she thought, *hearing voices when there is no one here.*

"And where did you get that funny hat?"

She turned around. He had come up behind her from the opposite direction. She looked at him, then put her hands over her face and wept. He took her in his arms and comforted her in the old way.

"I know, I know. There, now. There, Margaret, there, Maggie-Now."

"If you had only sent a line, a note, just a card with your name on it . . . something that I could have hoped on," she wept.

"I know, I know. Someday when we are old and have run out of things to talk about, I'll tell

405

you all about it. Why I must . . ."

"If you go away again, please, *please,* oh, Claude, tell me first. I won't keep you, I won't hold you, I won't . . ."

"If I go again, will you come with me, Margaret?"

"Yes! Yes! Anywhere . . . anyplace just so we are together."

He had brought back two small steaks which were wrapped up and pushed in his coat pocket. She made coffee and prepared to fry the steaks. He emptied his pockets and placed nearly thirty dollars on the table.

"I earned it," he said "and I want you to buy a dressing table so that, at night, I can lie in bed and watch you brush your hair and see you from the back and see your face in the mirror at the same time."

She put the coffeepot down. He was sitting, she standing. She took his head in her hands and held it against her breast, but all she said was: "Oh, Claude!"

He asked about Denny and about her father and said: "I hope he doesn't wake up and come out here. I'm too tired to spar with him tonight. I'll take him on tomorrow."

"I'll see that he doesn't bother us," she said.

She went up to her father's room. She was going to tell him under no circumstances to come out into the kitchen, that Claude was back and they wanted to be alone and, if he wouldn't let them be alone, she would leave with

Claude immediately.

"Papa, wake up!" He groaned. She shook him awake.

"*Now* what?" he said irritably.

"Claude is back and . . ."

"What?" he shouted.

"Sh! Don't holler. The tenants . . ."

"The hell with the tenants!" he shouted louder. "What did you say?"

"Claude just came home and I want you . . ."

He jumped out of bed. "If you think for one minute I'm going down there and give him the big welcome and sit there half the night talking to that bastid . . ." He was ranting and raving and cursing and stamping his foot like *Rumpelstiltskin,* the dwarf in the fairytale.

The tenant occupying the rest of the apartment banged on the wall, and yelled: "A little quiet in there. We want to sleep."

"Drop dead!" Pat yelled back.

"Yeah?" came the weary voice of the wife. "*You* drop dead!" Pat shook his fist at the wall and shouted: "I'll bury youse all!" After a while, Maggie-Now got him bedded down and quieted. When she got back to the kitchen, Denny was standing there in his pajamas talking a blue streak. Claude, almost asleep, was nodding his head from time to time.

". . . left back and I went to summer school and got promoted on prohibition" (he meant probation), "and I belong to a gang, The Rotten Roosters, and we got a password. . . ."

"Denny," she said sharply, "what are you doing out of bed?"

"I got up to say hello to Claude."

"Say good night."

"Good night."

"Now get back to bed."

"But . . ."

"Don't let me tell you again," she threatened. He went back to bed.

Claude fell asleep while he was eating his steak. She got up and pulled him to his feet. She pulled one of his arms over her shoulder and got him into the bedroom. ". . . sleepy," muttered Claude. "Don' know why . . . getting older . . ."

She sat him on the bed and got his pajamas from under the pillow where she always kept them. She got her nightgown from under the other pillow. But Claude had keeled over and was sound asleep. She pulled back the covers, got his legs up onto the bed, pulled his shoes off, and, not bothering to try to undress him, she got him under the covers. She undressed. She thought of the half-eaten food on the table and the unbanked fire and she didn't care. It was the first time she'd ever left the kitchen untidy.

She put out the light and got into bed beside him. She turned him on his side and got her arm under his shoulder, put his head on her breast and her hand on his cheek, pressing his head against her. She was utterly content. He felt like a baby in her arm.

He was up early the next morning and in

wonderfully high spirits. She brought him his breakfast on a tray and he made her sit on the bed and share it with him. He told her he was going out to get a job. She gave him his thirty dollars back and added twenty of her own and told him to get a suit and shoes and a hat. He refused at first, mentioning the dressing table. She said he could buy that for her out of his first week's pay.

She watched him fondly as he went down the stoop whistling.

He walked over to Henny Clynne's section. As he approached the super who was indoctrinating this snowfall's crop of "college men," Claude started to whistle: "High Above Cayuga's Waters." He whistled tenderly, nostalgically and with many trills. Henny's ears stood up; his nostrils quivered. He got the scent of a live one. His little eyes twinkled when he recognized Claude. He was seldom lucky enough to get the same college man two years in succession.

"Graduate from college yet?" he asked Claude.

"Oh, yes, sir. And now, I'm working on my master's. . . ." He paused and winked at Henny, ". . . you know what. And when I get finished with that," he looked around cautiously and dropped his voice to a whisper, "then I'll start on my pee aitch dee."

It sounded vaguely dirty to Henny. He snarled: "Don't get wise with me, college boy."

"Oh, no, sir," said Claude eagerly.

Henny heaved a shovel at him. Claude caught

it in one hand. He stroked the smooth wood. "Oh, sir," he said, "you don't know how I've dreamed of this. All year, cold and hungry, I dreamed you would put a shovel in my hand . . ." Some of the men started to laugh.

"Fall in, beautiful dreamer," ordered Henny. The men laughed louder. Henny was satisfied. If they *had* to laugh, let them laugh at *his* comeback.

". . . And I dreamed," continued Claude, "that I gave the shovel back to you, like this." Gently he put the shovel back in Henny's hand. ". . . And I dreamed I said: 'Stick it —— —— ——, you sadistic son-of-a-bitch!'"

Before Henny could recover, Claude was swaggering down the street, hands in pocket, and whistling: "Hail to the victors valiant. Hail . . ."

He went to a men's furnishing store and bought a cheap suit, a shirt, a pair of shoes and a hat. While the pants were being shortened, he went to a barbershop down the street and had a haircut and a mustache trim. While sitting in the chair, he read the want ads in the *Brooklyn Eagle*. He picked out a job for himself and went back to the store and got into his new outfit. The man asked couldn't he interest him in an overcoat. He couldn't. Claude had a khaki wool pullover left over from Maggie-Now's days of knitting for the Red Cross. That, pulled over his shirt, was as good as an overcoat, he thought.

He got home at three that afternoon and Maggie-Now threw her arms around him and told him he looked just *grand.*

"Just grand! But where are your old clothes?"

"In the store, Miss Practical. I'll pick them up tomorrow. Your grand husband feels grand because he has a grand job."

"No!" she said ecstatically.

"Floorwalker. In one of Brooklyn's biggest department stores. Basement," he added.

"Where, Claude? Where?"

"Downtown Brooklyn."

"Oh!" Her voice fell a little. *So he's not going to tell me,* she thought. "I see," she said inanely. She turned away from him. He turned on his heel and went out the front door. "Where are you going?" she asked, frightened. The door closed.

It opened almost immediately and he came in with a pasteboard box which he had left on the stoop. It said *Gage and Tollner* on the cover and it held six pieces of wonderful French pastry.

"For you," he said. "A surprise."

"Oh, Claude, I love you so much!" She was grateful. Her gratitude was mixed with relief. For a second, she had been afraid that he was going to leave her again.

I mustn't question him, she advised herself. *Even though a wife has a right to know where her husband works. But I must take him as he is and just be so glad that I have him back.*

"We'll have some right away," she said. "I'll make coffee."

"You will not! You will come to bed with me

411

right away. Last night, I fell asleep before I had a chance to kiss you good night."

"But . . ."

"But what? Don't tell me . . ."

"No. Not that. But Denny will be home from school any minute."

"Let him play outside awhile. It won't hurt him." He locked the door. "Oh, Margaret." He took her into his arms. "It's been such a long time!"

"Such a long, *long* time," she sighed.

She heard Denny try the doorknob. She grew rigid in her husband's embrace. "It's Denny," she whispered.

"Never mind," he said roughly. "He can look out for himself. I come first."

Afterward, she unlocked the door and looked up and down the street. "Now, sweetheart," Claude said, "stop fussing. You'll make a sissy out of him."

It was nearly six; supper was almost ready. She looked at the clock for the tenth time in five minutes. "I can't help it, Claude," she burst out. "I'm worried about Denny."

"I'll go out and find him, dear," he said.

He found him a couple of blocks away. He was with a gang of boys. They were throwing icy snowballs at a Jewish junkman. The man was in a rickety wagon pulled by a starved-looking dirty white horse. He was having a hard time getting the horse to pull the junk wagon through the street as the poor beast skidded from time to time on bits of ice left from the day's snow clearance. The boys were laughing and yelling and calling the junkman dirty names. Claude dispersed the boys, made Denny apologize to the man and say he was sorry, and took his hand and walked him home.

"Now, what devilment was he up to?" asked Maggie-Now crossly. Denny's hand twitched in Claude's.

"He wasn't doing a thing," said Claude. "He was only playing with some other boys."

Denny pressed his hand hard against Claude's hand. Maggie-Now saw the movement and she knew.

"Claude!" she said. It was a syllable of love.

"I have a very foolish name," said Claude to Denny, "and some people make fun of it. But when your sister says it, it sounds like a very fine name."

Denny smiled up at Claude.

Chapter Thirty-Nine

SHE was waiting on the stoop for him when he came from his first day of work. She kissed him, not caring if the neighbors saw, and pulled him into the house, where she kissed him again, this time more lingeringly. He was wearing a white carnation in his buttonhole. The flower was only a little bit wilted. She put it on the table in a wineglass full of water.

She had taken pains with this, the first supper the whole family would eat together since her marriage. She had boiled tongue with horse-radish sauce and asparagus with hollandaise sauce, and, with the hope of ingratiating herself with her father, candied sweet potatoes, a plain lettuce salad with oil and vinegar dressing, hard-crusted rolls, airy light inside, sweet butter, the pastries from Gage and Tollner, and of course coffee. (Only this time with real cream instead of canned milk.)

Pat came home and, to everyone's astonishment, greeted Claude heartily, Maggie-Now cheerfully and Denny with fatherly affection. He was so full of good will and kindliness and cheerfulness that he cast a pall over the supper. All worried, thinking he was either sick or drunk.

Thought Claude: *He's got something up his grubby sleeve. Throwing up that good-will smokescreen. I'll wait and see. This should be interesting.*

Thought Maggie-Now: *Papa knows I love Claude and that he can't do a thing about it. So I guess he thinks he might as well be nice about it. Only,* she worried, *Papa don't need to be so awfully friendly. I'd feel better if he was just not unfriendly.*

Pat's thoughts were along the same line as Claude's. *I'll treat him just like he was any other decent slob. He'll get so mad that I'm not interested in who or what he is that he'll spill the whole beans about himself, the bastid.*

Denny: *There's six cakes and four of us. Papa feels good and maybe he'll say to let the little boy get the two what's left.*

After supper, Claude told Denny he'd help him with his reading homework after the dishes were out of the way. Claude and Pat went into the front room.

"Sit down, son," said Pat benevolently.

"After you, sir," said Claude courteously.

Each sat at a window, their chairs facing each other. Pat lit up his clay pipeful of tobacco and Claude lit up a cigarette.

"I'm proud of you, me boy, and you getting the grand job the first day you look. Maggie-Now told me."

"Thank you, sir."

"And how much do they be paying you?" he asked mellowly.

"The usual salary." Pat was all ears. "A little more than *they* think I'm worth and a little less than *I* think I'm worth."

The bastid, thought Pat bitterly. He pulled himself together. *I must watch meself and not ask him anything right out. I got to go round-about.*

"I see you got a nice brown tan," said Pat.

Claude looked at one of his sun-tanned hands and said in simulated astonishment: "Why, so I have!"

"People what stay in the South for a time always get sunburned," said Pat.

"I envy you your room upstairs, sir," countered Claude. "You can see the sky while you lie in bed."

"Funny thing," mused Pat. "You can always tell when a man gets out that he's been in Sing Sing. Their skin is this here dead white because they never get out in the air."

"And," said Claude, assuming an eager naïveté, "their hair is clipped close to the head."

"Now down South," said Pat, dreamily sucking on his pipe, "you can't tell. When they put them in jail, they let them out all day to work on the roads. Then they get a good tan.

416

So, when they come out, nobody knows they're ex-convicts.''

Now he'll know I'm onto him, thought Pat.

"I read that in the paper," he added in a too offhand way.

"I read the newspapers, too," said Claude, dreamily contemplating the smoke from his cigarette. "I read that they put chains around their ankles when they work outdoors. And you can see white circles on the suntan of their ankles where the chains were."

In an absent-minded way, Claude pulled up a trouser leg and crossed that leg over his other leg. Pat's eyes, like a true-thrown dart, went to the exposed ankle. It was smoothly tanned all over; no white circles.

"Is there some other topic you would care to discuss, sir? We have the whole evening ahead of us. My, it's good to be home again," said Claude.

Claude brought home his first week's salary: fifty dollars! Maggie-Now could hardly believe it. Even Pat was impressed.

"That's good pay for a man what ain't got no steady trade," was his compliment.

Claude mentioned the dressing table but Maggie-Now said to wait until there was a sale. She put the money in the bank, all but ten dollars of it.

Claude seemed to like his work. Each night when he got home, he threw away the former day's carnation and put a new one in the wineglass. Each Saturday night, he gave her his pay intact. He asked nothing more than seventy-five cents a day for carfare, a luncheon sandwich and cigarettes. He seemed to want no material things for himself.

He gave lavish Christmas gifts to them: a meerschaum pipe in a satin-lined, carved-wood case for Pat, a pair of ice skates for Denny with a promise he'd take him to Highland Park to teach him ice skating, and a beautiful small gold and white dressing table, with an oval mirror, for Maggie-Now.

Pat pawned the pipe the day after Christmas and gave the ticket to Mick Mack, who did not smoke. But the little fellow considered the ticket itself, with Pat's name on it, as a Christmas gift and he put it in his wallet and treasured it for years.

The payday after Christmas, Claude brought no salary home. He had charged the gifts at the store. He asked her if she minded and, of course, she said she didn't.

In January, Father Paul, a missionary priest, came to give instructions to non-Catholics who wished to become converts. He would serve all the parishes in that part of Brooklyn and his headquarters were the principal's office in the neighborhood parochial school. Instructions would be given at night.

Father Paul was incredibly thin. His face

looked like skin stretched tight over a skeleton of bones with no flesh in between. He had spent his years in jungles and swamps and the brush and places not on any map. He had eaten the strange foods of savage people and been subjected to the strange ills of the jungle and had endured unheard-of hardships. He was worn as fine as a knife that had been honed too much. Every three of four years, he took a "rest" by carrying on his missionary work in America for a month or two.

Here, thought Claude, was no gentle, serene priest like Father Flynn; no priest who took a glass of wine before a meal or smoked a cigar or pipe for relaxation; who tapped a foot to the rhythm of a passing tune. Father Paul wore a long black cassock, and a six-inch crucifix, that looked like flashing gold, hung on the left side of his breast. He raised his hooded eyes to Claude and spoke in a strong, ringing voice.

"Your name, my son."

"Claude Bassett, Father."

"Religion?"

"I am a non-Catholic."

The hooded eyes flashed up and the cross trembled as he took a deep breath to bring out the full volume of his voice.

"Your religion!" he thundered. *Religion! Religion!* came back the echo of his voice from the corners of the room.

"Protestant," said Claude, awed in spite of himself.

"How long have you been married?"

"A year, Father."

"Is there a child?"

"We have not been fortunate enough . . ." began Claude.

"Has there been a child?" thundered the priest. The cross moved like a living thing and *Child! Child!* echoed in the room.

"No, Father."

"Is a child expected?"

"No, Father."

"Why?" Claude shrugged and smiled. "Why has your wife not conceived?" continued the priest.

"I beg your pardon, Father?"

"Do you do anything to prevent conception?"

"Really, Father," began Claude.

"Do you use contraceptives?" thundered the priest. The word echoed back.

A dark color came into Claude's face. He got to his feet and said: "With all due respect to you, Father, that's hardly any of your business."

The priest rose, also. The cross flashed like fire and the echoes of his thundering words made it seem as though there were three voices in the room.

"It is my business! It is the business of the Church! It is the holy duty of those who marry in the Catholic Church to produce children—children for the Church!"

"We might want them for our own pleasure,' said Claude a little flippantly.

"Your pleasure will be that you will be custodians of the children for Holy Mother Church!"

"Good evening, sir," said Claude suddenly. He turned on his heel and walked out of the room.

Maggie-Now greeted him eagerly. "Is it all settled?"

"As far as I'm concerned it is. For good!"

"Will you take instructions?"

"I had a heart-to-heart talk with Father Paul. He did the talking."

"Oh, Claude, can't you give me a direct answer? Can't you ever say a 'yes' or a 'no'?" She was nervous and tense. His conversion meant so, *so* much to her.

"I'll give you a direct answer," he said coldly. "No! I can never give a 'yes' or a 'no.' I don't believe everything in life can be settled by a monosyllable."

"Don't talk to me that way, Claude," she pleaded. "When you use words like that, I feel you are away from me."

Without another word, he went into their bedroom. When she got into bed later, he turned away from her and slept with his back to her all night.

The next morning, as he was leaving for work, he said: "Let me have twenty dollars."

She choked back the automatic question: "What for?" She thought she knew what for. He

421

was leaving her again and he wanted twenty dollars to start off on. She gave him the money. He pocketed it and put an arm around her and pulled her to him.

"It's time we celebrated our first wedding anniversary," he said.

"That was last week, Claude. I didn't say anything because I knew you'd forgotten."

"All men forget wedding anniversaries."

"But you're different, Claude."

"Not that different. Now here's what I want you to do: Pack your little red bag, put my stuff in too, and meet me in the lobby of the St. George at six. Bring a clean shirt. I'll go to work directly from the hotel."

She left two cold plates in the icebox for Pat's and Denny's supper and told Denny not to leave the house; his father would be home in an hour.

They had dinner at the same place. They didn't have the same room at the hotel but one almost as nice. It was like their marriage night except this time they undressed together in the bedroom. He got into his pajamas, looked in the glass, put the jacket inside the pants, took it out again, said, "The hell with it," and stripped off the pajamas and went to bed naked.

She went into the bathroom to wash up and clean her teeth and came out and stood before the dresser and started to brush her hair.

"Never mind the brushing tonight," he said impatiently. "Get into bed."

"All right, Claude." She picked up the

pajamas from the floor to hang them up.

"Stop fussing around so," he said crossly.

"All right." She dropped the pajamas back on the floor and got into bed with him.

It was a night of wild, almost insatiable passion. When morning came, she kissed him with great tenderness and said: "I *know* I'll have a baby now!"

"If you do, I know who'll be deliriously happy."

"Who?" she asked teasingly, assuming he'd say, "Me."

"Your Church!" he said bitterly.

She sighed. She guessed what Father Paul had said to him and she knew now that Claude would never come into her Church and her Faith.

They had breakfast in the hotel restaurant. "I'll walk you to the store where you work," she said.

"You're Daddy's little girl, aren't you?" he said with a sneer.

She flushed. "I don't mean to trick you into finding out where you work. I just wanted to walk with you. I never asked you to tell me. I never ask you questions any more. I don't want to know what you don't want to tell me. Just so I have you to love; just so you are with me."

He put his hand on hers across the table. "Margaret, from the time I was born, everyone kept things from me—things I had a right to know; that everyone has a right to know."

Intuitively, she knew he meant that no one would tell him anything about his parents or where he had come from.

"They put me off when I asked questions. . . . I grew up learning the trick of putting *others* off when they asked *me* questions. Now it's a habit I can't put aside."

"I know," she said.

One Saturday night in the middle of January, Claude came home from work as usual. "Where's your flower?" she asked.

"No more carnations for the wineglass. I'm fired," said Claude cheerfully.

"But why . . ."

"They needed me only for the Christmas rush and for the after rush—customers exchanging presents. And now they've all been changed." He gave her his final salary. "I'll get another job," he said.

"Sure you will," she said.

The first week, he read the ads and went out looking for a job. The second week, he didn't bother. He still read the ads but told her there was nothing for him. He got into a routine.

He'd get up after Pat had left for work, eat a leisurely breakfast, with Maggie-Now joining him for coffee, talk to her awhile and then go into the front room and sit at the window. At ten o'clock, he'd ask her for a quarter for cigarettes and a paper. She'd give it to him and tell him to come right back, and he'd say he would, and kiss her and be back in half an hour or so. Then he'd put in the day reading the paper and smoking.

On Saturdays, however, he always took Denny somewhere if the weather wasn't too bad. Maggie-Now gave them a dollar and they were off for the day. He took the boy to the Aquarium, to Prospect Park another Saturday, for a ride on the Staten Island ferry, to the Brooklyn Navy Yard, the Brooklyn Museum of Art, and other places of interest.

It was getting late into March. Maggie-Now woke up at dawn one morning, feeling strangely uneasy. She put on her robe and went out on the stoop. Yes, the south wind . . . the morning full of scented, tender promise of springtime.

She fixed him a special breakfast: broiled ham and eggs and poppy-seed rolls and sweet butter and coffee with real cream. After breakfast, he opened the window and leaned far out, feeling the soft wind on his face. He did not sit at the window that morning. He walked up and down restlessly.

Maggie-Now went into Denny's room and emptied his marbles out of their cloth Bull Durham sack. She went into her room and got the gold piece that her father had given her as a wedding present. She wrapped it in tissue, put it in the little sack and pinned it inside the breast pocket of Claude's coat. She pinned it top and bottom so that it wouldn't move about.

At ten o'clock, Claude said: "If you'll let me

have a quarter, love, I'll go out and get my cigarettes and the paper."

She fumbled in her pocketbook and gave him a five-dollar bill. "All I want is a quarter," he said.

"I have no change," she lied.

She held his coat for him and, when he had it on, she turned him around and buttoned it for him. "Come right back, hear?" she said as she said every morning.

"I will," he promised, as he promised every morning.

She took his hands in hers and pressed her cheek to his hands. "Oh, Claude, I love you so much!" she said.

He kissed her and went out for cigarettes and the paper as he did every morning.

But on this morning, he did not come back.

Chapter Forty

"NOW that he's out of the house, I'm going to move me bedstead downstairs," said Pat.

"Leave it where it is, Papa. You'll only have to drag it back up when Claude comes home."

She frowned over Denny's poor report card. "Oh, Denny, if you get left back again, what will Claude say when he gets home? He'll be so disappointed."

". . . every day, like clockwork, he'd show up for a pack of cigarettes and a paper."

"He's gone on one of his trips, Mr. Brockman. He'll be back again in the fall."

"Don't ask me *how* I know, Aunt Lottie. I just *know* he'll come back. In the war, women had to wait for their men to come back. I can wait, too."

". . . anything I can do, Father, to fill in the

time until my husband comes back."

"Perhaps Miss Doubleday over at the settlement house could use some help," suggested Father Flynn.

"You mean hand sewing? Oh, yes, I could, Miss Doubleday. I could teach them hemstitching and darning and fagoting and how to make buttonholes. I'd love it! Two hours, one night a week? That would be just fine! Only I must tell you that I'd have to give up the class in November when my husband comes home from his trip."

"He'll never come back," said Pat to Mick Mack. "Never! When he knew I was onto him, he got out before I had a chance to throw him out.

"You know, it got so I couldn't sit and talk with him no more. He gave me the willies. He asked them questions—about me mother and did I remember me father what died before I was born and did I know where all me brothers was. He eats off-a people was the way I figgered it out. He keeps chewing away at me life till he's got it all for hisself, but he don't give me nothing of his life; like where he was born and where his relations is now."

"Like that pitcher I seen," said Mick Mack. "Where them zombies climb out-a their coffins nights and go upstairs and eat the blood off-a people what's sleeping in their bed."

"You damn fool!" said Pat, contemptuously.

Maggie-Now was so sure Claude was coming back that she prepared for his return the day after he left. She sponged and pressed his new suit and hung it in the closet with a sheet over it to keep it dust free. She shined his new shoes and wrapped them in newspapers. She washed and ironed his few shirts and wrapped them in tissue paper and put them away in his drawer. She knitted a dark maroon tie for him and two pair of socks. She washed and ironed his pajamas and put them under his pillow and kept them there.

She made a sort of shrine of the little dressing table he'd given her. On it, she placed the little red suitcase he'd given her, *The Book of Everything* with his autograph, and the postcard with its message, *Wait for me*.

While she waited, she filled in her days as best she could. She visited Lottie each first and third Sunday of the month. She had her sewing class, and nearly every Saturday afternoon she had the little girl sewers over to her house for hot chocolate and crackers.

She sat in church one Sunday afternoon and saw Gina Pheid married to her Cholly. Outside the church, she shook Cholly's hand and kissed Gina and wished them both luck. Gina invited her to the reception but Maggie-Now didn't go.

A month later, at Mass, she heard the banns read for Thomas Pheid and Evelyn Delmar. She wondered whether that was the girl who had once given Sonny the go-by because he didn't have money to spend on her. Her name sounded like the name of a girl who liked spenders, thought Maggie-Now.

Maggie-Now did not go to see Sonny married. Not that she was jealous or anything, she assured herself, and not that she didn't know he'd marry sometime or other. She just didn't want to *see* him be married.

Denny caused her some concern that spring. He played hooky from school a couple of times. The first time Father Flynn brought him home; he had found Denny wandering around the streets. The next time, the truant officer brought him home and told Maggie-Now to see that it didn't happen again.

"There's a law, you know," he said.

For the rest of the term, she walked to school with Denny each morning and stood outside and waited until he was safely inside before she went home.

When she told Lottie, Lottie said that it was nothing. All boys played hooky now and then. Even her Widdy had. "I remember like it was yesterday. Timmy caught him and the next morning Timmy said: 'I want you to play hooky today and if I ketch you sneaking in school, I'll give you a licking you'll never forget.' So every morning, he made Widdy go out and play hooky, and the first thing you know, Widdy was sneaking back in school and he said: 'Don't tell

Pop that I'm going to school.'

"That Timmy!" Lottie smiled a tender, faraway smile of affectionate memory.

She pried ten dollars out of her father and sent Denny to camp that summer for two weeks. Denny had been gone but two days when Maggie-Now got so lonesome that she went over to Lottie's to try to get her to stay with her.

"You've never been to our house, Aunt Lottie, since the day I was christened. You can have Denny's room. I'll cook the things you like. You owe me a long visit."

"No," said Lottie. "I got to be here when Timmy gets home nights." Maggie-Now looked startled. "Don't look at me so funny. I only make believe he's coming home. I put out the pan of hot water with Epsom salts for his poor feet right in front of his chair. Don't think I'm funny in the head. When I was a little girl I used to make believe I had a little girl friend. I even gave her a name, Sherry. And I'd have a little tea party and talk to her and make believe she talked to me. Well, that's how I do with Timmy. Thanks anyway, Maggie-Now, dear. But I'd get homesick if I went away."

Well, Denny didn't finish out his two weeks at camp. He'd been gone only four days when Maggie-Now got a letter from the head counselor saying Denny wanted to come home; that he would not participate in the activities of the camp, had to be coaxed to eat; and his tentmates said he cried nights and said he wanted his sister. The counselor wrote that she was sending him home.

Maggie-Now knelt before Denny and put her arms around him when she noticed that his face had gotten thin in the time he was away and that there were black circles under his eyes.

"Why didn't you want to stay at camp, Denny?" she asked.

"Because I wanted to come home."

"Did you have fun, swimming and . . ."

"I wanted to be home with you."

"Denny, you're a big boy now, almost nine years old. You shouldn't be so dependent on me."

"I don't want to go no place if you don't come along."

Maggie-Now knew that she shouldn't be thrilled because he needed her so much. But she *was* thrilled and moved. *What will I do,* she thought in panic, *when he gets big and doesn't need me any more? Oh, I must have children. I must! I need so much to be needed.*

She went to see Father Flynn a few days later and asked him how she could go about adopting a baby.

"I'm afraid that's impossible, Margaret. Babies are not given out for adoption except to good devout Catholics."

"I try to be a good Catholic," she said.

"But your husband is non-Catholic." She hung her head.

"Couldn't I adopt a Protestant baby or a Jewish baby?"

"No, my child. Methodist orphanages permit only Methodists to adopt their children. And the Baptists and Lutherans and Episcopalians, the same. The Hebrew orphanages place their children with good, orthodox Hebrew families. You understand, Margaret?"

"Yes, Father," she whispered.

"We have an orphanage out on the Island and it boards out some of its children with foster mothers. The foster mother is given an infant and keeps it, and gives it a mother's love and care until the child is six, when it is taken back by the orphanage and put into school."

She leaned forward, tense and pleading and with her clasped hands extended to him in appeal. "Oh, Father, could you . . . would you ask . . . *please* if I could have one?"

"You should have your own children, Margaret. You're young and strong and healthy. . . ."

"But I don't have any!" she said piteously.

"Be patient a while longer, my child. Pray to our Holy Mother. And make a Novena. I will say a prayer each day for your intention."

"Thank you, Father."

It was December and still there was no snow. Nobody wanted snow but everybody was worried, thinking there would be no white Christmas. Snow or no snow, Maggie-Now prepared each day for her husband's home-coming. He came back on a cold, crystal-clear night full of stars, in the middle of December.

When she saw him, she held out her arms and smiled. She didn't ask him where he'd been. She didn't ask him never to leave her again. She hugged him tight and smiled and said: "What took you so long?" as though he had just stepped out an hour ago to go to the store.

She said: "I *knew* you were coming back. And I'm *so* happy."

She took him into the kitchen and shot home a small bolt she had set up some weeks before, so that her father or brother wouldn't walk in on them. He had brought home some meat: half a loin of pork.

"Pork?" she asked.

"Not pork. A symbol. It means that technically I'm your provider."

"I'll cut off some for chops and broil them because it takes all day to roast pork and you have to have applesauce which I haven't got." He started to laugh. "All right," she said. "So I'm practical. Laugh all you want to."

He grabbed her and hugged her tight. She felt the pressure of the gold coin in his pocket. *He didn't need it then,* she thought. She unbuttoned his coat and took it off and hung it over the back of a chair. He had a package under his pullover sweater. She pulled it out.

"What's this?" she asked.

"Open it."

She did so. It was a beautiful kimono of jade green, dull silk. "Oh, how lovely . . . lovely . . ." she said. "Oh, Claude!"

"I thought it was time that my little Chinee had a kimono. Put it on, love."

It looked beautiful on her. She held out her arms so he could see how wide the sleeves were. She looked up into a sleeve. She saw the label, *The Chinese Bazaar*. She couldn't read the street and number but the city was San Francisco.

So he was way out there, she thought.

She admired the kimono profusely and he admired her profusely and they had the broiled chops and coffee and he asked her what she had been doing with herself and she told him about the sewing class and Lottie and Annie and Denny. It was as if he had been away for but a day.

Early the next morning, he put on his good suit and shoes and went out job hunting. She took the gold coin out of his old coat and wadded up his old suit and shoes and hid them on the top shelf of Denny's closet. When he left in the spring, she wanted him to wear the good suit, because the old one was threadbare. Already, she was making preparations for his leaving in the spring.

He got a job on the third day out. He didn't say where or at what, but the first day he came home from work she saw tufts of cotton clinging to his shoulders. She smiled inwardly, but said nothing. He gave her his first week's pay, thirty dollars. The second payday fell on Christmas Eve. He didn't bring home his pay. He had bought Christmas gifts with it.

"I noticed, old sir, that you do not have the pipe I gave you last year," said Claude. "So I brought you another one. Merry Christmas."

It was a cheap pipe in a cardboard box. Pat muttered a reluctant thanks and, under his breath, he said: "The bastid!"

Claude gave Denny a Waterman fountain pen with a fourteen-karat-gold clasp. Pat eyed it enviously. Claude gave his wife a book. It was a beautiful book bound in smooth and supple blue leather, the pages were gold-edged and there was a fringed, blue satin page marker. The book was *Sonnets from the Portuguese*. Inside, in his fine hand, he had inscribed: *Sonnets for my little Chinee* and *Love* and *Claude*. At the bottom of the flyleaf he had written:

How do I love thee?
Let me count the ways.

Then Denny and Claude went out to buy the Christmas tree and Maggie-Now got out the ornaments. Denny was allowed to stay up and help trim the Christmas tree inasmuch as now he was too big to believe in Santa Claus. Pat sat in the kitchen with the boxed pipe in his hands. He was very angry because the pipe was too cheap to pawn. It was as if the cardboard box was magic, because every time he opened the lid the

436

word "bastid" came out of Pat's mouth. He promised himself that he'd find some way to get back at his son-in-law.

Maggie-Now called bedtime on Denny and Pat followed his son into the boy's bedroom. "I'll swap you this new pipe for that old fountain pen Claude gave you."

"I don't know what to do with a pipe," said Denny.

"Blow bubbles."

"I'm too big to blow bubbles."

"You can take this pipe on the street and swap it for something . . . marbles or a Daisy air rifle. It's a dear pipe."

"I'll go out and ask Maggie-Now should I," said Denny hesitantly.

"Never mind! Never mind!" said Pat hastily. He went up to his room.

As they were preparing for bed, Claude told her casually that he was out of a job; it had been merely a Christmas job. She said that was all right and he said he'd get another job and she said she knew he would.

Claude didn't bother looking for another job. He again took to sitting at the window and at ten o'clock asking for a quarter for cigarettes and the paper. Maggie-Now didn't care. *He'll be gone from me long enough,* she thought. *I want him here with me all day the few weeks he's home.*

One Monday morning early in February when Maggie-Now went up to wake her father, Pat said he wasn't going to work that day and not any day for two weeks.

"I'm on me vacation," he announced.

"Vacation?" she said aghast. "But you always take it in July."

"What do I do when I take it in July? I just sit by the winder in me stocking feet. If I got to sit through me vacation, I might as well sit in winter when it's cold outside anyhow."

"But . . . but Claude's home."

"I'll keep him company," said Pat.

As soon as Claude took his chair by the window, Pat took the one at the opposite window. The pipe Claude had given him for Christmas was prominently displayed sticking out of Pat's shirt pocket, while Pat smoked his stubbed clay pipe. Pat said nothing. He sat there staring at Claude. Claude stared at Pat's left ear lobe, meaning to disconcert him. But Pat knew that trick too. He stared at Claude's right ear lobe.

At ten o'clock, Claude signaled Maggie-Now to follow him into their bedroom. He asked for the usual quarter, explaining that he didn't like to ask her in front of her father.

While Claude was out, Maggie-Now said: "Why don't you sit in your own nice room upstairs, Papa?"

"It's cold up there."

"I'll put the little oil stove up there for you."

"I like it down here better."

Claude came back and resumed his seat. Pat

resumed his staring. Claude got up and, without a word, went into the bedroom. When Maggie-Now went in to tell him lunch was ready, she found him lying on the bed, hands clasped under his head, staring up at the ceiling. He refused lunch. She sat on the side of the bed and patted his cheek.

"Mister, did you know that two weeks ago we had been married two years?"

"I forgot again."

"*I* forgot. Let's go out tonight and celebrate."

"Fine!" He swung his feet over onto the floor and sat up.

"Let's go to that chop suey place you took me to, when you were still Mister Bassett to me. We had so much fun! I did anyhow. Remember how it rained?"

"Ho, hum." He tucked back a pretended yawn. "That was way back in my past. I can hardly remember."

"I'll make Papa cook his own supper, just because he's such a pest. And Denny's supper, too."

They had a wonderful time. After the chop suey dinner, they went to see the vaudeville show at The Bushwick. When they got out, it was nearly midnight.

"Let's end the celebration with our usual champagne or its equivalent."

"You mad at me?" she asked.

"Why?"

"Then don't use those dictionary words on me, hear?"

They went into a cider store. To prove that it was a cider store and not a speakeasy, there were a jug of cider and a bowl of apples in the window. They went through the empty store to the back room and each had a glass of needle beer. It cost thirty cents a glass and Maggie-Now thought that was a terrible price to pay and she liked champagne better, anyhow. And she wondered whether her father paid thirty cents for his weekly glass of beer, because he wasn't a person to throw his money around. Claude said Pat drank near beer and he drank it only when his little friend Mick Mack paid for it. Then they started to laugh about Pat staring at Claude all morning with the Christmas pipe in his pocket.

"He was hinting," said Maggie-Now, "that he hadn't wanted a pipe for Christmas."

"It was a nice, quiet hint, though," said Claude. And they laughed and laughed. . . .

But the next morning it was the same thing: Pat, pipe in pocket, smoking his blackened clay one, and staring silently at Claude's ear. At ten o'clock, Claude went out as usual for cigarettes and paper. An hour passed and he had not returned. Denny came home for lunch, ate, went back to school and still no Claude. Maggie-Now started to tremble inwardly. At two o'clock, she went in to her father. She addressed him with cold self-control.

"All right, Papa. You did it! You drove him away with your mean, spiteful ways. A big, grown-up man like you! Sulking for two months nearly because you didn't like your Christmas present! Shame! Shame! If you weren't my father, I'd horsewhip you! If he doesn't come back, I'm going to get my money out of the bank and leave here and go all over the United States looking for him. . . ."

Then she broke down and burst into sobs. "I love him so much; I love him so much. And I have him for just these few weeks and you have to drive him out. . . . I just can't go on living this way," she sobbed. "I wish I was dead!"

Pat was ashamed and a little frightened, too. "Aw, I was only fooling, girl, dear. I ain't on me vacation. I took meself two days' sick leave. I'm going back to me work tomorrow."

She throttled off her sobs. "You have my vote for the meanest man in the world. And Denny takes after you. He's growing up mean, too. Just like you. Give me that pipe!" she shouted. Before he could hand it to her, she grabbed it out of his shirt, tearing the pocket. She pulled his clay pipe out of his mouth and smashed it on the floor. "Another word out of you," she said, "and I'll break this new pipe over your head!"

Good girl! Good girl! he exulted to himself. *Oh, the beautiful temper of her . . .*

He got dressed and went out looking for Claude. He found him right away in Brockman's store. Claude was sitting at the counter on a stool, a glass of seltzer water at his elbow. Brockman was leaning over the counter. His voice was hoarse. He had been telling the story of his life

441

since ten o'clock that morning.

"So . . ." he was saying as Pat walked in, "my old gent never did learn to speak English. So he had this farm in Hicksville out on the Island. Land was dirt cheap in those days and . . ."

Claude saw Pat and pulled out a stool for him. "Mr. Brockman," he said, "I'd like you to meet my father, Mr. Moore. Old sir, this is Mr. Brockman."

Brockman and Pat clasped hands. "Seltzer water for all!" proclaimed Pat. "I'll treat." The seltzer water was served. Brockman resumed his saga.

". . . so my old gent use' to get up at four in the morning and wash the lettuce . . ."

"Take a rest, me good man," said Pat. Pat settled himself on the stool, cleared his throat and began: "I was a boy in County Kilkenny . . ."

They got home in time for supper. They walked in, mentally arm-in-arm. Maggie-Now had a grand supper ready for them.

The house was at peace.

Chapter Forty-One

THEN came that day in March, the day of false spring. While Claude sat in the kitchen eating breakfast in his pajamas, she slipped into their bedroom and pinned the gold piece in its cloth bag in his coat breast pocket, and laid out a clean shirt and underwear and socks for him.

I mustn't let him see me cry. I must act as though it were any other day.

He dressed, all but his coat, and went in to sit by the window. Maggie-Now finished her kitchen chores quickly, took a piece of sewing and went in to sit with him as she did every once in a while. She spoke to him from time to time in a low, quiet voice and he answered with a look or a smile.

He opened the window and leaned out. She leaned out next to him and the south wind lifted a tendril of her hair and she put her cheek next to his.

"It's a chinook wind," he whispered as though he didn't want her to hear.

"Yes," she whispered back. He didn't seem to know she was there.

She went out into the kitchen and came back walking heavily. He started at the sound of her steps and closed the window.

"If you'll let me have a quarter . . ." he said.

"Of course." She gave him the quarter and went in and got his coat. She helped him on with it and turned him around and buttoned it.

"Come right back, hear?" she said brightly.

"I will." He kissed her and was gone.

And this became the pattern of their lives.

He'd come home with the first snow and bring her something and he'd work a week or two and then not work and she'd be happy treasuring each day of his being there, and he was always so tender toward her and so kind to Denny and so patient with her father. And it was all so wonderful because she knew it was for such a very little time.

Then would come that day in March—a day like no other day. The next day, there might be a blizzard, but on this day there would be that sweet south wind. And people would walk along the street with their coats hanging open and a newspaper on somebody's stoop would unfold itself and its sheets would swoop into the air like kites.

And Claude would be restless and open the window and lean out and feel the wind on his face and close his eyes as though in ecstasy and listen as though he heard a faraway and well-beloved voice calling him. He'd whisper: *Chinook,* and bow his head as though making a promise. That was the day he'd leave her.

As he sat by the window in the winter, looking out on the street and up at the gray skies, was he waiting . . . waiting . . . for that day and that feeling he'd get that told him there was a chinook wind blowing over the mountains of Montana and that it was time for him to leave? And as he sat there, silent, waiting, watching, what was in his mind?

Did he dream great dreams of prairies with the wheat like flowing gold in the winds? Or how, where the great Rockies pierced the sky, you had to believe in God because the world was so grand? Did he get to the old Southwest and believe that he had walked into Spain? Did he think of a time he had followed a river to find out where it began or where it ended? Did he recall standing on a beach somewhere in southern Florida and looking out over the wide Atlantic Ocean and thinking that it was the same ocean that he smelled in Brooklyn just before it rained? And if he started walking north along the beach, in time he'd come to Rockaway—just an hour away from his dear love?

Did he go because those great dreams led him on? Or was it, as Father Flynn had deduced when he first spoke to Claude, that he roamed the country trying to find a name, a place or a human soul who would tell him who he was, what he was, where he had come from? Was he looking . . . searching for his birthright? Did he think of that in his hours by the window in the winter?

Or did he sit there all winter with no such thoughts, no such dreams—waiting only for cogs within him to mesh and put into motion that slow, patient walk that would propel him across the country for no reason at all except that that was his destiny?

No one knew. He told no one what his thoughts were.

When her father lashed out as he did from time to time and called Claude unspeakable names, Maggie-Now defended her love and tried to explain to her father that he roamed away because he was in love with the country, "Its rocks and rills," she quoted from a song she used to sing in school; because he was in love with rivers and mountains and cities. . . .

But Pat had his own version of where Claude spent his wandering months. He told no one but Mick Mack.

"He's got me poor daughter fooled," said Pat. "The bastid! The innocent girl thinks he goes away to look at the sky and smell the flowers. But I know better. You see, I'm the one what knows what men is. I'm a man meself." He waited.

"You are that!" said Mick Mack emphati cally.

"So I wouldn't be surprised a-tall if he ha'

446

another woman over in Jersey or somewheres. And he lives with her until cold weather comes when he has to put coal in the furnace and carry out the ashes. Then he comes back to me Maggie-Now and stays with her till it gets warm again and the furnace is out in Jersey. And I wouldn't be surprised either if he ain't got three or four kids by this here woman."

"Ah, poor, poor Maggie-Now," said Mick Mack.

"Me daughter don't want none of your sympathy," said Pat coldly.

Chapter Forty-Two

SHE missed him, as she would always miss him. But missing him had become part of her life now and she was able to stand it more or less . . . if she kept busy and didn't think about it too much. But she never adjusted herself to not going to bed with him. As far as sex went, her time with him was wonderful. For a few months each year, she had a fulfilling and contented love life. The lack of it anguished her terribly— physically, emotionally and mentally.

She tried to fill her life with substitutes. The sewing class again; the bimonthly visits to Lottie; stopping in at his store to exchange gossip with Van Clees; scrubbing and polishing up her home; shopping carefully and economically for family food and necessities; preparing meals carefully; going to Mass every day; getting Denny ready for his Confirmation; seeing to it that Denny served as altar boy at half a dozen Masses because she thought every Catholic boy should have the high and humble honor of serving as an acolyte sometime during his youth.

(Of course, Pat had something to say about that. "Don't try to make a priest out of the boy," he said.)

Maggie-Now ran into Gina on the street. Gina was pushing a beautiful white perambulator. Gina's baby was dressed like a valuable doll in lace and ribbons. The blanket, of fine angora wool, had been knitted on needles as thin as hatpins. The blanket cover was shell-pink silk topped with a pink satin bow. A pink rattle, with hand-painted blue forget-me-nots, hung by a pink ribbon from a strut of the perambulator hood.

"How beautiful she is," said Maggie-Now, "and how beautifully you keep her."

"You only have your first baby once in your life," said Gina. "My mother says wait'll I have three or four. I won't be so particular."

"What's her name?"

"Regina. After me. But Cholly—you know how Cholly is? He calls her Reggie. Honest! My mother has fits! Reggie! And, oh! Ev's expecting in October."

"Ev?"

"Evelyn. *You* know. Sonny's wife?"

"Oh!"

"You better catch up, Maggie. When you got married, I thought you'd have a baby every year, the way you're so religious and the way you're built for having children."

"Yes. Well . . ." Maggie-Now could think of

nothing to say.

"Come see us sometime, Maggie. We often speak of you."

"Thanks, I will." (But she knew she wouldn't.)

Soon after that, she went to see Father Flynn about taking in some orphans to live with her.

". . . and it's been a year, Father, since I asked you."

"The home has strict rules, Margaret. It will not give children to a family living in a flat or apartment. It has to be a house and yard. Of course you have that. And the child or children must occupy a separate room in the house."

"I have an empty room waiting."

"The home pays five dollars a week for each child. No foster mother must profit from that; nor divert the money to her own uses. It is for the child's food and necessities. Therefore, there must be proof that the husband works and has a steady income."

She bowed her head and squeezed her hands together in anguish. She did not have that kind of husband. The priest's heart went out to her.

"Of course, in the case of a widow, a son or daughter living at home and supporting the mother . . . or if she has a small legacy . . ."

"I own my own home," said Maggie-Now, with eager hope, "and I have rental property and it's my money and Papa has a steady job. And Claude brings home money . . . sometimes. And he always works for a while after he comes home and gives me every cent. . . ."

"You would surely get an 'A' on finances and on a suitable home," he said with a smile. "Of course, there must be no history of sickness in the family, like tuberculosis or congenital . . . well, social diseases."

"Oh, we're all so healthy," she exclaimed. "Nobody's ever been sick in the family with anything catching, except the time Denny and Papa had measles."

"That would be an easy 'A,' " he conceded. "However, . . ." he paused a long time before he continued. "The woman must have, or must have had, children of her own. She must be rearing, or have reared, children of her own."

"I brought up Denny ever since he was born," she said. "I have experience."

"Of her own," he repeated.

"I see." All the eagerness left her and she bowed her head again.

He rose, beginning to terminate the visit. She rose with him. "But you're a good mother, Margaret, even if you have no children of your own. If you have no child of your own within a year, come to me again. I'll speak to Mother Vincent de Paul and see what I can do. You can wait a year, Margaret?"

Yes, Maggie-Now could wait a year. She was used to waiting.

Denny got through that year without getting into too much trouble. He was grudgingly promoted.

451

The only thing, he took to hanging out on the streets with a bunch of slightly older kids. He'd stay out until ten o'clock at night if he could get away with it.

Claude came home with the winter. There was that same tender reunion. He brought her a pair of white buckskin moccasins to wear as bedroom slippers. The name of a shop in Albuquerque, New Mexico, was stamped on the inner sole. *At least,* she thought, *he was where it was warm.* The gold piece was still pinned in his coat and she knew he had not been in want.

Their reunion was tender and their love-making seemed new again, the way it had been on their honeymoon night.

He worked a few weeks, someplace or other. He gave her all of his pay except the money he used for Christmas presents. He gave her a singing canary in a lovely bamboo cage. She named him Timmy. It was a hard cross for Pat to bear. He was superstitious and instinctively his lips formed the words "rest his soul" whenever she called the bird by name.

Pat kept up a nudging feud with Claude all winter. To compensate, Denny openly worshipped Claude, and worked hard in school for good marks to get Claude's approbation.

It was a wonderfully happy winter for Maggie-Now. But he left again on that day when that certain wind called to him.

And she knew another year would pass and she would have no child.

Chapter Forty-Three

NOW when Maggie-Now made her visits to Lottie, she was, in a way, visiting Timmy, too. Lottie acted as though Timmy were in the same room with them and she had stopped saying, "I make believe."

"Well, Aunt Lottie, I guess I'll start for home before the rain comes."

"Oh, it's not going to rain. Do you think it's going to rain, Timmy?" She spoke to the empty chair. She waited. "There! Timmy says he thinks the rain will hold off until nighttime."

Once Widdy was there and he drew Maggie-Now aside. "I just happened to drop in," he said, "and Mom was eating her supper. But there was a full plate where Pop used to sit, and you know, Maggie, she was talking to him just like he was sitting there eating supper with her? Poor Mom!"

"Oh, I don't know," said Maggie-Now. "She's found a way to be near Timmy."

Denny and some other kids stood in front of Golend's Paint Shop. Out front was a big plate on a tripod. A scar of healing cement ran across what looked like a bad break in the plate. A chain went through a hole drilled in the plate and a heavy iron weight hung from the chain. It said on the plate that the cement was like iron and would hold the hundred-pound weight without breaking.

"I bet that plate would break right away if you even touched it," said Denny.

"Go 'head, then. Try it." One of the boys handed Denny a baseball bat. Denny tapped the plate.

Sure, it broke. It was made of cast iron, enameled white.

Maggie-Now heard the hubbub on the street. She went to the window to look. To her horror, she saw Denny being escorted home by a tall policeman. A bunch of kids and some adults were following after. When they got to the stoop, the young cop dispersed the crowd with a genial: "Why don't you all beat it, now?"

They stood in the front room. The cop removed his hat. Maggie-Now looked up at him. He was a clear-eyed young man with a nice, homely Irish face. He told about the plate.

"Golend was all for sending the kid to the electric chair," said the cop. "I talked him out of it. I said, let the kid's mother punish him. So here he is."

"I don't know how to thank you, Officer. . . .

Anyone else would arrest him. . . ."

"Oh, I expect to have kids of my own, someday," he said. "I wouldn't want a boy of mine crucified just because it was vacation and the kid was full of beans and got into mischief."

"I don't know how to thank you," she said again.

"Say, you look awful young to be the mother of such a big boy."

"I'm his sister."

"Well, that's fine! Just fine!" He grinned down at her. She looked up at him with her wide smile.

After the policeman had left, Maggie-Now started in on lecturing Denny. But her heart wasn't in it. She kept thinking how nice it was to have a man look at her with admiration.

The following Friday, she went to the fish store to buy a flounder for supper. She was waiting for the man to dress it into fillets when the policeman came in. The fish-store man's wife smiled at the cop.

"Where's my fish sandwich?" he asked.

"In a minute, Eddie," said the woman. She stuck a fork in a thick wedge of halibut which was browning in a cauldron of boiling oil. "In a minute."

A good Catholic boy, thought Maggie-Now. *Fish for him on Fridays.*

He recognized Maggie-Now. "Hello," he said.

"Hello," she answered. They smiled at each other.

"How's your brother?"

"Fine."

"That's fine."

It seemed they had run out of conversation until Maggie-Now said: "My father went around and gave Mr. Golend a dollar for the plate and Mr. Golend said he was satisfied."

"That's fine."

"Here you are, Maggie." The fish dealer pushed the package across the counter. "Fifty-two cents."

"Look," said the cop. "Would it be all right if I came around to see you some night? I mean in plain clothes?"

"I'm married," she said.

"Oh, I see!" The smile washed off his face. "I'm sorry," he said sincerely.

"I'll always appreciate what you did for my brother."

"That's all right," he said. She left the store.

"What do you want on your fish sandwich, Eddie?" asked the woman.

"Nothing," he said. "Just some catsup."

She prepared for bed as usual that night. She undressed, put on the Chinese kimono and the moccasins that Claude had given her. She went out and covered Timmy's cage. She sat before the dressing table he had given her and brushed her hair. She ran her hand over the smooth leather of the little red suitcase, read his postcard and read a line or two from the *Sonnets*. It was her nightly communication with her husband.

She lay awake in bed thinking. *Make believe,* she thought, *that I had never met and married Claude (and that would have been just terrible!). But make believe anyhow. Suppose I had married someone like this Eddie. I know I would've liked him—if I wasn't married. We would live in a house on the Island. We'd all go to Mass together on Sundays and sit in the back pew—so that in case the children got restless, they wouldn't annoy too many people back there. He would come home to me and the children every single night and . . .*

The next day, Saturday, she went about with a heavy heart. She had to go to confession that night and she had a grave sin to confess and she did not know its name. *I can't say I committed adultery in my thoughts: that I was lewd in my thoughts . . . what name can I give this sin?*

She went to confession late and let others go before her. She was trying to think of a name for her sin. The church was empty; she was the last one. She knelt in the dark confessional and confessed the usual sins in a whisper and then she came to the big sin.

"I lusted after a man, Father." It was the only way she knew how to say it. She thought she heard a snort from the other side of the tiny screened opening, but she wasn't sure.

"Explain, my child," said the priest.

"I thought how it would be if I were married to a man other than my husband."

He made no comment. She finished her

confession, and was kneeling in a pew saying her penance, when she saw Father Flynn come out of the confessional. He went to the altar and extinguished the candles. He genuflected and then knelt to pray before the altar.

When she left the church, Father Flynn was waiting on the steps. "Margaret," he said. "Monday I will take you to the home. I will do whatever I can to get you a foster child or two."

"Oh, Father!" she said, tears of joy coming to her eyes.

"I think it is time," he said.

Chapter Forty-Four

MAGGIE-NOW sat on a long bench while she waited for Father Flynn to confer with Mother Vincent de Paul. The room was combined office and waiting room. A nun sat at a typewriter briskly tapping out letters from shorthand notes. Another nun had six varicolored sheets and five carbons in her typewriter and was filling out forms. A very young nun stood at a filing case expertly filing documents and letters away. Another sat at a table and filled in a printed form with the answers of an applicant who stood before her.

All the clerical activity should have made it seem like an efficient office. But the habited nuns and a large picture of Christ holding a lamb in His arms gave it the feeling of a busy church. Aside from the woman having a form filled out, there were four other women with Maggie-Now on the bench. Two had children with them. The woman next to Maggie-Now was evidently foster mother to a beautiful child of six who quietly wandered about the room, returning to the bench at intervals. She addressed the woman as "Mama."

Maggie-Now struck up a conversation with the woman. "She's very pretty."

"Yes. I hate to give her up. My husband and I got very attached to her. We get attached to all of them. But she's six now and they have to take her back to put her in school. Well, in the twenty years I been a foster mother, I had to give up many a one I would have liked to keep. This one especially." She returned the smile the little girl gave her across the room before she resumed talking. She dropped her voice.

"This one's different. Her mother was a rich and beautiful society girl and her father was a poor artist. Her parents wouldn't let her marry this artist. But they had this child anyhow."

"Did they tell you that here?" asked Maggie-Now.

"Not in so many words," evaded the woman. But I *know.*" She whispered: "She's a love child. That's why she's so beautiful."

Father Flynn came out of Mother Vincent de Paul's office and instructed Maggie-Now to file an application. He stood by her side. The nun asked the routine questions and filled in the answers. Then she came to "Husband."

"Occupation?"

"He travels. . . ." Maggie-Now looked appealingly at Father Flynn.

"Traveling man," said the priest.

The nun's pen hovered over the blank space for a second or two before she wrote: "Travels."

"Income?"

"I live with my father. He's in Civil Service." She stated his salary. "And I get twenty-five a month from rental property and I own my own house free and clear."

"Husband's income?"

"He earns fifty dollars, sometimes thirty dollars a week." She paused. "When he works," she added honestly. The nun put a question mark in that space.

The nun picked up the application and said: "I'll take you to Mother Vincent de Paul. This way."

The nun put the paper on the desk and quietly withdrew. It was a small room holding only a desk and a chair. A large crucifix hung on the wall behind the desk. The mother wore bifocals and may have been in her sixties, although it was hard to tell the age of a nun; no matter what age, their faces were unlined and serene.

Maggie-Now stood quietly—she had not been asked to sit down—and waited. Without looking up, the mother said: "As you know, there are certain irregularities in your application." She pointed to the printed word "Children," and the inked "None" in the space following. "But Father Flynn spoke highly of you and we'll waive that. Do you agree to take two children?"

"Oh, yes! Yes!"

"Children must grow up with other children."

"Yes, Mother."

"When a child reaches the age of six, he will be taken from you. There must be no pleas, no tears, no requests to keep in touch with the child and no requests for adopting the child. Do you understand?"

"Yes, Mother."

"In due time, a nurse will visit you and examine the premises. If her report is satisfactory, your application will be accepted."

"Thank you, Mother."

The mother pressed a buzzer and a nun came in and took the application and went out again. Without looking up, Mother Vincent de Paul said: "Whatever became of your horse?"

"My horse, Mother?" gasped the girl, astonished.

"Drummer."

"Why, gone I guess, Mother," she said, bewildered.

The mother looked up at her. "I used to know Sister Mary Joseph," she explained. She smiled; Maggie-Now smiled back. "God bless you, my child."

Maggie-Now rode home on the trolley with Father Flynn. The priest read from his little black-bound book and Maggie-Now beamed happily at all the people in the car.

The nurse came in due time. She was a middle-aged woman in a tailored suit. She had a large black handbag from which she extracted a little book and a pencil. Maggie-Now, who had continually scrubbed, polished and painted the "nursery" while waiting for the nurse to call, greeted the woman cordially.

"Will you have a cup of coffee?" she asked.

"*O-o-oh,* no!" said the nurse with a rising and falling inflection. Her tone implied that she couldn't be bribed.

"Excuse me," said Maggie-Now, embarrassed.

The nurse made a thorough inspection of everything. She asked how the nursery room was heated. Maggie-Now explained that, since it opened off the front room, it was heated by the parlor stove. The nurse made a notation. Maggie-Now started to worry. Finally the nurse put her book and pencil away, straightened her coat and said:

"Now, I'll have that cup of coffee."

Maggie-Now knew it was all right, then.

Maggie-Now waited: one week, two weeks, three weeks. . . . Then Father Flynn came to see her. "Margaret," he said, "I've had a conference with Mother Vincent de Paul." He saw worry lines deepen in her forehead. "The home nurse turned in her report on your premises." She held her breath. "The word 'Immaculate' appeared four times in her report." Maggie-Now relaxed. "However," again the worried lines appeared on her forehead, "Mother and I agreed to put off giving you the children until spring."

"Why, Father, oh, why?" she pleaded.

"Your husband will be returning soon. He knows nothing of the foster children. It may be hard for him to adjust . . . then, the children will not have had time to be adjusted to the home and you. There may be emotional strain. In the spring, when he has gone, you will have the children. You'll have the spring, summer and fall, and when your husband visits you . . . returns in the following fall, you will have become accustomed to the children, there will be a settled routine . . ."

She was badly disappointed but she saw the logic of the matter.

"You can wait, Margaret?" he asked.

"I can wait," she said.

It was just as well. One morning after breakfast, instead of leaving for work, Pat settled himself in the chair by the front window.

"Aren't you working today, Papa?" she asked.

"Me working days is over. I put in me full time and today I start me retirement. Today I start drawing me pension."

Her first foolish thought was: *Now I don't have to wash those heavy, dirty uniforms any more.* She said: "But, Papa, you didn't tell me."

"Must I tell you everything?" he said.

"But, Papa, you're still young, just a little over fifty. What are you going to do with yourself all day?"

"Rest!" he said.

And he did. He slept late and Maggie-Now had to make a separate and lavish breakfast for him at ten in the morning. Then he sat by the window in his stocking feet, getting up only to go to the bathroom and to eat lunch, which now had to be dinner with meat, vegetables and potatoes instead of a simple lunch. After dinner he napped on the couch in the front room, and if she so much as turned on the tap to get a glass of water he shouted for quiet. After his nap, he took up his useless vigil at the window. When she came into the room, he asked her what she wanted now.

Maggie-Now was almost a prisoner. She had been used to having the house to herself most of the day. While dressing, she had often walked out to the kitchen in her slip to check on something that was cooking. Now she could never leave her bedroom unless she was fully dressed. When she went out, he asked her where she was going. When she came back, he examined her purchases and criticized the price she had paid and claimed she was cheated. When Denny went out, he gave him hell when he came back. When he stayed home, he asked what the hell he was hanging around the house for. In short, he was a pest.

When November came, Maggie-Now started to worry. Claude would be home soon, and with her father in the house all day, feuding with Claude, life would be intolerable. Claude would leave after a few days, she knew. She remembered the Christmas pipe incident.

One night she said: "Papa, when Claude comes you must go and board at Mrs. O'Crawley's while he's here."

"Oh, no, me girl."

"Yes, Papa. I mean it. You and Claude just don't get along. And for the little time that he's here . . ."

"I won't leave this house," he shouted, "till I'm carried out feet first. So help me God!"

It was the last week in November. The newspaper forecast snow for the next day. As Papa got up from the supper table, Maggie-Now said: "Papa, Claude will be coming back most any night now and . . ."

"And I'll throw him out the minute he steps foot in me door," he said.

She ignored that. "So I went over to Mrs. O'Crawley's today and rented a room for you."

"What!" he roared.

"A nice room and she likes you so much she's only asking seven dollars a week for room and board. And little Mick Mack can hardly wait. You can come back again when Claude leaves."

Pat made a terrible, hoarse cry. He tore open his shirt and gasped and his face turned purple. He spun around and would have fallen if Maggie-Now hadn't caught him.

"Run, Denny. Run for the doctor! No, wait! Let's get him to bed first." They got him into the hall but couldn't get him up the stairs. "My room! My room!" gasped Maggie-Now. They put him in Maggie-Now's dainty bed. "Now, get the doctor and hurry."

"No doctor," gasped Pat. "Too late. The priest! The priest! I want the priest! The priest!" he gasped faintly.

When Father Flynn arrived, a pale Maggie-Now with smudges under her eyes greeted the priest with a lighted candle. She genuflected and preceded him into the house. She took him into the room. He looked around with a glance of approval. Everything was in order. Pat lay pale and still in a clean nightshirt. She had washed his face and hands and feet. There was a clean linen towel on the bed table. On it stood a crucifix with a lighted candle on either side. There was a vial of holy water, a dish of salt, a saucer with clean bits of cotton for the holy oil, a tumbler of water and all the necessary things. There was a cushion on the floor at the head of the bed for the priest to kneel on. Father Flynn placed his small black leather bag and the Host on the cleared dressing table.

"Leave us, my daughter," he said. Maggie-Now left, walking backward out of the room, still holding the lighted candle.

Father Flynn performed the solemn last rites of the church. When it was all over, Pat said weakly, "I would not be calling you out in the cold of the night but the way me daughter . . ."

"You have been shriven of all your worldly sins, my son. Speak no more." When Pat would speak again, Father Flynn said: "Be at peace, my son."

He started packing his bag. "I will send the doctor," he said.

"No doctor," whispered Pat. "I am at peace."

"To sign the death certificate," said Father Flynn. "It is the law."

Father Flynn went out to Maggie-Now and Denny and prayed with them and left, after speaking words of comfort.

Maggie-Now, trembling and with tears falling unchecked from her eyes, went in to her father.

She found him frantically getting into his pants.

"Papa!" she cried out, shocked. "What are you doing?"

"I'm getting out of here!" he yelled. "Between you and the priest and the doctor, youse'll have me buried before I'm dead! I'm going to the widder's house where I'm safe!"

Maggie-Now had a beautiful, beautiful winter with her Claude.

Chapter Forty-Five

CLAUDE had come home. While they sat in the kitchen waiting for the two chickens he had brought to roast, he asked her, as was his custom, to tell him everything she had done during his absence. She told him everything except that she had made an application to take in children from the home. When she actually had the children, it would be time enough to tell him, she thought. Then there was always the hope that she'd become pregnant. She never gave up hope. Her mother hadn't given up hope and had had a child in her forties. However, she had sounded Claude out, hoping to get his reaction to having the children from the home.

"Claude, wouldn't you like children in the house?"

He gave a typical Claudian answer. "Every man likes children of his own about the house."

Unduly sensitive to his every reaction, she thought he stressed the "of his own" too much, and she didn't say anything more.

When he came home, he had brought her a dozen Dutch tulip bulbs. They were in a box marked *Tulips from Holland, Michigan,* so she knew he had been there. For his last three returns he'd brought her gifts with labels. It was as though he wanted her to know where he'd been but didn't want to tell her in so many words.

He said he'd wait a week before going to look for a job because he wanted to plant the bulbs in the yard. First, he said, he had to whitewash the old board fence. The tulips were red and needed a white background, he said.

He was whitewashing the boards one Sunday morning (he had one side of the fence done), when the tenant upstairs opened her window and called down to him.

"Mr. Bassett?"

He gave that quick turn of his head, which gave the woman a thrill, and looked up.

"That's going to look real nice."

"Thank you," he said and gave her his charming smile.

She closed the window. "I had to be halfway nice to him," she told her husband, "so's they don't raise the rent on us saying they made *improvements.*"

"Aw, you just wanted an excuse to talk to the bum," he said.

"He's not a bum. He's a gentleman."

"A bum!" he said. As an afterthought, he added: "Shut up!"

The ground was not frozen under the snow but it was as hard and barren as cement. Claude had to chop it up with an ax. He planted the bulbs. All during the winter, he garnered Maggie-Now's coffee grounds and tea leaves and potato peelings and the dottle from Pat's pipe and the ashes from the stove and other things and made a compost pile in the yard.

"In the spring," he said, "we'll plant zinnia and marigold seeds . . . things that come up the first year . . . later, perennials . . ."

He spoke as though he wasn't going away in the spring. Her heart lifted; then fell. If he stayed, would he let her have the foster children?

For Christmas, he gave her a big, beautiful garden encyclopedia. It had hundreds of colored plates. (It must have cost ten dollars.) He and Maggie-Now pored over it and he made a garden on paper and the list of seeds they'd need. He seemed obsessed by the garden. "This summer," he said, "we'll sit together in our garden in the evening—flowers smell better after dark, you know. . . ." Yes, it seemed that he wasn't going to wander any more.

But by January he had completely lost interest in the garden. Now when she got the book out, he frowned and said he guessed he'd go for a little walk. Once he asked her why she bothered. "Nothing will ever grow in that soil," he said. "It's hard as cement and just as barren." She didn't get the book out any more after that.

But it was a beautiful winter. He was a tender

471

and loving husband, and, as always, it was as though they were newly married.

That March day came and that softly demanding faraway wind blew over Brooklyn again. And Claude listened and gave his silent promise to something that was not tangible, and went away again.

This time her grief at his going was gentle and mixed with a tremulous inner excitement. She cried a little, but smiled as she cried and was stirred by a great anticipation. *I'll wait until twelve,* she thought, *to see if he comes back.*

But she waited only until eleven o'clock. She ran around to the furniture store and told the man he could deliver right away the two cribs and high chair she had been making weekly payments on since the fall. She went to another store and bought two thick white china bowls and two little spoons.

The store sent the cribs over. There was a two-drawer chest in the room that Maggie-Now had bought in the fall and enameled white. From a drawer, she took crib sheets she'd made from the best parts of worn household sheets and clean, worn blankets that had, so far, warmed two generations of babies: Widdy and Widdy's twins. (Lottie had said: "I forgot I still had those blankets until Timmy reminded me.") Maggie-Now was in a kind of ecstasy as she made up the little beds.

When Denny came home at noon, she gave him a makeshift lunch of bologna sandwich, milk and a wedge of crumb cake. She herself was too excited to eat.

"Did Claude go away?" he asked.

"Why, yes." Then she was dumbfounded! Claude had left only two hours ago and she had all but forgotten that she wouldn't see him again until fall.

"The flowers he planted in the yard are up. Did he see them?"

"Are they?" She went to the window. Yes, there were a dozen inch-high clubby spikes showing. "No, I guess he didn't see them."

As soon as Denny went back to school, she rushed over to Father Flynn's house. "Now, Father?" she asked. "Now? *Please,* now?"

He matched her tone. "Now!" he said.

"Honest, Father?"

"Honestly, Margaret. Mother Vincent de Paul has two little boys all ready for you."

"Honest, Father? *Honestly?*"

"One is four, I believe, and the other a babe in arms."

"When can I have them, Father? When?"

"I'll phone Mother and tell her you're on your way to the home."

She was out of the house and down the steps like a flash.

"Margaret!" he called. She paused in her flight. "Remember! In two years, you'll have to give up the first one."

"Yes, Father."

"And when you are sixty, you will have to give

473

them all back."

"It will be forever till I'm sixty," she called back.

I used to think so too, thought the priest.

Maggie-Now loved the beautiful ritual of getting breakfast for the children. Denny had gone off to school and her father was still sleeping. The sunshine poured in through the kitchen windows and the tulips were in bud in the yard and Timmy in his bamboo cage sang so lustily that the cage jiggled.

Mark, the four-year old, sat in the high chair eating his bowl of oatmeal with soft sliced bananas on top. From time to time, gently and patiently, she transferred the spoon from his left hand to his right. Just as patiently, the little boy transferred the spoon back to his left hand.

John, not quite a year old, was in her arms. She fed him with a spoon. He inhaled the oatmeal, gummed the soft banana and tried his best to drink milk from his mug with a sucking motion. He never took his eyes off Maggie-Now's face. He stared at her unblinkingly, moving his eyes only when she leaned over to change Mark's spoon.

The children were quiet children. Mark seldom spoke and the baby seldom cried. Mark obeyed any order instantly. The instant they were put in their cribs, they closed their eyes. They had been well trained at the home.

Maggie-Now had been astonished at the way

Pat took the news of the foster children. She'd had them three days when he came home from Mrs. O'Crawley's. She told him in one sentence and all in one breath. She ended up saying she would get five dollars a week to buy their food.

"For the two of them?" he asked.

"Five dollars each."

"Say! That's all right," he said. "Them two kids won't eat up ten dollars of food a week."

"The money is for the children and the children only," she said firmly.

Who knew the workings of Pat's mind? He got the idea that Maggie-Now got the babies to take the place of Claude and that now Claude was out of her life forever. He explained it to Mick Mack:

"Me daughter says: 'I got the chilthren in place of you. And now when you go away don't come back no more.' And he says: 'So now the chilthren have taken me place and I am no longer wanted.' "

"And you living at the O'Crawleys' the time he says that!" said Mick Mack. He was not doubting his friend's veracity. It was merely one of the little man's automatic compliments.

"I don't have to be Johnny-on-the-spot," said Pat icily, "to know what goes on in me own home. Anyways, warm weather comes and the bastid says: 'Nooky!' No, that ain't the word. Yeah! 'Chinook!' "

"And what would that be meaning?"

Pat had to think quick. "Why . . . why, it

would mean 'so long!' In the Eskimo language,'' he added. The little man looked as though he doubted that, but Pat clinched it. ''It stands to reason: First he says: 'Chinook!' Then he goes away. What else could it mean?''

It cannot be said that Pat fell in love with the children; he hadn't even fallen in love with his own children when they were small. But he got on with them; especially Mark. Pat was garrulous and, since his retirement, he had the whole day to talk in and Maggie-Now was not one to sit and listen. But little Mark listened. Pat told the boy all the things he thought his daughter should know—about the beautiful room he'd had at the widow's; the exquisite meals she'd fed him and, yessir, he'd marry her in a minute but what would his daughter and son do without him? Although he spoke to the little boy, he raised his voice so's Maggie-Now could hear him.

The little boy didn't know what Pat was talking about most of the time, but he listened with flattering concentration.

As for Denny, he was neither interested in nor indifferent to the newcomers. He was too old to play with them and too young to feel protective toward them. He gave them each a nickname: the baby, ''Pee Wee,'' and Mark, ''Snodgrass.'' That was the total of his relationship to the orphans.

Lottie was ecstatic about it. ''Now you'll have one of your own. I never known it to fail. As soon as a woman adopts a baby, bang! She gets in the family way. You wait and see."

"I didn't adopt . . ."

"It amounts to the same thing, Maggie-Now."

"I've given up hope," said Maggie-Now. "Soon I'll be in my thirties and it'll be too late."

"Don't talk foolish. Your mother had Denny when she was in the change. Take me: I didn't have Widdy till I was thirty-two. Of course, though, I didn't get married until I was thirty-one. I'll never forget it. We was on this picnic up the Hudson, and when I hollered to the boat that we was going to get married, the captain said all our troubles should be little ones. I wish you could've seen Timmy's face! Well, so we was married. . . ."

And Lottie was off, reliving again her wonderful life with her sweetheart.

The nurse came once a month to check the children and the cribs and the condition of the home. Her report was always favorable; extremely so. On one visit, she said: "Mrs. Bassett, you ought to have a furnace put in, you know. Your heating would not be adequate if we happened to have a severe winter. It would really pay you. You could get more rent for your upstairs apartment, you know." Maggie-Now said she'd talk to her father about it.

Fall came. Maggie-Now told her father he'd have to go to Mrs. O'Crawley when Claude came back.

"He ain't *coming* back!" said Pat.

"He *always* comes back in the fall."

"But you threw him out when you got the kids." By now, Pat believed the story he'd told Mick Mack.

"I did no such thing! That's all in your imagination."

"Well, I won't go."

"But all summer you're saying how wonderful it was there and how good the cooking was and how much you liked it."

"I still won't go."

"But why, Papa?"

"Because them orphans need me here."

"Oh, Papa!"

There was a little flurry of snow the third week in November. It didn't amount to much but Maggie-Now took up her nighttime vigil at the window waiting for Claude. She waited two nights and he didn't come. The third she sat there until midnight decided he wasn't coming that night and went out into the kitchen.

She always prepared the babies' oatmeal before she went to bed at night, got it started then left the saucepan on the back of the stove to simmer all night so that the cereal would be creamily well-done in the morning.

She heard the hall door open. She thought it was the tenant upstairs coming in late, then she thought of Claude! She stopped stirring the oatmeal, covered the saucepan and set it on the back of the stove. He walked into the kitchen.

"Oh, Claude! Claude!" She was in his arms.

"This is the first time you didn't run down the street to meet me. And I walked around the block three times. . . ."

"I was going to watch for you again as soon as I had this oatmeal started."

"Oatmeal? I haven't had that since . . ."

"Want some? It's good and hot."

"No!" he said sharply. "It reminds me . . ." His voice trailed off.

He had brought her a small silver stiletto that had the word *Mexico* stamped on the handle; to be used as a letter opener, he said. She smiled. She didn't get many letters: one a month, the electric bill; two a month in the summer when she used the gas plate for cooking; and one a year from the tax collector. Just the same it was a beautiful thing to have and to hold in her hand.

"I have to give you a coin for it," she said.

"You believe in that superstition that a coin must be given in return for a knife?"

"Yes. It's bad luck if you don't."

"Your luck is good. You gave me a coin some years back," he said. She knew he referred to the gold piece.

He had brought home a duck. She put it in the oven to roast and then went to sit on his lap. He patted her hip and then started to laugh.

"What's funny?" she asked. (As always, it was as if he'd been away only for the day.)

479

"You're funny," he said, "sitting here in your Chinese kimono and Indian moccasins, waving a Mexican dagger and roasting a Long Island duck." He kissed her long and hard; then said: "Tell me all you did while I was away."

"Well," she hesitated, "I went over to see Lottie . . ." Her voice trailed off.

"What else?"

"That's about all, I guess."

He wondered what *had* happened. Usually, when he asked her what she'd been doing, news literally poured out of her.

"You've been up to something, Margaret. Have you been a good girl?" he asked lightly.

"Oh, I forgot to tell you!" She was all animation. "The tulips came out. And they were beautiful, Claude. Just beautiful!"

"Did you plant zinnias and marigolds and . . ."

"No. I didn't plant anything."

"You're an odd girl. Here you cook and sew and love children and enjoy housekeeping and . . ."

"What's odd about that?"

"It follows that you'd enjoy working in a garden; making things grow. But you don't, do you?"

"Why, no, I don't, Claude."

"Why?"

"Oh, I don't know. I guess I like flowers in pots. You can put them in different places. love to see flowers in the florist shops. That' how I'm used to flowers, I guess. If I had a lot of flowers in the yard, I wouldn't enjoy so much going to the cemetery and seeing all the flowers on the street outside the flower stores. And in May, when Father Flynn's lilac bush is in full bloom, he invites me to sit on his bench a while and we have iced tea, and if I had a lilac bush in my yard then it wouldn't be so wonderful any more to see Father Flynn's lilacs and I would miss that."

"You'll always be a city girl, love. And now, speaking of bushes, stop beating around one and tell me exactly what you did while I was gone." Suddenly, she was tense in his arms. "What?" he asked.

"I thought I heard something."

"Your father?"

"He's at Mrs. O'Crawley's. Listen!" The sound again. It was the wail of a baby. She jumped to her feet. "He *never* cries. He must be wet and uncovered."

He jumped up too and grabbed her arms and shook her a little. "No!" he said in a high ecstatic voice—the way people say "No" when they expect a sure "Yes" back.

"Claude?" she said. It was almost a whimper.

"And I wasn't with you when it happened! I *am* a bastard; a pig." His self-reproaches were terrible. He got down on his knees and put his arms about her legs and pressed his cheek against the silk of the kimono.

She stood listening with her head turned, the

way he stood and listened for the voice in the wind on the day he left. She relaxed and breathed deeply. "There! He's gone back to sleep."

"I am nobody from nowhere," he said, his voice muffled against her kimono. "There is no one before me. But now one will come after me. A son . . . my name, a continuation of me . . . me! Who is a continuation of no one."

It was very hard for her to tell him that he had no son; that the child was one of her two foster children. He got up. His face was bone white.

"What have you done to me?" he asked in a reasoning voice.

"I don't know," she said, genuinely bewildered.

"I'll tell you," he said pleasantly. "All you did was tell the whole world that I could not get you pregnant." He was pleased when he saw her wince at the word. "All you did was tell the world that I couldn't support you and you had to take in bastards for pay."

"What world?" she asked. "Whose world?" The baby wailed again. She turned quickly and went out.

"You Goddamned peasant!" he hissed after her.

She came back carrying the baby. She pulled a chair close to the stove, spread her legs to make a large lap, and changed the baby's diaper. He looked on with distaste; even disgust. Mark called out, "Mama?" querulously from the nursery. She got up, put the baby in Claude's arms and went to Mark.

Claude held the baby. No miracle happened. The feel of the helpless child in his arms did not bring on a surge of tenderness; his heart did not turn over. The child, thumb in mouth, looked up at him with brown, unwavering eyes.

He looked down on the child and thought: *Whose spawn are you?* The child's eyes blinked once and he took his thumb halfway out of his mouth and put it back again. *But who am I to throw stones?* he continued in his thoughts. *Whose spawn am I for that matter?* Without his volition, his arm tightened convulsively about the child.

She came in leading the boy by the hand. "Claude," she said, "this is Mark."

Claude and the boy stared at each other. Neither said a word. *If,* thought Claude, *she says, And Mark, this is Papa, I'll throw the one I'm holding right in her face!*

She said nothing more. She took the baby from him and took both children back to their cribs. When she returned, she spoke to him as though continuing a conversation.

"And Claude, they are not bastards. Maybe they're orphans; maybe they're children that were not wanted by a mother . . . or a father. But they are not . . . what you say. They are God's children. They are Catholic children."

"Sit down, Margaret," he said gently. She complied. "Margaret, I want you to get a divorce and marry someone who will give you all the children you want."

"I can't, Claude."

"Why?"

"Because I love you and could never love another man in the way I love you. Because I slept with you and could never sleep with another man. And then, there's no divorce in the Catholic Church."

"The Church cannot prevent a legal divorce."

"No. But what good would it do? I couldn't ever remarry in the Catholic Church. I wouldn't want to marry any other way because it would be adultery."

"Nonsense!"

"Adultery. Yes! According to my Church."

He thought on that for a while. She put some more coals on the fire and basted the duck which was roasting in the oven.

"We are married then for life," he said.

"For eternity."

"That is, married until one of us dies. I am your husband. You love your husband."

"I love you, Claude. I do."

"Then send those children back to the orphanage."

"I can't! Oh, Claude, if you only knew how long I waited; had to wait. Because it was so hard to get them. If it hadn't been for Father Flynn . . ."

"The point is, you *did* get them."

"Yes. Father Flynn spoke up for me," she said proudly. "He told them I was all right."

And so you are, he thought. *And I'm as much of a sadistic son-of-a-bitch as that super who hires college men to shovel snow. But, by God, I'm not going to let those children take my place. I want her for me alone. I've got to have that. Someone who's all mine . . . who waits for me. . . .*

He grabbed her arms and held them so tightly that his fingernails went into her flesh. "You give them up. Hear me? Will you take them back where they came from or must I go to your priest and make him take them back?"

"If you make me, I'll take them back, Claude."

He was instantly mollified. "Yes, Margaret, that's best."

"But you know that, as soon as you go away, I'll get children again. If it's too hard to get them from a home, I'll manage somehow to have one of my own." She hardly knew what she was implying.

But he knew. He knew of many women, many barren wives who got with child by another man and the husband believed the child was his. Claude was afraid.

"Margaret, love, I'll never leave you again. I've had my lesson. I have been too careless of you. But a man can change. I'll get a job. I can always get a job. We'll be together all the time as married people should—not for just a few weeks in the winter. We'll have a child. If, after three or four years, we don't, we'll go together and adopt one or two. I'd want them to take my name. But I swear it, Margaret, I'll never go away again if you will only send those children back."

"You will always go away," she said quietly. "Because it is *in* you to go away. The way it's *in* me to be a Catholic. The way it is in me to want children, to need them so bad that I'll get them any way I can."

I've lost, he thought. *But then, I had no right to win.*

"The duck's done," she said.

"The hell with the duck," he said wearily. *I hate her,* he told himself.

They went to bed, and, because essentially and in spite of everything they loved each other, and because they loved to make love to each other, and because they had not been with each other for so long, everything was new and wonderful again.

Afterward, he drifted off to sleep. She prodded him awake. "Claude," she asked, "what's so wrong with being a peasant?"

He laughed and he found that he didn't hate her any more. "Nothing, my little Chinee," he said. "Nothing."

Chapter Forty-Six

CLAUDE got up next morning to say hello to Denny before the boy left for school. He kept the boy company with a cup of coffee. Claude didn't speak to Maggie-Now, and when Denny went off to school Claude went back to bed.

It was nearly ten when Claude got up and dressed. He went into the kitchen and had a cup of coffee and a roll. Then he went into the front room. The baby was sitting in the high chair at the window with a rattle in his hand. Mark was on the floor quietly playing with some of Denny's discarded blocks.

"I'll fix your breakfast," called Maggie-Now from the babies' room, "as soon as I finish making up the cribs." He didn't answer her.

Claude walked around the room restlessly. The baby's eyes followed him. Claude walked diagonally, the eyes followed him. He walked behind the high chair and, awkwardly, the child turned its head and body to keep him in sight. He came around to face the child. The child looked up at him, still clutching the rattle. He didn't play with the rattle or make it jingle, he just clutched it.

Claude looked down at the child and thought: *Spawn.* As he thought the word, he had a curious feeling of tenderness toward the baby.

He looked down at Mark. "What are you building?" The child didn't look up. The child didn't answer. "A house?" No response from the child. Claude clapped his hands loudly. The baby dropped the rattle on the high-chair tray but Mark neither looked up nor started. He picked up another block. Claude had an instant of fear. He went in to Maggie-Now.

"Is that boy dumb?" he asked. "Deaf and dumb?"

"Oh, he can talk when he wants to," she said. "You heard him call me Mama last night." Claude was disgusted at the feeling of relief he felt.

She heard a clock strike ten. She dropped her work and went into her bedroom. When he followed her in there, he saw that she had put a quarter on the dressing table and was pinning the gold piece back into his coat.

He crushed her in his arms. "No, no, no," he kept saying. "No, I'm not going away. I just got home."

"But you *said* . . ."

"Why must you take everything so literally?" he asked desperately. "I was shocked; angry. I said a lot of things. . . ."

"But you told me . . ."

"Hush, now. Hush! I always wanted a family. You know that. You gave me a father and a brother. And now, my sweet love, you throw in a couple of sons that I don't deserve."

She broke down and cried.

"Listen! Listen now! Listen, Margaret! Listen, Maggie-Now!" He got her quieted down finally. "Listen, Margaret, what do you want more than anything else in the world? Aside from me and children?"

"A furnace?" she said tentatively.

He had to laugh at that. She told him the nurse had said a furnace was needed with the children in the house.

"Your husband will get you a furnace," he said gallantly. "Where are my old clothes? I'm going to get a regular job; a hard-working job with good pay."

True to his word, he got a job which paid seventy-five dollars a week. This seemed like fabulous pay to Maggie-Now. He didn't tell her what he worked at but she noted his broken fingernails and, after he combed his hair, she saw little grains in the teeth of the comb. Marble dust? Grains of cement? Flakes of plaster?

She gave him a dollar a day expense money and used some of his salary for food and household necessities. At the end of a month, there was one hundred and eighty dollars left of the three hundred he'd earned. Claude decided that was enough to start the furnace on.

A man came and gave an estimate. A hot-air furnace with registers would be cheaper than steam heat and radiators. Three hundred was his price: half down now and the balance after the heating had been installed. The deal was made; the hundred and fifty dollars paid. Then terribly cold weather set in and it was agreed that it was a bad time to tear up the house to install the furnace. It was put off until the spring.

After the deal with the furnace man, Claude, no doubt feeling that he had accomplished his mission, stopped working. He took up his old place at the window and waited. One day that wind came and she pinned the gold piece in his pocket and gave him the quarter for cigarettes and the paper. He didn't come back.

Well, she was used to Claude's leaving by now. And she would have to get used to Mark's leaving. She counted the months, the weeks, the days until he'd be taken from her. *I must expect it,* she told herself. *I know it must come.* She did her best to prepare herself for the time.

They put the furnace in. She didn't have the money to pay the balance. She pried twenty-five dollars out of her father on the grounds that he had not paid for Denny's keep while he, Pat, was at the widow's. She paid off the rest, five dollars a month. She was able to get five dollars more per month rent for the upstairs. That paid for some of the coal. Her taxes on the house were raised a little on account of "improvements."

Chapter Forty-Seven

THE pattern of Maggie-Now's life seemed set now. She took Mark back to the home when he was six and, in spite of Mother Vincent de Paul's orders, Maggie-Now wept and Mark wept and clung to her. They gave her another baby. He was six months old and his name was Anthony. She counted up the years and months, days and weeks. She'd have Johnny three years more, and Anthony five and a half years. That was a long, long time, she thought. She was content.

Claude came home each winter with his gift and with meat or fowl. Sometimes he brought a little money. Pat went to the widow's each winter but one, and sent for the priest each night before, save one. Father Flynn was in the hospital having a kidney stone removed at the time. Another priest served the parish temporarily. Pat didn't want this other priest. He was afraid he'd give him Extreme Unction.

One winter he didn't go to Mrs. O'Crawley's

because she closed up her boardinghouse for a few months while she took a vacation in Florida. Pat worried. There were men down there. They'd know she had means, else how could she afford a Florida vacation? He was afraid someone would marry her for her property.

When she came back after Christmas, unmarried, Pat was so relieved that he bought her a five-dollar vanity case as a present. She gave him a present in return—a knotty shillelagh, a treasure that had belonged to her first husband. He was proud of it, Pat was, and carried it with him whenever he went out, wishing he could get into an argument and make use of it.

Maggie-Now worried about Lottie. Gracie and Widdy came to see her one Sunday afternoon. "Widdy's mother's not 'right' " said Gracie. "And Widdy and I don't think she should live alone. It would be better if she went to some old ladies' home where she could be with her contemporaries. She could turn over her pension to the home and get special privileges. Some of those homes are real nice."

"But you see, Maggie, Mother won't go," said Widdy, "and we thought since she likes you so much and depends on you, in a way, that you could talk her into it."

"I'll do no such thing," said Maggie-Now angrily. "And shame on you, Widdy, and you too, Gracie, putting your mother in an old ladies' home. Don't you tell me she'd be better off with her con . . . con . . . with people her own age. Let her have her home where she was so happy with her Timmy—where everything reminds her of him so much that it's like he was still there.''

"But, Maggie," said Gracie gently, "we worry about her. She might get sick and die there alone. And it's not fair, Maggie, that we should worry. We have our own children and . . ."

"Worry then," said Maggie-Now bitterly. "It will do you good to worry about somebody else for a change. When I think of how your mother took the twins off your hands when Widdy was in the war and you were gadding around . . ."

She got them to promise that one or the other would drop in on Lottie once each day. Maggie-Now, herself, went to see Lottie twice a week—if she could talk Pat into staying with the babies for a few hours.

On one visit, Lottie seemed distraught. "Timmy was looking all night for that china dog with the nursing puppies and he couldn't find it. Somebody must have stolen it," she said.

On her next visit, Maggie-Now surreptitiously slipped the china dog back on the mantelpiece.

Chapter Forty-Eight

DENNY was nearly sixteen when he finished second year high. He left Eastern District High without a backward glance and with no tender memories. He was glad to be done with school.

He went to work. He got a job with the druggist for whom he had worked the last two summers. He washed out citrate of magnesia bottles that had been returned for the nickel deposit, filled them from the formula in the big gallon jugs, and delivered prescriptions, stocked the shelves with patent medicines, swept out and did various other odd jobs.

He came home the first Saturday night and his father said: "Hand over your pay."

The boy gave him twelve one-dollar bills. Pat gave the boy two dollars back and handed the ten dollars to Maggie-Now.

"Is that all I get?" asked Denny. "After all, I worked like a dog all week and . . ."

"That's all," said Pat. "And that's too much, if you ask me."

"What's the use of working, then?" asked Denny. Before his father could answer, he went out, slamming the door hard.

That job lasted three weeks. He came home and told Maggie-Now: "I threw up my job."

"Why, Denny? Oh, why?"

"I figured what was I working for? Peanuts? Two dollars' spending money!" he said contemptuously.

"But, Denny, when you're eighteen, you'll get half your salary back. And when you're twenty-one, you can keep it all."

"I'll wait," he said.

"But, Denny, you have to work."

"Give me one good reason."

"Everybody has to work: to buy food and clothes and pay rent."

"Papa doesn't work."

"For thirty years, your father worked steady. Now he has a pension. He still provides money for us."

"Claude doesn't work. Not that I have anything against Claude," he added quickly.

"When Claude isn't here, he pays his own way, wherever he is. When he comes home, he brings money . . . sometimes. And he always works a while when he first comes home."

"But he doesn't plunk down a salary on the table every Saturday night of the year, does he?"

"What Claude gives me," she said, "is worth much more than a man's steady salary. He gives me a whole world . . . oh, Denny, sometime when you're a man and are going to be married, I'll tell you all about it."

"I want to say it again," said Denny. "I've got nothing against Claude. I *like* Claude."

"Why, Denny?" she asked quietly.

"Because. Well, because he makes me *feel* like somebody . . . like somebody important. Other people make me feel like a worm."

Maggie-Now smiled tenderly. Back down the years she heard herself saying . . . *because you make me feel like a princess.*

After a while Denny got a job in Manhattan: messenger boy in a brokerage office. He earned twenty dollars a week and Maggie-Now gave him five out of it. He seemed satisfied. He loved working in the big city and wished he could live there. He seemed to like his job.

He had been working there a couple of months when he found out that the other messenger in the firm was getting twenty-five a week. He went to his boss and asked for a raise.

"I'll see," said Mr. Barnsen.

Denny waited three days. Then he went back to the boss and asked, a little flippantly, "Did you *see* yet, Mr. Barnsen?"

Now Mr. Barnsen had just about decided to give Denny a two-dollar raise. But he changed his mind. He didn't like the boy's attitude.

"Yes, I saw," said Mr. Barnsen. "And I saw that I don't like your attitude."

"What else did you see?" sneered Denny.

"I saw that the firm could very well get along without you."

"You mean I'm fired?"

"We like to say 'dismissed,' " said his ex-boss.

"Why? Why?" asked Maggie-Now when Denny told her.

"He said he didn't like my attitude—whatever that is," replied Denny.

Chapter Forty-Nine

SUNDAY afternoons, Denny hung out with some fellers around the newsstand of a corner candy store. Denny had an act, the purpose of which was to give the fellers a good time. Strolling girls were the stooges of the act. Denny'd see a girl approach. As she passed, he'd say something like: "Oh, you kid with the bedroom eyes." The girl would pause, startled, and say something like: "You fresh thing, you!" This put the fellers into hysterics.

He used a different routine for the next passing girl. He took off his hat with a flourish, bowed and said: "How do you do . . ." When the girl stopped in surprise, he'd continue. ". . . that trick with your hat? Like this?" He'd twirl his hat around on his forefinger. Laughter from the crowd.

One day, Denny saw a pretty girl coming along. She had a cute shape, too. As she was passing, he said: "Hello, good-looking." When she turned to give him an indignant look, h said: "Can't you take a joke?" Instead of tossing her head and going on her way, the girl came right up to him.

"Dennis Moore! You ought to be ashamed of yourself, hanging around on the corner like a loafer and insulting girls, and you with such a nice sister and such a nice home and all."

She lectured him for a good five minutes. Dennis was charmed by the way her eyes sparkled and how a pink color in her cheeks came and went. He was sorry when she walked away.

One of the boys said she was a peach and she lived on his block and her name was Tessie Vernacht.

Dennis thought he had heard his sister mention that name. And how did the girl happen to know his name?

He went home and asked his sister. She said, yes, she had once spent an evening with her mother, Annie, when Dennis was just a little boy. And she had seen her working in a dime store but Mrs. Vernacht hadn't recognized her.

"Are they Catholic?" he asked.

"Everybody around here is Catholic," she said. "Why do you want to know?"

"Oh, she saw me on the street and she said, 'Hello, Dennis,' and I thought maybe you knew her mother or something."

The next Sunday he went to every Mass, starting with the six o'clock one. After each Mass he came out and stood on the step waiting for Tessie to come out. She came out from the twelve o'clock Mass.

He grabbed her arm. "Look, Tessie, I'm sorry I said that to you that day. I didn't know it was you. You did right to bawl me out and I'd like to make up for that. Would you go to a movie with me sometime?"

Tessie was pleased with his apology and was sorry she had called him down in front of his friends. She said, "I'd like to, Dennis, but first I'll have to ask my mother."

He was waiting for her the following Sunday. "Did you ask her?"

"Yes."

"What did she say?"

"She said I couldn't go out with you."

"Did she say why?"

"She said you were too wild, Dennis."

"Gee, Tessie, you're old enough. I'm eighteen and you must be nearly that. You can go out with me without telling your mother."

"I'd like to go out with you, Dennis. But if I fooled my mother, you'd start thinking that maybe I was fooling you."

"You talk like Maggie-Now."

"I'd be proud if I was as good and decent as your sister."

"Listen," he said, kicking at a nonexistent pebble. "Maybe I am what your mother calls wild. But if I had a girl—a good girl like you—maybe I'd be different."

"I'll ask her again, Dennis."

"I don't want to be the way I am," said Denny inarticulately. "But I don't know any other way to be."

"I'll ask her," she repeated.

"No!" said Tessie's mother. "You don't go out with that feller."

"But Mama, I'm eighteen."

"I say, no!"

"But why?"

"He is too wild for a good girl like you."

"Sometimes a good girl can make a wild boy change."

"I didn't bring you up to make angels out of devils."

"But, Mama . . ."

"I say, *no!*" shouted her mother.

When they met the next Sunday outside the church, she told him that she couldn't go to a movie with him. Tessie said she was only eighteen and had to do what her mother said. But if he could wait until she was nineteen, she'd go to a movie with him.

He took to walking her home from church, but left on the corner near her house so that her mother wouldn't know.

But one Sunday he forgot and walked her to her door. Her mother saw them and came out and gave him hell.

"You stay away from my Tessie. You hear? She is a good girl and not for bummers like you."

"But I go to church. Does that make me a bum?" he said.

"You go only because so you see her. You stay away from her, you hear?"

But Dennis did not stay away. And Mrs. Vernacht went to see Maggie-Now.

"Maybe you don't know me no more," she said to Maggie-Now. "But . . ."

"Of course I know you, Mrs. Vernacht. I remember I went to your house when Denny was only a baby. And I saw you once in the dime store and you didn't know *me*. Will you sit down?"

"For what I must say, I must stand up. About your brother."

"Dennis?"

"Him. I don't know how I say it but . . . your brother—he is after my girl, Tessie, and she is a good girl.

"I'm glad of that."

"You don't know it, that she is too good for your brother."

"I *beg* your pardon! My brother is good enough for *any* girl!"

"The way he hangs out in poolrooms? The way he plays craps on the street? And the way he won't work, the loafer?"

"I guess you can find your way out," said Maggie-Now.

When Dennis came home, his sister told him about Mrs. Vernacht's visit.

"As far as I am concerned, Denny, you're good enough. But so long as her mother doesn't want you to see Tessie, I think . . ."

"Okay! *Okay!* I only felt sorry for the poor girl. All I did was ask her to go to a movie. You tell the old woman not to worry any more—from now on her baby is poison to me."

Then he added, "All you got to do is say hello to that Tessie and she thinks she's engaged to you." Remarks like that.

He likes her, deduced Maggie-Now.

Denny got to staying out late nights. Pat got tired of telling him to get home early. He issued a simple ultimatum: "From now on, if you ain't in the house by ten o'clock, I'll go looking for you with me big stick."

Denny took the easy way out and got home before ten. His father was always sitting by the window with his shillelagh between his knees, his expression black with disappointment because Denny got in on time and he couldn't go out looking for him.

One night, Denny wasn't home by ten and Pat went out looking for him. He found him in the areaway of a vacant store. Denny and four other boys were kneeling in a circle. They were shooting craps. Facing Pat was a fat backside straining at the seat of a pair of pants. It was as though Pat had been waiting all his life for that. He gave it a good whack with his thorny shillelagh. The boys scattered, except Denny, who knew it was no use to run, and the fat boy, who was in too much pain to run.

Pat spoke gently to his son. "Here, me boy. Hold me stick." Denny held it while Pat got down on his knees and scooped up the nickels and dimes.

"Hey, mister," whined the fat boy, "that money belongs to us."

"I will give it to the Church," said Pat, "for the sins of all of youse."

(Of course, the Church never saw the money.)

After that, Denny took to hanging out in the pool parlor. In those prohibition days, nearly every poor section of Brooklyn was the headquarters of some crime syndicate or some gangster corporation. The poolroom where Denny hung out was a front for the neighborhood gang lord.

Sal (The Gimp) Hazzetti (he got his nickname because one of his legs was a half inch shorter than the other) used this poolroom as a sort of gangster college. Entrance requirements were simple. A kid had to be a punk to matriculate.

From time to time, Denny was approached and asked if he'd like to make an easy "ten." Sure, Denny would have been glad to make an easy ten, but not that way. He always said "No." Why? He was afraid of Father Flynn. Denny went to confession each week. He had been doing so since he was eight years old. It was as much a part of his life as eating dinner at noon and supper at six. He'd have to confess to Father Flynn. The priest would not violate the confessional but he might withhold absolution until Denny went to the police and confessed. It never occurred to Denny *not* to go to confession or to falsify a confession.

Then he was afraid of his father. He always had a feeling that his father was waiting . . . waiting for him, Denny, to do something real bad so that he could beat him to death with his shillelagh.

So while he did nothing worse than sit in the poolroom, it got around in the neighborhood that he was in bad company and he was tarred, bad.

Eventually, his father saw to it that Denny got a job working for a greengrocer.

Chapter Fifty

DENNY'S boss, Ceppi, the greengrocer, always brought his lunch from home. But one day he left it home standing on the sideboard and never missed it until noon. He called Denny out from the back room where the boy was sorting tomatoes: the firm for salads and eating out of hand in one basket, and the soft ones for soup or stewing in another basket.

"Hey, *Wal-yo,*" called the boss. "Go by Winer the butcher and buy me six slice' hard salami slice' thin like tishy paper only to Winer you say *dinny* because he's a Heinie."

Otto Winer, in white apron, white coat over a sweater and straw cuff protectors and wearing a straw hat as all butchers did, even in winter, had taken advantage of the noon lull in trade to eat his steaming hot dinner in the room adjoining his store.

Denny walked into the empty shop and saw Winer eating in the back room. "Hey, Otto," he yelled, "Ceppi the Boss wants six slices of hard salami sliced *dinny.*"

"For a penny profit," said Winer coldly, "I don't let my dinner stand."

"Aw, come on. Chop-chop! That means get the lead out in Chinese."

"Listen! Go by Blyfuss, the butcher, for your wurst."

"The boss said to get it here. Have a heart. I'm only trying to make a living.

While he was waiting, he jiggled his way in back of the meat counter. He looked at the meat-cutting block. He remembered coming to this same store when he was a little kid, the time Maggie-Now came here to buy a leg of lamb for Claude's first dinner at the house. He remembered vividly how he had been entranced with that meat block then.

Now he took his fill of looking at it. The hardwood was whitely clean and had a slight hollow like a big, shallow bowl. He ran his hand over the smooth wood and a thrill—a shiver—went down his spine. He fell in love with the block. He looked at the rack of sharp knives fastened to one side of it. He had an impulse.

"Hey, Otto," he called, "would you let me cut the salami for you?"

Now, whether there was something in the timbre of Denny's voice, or Winer's conscience bothered him because he had been rude to a customer, or he felt generous because he was replete with good, sound food, he made an answer which had a tremendous effect on Denny's life.

He said: "Go 'head!"

"Where's the salami?"

"Is in icebox."

The icebox was a small room lighted by a small barred window high in the wall. Two huge blocks of ice stood on the sawdust-covered floor. Denny looked around reverently like an art connoisseur in an art museum.

The focus of interest was a large, cleaned, split hog crucified from a rack by a hook in each front foot. There was also a quarter of beef hanging up and legs of ham and legs of veal. Also there was something he had never seen before. It looked like a rubber washboard.

"Gee!" he breathed admiringly.

He found the salami hanging with other bolognas, near the door. He brought it out to the block. He took a knife from the rack. It was as big as a saber. He walked twice around the block, half afraid to start cutting the salami.

"Hey, Otto," he called. "How do you make it dinny?"

Otto sighed, put down his bread and came out into the shop. He snatched the saber from Denny, gave him a dirty look and said "Dockle!" He replaced the saber and withdrew a long thin knife from the rack. It had been honed so many times that it was down to a quarter inch of blade.

"Watch!" commanded the butcher.

He inserted the fingernails of the middle and

forefinger of his left hand deep into the salami near the edge of the roll. He leaned the knife blade against his fingers and sliced. He held the slice up to the light. It was transparent! Even a little seed in the salami had been cut in half.

"My God!" said Denny in admiration.

"*Dinny!*" proclaimed the butcher.

Winer handed him the knife. Denny dug his nails into the salami, wishing they were cleaner, and placed the knife blade against his fingers. The hand holding the knife started to tremble. He looked an appeal at Winer. The good man understood.

"I ain't done eating yet," he said. He went back to his bread and broth and beer.

Denny breathed easier. His hand stopped trembling. He cut through. He held up the slice to the light. It was almost as transparent as the butcher's!

"Gee!" he whispered, thrilled.

He cut four more slices, testing each against the light. The fifth slice was opaque. He had grown too confident. He popped that into his mouth and cut the last two slices perfectly. He arranged the slices overlapping on a bit of oiled paper. He thought he had never seen anything so beautiful. He carried the salami roll back to the icebox and hung it up. Still holding the knife, he went over to the hog and stared at it.

"You like the hog?" said Winer, who had come in behind him.

"It's a ditzy," said Denny.

"Go 'head," said Winer. "Tell me kinds of pork it gives from a hog."

Denny touched the hog with his knife. "Pork chops?" he asked hesitantly.

"Sure."

"Honest?" said Denny, all aglow.

Otto Winer felt a distinct thrill. He recognized immediately a meat aficionado. "Go 'head! Show me more."

Denny touched a haunch with the knife. "Fresh ham?"

"Good!"

"Shoulder ham?"

"Good!"

"Pigs' knuckles?"

"Good."

"Spareribs?"

"*Sehr* good!"

"But where's the bacon?" asked Denny.

"Smoked. Hanging on the hook by the window," said Winer, scathingly. *"Dockle!"*

Denny drew himself up to his full height and even stretched a little. He looked Winer right in the eye. "Listen," he said, "I don't like that name *Dockle*. Call me Dennis."

Winer measured him with a look, then said, "All right, Den-iss."

"What's that white wrinkled skin hanging there?"

"Tripe."

"Tripe? I always thought that was a word meaning no good."

"I don't like tripe, needer," said Otto.

"Do you ever need a helper?" asked Denny.

"When I'm busy, I need, when I ain't, I don't."

But thoughts raced through Winer's mind. *I know a lot of things about meat,* he thought in German. *It is not right that, when I die, nobody lives no more as knows what I know. For forty years, the meat is my life and I learned many things by myself. About cutting meat. This boy here, I could teach him these things. A son I never had. But this boy . . .*

Denny broke in on his revery. "Well, if you ever do need a helper, think of me. The name is Dennis Moore."

"I don't hear good from you," said the butcher. "You go by the poolroom every night."

"I quit that."

"How long ago you stop?"

"Starting now."

He don't lie anyhow, thought Winer.

"But where you work, you don't stay long. You get fresh with the boss and you be lazy."

Denny put away the fresh retort which came so handily to his mind. He took his cap off and wrung it in his hands, looking away from Winer.

"I've been working since I'm sixteen. All the things I've worked at, I never liked. I don't like to work at jobs I don't like. So I get fresh so I can get fired. But here . . ." He looked around at the sides of meat. "To work here, it would be like going to Coney Island every day in the summer."

It was done! Winer knew it and Denny knew it. But there were certain formalities.

"How much does Ceppi pay you?" asked Winer.

Denny was going to lie and say twenty dollars. He decided against it—not that he believed in the truth, but he thought it would be bad luck if he lied now.

"Eighteen dollars," said Denny.

"Maybe I could pay that," said Winer. But he sounded doubtful.

"I get eighteen dollars. *And* tips for deliveries."

"Eighteen dollars I give you and no more," said Winer firmly. "Your tips is that I learn you a good trade."

Denny's heart jumped. He was hired! He had never expected . . . why he would have worked for nothing. . . .

Winer mistook Denny's introspection for hesitation. He felt he had to add something. "Never will you starve are you a butcher because always people must eat and always they like to eat meat."

"Eighteen dollars is fair enough," said Denny.

They shook hands clumsily over the deal. Both were embarrassed with being so secretly delighted. "You start Monday?" asked Winer.

"First, I must tell Ceppi and my sister."

"That's a good boy," approved Winer.

"But are you sure, Denny? 'All my life' is a long time when you're only nineteen."

"I'm sure. I went in there and there was this cat in the window and clean sawdust on that clean floor, and the wood block and the good knives that he keeps sharpened. . . . I wish I could get it over to you, Maggie-Now, but I can't. Anyway, I knew all of a sudden that that was what I wanted to do all my life. This is a dopey thing to say, but I felt that I'd been born just for that."

She smiled. Maggie-Now had never expected Denny to grow up to be President of the United States. Still and all, she'd had a dream or two for the baby her dying mother had put into her arms; a dream for the vulnerable little boy who had sat on his cot alone the day she married; who had said: "I want to go with you." No, she had never expected him to become President or even a governor. Yet . . . yet . . .

"I'm glad you found what you want to work at, Denny. I think it's a fine trade for a man."

"Ceppi," asked Denny brightly, "do you think you could do without me?"

"Anytime. All-a-time," said Ceppi.

"Because after Saturday you won't see me any more."

"Sure, I see you. Ever' Sunday I come see you in reform school and I bring orange for you."

"All kidding aside," said the boy. "I'm quitting Saturday night. I'd quit now but I don't want to leave you holding the bag."

Ceppi snatched a bunch of soup greens out of Denny's hand. "Go! Go now!" he said passionately. "Beat it!"

"I'll stay to the end of the week. You might have trouble getting another boy."

"Ha! You think? Oh, no! There's plent' more loafers where you come from."

Denny came home with half a week's pay.

"Oh, well, you were going to leave Ceppi's anyhow, Denny," said his sister.

"Sure! But he didn't have to kick me out while I was resigning. And he didn't have to give me that loafer and reform-school routine, either. But I'll show him! I'll show them all," vowed Denny. "I'll be the best damned butcher in the whole damned Borough of Brooklyn!"

That was Denny's version of his father's far-flung challenge to the world: "I'll bury youse all!"

Chapter Fifty-One

TO Denny's disappointment, he wasn't allowed to cut meat right away. Winer said he had to work his way up from the bottom and he meant it literally. Winer, like many a lonely person, was scrupulously neat about himself and the store and first Denny had to learn to carry out Winer's ideas of neatness.

Each night, after the store closed, the sawdust had to be swept out and fresh sawdust sprinkled on the floor. Each day, the marble block that was the store window's floor had to be scoured and rubbed with a cut lemon; the cutting block had to be cleaned daily, with salt and a wire brush; the knives had to be washed and honed daily. The meat-grinding machine had to be taken apart and washed after each usage, and it was used ten or fifteen times a day. The counter scrubbed; the store window washed once a week; the walls swabbed down every so often. Clean, scrub, polish . . . Winer was fanatically neat.

Winer tossed all fat scraps into a barrel. Winer

sold the fat to a soap manufacturer. Once a week, Denny risked getting a double hernia carrying that barrel out to the curb to be picked up by the soap people.

And Denny loved every bit of work connected with the butcher shop.

The second week, Winer let him cut meat from bones and cut up scrap meat and grind it into hamburger, which was called chopmeat in the neighborhood. It fell to Denny to place the sprig of parsley in the center of the artistically arranged swirls of ground meat on the gray agate platter. Winer let him sell soup bones: a marrow bone, a knuckle bone and a straight bone, all for a nickel. He let him slice bologna. He let him give away dog meat and dog bones free—but only if the customer made other meat purchases.

"When they ask for dog meat," instructed Winer, "you must say should you wrap it or do they want to eat it here."

"But that gag's got hair on it," said Denny. "It's that old."

"Just the same, the customers like it. It belongs with giving away dog meat."

Now Denny knew that hamburger was one hundred per cent profit; being made from meat that couldn't be used any other way. He asked Winer wouldn't it be better to urge the already ground hamburger on a customer when she asked for a pound of chuck or round ground to order.

"That's out of date," said Winer. "Here's

516

how you sell chopmeat off the plate. A lady wants a pound of round ground. You make out like you're very happy to do this. You grind it right in front of her. When you put it on the scale, you look mad like you grind too much meat. You take a *lumpen* off and throw it on the chopmeat in the showcase like you don't care. The lady and any other ladies in the store will tell theirselves: I should pay thirty cents for ground round when I can get the same off the plate for eighteen cents. And I know it's the same. I saw the butcher put some on the plate from my thirty-cents-a-pound ground round."

The bane of Winer's life was a woman coming in and asking for half a pound of sirloin or one lamb chop or any other quality meat which meant cutting into a whole side of meat for little profit. Winer instructed Denny.

"A lady comes in and wants only half pound sirloin, it should be cut thick. You then go in icebox and come out and you are carrying a side of beef on your shoulder. You make your legs bend like is the beef very heavy. You put it on block and put hand over your heart like it hurts a little from carrying. Then is the lady so ashamed, all that trouble for half a pound, she says she may as well take whole pound steak."

Winer instructed further. "People buy kidneys and hearts and pigs' feet. Maybe they is shamed they buy such. They all make the same fun about it but all thinks he made up the fun in the first place. Like a lady says: 'You got kidneys?' "

"So I tell her," said Denny, "not to get personal?"

"No. That's fresh. You say, like this: 'I hope so.' Then you smile and make a wink. They think, ain't he fresh! But they like it all the same. Also on all the old ladies and middle ones, you should smile and make a wink even without the kidneys."

"Yeah. But I don't see you winking, Otto."

"That I cannot do. They think I got dirty feelings because I am a widder man living by myself in the back. But for you what is so young and nice-looking, it is a present, the wink, to the ladies what ain't so young no more."

Just then, Denny saw Maggie-Now turning in to the store.

He knew that Winer did not know Maggie-Now. He said, "Otto, let me try the wink and the smile on this customer." Otto gave permission.

Denny gave his sister a big wink. To Otto's consternation, the lady winked back. "What can I do for you, Tootsie?" asked Denny.

Otto, shocked, whispered: "Say 'Missus.'"

"*Missus* Tootsie." said Denny. "What's yours?"

"Do you have spareribs?" she asked.

He made a great to-do about clutching his ribs and feeling his back. "I thought I had some," he said. "But I must have left them home, hanging up in the closet."

That was better, thought Otto. He beamed.

Denny weighed and wrapped the ribs and Maggie-Now asked, "How much?"

"I'll let you have them for a nickel," said Denny, "if you'll give me a big hug and a big kiss."

"You go too far!" shouted Otto. "Excuse, lady," he said to Maggie-Now, "but the boy is new here."

"That's all right," smiled Maggie-Now. "I'm his sister."

"No!"

"This is Maggie-Now. I'm her baby brother."

"He is lucky baby, Missus Now," said Winer gallantly.

Denny laughed. "Mrs. Bassett. We just call her Maggie-Now."

"By me," said Winer, "she is always Missus Now."

In time, he taught Denny how to cut meat. Denny learned fast. He had a great aptitude for meat. Denny became very popular with the customers. Mothers told their children: "When you go by Winer's ask that Denny should wait on you. He don't skin people."

Winer called Denny "Dinny," because Den-iss was too difficult for him to say and the name Dinny was like an affectionate souvenir of the fate that had sent Denny to his store that day.

Winer depended a lot on Denny. Winer found he could take things a little easier now. He experimented with new combinations of food, because Denny ate lunch with him now and

Winer liked to surprise him. Winer took walks in the morning and naps in the afternoon while Denny tended the store alone.

Came the time when he left Denny in charge of the store for a whole day. Winer was going over to Yorkville to spend the day with a *Landsmann,* also a butcher. Denny had long since been promoted to sweater, straw cuffs and white bib apron. On this day, he got his stripes—a straw hat to wear in the store.

"There," said Winer, placing it on Denny's head with two hands as though it were a crown. "Today you are full butcher. Now I go to Yorkville and I would not stay all day if I did not trust you, Dinny."

Denny was so accustomed to being mistrusted that he didn't know whether Winer's remark was a compliment or a warning. Denny tipped his new straw hat over one eye. Winer frowned and set it straight on his head. Denny always wore it straight after that.

Denny had always wanted to know why butchers wore straw hats in the store even in winter. At first, he thought it was to prevent dandruff from falling on the meat. Then he decided it was to prevent a butcher from running bloody hands through his hair. Now he had a chance to find out the truth.

"Otto," he asked, "why do butchers always wear straw hats in the store?"

"So people should know they're butchers," said Otto Winer.

Chapter Fifty-Two

THE neighbors who once eagerly discussed Denny's bad ways, because they had to talk about *something,* now discussed his success just as eagerly because they still had to talk about *something.* They used to warn their boys not to be like that Denny Moore, now. Now they asked their kids, why *couldn't* they be like Denny Moore? Once it had been agreed that he'd end up in Sing Sing. Now it was agreed that he'd own his own butcher shop before too long.

Mothers of marriageable daughters put off buying meat until the daughter came home from work. Then it was: "Go to Winer's before they close and tell Denny you want four loin pork chops." At six each evening, there was always a rush of girls in the store. Each time a girl came in, Denny hoped it wasn't "That" Tessie and when it wasn't Tessie he was disappointed.

Maggie-Now and Winer laid the foundation for a teasing friendship. She bought all her meat at Winer's now, and brought her foster children along when she shopped.

Nearly every Saturday night, Winer gave Denny some delicacy to take home to Missus Now: a couple of veal kidneys or a sweetbread or a Delmonico steak. She was touched and grateful. And she told Winer so.

He said: "I ain't so dumb like I look. If I give Dinny meat to take home, how can he ask me for a raise?" And he knew Maggie-Now didn't believe that.

She said: "Why, Mr. Winer! You're just terrible!" And she knew Winer didn't believe that.

Pat, of course, had to take a dark view of Denny's profession. "Do you know, me boy," he said, "that when you went in the butcher business, you gave up your great right as far as the constitution is concerned?"

"No, I didn't. I can still vote when I'm twenty-one."

"I mean the right to serve on a jury. In a murder trial, they don't take butchers on the jury, because a butcher is use' to blood and chopping off bones."

"Were you ever on a jury, Papa?"

"No. I had better things to do with me time."

"Gee, Papa," said Denny, "if I live until I'm a hundred, I'll never understand how you figure things out."

"I'm deep," explained Pat.

One Sunday morning, Denny just happened to wander over to the church. And it happened that

Tessie came out with a young man. She smiled and said, "Hello, Dennis." And he said, "Hello," and turned away. Tessie said something to her young man, and he tipped his hat and went on his way.

Tessie went over to Dennis and they started to walk to her home. She asked how he was getting along, and said she missed seeing him at church. When they came to the corner he stopped and said, "Here's where I get off."

She said, "Oh, come on. Don't be silly. Mama won't bite you."

"What's the matter? Did she lose her teeth?"

"Now don't be flip. Mama thinks a lot of you."

"Since when?"

"Since you changed and settled down. And since Mr. Winer told her what a good worker you are and how he couldn't do without you."

"Honest, Tessie?"

"I wouldn't lie after I received Holy Communion. Ah, come on in and say hello to my mother. She said she'd like to see you. Come on!"

"No. I got my old suit on and I need a haircut and I want to make a good impression. How about next Sunday, when I'm all dolled up?"

"Okay, Dennis." She smiled. "I'll be waiting at the church for you."

"I hope you'll be waiting at the church for me for good," he said gallantly.

She said, "Oh, go on!" and gave him an

affectionate push.

He cynically told Maggie-Now about it.

"Are you going, Denny?"

"And get the gate?" he said. "Nothing doing."

"Now listen. I've seen a lot of Annie Vernacht lately and she has sure changed her mind about you. She thinks you are 'It.' "

The next Sunday, he had dinner with Tessie and her mother and James, her brother. Dennis wore his good suit and his shoes were polished and his fingernails cleaned and his hair cut a little too short.

There was a little small talk. Annie said how much she liked Maggie-Now and recalled the visit when Dennis was just a little boy and Jamesie had not been born then, but now they could be brothers. And how the butcher had praised Dennis, and so on.

When it was time to leave, Dennis said, "Mrs. Vernacht, would you mind if I took Tessie out once a week?"

"Take my Tessie out?"

"Take your Tessie out," he repeated.

"She has the say of that," said the mother.

He asked, "What do you say, Tessie?"

She said, "Let's not wait 'til next week."

In this way was the pact between them made and it would endure for all of Tessie's life.

Tessie's mother knew the inevitable. She sighed as she thought, *He ain't rich. But he has a good trade and now he is a good man. What more could a mother ask from God, only that her daughter gets a good man?*

A two-year courtship started with their first date. They made plans.

"We'll be different," they told each other. "I won't be like some women," said Tessie, "and get sloppy as soon as I have you for good. No matter how much housework there is—how many children there are—my hair will be curled and my nails manicured when you come home from work and I'll treat you like you was company."

"And I," said Dennis, "will be just as polite to you as though you were a girl I'd just met and was anxious to make a little time with."

"And," said Tessie, "we'll have dates, pretending we're not married but just going steady. And we'll get dressed up and go out on Saturday night to a show or a dance or a nice dinner someplace like we do now."

"And I will respect your mother," he said.

"And I will keep on loving your sister the way I do now and I will be nice to your father."

"Yes," they agreed. "We'll be different."

Chapter Fifty-Three

AT the turn of the century, Winer had bought two acres of farm land in a sparsely settled place out on the Island, called Hempstead. He had only paid a hundred dollars for the land. But now Hempstead was growing into quite a city and Winer had a notion that a de luxe butcher shop would do well out there.

"Otto wants to sell choice meats there and stuff from all over the world like Italian pepperoni and Westphalian ham," Denny explained to his sister. "He wants a cheese department with fancy cheese from every nation in the world. And caviar and even snails, I guess. Truffles, he said, too. A lot of people in Hempstead are well off and would go for stuff like that. At least, that's what Otto thinks."

"What do you think about it, Denny?"

"Oh, he wants Tessie and me to move out there after he sets it up. He wants me to manage it for him."

Maggie-Now's heart fell. *Now he will go from*

me, she thought, *like Claude and the children. At first they'll come in to see me once a week, then once a month, once every three months and then it will be once a year at Christmas or my birthday.*

"Are you?" she asked.

"Oh, I'd like to fine," said Denny. "Only Tessie doesn't want to be so far away from her mother. So I told Winer I wasn't interested."

Mixed with her relief that he wasn't going (although if he had said he was, she would have encouraged him to go) was indignation that Tessie would stand in his way. *He should tell her that's what he wants,* she thought. *She'd go with him.*

"Anyhow, it's still only an idea in Otto's mind."

The wedding was set for the coming June. In the beginning of March, Denny asked Claude would he be his best man? Claude seemed very pleased and flattered and said he'd be honored.

Denny told Maggie-Now that Claude had accepted the role of best man. "That means he won't go away this spring. And you'll have him around to take the place of me pestering you all the time," he said affectionately.

"Don't count on it, Denny. He'll go away again in March."

"Not after he promised."

"He'll go. He'll always go."

"Listen, Maggie-Now. People change, you know."

"Not at our age, Denny. Claude's and mine. Things are set with us."

Claude went away in March.

Plans for the wedding went forward. Annie and Maggie-Now sat together many an afternoon and sewed for Tessie. Annie made her daughter an oval rag rug and Maggie-Now admired it so much that Annie made one for her, too. Denny and Tessie found a modest three-room apartment that was halfway between Annie's home and Maggie-Now's house.

The girls at Tessie's dime store gave her a shower and Winer said that after Denny married he could take home from the store all the meat he needed at wholesale prices. That was his wedding gift. Tessie even got a present from her boss, a brand-new five-dollar bill set in slots in a flowered folder that said, *Congratulations!* This unexpected kindness gave Tessie the courage to ask if she could keep her job after marriage. He said, no, business was awfully slow.

"Then who'll bring the girls change after I'm gone?"

"Me."

"Will you dust the hardware counter, too?"

"No. The girls will take turns doing that. Whenever they go to the washroom, they can stop a second on their way back to dust."

"You never needed me in the first place, then," she said.

"First off I did," he said. "But I don't now. They say this depression is only temporary—that business will pick up again by Christmas. But I don't know. I should have laid you off but I didn't because I thought you'd need the money—getting married and all. And besides, I kept you on for Auld Lang Syne like they say New Year's Eve. You see, Tessie, your mother worked for my father and you worked for me, maybe a daughter of yours might work for my son, someday."

Tessie told Maggie-Now: "He said he didn't need me. It's sad to think that you weren't needed—even in a dime store."

"I know," said Maggie-Now. "Everybody likes to be needed."

"And you know what else he said? He said that maybe a daughter of mine will work for his son someday. Imagine!" she said indignantly. "No daughter of mine will ever work in a dime store!"

That's what her mother said, thought Maggie-Now, *when Tessie was little. Ah, well* . . . She sighed just like Annie.

"Here's a last-minute present for you and Denny. It's from Lottie. You heard us speak of her?"

"Yes, and I'd love to meet her sometime," Tessie said automatically.

The present, of course, was the china dog with

the nursing puppies. Tessie laughed hysterically. "That's the funniest thing I ever saw," she said.

"I have to tell you, Tessie, it's not for keeps. Lottie forgets. In a little while, she'll forget she gave it to you and Denny and she'll think it's lost and she'll go around the house looking for it and crying. I'll have to sneak it back."

"Of course," said Tessie.

"But she did think of you."

"That was nice," said Tessie. In an offhand way, she added: "Poor thing!"

It was June, it was a Saturday night, and it was the night before the wedding. There was an excited hush in the house, the same excited hush that fills a house at a birth, a wedding and a death. Each member of the household goes about with a private look on his face as though recognizing and acknowledging the great verities of birth, marriage and death.

The boy came from the cleaner's with Denny's suit. Maggie-Now brought the suit in to her brother. He was sitting in his room on his cot. She remembered how she had found him there the day she married Claude and he had said he wanted to go with her and she had knelt down before him. . . .

"Your suit," she said.

"Thanks." She hung it in his closet. He said: "Sit with me a minute before you put the kids to bed." She sat next to him on the cot. He put his arms around her. "My mama, my sister, my Maggie-Now."

She smiled. "Remember how you stole the little flags from the cemetery?"

"A man *gave* them to me," he said in pretended indignation.

"Happy?" she asked

"Can't tell you how much," said Denny.

"Denny, it's your last night home. Go upstairs, and talk to Papa for a while."

"He and I have nothing to talk about," said Denny shortly.

"Just the same, he's your father and you can overlook his ways one more time."

"All right." Denny went up to say good-by to his father.

Tessie's brother Jamesie gave her away and her other brother, Albie, was Denny's best man.

Van Clees, who had known and loved Tessie and Denny since they were born, treated the wedding party to a duck dinner out on the Island. That was his wedding gift.

At the end of the dinner, Van Clees presented Denny with a box of fine, hand-rolled Havana cigars. He made a courtly little speech.

"I give you these that you should share them out to all your friends what was not lucky enough to marry Tessie."

Of course, Pat had to have one then and there. Motivated by some black thing in his soul, he took the cigar apart and stuffed the expensive tobacco in his five cent clay pipe, and smoked it. Van Clees held back his tears.

Denny and Tessie had a few hours of honeymoon—a night in a reserved room at the Pennsylvania Hotel over in Manhattan with breakfast served in their room the next morning. They had a night and morning of undreamed luxury for ten dollars and tips.

They came together, they loved and they married. In innocence, and never dreaming how courageous they were, they started a new life together and a new generation of their own.

It was late in the following November. Claude had been home a week. He had brought with him a half-grown Siamese cat that someone had abandoned. They sat in the kitchen watching the cat lap up a saucer of evaporated milk.

"Tessie's going to have a baby in May," she said.

"I know," said Claude. "They asked me to be godfather," he said proudly.

"But that will be *May*."

"Of course."

They asked him, she thought, *so that he'd stay this spring. But he won't.* She sighed.

"If it's a boy, they're going to name him . . ."

"Claude?" she interrupted.

"Good Lord, no! John Bassett Moore."

"That's a beautiful name!"

"My name! Bassett!" he said with deep satisfaction.

Maybe he will *stay,* she thought hopefully.

Christmas was a little sad with Denny gone but Maggie-Now and Claude trimmed a tree for the home children and he gave her a cuckoo clock for Christmas. The children were entranced by it as was the canary, Timmy Two. (The first Timmy had died some years ago.) When the cuckoo came out to call the hour, the bird sang hysterically in competition and the cat lashed his tail and the little boys laughed.

Chapter Fifty-Four

IT was early in March. "I saw Tessie in the store today," Maggie-Now told Claude. "She expects the baby in May. She told me to remind you that you promised to be godfather."

"She did?" he said absently.

"You remember. Denny asked you way back in November—right after you came home. They're going to name it John Bassett."

"It will be a girl, of course."

Her heart sank at his indifference. She had hoped against hope that he wouldn't go away that spring—or would at least stay until the baby was christened. He had seemed so pleased in the winter about the child's name. Now her hopes were gone.

When that day came in March, he left.

The baby was a girl. To Maggie-Now's relief, Tessie had an easy time of it. Maggie-Now had worried. Tessie always looked so frail. But Tessie came out fine. While she was at the hospital, Denny stayed with Maggie-Now. He slept on the lounge in the front room. Maggie-Now was happy. It seemed like old times having Denny home again.

When it was time for Tessie to leave the hospital, Maggie-Now suggested that Denny and Tessie and the baby stay with her a week or two—until Tessie got on her feet. Tessie accepted the invitation gratefully and they all moved in.

Denny and Tessie had Maggie-Now's bedroom with the baby in a pillowed wash basket on the dressing table. Maggie-Now slept on the lounge in the front room. It was a very happy two weeks for Maggie-Now. The house was full and it was wonderful to her to cook large meals. The only thing was that Maggie-Now wanted to hold the baby all the time and Tessie, a modern mother who put her baby on a strict schedule, didn't let Maggie-Now hold and cuddle the baby.

Annie came over and they tried to decide whom the baby looked like. Tessie thought she looked like Maggie-Now and Denny thought she looked like Tessie, and Annie thought she looked like Gus.

Annie fretted because the baby was ten days old and hadn't been christened. Tessie had decided to call her Mary Lorraine. Mary, after Denny's mother, and Lorraine, a name that Tessie would have liked for herself. The christening was delayed because Tessie wanted a godmother for her child named Mary. There was no one in the family named Mary and none of the women had a friend named Mary. It was

535

Maggie-Now who suggested they ask Father Flynn to find a Mary.

"Good day, Father," said Maggie-Now. "We came because Tessie wants to ask you something."

"Come in the house, do," he said, "and sit down."

Tessie had never seen Father Flynn outside of the church. She was surprised at how old he looked.

"Yes, Theresa?" said the priest.

"It's this way, Father. I want to christen my baby Mary. I need a godmother named Mary but I don't know anyone named Mary."

"So we thought, Father," said Maggie-Now, "that you might know someone in the parish . . ."

"Ah, there are many Marys," he said. He riffled through his memory. "Mary O'Brien . . . No, they moved out on the Island. The Bacianos have one. No. That's a Mario; a male. Yes! Ah!" He put his pipe aside, leaned back in his chair and smiled. "I have your baby's godmother, Theresa." He waited, enjoying the suspense. "Mrs. O'Crawley."

"Who, Father?" asked Tessie.

"Margaret knows Mrs. O'Crawley, don't you, Margaret?"

"Her name is Mary?" asked Maggie-Now, surprised.

"I have told you so, Margaret."

"I mean," said Maggie-Now, "it just seems funny that I never knew her first name was the same as my mother's."

"How would it be, now, if I asked her?" said the priest.

"Oh, Father!" breathed the two women simultaneously in gratitude.

"Settled! Baptism this Sunday coming at four. You have a godfather, Theresa?"

"My brother Albie."

"Good!"

They prepared to leave. "Thank you, Father, for giving us your time," began Maggie-Now.

"A moment," said the priest. He raised his voice. "Father?"

A very young priest with a thin, serious face, and wearing eyeglasses, came into the room. Maggie-Now and Tessie stood up and remained standing. They had heard that a new priest had come to the parish to help Father Flynn.

"This is Father Francis Xavier Clunny."

How young he is, thought Tessie. *No older than Dennis and all that education behind him!*

"Father, this is Margaret Moore. I should say Bassett," he corrected himself. "I christened her."

Father Francis stared at the tall, buxom, motherly-looking woman and then stared at Father Flynn as though astonished that the frail little priest had managed to baptize her.

"And Theresa Moore," continued Father Flynn. "She married Margaret's brother about a year ago." The young priest murmured the names as though memorizing them. "Margaret," continued Father Flynn, "goes by the name of Maggie-Now."

"Maggie who?" asked Father Francis.

"The name was put on her because she was wild as a girl." Maggie-Now blushed, ashamed, yet pleased at the attention she was getting. "Oh, you never heard the like of it," continued Father Flynn. "Always her mother calling through the house and up and down the street:

" 'Maggie, now come and study your catechism!'

" 'Maggie, now stop being such a tomboy!'

"Maggie, now this, and Maggie, now that. And one day her mother said: 'Maggie, now you have grown up into a good girl.'

"It was then her dying mother put her new-born baby in this good girl's arms," said Father Flynn.

Remembering, the always easy tears came to Maggie-Now's eyes. All was quiet in the room for a while. Father Francis was arranging all the information he'd received.

The mother died, then, he thought, *and this girl . . . woman reared the baby and the baby must have grown up to marry the younger woman . . . both surnames the same before the older woman married . . .*

The sun was almost gone and night was coming on. Back in the kitchen another in the series of Father Flynn's aged housekeepers was banging pots around as her predecessors had done.

A feller passed on the street, whistling "Ma, He's Making Eyes at Me." Unknowingly, Father Flynn's foot tapped out a bit of the rhythm. Father Francis frowned fiercely until the whistling faded away.

"Father Francis has lately been ordained," said Father Flynn. "He was sent here to help me. My parish is growing all out of bounds and I am growing old." He sighed and looked about the worn and mellow room as though he loved it very much. "Father Francis will be your priest after I'm gone."

"You're not thinking of dying yet, Father, are you?" asked Maggie-Now politely.

"No. But I'm thinking of a vacation. If my Bishop will grant it. I'd like to go to Quebec. The snow . . . You see, I was quite a skier many years ago when I was a boy."

Father Francis made a sound of surprise and admiration as though the older priest had admitted that he'd scaled the Matterhorn. Maggie-Now remembered the skis she'd seen in the church basement long ago.

"Of course, that's all behind me now. It was fifty or more years ago. And now, for a little while, I'd like to be where it's cold and there are hills and where the snow is hard and dry and powdery—I like the snow, you know. And I'd like to watch the young people ski. Well . . ." he rose, signifying that the visit was over.

"Father Francis will be saying his first Mass here, Sunday. Eleven o'clock. You will be there, both of you, and see to it that all members of the family attend." It was an order. "At four, Father Francis will perform his first baptism, your child, Theresa."

He walked to the door with them and gave each his blessing and a Sacred Heart scapular.

Outside, there was a wooden box nailed to the door. A card above it read: *Coal Fund, for Parish House.* Maggie-Now groped around in her pocketbook for a dime.

"But Maggie-Now," said Tessie, "that's for last winter's coal."

"I suppose they'll need coal for next winter though." She dropped a dime in the box.

"Many years ago," said Father Francis, "when I had my vocation, I never thought it would lead me all the way to Brooklyn." Father Flynn smiled. "I'm glad I was sent to this parish. There's work needed here, much work."

And what does he think I've been doing here all these years, thought Father Flynn.

"I've never thought of it as 'work,'" said Father Flynn. "My duty? Yes. My obligation? Yes. And sometimes my pleasure."

"I meant work outside the Church," explained Father Francis. "These are the facts: This is a slum area; the standard of living is low. Cultural values . . ."

"Sociology 2, they called that course when was a freshman," said Father Flynn with a smile.

"But seriously, Father . . ."

"Seriously, my son, I will not have my people patronized or labeled 'Underprivileged' or referred to as the 'Little People.' They are decent and hard-working, most of them, and their sins are venial for the most part."

"But they are poor," insisted Father Francis, "and . . ."

"So in the end was your namesake of Assisi poor. Now my son," continued Father Flynn, "if the people, themselves, have not realized by now how poor they are, it's not up to you to tell them."

But, thought Father Flynn, *I talked just like him when I came here to my first parish. Poor Father Wingate! What he must have put up with from me!*

"Did I sound so pompous?" asked the young priest, seriously concerned.

"No more than I did when I first took over here. Father Wingate warned me not to try to change the world in an hour. I recall that he said a young man wanting to change the world is a reformer; a middle-aged man who would do the same is a meddler. But when an old man tries it, he's an eccentric and a fool."

"I had not thought to reform . . . but to make things a little better . . . yes."

"Vanity," said Father Flynn.

"I ask forgiveness for my sin," said the young priest.

"It is right that you wish to work to make

things better, but don't do it by making the people dissatisfied with what they have. Take them as they are and for what they are. Find them good, *but* needing correction from time to time."

"Needing correction from time to time," repeated Father Francis as though memorizing a lesson. "Thank you, Father."

The housekeeper came in and announced bitterly: "Supper soon. In case you want to wash up." She went back to the kitchen.

"I like a glass of wine before my supper," said Father Flynn to the new priest. "Will you join me?"

"Thank you, but no. I don't believe that wine, except as used in Holy Communion . . ."

"Ah, Francis, you make me feel like a satyr with my bit of wine once a day."

"Oh, no! Who am I to . . . it so happens I have a little satyr in me," confessed the earnest young man. "I like a good cigar, myself, once in a while," he said airily.

"How many do you smoke?"

"Three a week. One every other day, Sundays excepted, of course."

"What kind?"

"Corona."

"Corona-Corona?"

"No. The one-word kind. They cost five cents each. But I've been thinking of changing to Between the Acts. You get more."

"We will spare you that sacrifice. Our good

Lutheran friend, a fine cigar maker, will keep you supplied with good Havana cigars. And it will give him great happiness to do so."

"I prefer not to accept gifts. The people of this parish can't afford . . ."

"Yes, it is a poor parish," agreed Father Flynn. "All the more reason we should accept with grace the small comforts that come our way."

Father Flynn looked in turn at the humidor of tobacco, his rack of pipes, the decanter of wine, and at the lilac tree in bloom outside the window. All were gifts of parishioners or of non-Catholics who happened to like him.

"Small comforts," continued Father Flynn, "do much to lessen the strain of making ends meet. Small comforts give a certain serenity to life and a serene man is a tolerant man. A harried man is not a tolerant man."

He sipped his wine.

"I would not deny a poor man the privilege the rich man has—the privilege of being generous. I would not deny the poor man the grace he feels when he is graciously thanked for a gift graciously given. It makes him feel like a king."

"I have my own way of looking at things, Father," said the young priest earnestly. "In time, I may see things as you do. But it has to come to me in my own time and my own way."

Father Flynn finished his wine. "You are a good boy, Francis," he said. "And after supper would you let me try one of your Coronas?"

Father Francis had but two in his pocket. Eagerly, he gave one to Father Flynn. The old priest sniffed it and admired its shape.

"Not bad! Not bad at all! It will be a welcome change from pipe smoking. Thank you, my son. I hope you won't run short?"

"Oh, no! No!"

Father Francis glowed all over at Father Flynn's thanks. He felt like a king—in a sort of humble way.

Chapter Fifty-Five

EVERYONE went to Father Francis' first High Mass, except Tessie, who had gone to an earlier Mass in order to stay home and mind the children. Even Mrs. O'Crawley, who was a member of another parish, came. After the service they stood outside the church.

"He sang the Mass beautifully, just beautifully," said Mrs. O'Crawley, holding up her hand to button her tight kid glove.

"He has the voice for it," said Maggie-Now.

"Better than Father Flynn, anyhow. He's tone-deef," said Pat.

"Patrick! Is that nice?" said Mrs. O'Crawley possessively.

"Did I *say* it was nice to be tone-deef?"

Pat was in one of his argumentive hair-splitting moods. He was going to make somebody pay for making him go to a long High Mass instead of one of the shorter ones.

"Will you stop at the house and have a cup of

coffee with us, Mrs. O'Crawley?" asked Maggie-Now.

"Thank you, Mrs. Bassett, but I must get home. I'm making a veal shoulder with a pocket for dressing, for dinner. And, Patrick, I'll expect you at one for dinner. After, we can walk to the church together for the christening."

After the baby had been christened, all went to Maggie-Now's house for coffee and cake. Except Annie, who went over to straighten up Tessie's apartment because the little family was going back to its own place to live.

"It was beautiful, just beautiful!" said Mrs. O'Crawley as she skinned off a tight kid glove. "The way Father Francis said that about renouncing Satan and all his angels . . . Just beautiful!"

"I can't thank you enough for the locket," said Tessie.

"It was nothing! Nothing!" said Mrs. O'Crawley. "Just a little something."

"And for being godmother," said Denny.

"It was an honor."

"Yeah. But don't let that give you the idear that you own me, O'Crawley," said Pat.

To divert Pat, Maggie-Now said: "And Albie made a fine godfather."

"Beautiful!" agreed Mrs. O'Crawley.

"Thanks!" said Albie hoarsely. "I got to go now. Good-by." He was off.

Pat left with Mrs. O'Crawley. Denny and

Tessie packed and got ready to leave.

"You've been awful nice to me, Maggie-Now," said Tessie.

"You spoiled her, Maggie-Now," said Denny. "She won't be fit to live with."

"I wish I could stay here," said Tessie wistfully. "It's lonely in that apartment—Dennis away all day. Only home an hour for lunch."

"Come over anytime," said Maggie-Now. "And bring Mary Lor-rainy."

"Lor-*raine!*" corrected Tessie, a little sharply.

"She's tired," said Denny, apologizing for his wife.

"Here!" said Tessie, immediately sorry. "You can hold the baby a minute, Maggie-Now."

After they had left, Maggie-Now changed the sheets on her bed and put her little possessions back on the dressing table. (She had put them away while Denny and Tessie used her room.) She bathed her two foster babies, gave them their supper and put them to bed. She had a sandwich and a cup of coffee for her supper. No use cooking for only one, she thought. She ate standing up and from the top of the washtub. She couldn't bear to sit alone at the big table where so many had sat the last week or so.

She went through the rooms looking for something to do. Everything was in apple-pie order. It was too early to start the oatmeal. The cuckoo clock struck once, and Timmy the bird answered with a tired chirp. It was only six-thirty. She covered the birdcage and went in to sit by the front window. It was going to be a long, lonely evening for her.

Maybe, she thought hopefully, *one of the children might wake up and need something.* She sat and waited . . . waited to be needed.

In September when the nurse came from the home for her monthly inspection, she asked Maggie-Now wouldn't she like to take another baby? She had a nice empty room, observed the nurse, and there was no reason why she couldn't have a third foster child if she wished.

Maggie-Now was delighted. She said she hoped he'd be a very young baby so that she could have him a very long time.

A few weeks later, the nurse brought her a three-month-old baby. His name was Matthew; Matty for short. He had a large birthmark on his little cheek. The nurse said it didn't matter so much with a boy. But it would be bad on a girl. But, added the nurse, as soon as he was old enough, the home would see about having it removed.

Chapter Fifty-Six

EVERYONE said that the November of that year was the coldest they remembered. On one of the coldest days, when there was an icy wind blowing and the very hair in one's nostrils froze, Father Francis set out to make some parish calls. Toward evening, an icy rain began to fall. Father Francis came home with wet shoes and four dollars and thirty cents in contributions for the parishhouse coal fund. The young priest took off his wet muffler and his wet coat and his wet shoes. He put on his slippers and went down and put some coal on the furnace fire and shook down the ashes.

"If we go to bed immediately after supper and prayers," suggested Father Francis, "we can save on coal."

"No," said Father Flynn. "We may be needed this night. The cold spell has held on too long and there are old people who may be dying and we must be available."

"I had better get my shoes dried then." He

stuffed wadded papers into his shoes. He had but the one pair. "Has the doctor been by?"

It was the kindly custom of one of the neighborhood doctors to inform the priest, the rabbi and the Methodist minister, by phone or personal call, when one of their parishioners was seriously ill.

"No, he hasn't. But, mark my words, Patrick Dennis Moore will send for me before the night is out. For the past ten years now, when the cold and snow of winter sets in, he has the idea he's going to die and he wants the Church. Well, one of the times may be *the* time."

And sure enough! While they were eating their supper, a neighbor boy came and said Maggie had sent him because her father was dying and asking for the priest. Poor Father Francis took the paper out of his still-wet shoes and shrugged into his still-wet coat.

It was beginning to snow as they left. *Ah!* thought Father Flynn. But he said nothing. A pale and quiet Maggie-Now met them at the door with a lighted candle. She genuflected and preceded them into the house in the proper way and took the two priests up to her father's room. The bedside table was prepared with crucifix and candles and the needed things.

As in other years, there were clean sheets on the bed and dried blood on Pat's face from Maggie-Now's inept barber work.

Pat started talking right away. "You will forgive me, Fathers," he said, "for getting you out in the weather."

And one of youse would have been enough, he thought.

"But I'm not long for this world and I want to make me peace with me God and me Church before I go."

"You are prepared then, my son?" asked the young priest of the man almost old enough to be his grandfather. And there was no incongruity. The young priest was the older man's spiritual father.

"I have enough insurance to bury me," said Pat. "And a bit of money in the bank to pay for Masses for the sake of getting me out of purgatory *when* I go," said Pat. No one but Father Flynn noticed he emphasized the word *when.*

"Be no longer concerned with things of the world," said good Father Francis. "Prepare yourself spiritually." Father Francis got his stole out of his black leather bag.

He believes me! thought Pat in a panic.

Maggie-Now started to cry. Father Flynn touched her arm and said: "Come, my child." They started to leave the room.

"Where are you going, Father?" asked Pat, really scared now.

"Downstairs. I leave you in the good hands of Father Francis, my son." The door closed after his daughter and Father Flynn.

Pat heard them in the hall. He heard a sob from Maggie-Now and the murmurous voice of

Father Flynn saying, ". . . a speedy recovery or a happy death."

They all believe me, thought Pat in despair. *And all I wanted was to tell me priest me troubles.*

Father Flynn noticed that Maggie-Now's kitchen was freshly scrubbed. There was a new white oilcloth cover on the kitchen table. The chintz skirts that masked the ugly built-in soapstone washtubs had been freshly washed, starched and ironed. There was the good smell of good cooking in the house, and, furnace or no, Maggie-Now had a wonderful fire burning in the kitchen range and a pot of coffee simmering on the back.

As she poured a cup of coffee for her priest, Father Flynn noted a strand of gray in one of the braids of her brown hair. Yet she had an expectant air, subdued as was natural with a dying man in the house or one who she thought was dying. There was something radiant about her—like a bride waiting for her bridegroom.

"Have you had the doctor, Margaret?"

"Papa wouldn't let me send for the doctor."

"When was he taken like this?"

"After supper. And he ate such a good supper, too. He asked for a clean nightshirt and went to bed. He asked me to shave him. He said he was too weak. Then he said to send for you because he knew he was dying."

"Like he did last year," said Father Flynn.

"Like last year and all the other years

when it starts to snow. I'm afraid not to take him seriously because every time I think it is real.'' She rubbed a tear from the corner of her eye.

"When do you expect your husband back?"

"Any night, now."

They talked some more. Maggie-Now told him little anecdotes about the children and made him smile. After a while, Father Francis came down from upstairs.

"He rests quietly," reported Father Francis.

"I'll go up and look at him," said Father Flynn. "Margaret, why don't you show Father Francis your children?"

She took the young priest into the bedroom where two of the children slept. Then she took him into Denny's old room, where the newest baby had his crib. The children smelled fresh and clean and wore freshly washed and ironed nightgowns. The rooms were bare but immaculately clean.

Back in the kitchen, she called his attention to the shelf which ran the length of the room. On it was a row of heavy white china bowls—three of them—three spoons, three mugs and three bananas. There was a large pot of oatmeal simmering on the back of the stove. She explained that, in the morning, the bowls would be filled with the hot oatmeal, sugar and milk added and a banana sliced on top of each bowlful, and that and three mugs of warmed milk would be breakfast for three babies.

"Is it all right, Father?" she asked anxiously. "The way I do for the boys from the home?"

Father Francis had a flash of prescience. He knew that often in the years to come a picture would come to him unbidden: a picture of three mugs and spoons and bowls and bananas. And prescience told him that he would have that same impulse to weep as he had now. But he spoke in a detached and judicial way.

"You do well with our orphaned children, Margaret. They are safe, warm, well-fed and well-loved."

"Thank you, Father. I am pleased and rewarded."

Pat lay very still, scarcely breathing, until he saw it was Father Flynn who came in—not the other priest. Then Pat sat up and began to talk indignantly.

"Ah, Father, the curse of ungrateful chilthren!"

What now? thought Father Flynn.

"I speak of me only son, Dennis Pathrick. He was sent for, but do you think he comes to see his only father and he at death's door?"

"Dennis might think, possibly, that you're crying wolf again."

"Wolf?"

"I told you the story often enough."

"It slips me mind."

The priest told him the fable again, concluding: "And someday, you'll really need help and no one will come."

"Is it becoming," asked Pat, "for a holy father to frighten a poor soul who has no one in the world-a-tall . . . but his priest and his chilthren?" He sighed piteously. "But 'tis true. No one cares for a man that is old."

"True, you are old, my son. True."

"I ain't so old, Father," said Pat indignantly.

"Too old," continued Father Flynn, "to act the foolish way you do."

Pat felt the sudden need to mend his fences. "I am no good a-tall. But I will do better from this day on."

"You can," said the priest patiently. "You can do better if you try."

"And I *will* do better, Father. Yes, I will! Providing," he bargained, "our Lord lets me live a long, long time."

"You will start doing better tomorrow morning."

"Yes, yes," agreed Pat. "I'll get me a good night's sleep first and . . ."

"You will be at the church at six tomorrow morning prepared to make a good confession."

"But I did! I did! This very night!"

"You will confess that, after receiving Extreme Unction, you started sinning all over again in word and in thought."

"Could you not make it nine o'clock, Father?"

"Six o'clock."

Denny and Tessie didn't get over until eight that

night. Tessie made him eat his supper first. They had to wrap up Mary Lorraine in a blanket and carry her with them because there was nobody to stay with the baby.

Denny was on edge from worrying about his father. He never believed his father was faking in spite of the fact that Pat always put on the dying act when he wanted attention. Yes, like Shakespeare's coward, Pat died many times before his death.

"He's fooled you and Maggie-Now before," said Tessie. "What makes you think it's real this time?"

Denny pushed his plate away. "I'm not hungry," he said.

What that man does to his children, thought Tessie in exasperation. *Always feeding off their lives. And when I think of my mother! If she was really dying, she'd deny it so's we wouldn't be worried.*

Denny seemed to know what she was thinking. He said, "Now, Tess, you don't have to go if you don't want to. The drizzle's turning into snow and no one would blame you."

"Oh, I'll go with you, Denn. Maybe he is real sick this time. And I couldn't live with myself if I was mean and didn't go and he really died."

When they got to Maggie-Now's house, Tessie was fussing because the baby's blanket was wet and she was worried about her taking cold. Maggie-Now hung the wet blanket on a chair in front of the stove and placed Mary Lorraine in the middle of her own bed.

"How's Papa?" asked Denny.

"Father Flynn and Father Francis just left."

"Do you think I can see Papa?" asked Denny.

"Now, Dennis," said Tessie. "What do you think he sent for you for?"

Denny smoothed his hair and pulled his tie knot closer and examined his fingernails. He was very nervous. When he came into the room, Pat pretended to be asleep. He tried to throttle down his breathing. He almost laughed aloud when Denny cautiously placed a hand over his, Pat's, heart to check on his father's breathing.

Let him worry his head off about me, thought Pat. *It will do him good.*

"Papa?" Denny sounded worried. "Can you hear me?"

I've got him going, thought Pat.

Denny tried his best to get through to Pat. Finally the boy gave up. He tiptoed out of the room and closed the door carefully.

I hope he's good and scared, thought Pat. *That'll learn him to neglect his father.*

Back again downstairs, Denny said to his sister, "I'm sort of worried about Papa."

"He'll be all right," said Maggie-Now.

"Why did you send for the priest then?" asked Tessie. "After all!"

"Because I always get the priest when he asks. I wouldn't want the responsibility of *not* getting him. In case something happened."

"That's all right, Maggie-Now, as far as

you're concerned. But what about us? Denn works hard all day and then he can't eat his supper—he's so worried."

"Now, Tess," said Denny soothingly.

"And then we had to drag the baby out in the snow."

"Tessie, I told you! You didn't have to come."

"I'm sorry I did. I should have thought first of my baby, who has her whole life before her, than of some old man who has to die anyhow sometime."

"Denny has some obligation to his father," said Maggie-Now evenly.

"His first obligation is to me and the baby," said Tessie.

"And," said Denny, finally losing his temper, "after that to your mother and your brother . . ."

"Why, Denn!" said Tessie, immediately hurt.

Denny loosened his tie, ran his fingers through his hair, started pacing and said: "The sooner Otto builds that place in Hempstead and the sooner I get out there away from all this, the better I'll like it!"

Tessie was instantly ashamed of herself. "Aw, Maggie-Now, honey, I'm sorry for blowing up. But you're so swell that it makes me as mad as anything the way you give in to your father."

"Oh, I don't mind humoring him, Tessie."

"That's all right for you!" Tessie flared up again. "But it makes it hard for Dennis and me. *You* give in to your father, he expects Dennis to give in. You cater to him and everybody else has to."

"Papa's dependent on me and I'm used to it, I guess."

"Get unused to it," said Tessie. "Because it's going to be tough for you when you get old and nobody . . ."

"I'll always treat you as though you were company," quoted Denny, "Remember, Tess?"

"Yes. And," she quoted, "I'll always treat you like a girl I just met and that I'm anxious to make a little time with. Remember when you said that to me?"

"You said, I will always love your sister and . . ."

"And I do! I do!" She put her arms around Maggie-Now and started to cry. "I didn't mean it, Maggie-Now. Honest! I'm so wrong. I shouldn't talk to you that way. But I'm so on edge all the time. The baby cries all night long and I get behind in my housework and I'm alone all day and . . ."

"Listen," said Maggie-Now. "How long since you and Denny went out together?"

"Why . . . why it must have been last February. Yes, I remember. I was showing so much by then I didn't want to go out and then the baby came and . . ."

"Look! You and Denny go out tonight. You can catch the last part of the show at The Bushwick. Or have coffee and waffles some-place. Anything to get out together."

"But the baby!"

"Leave her with me overnight."

"I couldn't!"

"You can and you will," said Denny.

"But the baby needs . . ."

"Maggie-Now's been taking care of kids all her life."

"But I mean the formula and the diapers."

"Matty's about the same age as Mary Lorrainy," said Maggie-Now. "I can use the same formula. And I've got hundreds of diapers. Now you and Denny go out and have yourselves a time."

Tessie held out until Denny said: "Let's go out and celebrate our first big fight."

There was a thin covering of snow on the ground now. Maggie-Now watched Denny and Tessie go down the street. Tessie took a running slide but her high heels threw her off balance and Denny caught her and washed her face with snow. She broke loose, scraped up a handful of snow to throw at Denny. He caught her arm and made her drop it and she squealed and he laughed and they ran off down the street, hand in hand.

Maggie-Now watched them out of sight. Just kids, she thought tenderly. She took a moment to watch the snow dancing about the lighted orange globe on the corner. The globe meant there was a fire alarm box there. The white snowflakes flashed orange as they went past the light.

She went back to the kitchen and added half a cup of water to the simmering oatmeal because it was getting a little thick. She checked the orphans, arranging the covers more securely on one and turning another, who was sleeping upsidedown, the right way. She felt of Mary Lorraine, whom everybody was beginning to call Rainy, to see if she needed changing. Lastly, she went up to her father's room. He was on his knees on the floor, half under the bed.

"Papa! What *are* you doing?"

"Looking for me pipe."

"Get right back in bed! Crawling on the floor and all. I wish you'd rest more, Papa." She got him back into bed.

"Rest, she says! And how can I be resting with me room full of priests praying over me and me family downstairs hollering and fighting and me only son out on the streets with his German girl, jigging and hollering and doing I don't know what."

"Oh, don't begrudge them a little fun."

"I begrudge nobody nothing. All I ask is that me chilthren leave me body get cold, first, before they hold me wake." He jumped out of bed.

"Get back in bed! I've had enough out of you for one day. Get your sleep because you're moving to Mrs. O'Crawley's in the morning."

"No you don't, me girl. No one is shoving me into the O'Crawley's arms. I'll find me own room. I'll find a room in some widder woman's house; a widder woman who'll be glad to marry the likes of me with me pension and all and carrying insurance.''

''Mrs. O'Crawley's a widow,'' she suggested.

''Too old! She's fifty-five.''

''You're sixty-four yourself.''

''How did me age get in the conversation?''

''Oh, Papa,'' she sighed, ''if you only would marry again!''

''What would you do without me insurance then? Answer me that.''

''I don't want your insurance, Papa. I hope you live many years to come.''

''That I will! That I will!'' he shouted.

''You don't have to holler so.''

''I'll holler all I want,'' he shouted, ''and I won't die, either. I'll live! I'll live just for spite!''

''Live, then!'' she hollered back. ''Who cares?''

''I'll bury youse all!'' he roared. ''I'll live to bury youse all!''

His curse rang through the house. The little orphan boys downstairs trembled in their cribs. Mary Lorraine Moore whimpered, wet her diaper, woke up and cried.

Maggie-Now changed the baby's diaper, pulled a rocking chair up close to the kitchen range and sat there rocking Mary Lorraine and talking to her.

''I'm going to hold you all I want tonight and rock you and sing to you. Because you're *my* baby. My brother is your father and my father is your grandfather and your grandmother was my mother. You have the same blood and bones and flesh that I have. So you're my baby. At least, until tomorrow morning."

Chapter Fifty-Seven

PAT left the next day for Mrs. O'Crawley's. At last, he had decided to marry the widow. He would have to figure out the best way to *tell* her. It never occurred to him to *ask* her. He would have told her some time ago but for one thing: She had two dead husbands and Pat, being superstitious, believed that everything came in threes.

He rationalized his decision to marry her: *Every year a priest comes and gives me the last rites and me family leaves me for dead. I can lick that. But when two priests believe I'm dying, that's tough. With the widder now, I'll only die the once, instead-a every year.*

Tessie came to pay a visit to her baby's godmother and Pat. From his window, Pat saw her arrival. He sent Mick Mack back to his own room, saying, "Here comes me daughter-in-law, the Informer." Pat turned off his radiator. *The Informer will tell me daughter that I sit in a cold room and Maggie-Now will worry her head off,* he thought with satisfaction.

She left the baby with the widow and came up to see Pat. "I brought you some new clay pipes," she said.

"Where's the tobacco?" he asked.

"You've got tobacco."

"What'd you come here for?"

"Just for a visit."

"You came so you could inform on me to me daughter."

"I did not!" she said hotly. "I know you don't like me. And I don't like you either. I come to see you only because it pleases Dennis when I do. Well, I've paid my visit. Good-by." She left.

She's got spunk, that one, he thought. *Me son's in good hands.* After a while, his room got cold. He forgot that he had turned off the heat. He grabbed his shillelagh and banged on the radiator pipes.

"Heat, O'Crawley!!" he bawled. "Heat, Goddamn it!" She came up to his room. "Where's me heat?" he hollered.

She knelt down and turned the valve. There was an immediate hiss and gurgle. "You turned it off," she said reproachfully.

He looked at the slender, aging woman kneeling there, her small, work-worn hand resting on the valve. There was something tender and vulnerable about the arch of her slender, bent back.

And so had a young girl, long ago, knelt in a field in Kilkenny County to pluck a daisy to put in his buttonhole and her young back had had that same tender and vulnerable look. He thought briefly of Maggie Rose and lingeringly of Mary Moriarity.

"Me first wife was named Mary," he said. "And the one I'm taking for me second wife is Mary, too."

She got up and clasped her hands ecstatically. "Oh, my man, dear!"

"No fancy wedding, now," he warned her.

And it was done and he made his permanent home at the widow's house. When Maggie-Now realized her father had moved out for good, she felt strangely depressed.

That year Claude came home late, the second week in December. Maggie-Now was shocked at his appearance. He had gotten quite thin and his clothes were nearly in rags and he had an irritating cough.

He went away too far this year, she thought in dismay. *Where it was too cold. And he must have had a hard time getting back.*

In her presence, he unpinned the gold piece and took it out of his pocket. "I almost needed it this time," he said. "But I managed to get through without it." He put the coin in her hand. "You'll never need to pin it in my coat again. I'm never going away again."

He pulled a package from his pocket. "My

last coming-home present to you. Open it.''

It was a beautiful thing; a sea gull made of alabaster. It was poised in flight on a bit of ebony wood. The whole thing was only six inches high.

"It's so beautiful,'' she said, "that it hurts to look at it.''

"Of all the creatures of creation, the gull is the loveliest. And the most free. The blue sky and the bluer sea and a gull poised in the wind . . . alone . . . free . . . nothing but sky and sea and wind and bird . . .

"Oh, if there is a life after death; if one could return to earth in another form, I would be a sea gull!''

She shuddered. "You'll always go,'' she said sadly. "And I'll always miss you.''

He took her by her arms and pulled her close to him. "Margaret, look at me! I will never go away again. There will never be a *reason* for me to go.''

Timidly, she ventured a question. She asked it in a whisper: "Did you find what you were looking for?''

For the first time in their life together, he gave her a definite answer. He said: "Yes.''

He said no more and she asked for no more.

Later they went to bed. As the years had gone by, their lovemaking had imperceptibly changed. Once it had been a wild, passionate thing; as if there had to be a surfeit of love. Now, it was a wonderful surcease from not having had love for so long—all during the months he'd been away.

Two days later Claude became very ill. It seemed like a routine cold at first. Only it didn't respond to the usual home treatment. When his fever went high and he babbled of inconsequential things, she sent for the doctor.

"It looks like flu," said the doctor. "Yes, Spanish influenza. That's strange, though. We haven't had any of that since the World War. Strange . . .

"Have the children shown any symptoms?"

"The children?"

"It's very contagious and I'm afraid the children must leave, Mrs. Bassett."

"No!" she cried out.

"They're too young to survive if . . . You wouldn't want anything to happen to any one of them, would you?"

"No, oh, no!"

"I'll have to notify the home." He was the home doctor for the children.

In two hours, the home nurse and an assistant came in a car for the babies. They wouldn't let Maggie-Now dress the children. They brought blankets and clothes from the home. They put masks on when they went into the babies' rooms. The nurse was very severe with Maggie-Now—telling her sharply that the home should have been notified earlier. Of course, Maggie-Now couldn't even tell the children good-by.

Suddenly it's all over, thought Maggie-Now. *I*

mustn't think of the children. I have Claude. Please God, she prayed, *don't let anything happen to him. Holy Mary, Mother of God, I beseech thee . . .*

Claude got over the flu. It left him weak. And no matter how she tended him, how many custards and how much chicken broth she made for him, he didn't improve. She put the rocking chair near the coal range and put pillows in it. He sat there and she gave him a footstool to keep his feet off the floor and put a blanket over his knees

He was content to sit there holding on his lap the little Siamese cat he had once brought her and to watch Maggie-Now at her household duties. He watched the time go by, smiling when the cuckoo clock struck and the canary in its cage rapturously burst into competitive song.

"We are alone together, love," he said. "For the first time. Your father's gone and Denny . . ." He didn't mention the children because he knew she'd cry.

"I'm glad I've got you, Claude. So glad! And you are my father, my brother and my children—all in one. If I have you, I need no one else."

"Were you frightened, love, when I was sick?"

"No. I was worried though."

"I was frightened," he said. "Oh, not of dying. I'm no fool. I know we'll all die someday—just as sure as we're born. I was

569

frightened of being put in a covered box and being put in the earth."

"Don't talk that way, Claude," she moaned.

"Let me. I've always been free. I hate darkness and small places; small dark rooms with closed doors. I never want to be tucked away somewhere."

"It's getting cold in here," she said. "I'll poke up the fire."

"No. Listen, Margaret. Where is that little gull I brought you?"

"I'll get it for you."

He held it in his hand and ran a finger over the spread alabaster wings.

The little cat on his lap got up, arched its back, gave the canary in the cage a baleful look, and jumped to the floor. Maggie-Now picked up the cat and held it close.

Claude spoke all in a rush. "I wouldn't be so frightened—I'd even be contented—if I were sure that my ashes would be thrown to the winds over the sea where gulls are flying."

She trembled so much that the cat struggled to get out of her arms. She held the cat against its will. "No, Claude. No! I won't do it! If there is a life after death—and I know there is—I want us to be together in it. And that couldn't be if you . . ."

"Do you love me, Margaret?"

She let the cat go then and went over and held Claude tightly. "My darling, my dear, my love my everything," she said. She was trembling.

"There, Margaret! There now, Maggie-Now. There!"

After a while, she said: "Mr. Van Clees sent over a bottle of very fine cognac for you. And Annie made some wonderful calf's foot jelly for you. How about a nice hot cup of tea with lemon and sugar and half cognac? And toast and sweet butter and calf's foot jelly spread on top?"

"Wonderful! Will you have some too?"

"Of course. You don't think you're going to have all of it, do you, Mr. Bassett?"

"No, Mrs. Bassett."

That night, after tucking him into bed, she undressed, brushed her hair and got in beside him. She put her arm under his shoulder and put his head on her breast.

"Margaret," he said, "if you happen to see your father, ask him to come over. I'd like to talk to him awhile."

"All right," she said.

Pat came over a couple of mornings later and went into the kitchen where Claude was sitting. Pat closed the kitchen door after him. Maggie-Now went into the bedroom to make up her bed. Pat didn't stay long with Claude. Pat opened the door and paused to say:

"I said I would. And I will. In fact, I'll bury youse all!"

Maggie-Now accompanied her father out to the stoop. "Oh, Papa," she said, and the ready tears came to her eyes. "Why do you fight with him? And he's so sick."

"Well, I ain't sick," said Pat. "I didn't like him when he was well. Should I insult him by liking him just because he's sick? No! Furthermore," he burst out, "I don't like that damned skinny cat and that lousy canary and that dopey clock. That's why I married the widow," he said illogically, "so's I wouldn't have to put up with all that stuff. And statures of pigeons, too." He stalked down the street.

Claude must have said something to upset him, she thought.

She went in to Claude. He was smiling. "Your father!" he said. His voice was full of admiration.

Chapter Fifty-Eight

THERE was a warm day in February and Claude wanted to sit by the front-room window. Maggie-Now set him up there and then she knelt down and put her arms about his waist.

"Claude," she said, "I always knew when you were going away but I never let you know that I knew. But now I will speak out. My dear darling, don't go away this spring. You're not well yet. Later on in the summer, if you have to go, I won't try to hold you. But don't go! Please, don't go! And if you do, I'll have to go with you. Because now there is no one but you."

"I told you, Margaret, that's all over. I don't want to go any more. But I would like to sit at the window. I like to see the sky and the street and watch the people go by."

"But the day that wind comes, you'll go again."

"I promised you . . ."

"Could you say it in some way that I could know it's for sure you won't go?"

573

"I'll tell you why I had to go away and why I don't have to go any more. Once I told you that when we were old and had nothing more to talk about . . ."

"That you'd tell me the story of your life," she interrupted. "But we're not old yet."

"We'll pretend. God knows I feel old. Tonight, when it's dark and we're closed in, I'll tell you. But for the day, let me sit by the window."

That night, she gathered all the pillows in the house and she and Claude sat propped up in bed. She put her arm around him and made him lean against her. She had a moment of uneasiness when she felt that his heart was beating too fast.

"If you don't want to tell me, Claude, it's all right."

"No, love. I want to—I *need* to tell you.

"Well," he began, "soon after I was born, I was placed in a private institution for orphans in Detroit. It was denominational, Protestant, and someone paid for my care. From that, I knew these things about myself: That I was white, a Christian, and that someone had enough of a conscience to pay for my care. Who? Father? Mother?"

He was not treated badly at the institution, but with a lot of little boys and an inadequate, overworked staff there was no time for love and understanding.

When he was eight he was sent to a boys'

boarding school. Here there was a difference. Some of the boys had parents, though many were orphans placed in the school by an aunt or older sister. A good many were children of divorce. In all his time there, Claude was the only boy who did not have a visitor.

It was here he learned to parry questions. "Hey! When's your mother coming?"

"Wouldn't you just like to know!" or,

"Hey! You got a mother?"

"How do you think I was born?"

At the age of twelve, he was sent to a modest preparatory school. He had a little surcease there. No one seemed especially interested in his parentage.

Parents or guardians deposited money with the headmaster and, once a week, each boy received fifty cents' pocket money. Claude got his fifty cents along with the rest. There was but one thing different about him: He was the only boy in the school who never received a letter.

One day he came across a writers' magazine in which was a tiny ad that said: *Letters remailed from Chicago . . . 25¢ each.* He wrote a letter to himself, starting, *Dear Son,* and signed it, *Your Father.* He addressed it to himself and sent it off in another envelope with the quarter. In due time, his letter came back, postmarked Chicago. From that time on, he got a letter once a month from Chicago. Once in a while he displayed a letter with elaborate casualness and was not above quoting a pithy sentence or two.

There came a time when he went to the headmaster. "Sir," he said. "I know someone pays for me here and I would like to know who . . ."

"You want to know who you are. Is that it?"

"Yes, sir."

"You may not know who you are, Bassett, but I'll tell you *what* you are: a very lucky boy. Through no efforts of your own, you are being provided with a good education in a good school. . . ." He talked on and on.

"Then you won't tell me, sir, who is responsible for me?"

"I *can't* tell you, Bassett. Your benefactor wishes to remain anonymous."

When Claude finished prep school, the headmaster told him he had been registered at a small denominational college in upper Michigan. His tuition would be paid and rent on a room in the dormitory and meals at the college cafeteria. There would be a small sum available for textbooks. . . .

Claude matriculated there. After a few months he went to the bursar of the college.

"Sir, he said, "I should like to know who is paying my fees here."

The bursar got up and took a file from the filing cabinet. The folder had two sheets. The bursar read the papers, closed the folder and put his hand on it.

"Evidently," he said, "your benefactor wishes to remain anonymous. I can tell you this much, however: A small trust has been set up for you. It will terminate when you graduate from here.''

"Sir, may I know the name of the bank or firm . . .''

"I am not in a position to give you that information.''

Claude looked at the folder under the man's hand. *Everything I need to know is in that folder,* he thought. *I could grab it, run off with it. . . .* But he was not aggressive enough to make a deed out of his thought.

In Claude's sophomore year, the little college won an important football game and some of the boys in his dorm had a beer bust. They all got a little high and someone inadvertently called Claude a bastard. Claude hit the fellow and a free-for-all fight started. They smashed beer bottles over each other's head. Claude woke up in the infirmary with a row of stitches in front of his right ear and they were picking glass fragments out of his ear. Probably his defective ear resulted from that fight.

At graduation, he slipped out of the auditorium as soon as he received his diploma. He stood on the steps and scanned the face of each one who came out. He had a strong feeling that his mother or father had come to see him graduate. He saw a man standing alone and the man's eyes searched the crowd. *This is my father,* thought Claude, *and he is looking for me.* The man's eyes rested on Claude and the man's searching look was replaced by a smile. He held out his hand and Claude started to go to him. Then he found that the smile and the outstretched hand were for a young man standing behind Claude. The father put his arm about the young man's shoulder and they walked away together.

Claude stood there in his cap and gown, holding his diploma, and he waited until all the people had gone.

He got a job that fall, as English teacher in a small-town high school in South Carolina. He loved the town, and he fell in love with a girl there. She was nineteen and he was twenty-four.

"I would like to live here all my life. If you will marry me," he said.

"I will, Claude," she said. "But first you'll have to speak to Daddy."

"Why?"

"Because that's the way we do here."

He sat on the porch with the girl's father. It was a spring night. There was the smell of mimosa and the smell of woodsmoke. Claude noticed a broken board of the porch floor. *Tomorrow*, he thought, *is Saturday. And I will come and fix that board for them. And in spring vacation, I will come and say, Let me paint the porch for you.*

He told the girl's father all he knew about himself. The father was much moved by Claude's story. But he spoke of heritage; he spoke of lineage, proud and poor, but pure. He spoke in firm words of uncontaminated, white lineage.

"But, sir," said Claude. "I am a man in my own right. I have my own kind of honor. . . ."

"But this is the South," said the father. "And we have to know."

"What was her name?" asked Maggie-Now.

"Who?"

"The girl."

"Oh, Willie May."

"I guess I don't like her," said Maggie-Now in a miserable voice.

"Because she wouldn't marry me?"

"Because you once loved her."

"Oh, Margaret," he said patiently, "that was so long ago. It shouldn't matter now."

He left his town, his job and his girl and started on his wandering search. He went to Detroit first because there he had started as an infant. He got a job as hotel clerk and in his free time he wandered over the city and its raw suburbs and looked in phone books, directories, libraries (to read old newspapers, looking for the name), and examined the boards in office buildings and looked up names of professional people and firms. He found a Bassett or two but they were not the right ones. He tried to approximate the year of his birth and sent for a birth certificate. There was no record.

He went to Chicago and stayed there a fall and a winter and again it was the same. Each state he went to, he wrote and asked for a birth certificate. Some states had no records prior to 1900, in others, the records had burned up, and in other states there was no record.

He got out to the West and he loved it there. He loved the mountains and the sky and the great loneliness of it. *Here,* he thought, *a man could live. No one would ask who he was or where he came from. A man could start his own dynasty here,* he thought grandly.

It was out there in Idaho that he first felt the chinook blowing. And he fell in love with it. After that, no matter where he was, he left the place and set out westward when he judged the chinook wind was blowing over the Rockies.

And as the years went by, it was so that the wandering got to be more important than the searching.

He made his way to Manhattan. . . .

"Then I got over to Brooklyn and found you," he said. "And I knew you were the one. You were the one. And you took me without question."

"You could have told me," she said. "And it would have been all right. I wouldn't have cared. And perhaps you wouldn't have needed to go away any more."

In the summer just past, he had gone back to Detroit again. There he got the idea that perhaps Canada was the place. He walked over the bridge into Canada and worked his way north.

One night, he registered at a small, inexpensive hotel in one of the smaller cities. The old desk clerk read off Claude's name slowly. He adjusted his spectacles to look at Claude. Claude had a sudden sense of awareness. "You have people here, Mr. Bassett?"

"No. I'm from the States."

"I inquired because a gentleman of the same name used to live here."

Very quietly, Claude asked: "Where does he live now?"

"Oh, he passed on. Fifty years ago. I was a lad of twenty, then."

"What," asked Claude carefully, "became of his children?"

"He had but the one. A son. Kenmore. He would be my age now."

"And this Kenmore: Where is he now?"

"That, I do not know." The old man suddenly became loquacious. "Kenmore never did have children. He was married, though. He was a professor in one of those big colleges up in one of the northern provinces. I don't remember which one, now. Used to know, though. Some things come back to me. I remember he had a year's holiday. You call it . . . ?"

"Sabbatical year."

"Thank you, sir. He went to the States for that year." The aged clerk started counting the coins in the cash drawer as though the conversation was ended.

"And when he returned . . . ?" asked

Claude nudgingly.

"Pardon me, sir?"

"When Kenmore Bassett returned . . ."

"Oh, he never did come back from the States. Here's your key, sir, and we like our guests to pay in advance."

"I would appreciate any information you can give me about Kenmore Bassett," said Claude earnestly.

"Let me see: His wife didn't go to the States with him, you know. He wrote her. Yes, I remember now. He wrote and asked her to divorce him."

"Did she?"

"No, sir. You see he wrote that there was a young lady in the States whom he wished to marry. And that did not go down well with Mrs. Bassett. Oh, my wife could tell you everything. You see, sir, she was in service. She worked for Mrs. Bassett until that lady passed on."

"May I speak to your wife, sir?" asked Claude, feeling he had come to the end of the trail at last.

The old clerk shook his head sadly. "My wife passed on ten years ago."

"You believe then," said Maggie-Now, "that this Kenmore was your father?"

"I can make myself believe it if I wish."

She thought: *Oh, all the wasted years of life!* But she said: "And now, you'll never need to go away again."

"Never more will I go," he said lightly.

But he had a stab of anguish. Never again to live a while in a sun-baked adobe house of the dreamy Southwest . . . never again the thrill of seeing for the first time one of the magnificent big cities of America. Never again the eternal mountains against the wide and infinite sky . . . the miles of golden wheat rippling in the sun . . . the blinding blue of the great Pacific Ocean. Never again . . . never.

"And you're happy—now that you know?"

"I don't know, Margaret. If we were younger I'd want children now. I feel right about becoming a father, now that I know. But for twenty-five years that has been my way of life—the wandering and searching. Now that that's over, I don't know any other way of life."

No, she thought, *he doesn't know any other way of life. But how, all of a sudden, can he tell himself that he's through with it? I know! Oh, dear God, his strength is failing and he knows he can't make it any more.*

He said that now that he knows, he wants children; would feel right about having children. Did he mean . . . Why wasn't it right before? Could it be that he, like all men who never settle down, didn't want to be tied down by children? Or was it that he had to know who his father was first?

She felt oddly ill at ease with him now—as though he were a stranger with whom she had nothing in common. She felt vaguely inferior as

583

though she were an illiterate peasant. Then she remembered that, this last time he had come home, he had asked her nothing about what she had done in the summer.

He used to need my life, she thought, *to fill in his own. Now he doesn't need that any more. He doesn't need me in that way any more. Oh, I'm sorry he told me!*

She said: "Claude, in a way, I'm sorry you told me."

Chapter Fifty-Nine

IN the days that followed, Claude sat by the window and Maggie-Now sat with him and there was little to talk about. From time to time, he'd reach out his hand and she'd take it and tell him she loved him. Sometimes he'd ask her if she missed the children. She'd hesitate a moment before she told him, no, now that she had him . . .

About a week later, Denny came over in his lunch hour and ate with them. He brought news. The new store in Hempstead was ready and they were going to move in March first. They had already given notice to their landlord.

"Does Tessie feel better now about moving out there?" asked Maggie-Now.

"Well," said Denny, a little evasively, "I made her see that it was for the best."

Denny spoke excitedly about the new store. He described the fixtures, the floor plan and some of the exotic meats and cheese that already had been delivered, and . . .

While Denny was speaking, Claude started to moan. Suddenly his face contorted in severe pain.

"My head!" he gasped. "The pains . . . get . . . something . . . Margaret . . . please . . . I can't stand . . ."

"Oh, darling . . . dear . . . dear darling!" she said. She ran into the bathroom. There was nothing for a headache in the medicine chest, only a tin of aspirin. She knew that wouldn't be enough. She ran back to the kitchen. She spoke to him as though he were a child.

"There, my darling, Margaret will get you something and Denny will stay with you while I'm gone and I'll be right back." She kissed him and rushed out.

Fortunately, the doctor was home. He was having lunch with his family. "How often does he get these headaches?" he asked.

"He never had one before in all the years we've been married."

"I'll give you a prescription. . . ."

"That will take too long, Doctor. And oh, he seemed to be suffering so terribly! He could hardly talk, and . . ."

"I'd better take a look at him," said the doctor. They drove over in the doctor's car.

Denny was on the stoop waiting for them. He seemed terribly distraught and kept putting his hands up to his head.

"Something terrible happened, Doctor," he said. "Something awful . . ."

"A stroke," said the doctor succinctly. He gave what comfort he could: "If he had to go, it was better this way. A few moments of pain and it was all over."

Maggie-Now was too shocked to comprehend. "But he said he wouldn't go away," she kept repeating. "He *promised!*"

"If you loved him," said the doctor, "you'd rather have it this way. You wouldn't want him to suffer and die by inches—stroke after stroke."

"But he told me he wouldn't leave me," she said like a bewildered child.

"I'm going to give you something, Mrs. Bassett," said the doctor, "to get you over this first shock." He broke an ampule and filled the hypodermic needle.

When she awakened, Claude was no longer there. The house seemed full of people. She heard Annie's voice saying she'd take care of everything.

The talking ceased when Maggie-Now came out of her room. She went into the kitchen. Annie had the range going full blast. She was mixing a cake and preparing a beef rib roast for the oven. Potatoes and vegetables were on the table waiting to be prepared. Annie knew it was right to have food ready for the people who would come.

"He's gone, Annie," said Maggie-Now.

"Is better if you cry, Liebchen," said Annie. "But he promised . . ."

She went into the front room. "Papa, he said he wouldn't go . . . he promised."

"Ah, me Maggie-Now," said Pat. "Me poor Maggie-Now!"

Denny gave her a glass with some pinkish liquid in it. "The doctor said you're to take this, Maggie-Now."

"I don't want it," she said.

"You must!" He started to weep. "The doctor said I must make you take it."

"Of course," she said soothingly. "Don't cry. I'll take it."

"Maggie-Now," said Pat, "you must put yourself together, girl, dear. We got to fix it about the funeral."

"Funeral?" she said vaguely. "But I haven't any money."

"I have a bit put away," said Pat. "I'll pay for it."

"But, man, dear!" For the first time, Maggie-Now noticed Mrs. O'Crawley was there. "Man, dear, wouldn't it be better for Maggie to take care of that?"

"I *said* I'd bury him and I *will*," said Pat. "Goddamn it!" he added for no reason at all.

Maggie-Now's innate thoughtfulness broke through her shock. "It won't cost much, Mrs. O'Crawley," she said. "We have our own plot and he can be with Mama and Grandfather. And I'll pay Papa back as soon as I can."

"He ain't going to be put in the ground," said Pat. "He wants to be ashes and the ashes to be thrown away in the wind where birds is flying."

"No!" screamed Maggie-Now. "No!"

"He told me the last time I was here and I said I would do that for him."

"I won't allow it!" she screamed. "It's against our religion."

"Maybe it ain't against his," said Pat.

"No, Papa," she said more quietly. "I have the say and I won't allow it."

"Look, Maggie-Now," said Denny. "You always gave Claude everything he wanted. You'd have ways to find out what he wanted and he could have it. You let him go when he wanted to and you never said no to anything he did or wanted. Why don't you give him this one last thing he wanted? It's nothing I'd want." He shivered. "But he wanted that."

"Yes, Denny," said Maggie-Now quietly. "That's right."

"Sure," said Pat. "And I'll take care of everything for you. Everything."

"Thank you, Papa," she said. Now she seemed to get control again. "It was nice of you to come, Mrs. O'Crawley. I think Annie made coffee. Will you go out in the kitchen and have a cup?"

"Thank you, I will," said Pat's wife.

She turned to Pat. "And thank you again, Papa. And why don't you ask Mick Mack to stop over? I'd like to see him."

After they had left, she went out to the kitchen.

"Ah, Annie, you're so good," she said.

"Is nothing," said Annie. "Someday, maybe you do the same for me. Is right people do so for each other."

Maggie-Now put her coat on. "You go out, Maggie?"

"I want to talk to Father Flynn."

"Then you go by the church. Yes?"

"Yes, I will."

Maybe she will cry there, thought Annie.

Maggie-Now didn't go to the cremation. Pat and Denny went; no one else. Pat brought her the cheap urn that the crematory provided.

"I thought maybe you wanted to keep this awhile," said Pat.

"Papa, it would be all right to bury his ashes with Mama, wouldn't it?"

"I gave him me word I would throw his ashes in the wind. I'll wait for the right day and then I'll come and get him and go out on a boat to where birds is flying, and I will do it."

"All right, Papa," she said, obediently.

It was terrible, *terrible,* for Maggie-Now to be alone; to have no one to care for. The house echoed with emptiness. All, all were gone. No tenants occupied the rooms upstairs. Denny was gone, her father was gone, the children had been taken from her. And now Claude.

She walked from one empty room to the other, moaning, *How can I live? How can I live alone? There was always someone. And now no one.*

Denny knew how it was with his sister and he was anguished for her. And he was the one to come to her aid.

"I'm not going to take over the new store in Hempstead," he said. "Well, Tessie and I talked it over. We want to rent the rooms upstairs from you and live here."

"Honest, Denny? Honest?" Tears of happiness came to her eyes.

"Tessie is tickled to death at the idea. She says no one can handle Rainy like you can. We could all eat together—Tessie doesn't like to cook especially. And we'd all be safe together and . . ."

How wonderful! How wonderful! thought Maggie-Now, *to have them here with me! I could take care of Rainy and I could cook again: cook for someone else besides myself . . . I'd have someone to talk to. . . .*

"Are you sure that's what *you* want, Denny?"

"I would have liked to manage the new place and live out there. Yes, I would! But in the first place, Tessie doesn't want to live so far away. In the second place, you can't stay here alone and starve. And then Tessie says her mother needs her."

"It's the other way around," said Maggie-

Now. "Tessie needs her mother—or thinks she does."

"Oh, well!" Denny shrugged and smiled.

Maggie-Now took a little time to savor this wonderful idea of Denny's before she gave it up. *It would be like a dream come true. Tessie would let me take care of Rainy and it would be like having my own babies. And I'd have the brother I love with me. And Tessie! I could teach her how to sew . . . And Annie would come over often, and . . . Oh, it would be just too wonderful.*

She said: "No, Denny! I'm not going to let you do it."

"What?"

"Don't be such a damned fool!" It was the first time he'd ever heard his sister use a curse word. "Now look here! Annie can take care of herself. She's got Albie for the time being. And I'm around if Annie has trouble."

"But what about you?"

"I'll manage. I've always managed. The rooms will be rented again. I'll find something to do. Maybe I'll rent out the whole house or close it up and go to Atlantic City or somewhere to find work. I've never been outside of Brooklyn except twice—when I went to Boston with Mama and when I went to Manhattan with a boy many years ago. Maybe I'd like to see other places."

"You mean you don't want us?" he said, aghast.

"Yes, I do want you and your family. But it's

not good for me to want that. And it's not good for you to give it."

"But Tessie wants . . ."

"Tessie's a wonderful girl. And she's a smart girl, too. She has one beautiful fault, though. The fault of being very young. Don't ask her what *she* wants, tell her what *you* want. Tell her how wonderful she is; how lucky you are to have her. Tell her you couldn't live without her, and then tell her that you are all going to move out to the new place because it is the best thing for all of you. *And move out there right away.*"

Denny got up, put his hands in his pockets, grinned and started to swagger around the room. Then he went to Maggie-Now and gave her a big hug.

"If Tessie makes a fuss, tell her I'm tired of looking after people. I want to live my own life for a while. And tell her if she gets out of her mother's way, maybe Mr. Van Clees might have a chance with Annie."

After Denny had left, Maggie-Now sat in the kitchen and wept. *What am I going to do?* she asked herself. *What am I going to do alone here?*

Chapter Sixty

PAT and Mick Mack had just finished the ample breakfast served to them by the neat and taut widow.

"Man, dear," she said to Pat, "it's a wonderful day for beating the carpet. Just wonderful!" She handed Pat two rattan carpet beaters. "And I'm sure Mr. Mack will be delighted to help you."

Mick Mack carried the carpet out into the yard. Pat followed, carrying the carpet beaters. "Get the damn dusty thing up on the washline," instructed Pat. Mick Mack started to struggle with the carpet. There was a soft wind blowing.

"Hey, Mick Mack!"

"And what is it, Pathrick?"

"You feel that wind? A kin-nooky . . . what did the bastid call it? Oh yeah! Chinook!"

"So long," said Mick Mack.

"Where you going?"

"I just said that means 'so long' in Eskimo. Did you not, yourself, tell me so?"

"To hell with the carpet. This is the day. Come on."

They went back into the house. "Listen, O'Crawley," said Pat to his wife, "we can't beat your carpet today."

"And why not, man, dear?"

"Because I got to bury me son-in-law."

"But he's been dead three weeks now."

"It's time he was buried then." He grinned in delight when he saw his wife's shocked expression.

"Perhaps Mr. Mack will do the carpet while you're gone?"

"He's got to go with me. I got to have a witness."

Pat carried the urn holding the ashes in a paper bag. They beat their way by trolley and subway over to Manhattan.

"Where you going to bury him?" asked Mick Mack.

"Off-a some high place where there is wind and birds."

"Off-a the Woolworth Building?"

"You damn fool!" said Pat coldly.

They got on the little boat that would take them to Bedloe's Island. Pat was astonished that they had to pay for the boat ride. "You pay," he instructed Mick Mack. "I left me money in me other suit."

Mick Mack knew that Pat didn't have another suit, but he paid all the same.

"You going to bury him from off-a the

boat?'' asked Mick Mack.

"No. From the top of the Stature of Liberty. We're going to go up in the torch and do it.''

"But I'm afraid of heighths,'' said Mick Mack.

"A fine time to wait and tell me.''

"But you didn't tell me we was going here.''

"Why do you always have to argue?'' asked Pat.

The elevator took them as far as the pedestal, then they had to climb the winding stairway. Mick Mack started to lag behind. Pat looked back. The little man was pale and his hand was pressed to his heart. He seemed to have trouble getting his breath.

Pat felt a stab of pity. *I never saw before how old he's getting,* thought Pat. *And he don't look so strong, either.* He went back to Mick Mack.

"Me old friend,'' he said, " 'tis shamed I am, making you climb up here and you with no stren'th a-tall. Do you let me put me arm around you and I will help you up.''

To Pat's surprise, he saw that Mick Mack was crying. "Is it a bad pain you have, me friend?'' he asked tenderly.

"No. It's because of the soft way you spoke to me; the kindness of your words. It puts a strangeness on you. I don't know you no more, you black-hearted stranger.''

Pat lost his temper. "That's what a man gets—trying to be decent to the likes of you. Here! Carry this, you damned fool!'' He thrust the urn into Mick Mack's hands. "Making me do all the work! Come on, now! And let me hear no more complaining out of you."

The little man looked up at Pat and beamed.

In those days, people were allowed to go up into the torch. Pat and Mick Mack slowly made their tortuous way up through the arm. The torch could hold twelve people but Pat and Mick Mack were the only persons there at the time.

The wind was terrific. They had to hold on to their hats and the wind tore the paper bag off the urn.

"Give me that," yelled Pat angrily against the wind, "before you drop it." Mick Mack gave him the urn.

Hundreds of gulls flew around the head of Miss Liberty, and wheeled and banked and swooped and screamed. "Look at all them pigeons!" said Mick Mack.

"They ain't pigeons!" hollered Pat.

"What are they then?" screamed back the little fellow.

"Whatever they are, they *ain't* pigeons! Take your hat off!"

"What?"

"Take your hat off! And hold mine." The wind made the hair stand up on their bared heads.

Pat lowered his head and spoke silently to the urn. Mick Mack thought he was saying a private prayer for the dead. Mick Mack lowered his eyes and said his own prayer. Pat wasn't praying, he was telling his daughter's husband good-by.

You wanted to be buried off a high place, Claude, and this is the highest I can get. And you wanted to go out over the sea. Well, here's the whole ocean. And there is birds here—the kind you like. And may God rest your soul.

He removed the cover from the urn. Before he could scatter the ashes, the wind scooped most of them out of the urn. Pat had an instant of terror. The gulls, the screams, the wind and the infinity of sky and sea, and he was such a tiny dot.

There is things I don't know, he thought, *and God forgive me all me sins.*

Mick Mack was screaming. "Say something!" he screamed. "For the love of God say something! Don't let him go without a word! Say something!"

"What?" hollered Pat.

"Good-by! Good-by!" shouted Mick Mack. He waved the hand that held Pat's hat. The wind caught Pat's hat and blew it out to sea.

It was more than Pat could stand. He took the urn, which still held some of the ashes, and with all his strength he hurled it into the wind. He shook his fist at the sky and the sea and the wind and the gulls.

"I'll bury youse all!" shouted Patrick Dennis Moore.

A note on the text
Large print edition designed by
Lynn Harmet.
Composed in 16 pt English Times on a
Compugraphic 7700 by
Debbie Nelson of G. K. Hall Corp.
Printed on 40# Miami Book Smooth paper
and bound by The Book Press.